THE CLARKS FACTORY
GIRLS AT WAR

MAY ELLIS

Boldwood

This edition first published in Great Britain in 2024 by Boldwood Books Ltd.

Cover Design by Colin Thomas

Cover Photography: Colin Thomas

A CIP catalogue record for this book is available from the British Library.

Paperback ISBN 978-1-83533-019-7

Large Print ISBN 978-1-83533-020-3

Hardback ISBN 978-1-83533-018-0

Ebook ISBN 978-1-83533-021-0

Kindle ISBN 978-1-83533-022-7

Audio CD ISBN 978-1-83533-013-5

MP3 CD ISBN 978-1-83533-014-2

Digital audio download ISBN 978-1-83533-017-3

Boldwood Books Ltd
23 Bowerdean Street
London SW6 3TN
www.boldwoodbooks.com

This story is dedicated to the thousands of men, women, boys and girls who have worked for C & J Clarks, making shoes, boots and slippers for the world since the business began in 1825 to the present day.

1

AUGUST 1914

'I can't believe we've been at Clarks for two years already,' said Louisa. 'Do you remember our first day? We thought we were so grown up, didn't we?' She laughed. 'We were so wet behind the ears. We've learned a lot since then.'

Her friends Jeannie and Kate laughed with her as the three of them climbed the stone steps to the Machine Room where they worked on the third floor of the main factory building. Above and below them was a steady stream of women and girls, all heading in the same direction. The three of them linked arms, their heads close together so they could hear each other above the noise of boots on the steps and the women's chatter, as they'd done every day for the past two years since they started work together on this very day.

'Oh, my word, I was so scared,' said Kate. 'I was so glad you two were with me, or I'm sure I'd have turned tail and run.'

That surprised Louisa, because Kate always seemed so fearless. She was the first to argue, the last to back down and she had the loudest laugh of the three of them. 'Why were you scared?' she asked.

Kate shrugged. 'I stood in the doorway, looking around that huge room. It was noisy and smelly and... I don't know... overwhelming, I suppose.'

'I know what you mean,' said Jeannie. She was the quietest of the trio, brought up in a Quaker family, generations of whom had worked for Clarks and worshipped alongside the family who owned the factory. She had a calm and thoughtfulness that Louisa appreciated and didn't often find amongst her other acquaintances.

'I always knew a lot of women worked in here,' Kate went on, 'including my sister Peg until she got married, but seeing all three hundred of them in the one big room was a shock.'

Jeannie nodded. 'The smell of the machine oil and the leather made me feel sick. I was sure I'd skewer my hands on the machines the first time I used them, and the foreman scared me to death.'

The industrial sewing machines on which the girls were trained to stitch shoe linings were big and fierce, as was Mr Briars, the foreman. It had taken some getting used to, and many a week had passed before they got the hang of the machines and didn't lose a good portion of their wages by being charged for wasted thread when they made mistakes and had to unpick their pieces.

'I'm glad we started together,' said Louisa, remembering her own nervousness on her first day at work.

'So am I,' said Jeannie. 'Being with you both, my best friends from school, made it more exciting than frightening. And it was lucky Mr Briars used the same system as our teachers of putting girls in alphabetical order, so we got to stay together – Jeannie, Kate and Louisa – J. K. L.'

Louisa squeezed her arm. 'I remember our first day at school. I knew Kate from church, but you were a stranger to me. But then I fell over in the playground and scraped my knee and you helped me up and gave me your apple to cheer me up. I was so glad you ended up sitting with us.' The girls had been inseparable ever since.

'Yes,' said Kate. 'It was a relief when Mr Briars put us together again. I wouldn't want to work next to anyone else. But, you know, Louisa, I was always surprised you didn't stay on at school. I mean, your pa's a foreman and you don't have any brothers and sisters. Me and Jeannie both had to work to help put food on the table, but you didn't.'

Louisa pulled a face. 'Ma and Pa wanted me to stay on, but what was the point? You know me. I'm not the brightest spark. I like reading and drawing, but I was forever struggling with my lessons.'

'But you always did well,' Jeannie protested.

'Only because Ma stood over me and made me study really hard,' she confessed. 'By the time I got to fourteen and you were both leaving school, I couldn't bear it any longer.'

'Oh, my,' said Jeannie. 'You never mentioned it before. What did they say?'

Louisa laughed. 'Plenty! I didn't mention it, because I didn't think they would ever agree to it. But I stuck to my guns and in the end, they gave in. I mean, they both left school when they were twelve, and they've done alright for themselves, so what was wrong with me leaving at fourteen? In fact, I was almost fifteen by then, wasn't I, on account of my late-summer birthday? Anyway, I don't regret it. I love working with you two, even when Mr Briars is breathing down our necks, telling us to work more and chat less.'

'Mmm,' said Kate, frowning as they reached the top of the stone stairs that were worn down in the middle by the feet of thousands of workers over the decades. 'I expect they'll want us to work us even harder if all the lads are going to rush off to fight. I can't believe Mr Asquith has declared war. It's not like England has been attacked, is it? It's the folks on the Continent who are in dispute, not us.'

'Pa says it's because we had a treaty with Belgium to protect them if they were invaded,' said Louisa. 'The Kaiser has sent his troops through Belgium on their way to France, so the Prime Minister had no choice but to honour the treaty and enter the war against Germany.'

'But war is never the answer,' said Jeannie. 'They should be talking, not fighting.'

Louisa knew that the Quakers – or *Friends* as they referred to themselves – adhered to a Peace Testimony that meant they were against all forms of violent conflict. 'I'm not sure we have a choice,' she said gently. 'But Pa says we'll soon chase them out of Belgium and France, then things will settle down again.'

As they entered the vast Machine Room, she was aware that the conversations around them were all focusing on the news that the country was at war. Some sounded excited, others fearful. Louisa felt uneasy, but at least she didn't have brothers who might be sent off to fight like Kate and Jeannie did. Her unease grew when she saw that Miss Alice Clark, one of the directors of the company, was waiting to speak to them. It took a few minutes for everyone to be gathered together and a step to be found for Miss Alice to stand on so that all the women could see her.

'Ladies,' she greeted them, her tone solemn. 'This is a sad day. Our country is at war. This is particularly painful for the Friends among us who adhere to the Peace Testimony, and no doubt to every woman who faces the prospect of her menfolk being forced to fight. I urge thee all to pray for peace and for the Kaiser to change his ways in the face of the worldwide condemnation of his actions. War is *never* the answer. We must urge our leaders to pursue a peaceful resolution.'

No one spoke as she paused, looking around at the women and girls standing in the aisles between the machines. One or two fidgeted. Louisa knew that the women on piecework would be itching to get on to ensure they didn't lose any wages. She was glad she was still paid on a day rate, which meant she received a steady wage – albeit lower than she might earn on piecework. She and her friends had been told they might be promoted onto piecework soon if they continued to work well, and their wages would go up provided they worked hard.

'As for our lives here in Somerset,' Miss Alice continued, her voice clear and firm, 'we must continue as usual, living and working as God would expect us, in service and kindness. We shall go forward with forti-tude. But be warned, ladies, we at Clarks will not tolerate any warmon-gering on these premises. Whatever thy beliefs, and those of thy menfolk, I urge thee all to look within yourselves for divine guidance in these diffi-cult times.'

She spoke for a few more minutes in the same vein, then sent everyone to their machines to work.

'Well, that's told us,' said Kate under her breath. 'Keep quiet, pray for peace and get on with your work.'

'I thought it was a good speech,' said Jeannie.

'You're both right,' said Louisa. 'There's nothing we can do but pray and carry on as usual and Miss Alice put it very well, even though I still find her way of speaking a little old-fashioned.'

'A lot of older Quakers use *thee* and *thou* in their speech,' said Jeannie. She shrugged. 'I suppose I'm used to it.'

Louisa nodded. 'It doesn't matter. It's the sentiment behind her words that is important. Let's hope my pa's right and it will all blow over quickly.'

'I hear there's already a few lads in Clicking who want to enlist,' said Kate. While Louisa's pa was a foreman in Clicking, Jeannie's brother Lucas, and one of Kate's brothers, her brother-in-law and her pa also worked there, the latter staying firmly on day rates as he never wanted to make the effort to earn more on piecework. It was officially called the Cutting Department, where the leather skins were cut into the components of Clarks shoes and boots, but everyone knew it as the Clicking Room, on account of the noise made by the cutters – or Clickers – as they snipped through the hides. 'My pa's all for them going. Says he'd go himself if he wasn't too old.' She laughed. 'He's not just too old, but he's hardly fighting fit either. He's had too many ciders over the years for that.'

'What about your brothers?'

Kate had two older brothers, George and Fred, who were already married. George worked at his father-in-law's haulage business while Fred was the Clicker.

She shrugged. 'I think they've got more sense than to sign up if they don't have to. They've both got kiddies now, so I expect their wives will have something to say about it as well.'

'I'm worried about Lucas,' said Jeannie. Her older brother was eighteen and unmarried, so would probably be expected to fight. 'He says he won't go, but what if he's forced to? In other wars, Friends have been persecuted – some have been jailed and others even executed.' She blinked rapidly, tears welling. 'It would kill Ma if anything happened to him. And if this war goes on too long, the twins might face the same fate.' Her younger brothers, Peter and John, were thirteen.

'I'm sure it won't go on that long,' said Kate, but she didn't look convinced. 'Let's not invite trouble. I'm sure the Clarks will protect their workers. They're not going to want anyone to go off and fight.'

None of them addressed the question of whether Lucas might face punishment for refusing to fight. Louisa couldn't imagine it. Surely the Clark family would have some influence and be able to save Quaker lads from such a fate?

'You mustn't invite trouble by worrying, Jeannie, love. I'm sure this will all blow over. No one wants a full-blown war, do they? Anyway, we'd better get on. Mr Briars is giving us the evil eye.'

The girls worked steadily through until lunch time. They'd all brought some food and sat outside on the grass between the factory buildings to eat in the good weather. None of them had the heart to talk about the war again, even though it seemed to hang over their heads like a dark cloud.

'I need some advice,' said Louisa after they'd finished eating and were enjoying the August sunshine for a few minutes before they had to go back to work.

'About what?' asked Jeannie.

'My ma's got a bee in her bonnet now I'm nearly seventeen. She seems to think that, as I'm not going to be a teacher like she wanted, I should be looking to get married as soon as I can.'

'But that's daft,' said Kate. 'There's no rush, surely?'

'I know. That's what I said. But she keeps going on that she doesn't want me working in the factory all my life and I should make a good marriage to a man who can look after me like Pa looks after us.'

'I'd love to get married,' said Jeannie, her expression dreamy.

'Really?' asked Kate, looking appalled. 'I want some fun before I settle down.'

'If you marry someone you love and who loves you, it should be fun, shouldn't it?' Jeannie asked, her expression earnest.

Kate laughed, although she didn't look amused. 'There's not much fun in cooking and cleaning and fetching for a man and then having to ask him for money to buy yourself a well-deserved treat. Ask my ma. I'm not in any rush to end up like her. I'm definitely not keen on getting married any time soon.'

'I don't mind the idea of getting wed eventually,' said Louisa. 'But I'm like you, Kate. I want to live a bit before I settle down. And anyways, I want to choose my own husband. Someone handsome, who I love and who loves me.'

'Got your eye on anyone?' Kate grinned.

She tried not to look too coy. 'I might have. There's a certain lad I see on the way to work and back. I've seen him around, but he's a couple of years older than us, so I don't know him. He lives in The Mead. He's really dreamy, brown hair, tall and handsome, with beautiful eyes.'

'Hang on, you're not talking about Mattie Searle, are you?' asked Jeannie, sitting up a little straighter.

'I think that's his name,' Louisa confirmed. 'Why?'

Kate laughed. 'He's my sister Peg's brother-in-law. She's married to his older brother Will.'

'And he's Lucas's best friend,' said Jeannie, her voice quieter than usual.

Louisa glanced at her, her heart sinking. 'Don't you like him?' she asked.

Jeannie shrugged her shoulders, not looking at her friends. 'I like him well enough. He's a nice lad,' she said. 'But you know he's a Friend, don't you?'

'Do you mean a Quaker, or a pal?'

Kate giggled. 'She means a Quaker, of course. Pa was spitting mad when Peg announced she was marrying Will, seeing as how we're Anglican. Not that Pa bothers going to church these days, but he still wouldn't have anything to do with Peg marrying Will, so they had a ceremony at the Friends' Meeting House. Pa wouldn't even come to the wedding. But Ma was alright about it as she and Mrs Searle are good friends. They're like us – went to school together and started at Clarks together. Mrs Searle is a widow now and came back to work in the Trimmings Department after her husband died and her boys started work.'

Louisa frowned. 'I don't think my Pa would be happy with me courting a Friend.'

Jeannie nodded, looking sympathetic. 'A lot of Anglican folks don't like their children courting Friends.'

'And vice versa,' said Kate. 'I think our Peg and her Will are the exception, although it wasn't easy for them.' She sniffed. 'It seems a bit strange that all the churches preach loving our neighbours, then get their knickers in a twist when we do just that. Our vicar acts like Peg's not there if he passes her in the village. He gave Ma a right telling off for letting her marry outside the church.'

'What did your Ma say to that?' asked Louisa.

Kate sighed. 'She tried to explain that Will is a good man, but he wasn't having any of it. Told her he expected her to bring Peg back into the fold and to be at services on a Sunday. That he wouldn't consider her legitimately married until she brought her man into the Anglican faith and entered into a marriage in the church. 'Course, our Peg isn't having any of it and I don't blame her. The Quaker marriage is as legal as anything at Holy Trinity. It's not like she's committed a sin or anything.' Her friends nodded. 'But what with the vicar, and Pa giving her grief, well, Ma was in tears over it all.'

'Your poor ma,' said Louisa.

'I know,' said Kate, looking fed up. 'I've told her she should pay them no mind. Peg and Will are perfect for each other, and that's that. I said we should start going to the Methodist Church where my brother Fred goes with his missus, but she won't have it.'

Jeannie nodded, her expression solemn. 'That happens all the time. Why, even the Clarks refused to accept a marriage of one of their own when he wed an Anglican lass in her church. It wasn't until the bride joined the Friends that they relented. Then *her* family got upset.' She shook her head as she looked at Louisa. 'It's difficult. Don't expect your ma and pa to accept you courting a lad who's a Friend, Lou. It's not like Mattie would join the Anglicans, even for love.'

Louisa pulled a face. 'But he's so handsome. I've never seen anyone who makes me feel so… *shivery* inside.'

'There must be some nice lads at Holy Trinity, or what about the other churches?' There were a couple of non-conformist churches, plus the Salvation Army and even the Tin Church – a sister church to the parish church of Holy Trinity. It had been built as a temporary structure at the other end of the village as the community grew around the factory, but it was still in use decades on.

'None of the lads at our church are worth a second glance,' Louisa replied. 'Especially not the one Ma wants me to go to the summer picnic with.'

'Why, what's wrong with him?' asked Jeannie. 'Is it just on account of your ma liking him?'

'Of course not!' She pulled a face. 'Well, partly, I suppose. But he's not handsome. In fact, he's greasy and spotty and laughs like a donkey.'

Kate giggled. 'Do you mean Horace who works in the office?'

Louisa pulled a face. 'Yes, that's him. Ma thinks he's a good prospect, seeing as he's a pen pusher. She keeps saying he'll grow out of his faults soon enough. But I've spoken to him. He's the most boring lad I've ever met in my life. I don't see how he can grow out of being dull.'

'Oh, you poor love,' said Kate, trying not to laugh.

'At least he'll come home clean and tidy,' said Jeannie, always the one to look on the bright side. 'The lads from the Clicking Room reek of leather and machine oil.'

'So do we,' pointed out Kate. 'Although I suppose we're not as sweaty as the lads. At least we get to sit down while we work.'

'Anyway, Ma says I should go to the picnic with him.'

'Has he asked you?' asked Jeannie.

Louisa shook her head, looking disgusted. 'No, of course not. I don't think he's any keener than I am. It's our mothers who are planning it all.'

'Do you have to go at all?' said Kate. 'I'm not going. They used to be fun when we were kids, but I told Ma I'm too old for it these days. Sunday is my only day off, so apart from going to services with her, I'm not inclined to waste the rest of the day there.'

Louisa frowned. She hadn't thought of that. 'Do you know, you're right. I don't see why I should go either.' Even as she said it, she knew her parents would disapprove. But she'd rather face that than spend an afternoon with the lad her ma was pushing her towards.

'Why don't we have our own picnic?' said Jeannie. 'We could walk up Collard Hill to the Hood Monument.'

'Or Glastonbury Tor,' said Kate.

Jeannie wrinkled her nose. 'There's always people up there. There's more space at Collard Hill and if it's too hot, we can find shade in the woods.'

'Good point.'

Louisa was thoughtful. 'I don't suppose you'd invite Lucas and his friend?' she said, knowing her cheeks were going pink as she thought about the handsome Mattie Searle.

'I doubt they'll come,' said Jeannie, not looking at Louisa. She wondered what was bothering her. 'Lucas still thinks I'm a kid, so he's not likely to want to spend time with us.'

Kate snorted. 'Huh. You're as mature as he is. Stupid lads think that, just 'cause they're a couple of years older, they're smarter and better. Truth is, we're the superior sex and one of these days they'll start to realise it.'

Louisa grinned. 'Have you been reading those suffragette papers again?'

She lifted her chin. 'What if I have? Even Miss Alice Clark believes women should be given the vote. Maybe if women were in charge, the country wouldn't be rushing headlong into war.'

The works hooter sounded, reminding everyone that they had five minutes to get back to work. The girls got up and brushed off their skirts before hurrying back to the Machine Room.

Louisa had a feeling that something was bothering Jeannie. She wondered if she disapproved of Louisa wanting to get to know the Quaker lad. It wasn't like Jeannie to judge. But their break was over, so she didn't have time to ask her. It occurred to her that Jeannie might like him too and her heart sank. If her friend really did like the lad, Louisa couldn't in all conscience ignore that. They'd been friends for too long. She'd have to put her own feelings aside for Jeannie's sake.

Yet this lad, this Mattie Searle, this Quaker boy, was the only person who had ever made Louisa's heart race just at the sight of him walking down the lane. He was the only one who made her blush when he smiled at her. What if he was the only one who could ever make her feel like this?

2

'What's this your mother tells me about you not going to the church picnic?'

Louisa closed her eyes briefly, trying not to groan in frustration. Her mother always got her father involved in their arguments. Ma had gone to visit someone from the parish who was poorly this evening, no doubt to give Pa a chance to have this conversation with their stubborn daughter. 'I've been invited to go out with my friends from work, Pa. We're going to walk up Collard Hill and have our own picnic.'

He frowned. 'You see your friends every day at the factory. Sunday is family time. Your mother's upset that you seem to want to spend more time with other people and not with her.'

She sighed. 'We might see each other at work, but we never get a chance to talk for more than a few minutes at break times, do we? Ma should know that – she worked there before I was born, didn't she?'

'She did. And she devoted her Sundays to her family.'

Louisa was beginning to think she'd never get the chance to go out with her friends – or to get to know Mattie Searle. The thought of having to spend time in the company of that spotty Horace at the church picnic, just because her mother thought he was a 'good prospect', filled her with dread and revulsion.

'It's only this Sunday, Pa. Please. It's not as though Ma is planning on being with me at the picnic. Have you seen the lad she wants me to go with?' She shuddered and pulled a face. 'I can't bear to be near him.'

He tried to look stern, but she could see a glint of amusement in his blue eyes that were so like his daughter's. 'Young Horace is from a good family.'

'So are my friends,' she countered, feeling a little braver. 'And they don't smell or laugh like a donkey.'

Her father raised an eyebrow but didn't disagree with her description of the lad. 'I wouldn't say young Kate's family is quite our kind of people. Reggie Davis isn't what I'd call a good man. He's a little too fond of his cider and has never been a grafter.'

'But Kate's not like her pa. She's like her ma, who's a very good woman. Mrs Davis is lovely – you see her in church every Sunday without fail. She isn't making Kate go to the picnic with her.'

'Mmm,' he grumbled but didn't argue. 'And I suppose your other friend – that Quaker girl – is in on these plans?'

Louisa nodded. 'Jeannie's coming too. The Musgroves are good people too. It's been hard for them since their pa was killed in that accident at the factory all those years ago.'

He still didn't look pleased. Louisa had learned to stay silent about her Quaker friends from an early age, but it didn't mean she agreed with her father.

'Anyone else?' he asked.

She felt her cheeks warming but couldn't stop it. 'There might be a few others,' she said, looking away. 'Just a few friends from work.'

He was silent, studying her, no doubt knowing what she wasn't saying. 'So why don't you invite Horace to go with you and your friends?' he said after a few moments. 'He works at the factory as well.'

'What?' Louisa almost shrieked the word. She was horrified. 'No! The whole reason I want to go with my friends is to avoid him! Please, Pa, don't suggest this to Ma. If you do, I'll just take to my bed and refuse to do anything.' She crossed her arms over her chest, glaring at him. Could this get any worse?

Her father narrowed his eyes and sighed. 'Louisa Clements, I swear you'll be the death of me. So, you're going on a walk up Collard Hill with young Kate and Jeannie and some lads, eh?'

She gulped, wondering how she could avoid admitting it. 'What makes you say that?'

He glared at her now as she tried not to squirm in her chair. 'If you were just going with a group of lasses, you would have said so and no one would have expected you to ask Horace to tag along.'

Her heart sank as she realised her mistake, but she was her father's daughter and she wasn't about to give up now. She raised her chin and looked him in the eye, praying her warm cheeks would settle down. 'Jeannie's brother will likely come,' she admitted. 'You know Lucas. He works for you. He's the man of the Musgrove house since their pa died. He'll make sure we don't get into any mischief. Not that we would, anyway. We're not children any more, Pa. We just want to spend some time with our friends outside of work.' When he didn't say anything, she huffed. 'And it's Ma's fault. If she didn't keep trying to push me into talking to lads I've no interest in, it wouldn't be a problem.'

'She just wants to see you settled, lass,' he said, his tone a little gentler. 'As you say, you're not a child any more. The sooner you're safely married, the better.'

Louisa frowned. 'There's no rush, is there? I'm hardly on the shelf yet.'

'I'll not have lads sniffing around you like dogs on heat,' he grumbled. 'You make sure you don't let Lucas Musgrove or anyone else touch you, my lass, or there'll be trouble. Your ma is looking out for you, trying to find you a good Christian lad.'

'Quakers are Christians too, Pa.'

He scowled. 'Not in my book,' he said. 'They might be good people – the Clarks are testament to that with all the good works they undertake. This village wouldn't be what it is without the Clark family. But they and their *Friends* don't pray or worship like we do. They don't even accept the Nicene Creed or say the Lord's Prayer. And they'll be hiding behind that Peace Testimony of theirs now that there's a war on, refusing to fight. It's not right. Everyone will have to do their bit to defeat the Kaiser. So don't you go having any ideas about courting lads outside of our church, Louisa. I'll not have it.'

She closed her eyes, disappointment making her ache. 'Does that mean I can't go out with my friends on Sunday?' She didn't add that she would not under any circumstances go to the church picnic now. She'd already made that clear. She'd rather stay home on her own. But her father must have realised it anyway.

'You can go,' he said, although it was clear from his tone and his scowl he wasn't happy about it. 'But don't go making plans for any other Sundays, my girl. It's a day for God and family, not gadding about.'

She nodded, keeping her gaze downcast so that he wouldn't see the delight and excitement in her eyes. 'I won't. Thank you, Pa.'

She took herself off to her bed before her mother arrived home. She'd leave Pa to tell her that her plans had been thwarted this time. Louisa didn't doubt there would be another battle over Horace or some other lad from church sometime soon. But right now, her thoughts were more engaged with the prospect of her outing on Sunday and maybe getting to speak to Mattie Searle at long last.

3

Kate was thoughtful as she walked home from the factory the next day. Louisa had been triumphant that her father had given her permission to miss the church picnic for the first time in her life. It seemed strange to her that Louisa's parents were so strict about her attending church services and social events. Kate's pa never went near the church, and her ma was happy when she accompanied her to church, but she never forced Kate – or any of her siblings when they'd lived at home – into going every time.

'You must make your own choices,' she'd said. 'Our church gives me comfort and hope, but I know that others are just as content in the Meeting House or in one of the other denominations. So long as you love God and respect His wishes for us, that's fine with me. We're all His children, after all. It doesn't matter where or how we worship Him.'

The Davis siblings had taken her at her word. Her brother George and his wife Ada attended the parish church services, although they didn't get involved with much else there. Older brother Fred and his wife Vi went to the Methodist Church where Vi's family had always worshipped. Her sister Peg had joined the Friends at the Quaker Meeting House as her husband Will was born a Quaker. Kate's ma was happy that all of her children regularly worshipped God in their own ways and lived good lives.

But Louisa's parents were a different kettle of fish. As far as they were concerned, if you weren't an Anglican, you weren't a proper Christian. It seemed strange to Kate, given that their employers, the Clarks, were Friends and led their lives according to the Quaker ethos. While Mr Clements was a loyal employee at the factory and had done well for himself there, Louisa had confided to Kate that she often heard him sneering about the Friends in the privacy of his own home. And now Louisa's ma and pa were going on about her finding a 'proper Christian' husband.

As she approached the Davis family home, Kate shook her head. She couldn't understand why Mr and Mrs Clements were so two-faced about the factory owners. Her own pa was almost as bad, constantly complaining about them, although in Kate's opinion, that was simply because he would rather spend his time drinking cider than working, while the Clark family were mostly teetotal and members of the Temperance Movement. It amused her that both of their fathers grumbled about the same thing but for very different reasons.

The Clark family not only provided good jobs for thousands of people in Street and the surrounding areas, but they were good people. They'd built the schools as well as the community centre at Crispin Hall, and they were talking about building a new library soon. They had just started sending the younger factory lads and lasses to the new Day Continuation School for a couple of half-days a week while they were aged between fourteen and sixteen. Kate had missed out on that, but Jeannie's twin brothers would get some extra schooling that way when they started working at the factory next year. Clarks looked after their workers better than a lot of factories; Street was thriving, with a growing population. Without the Clark family and their generosity, Street would be a poor, small rural community with few prospects for work.

The cottage was silent when she entered, which surprised Kate. Her ma was usually singing as she worked in the kitchen, getting supper ready for when Pa walked through the door. He hated to be kept waiting and expected a hot meal on the table when he got home from a hard day's work, mainly so that he could eat it then take himself off to the Street Inn for the evening.

'Ma?' she called out, heading through the parlour to the kitchen at the back of the house. 'Did you lose track of the time? You know Pa will only be five minutes behind me. What can I do to help? Oh!'

She gasped in shock at the sight of her mother lying on the stone flagstones of the kitchen. 'Ma!' She rushed to her side, falling to her knees. She put a trembling hand on her mother's forehead, gently brushing a few stray locks of hair off her face. Her skin was cool and clammy. She looked so pale.

'Oh, dear lord, Ma. Please be alright,' she whispered.

Her mother groaned and opened her eyes. Kate nearly wept with relief.

'Ma, whatever's happened?' she asked.

She looked confused for a moment, squeezing her eyes shut and grimacing. 'I... I'm not sure. I was taking the pot off the range...'

They both looked towards the range, where a pot of what must have been stew had tumbled to the stone hearth. It had cracked and split into three large pieces. Meat and vegetables and gravy were pooled on the floor between where her mother lay and the black, cast-iron range where she cooked all their meals.

'Oh, no!' her mother cried. 'Kate, love... help me up. Whatever will your father say?'

Kate gently helped her to stand and led her to a chair next to the table. 'Sit down, Ma. I'll clear this up.'

'But what are we going to feed your father? And that was my best stew pot. I'm so stupid. He'll be hungry and there's nothing ready.'

Kate was more concerned about why her mother had collapsed, but she could see that she was getting het up at the thought of the ruined meal. She urged her mother into a seat. 'Don't worry, Ma. Let's have a look at you. Have you hurt yourself? Do you remember what happened?'

The older woman slumped into the chair Kate had pulled out and leaned her elbows on the table, putting her head in her hands.

'I'm alright, lass,' she said, raising her head to give her daughter a reassuring smile that Kate did not for one minute believe – not when her ma's hands were shaking so. 'I can't for the life of me think what happened. I must've slipped on something. One minute I was picking up the pot, then there you were, leaning over me and I'm lolloping on the floor.'

Kate frowned. She hadn't heard a crash as she'd come in the cottage. That pot would have made a heck of a racket when it smashed. The spilt food wasn't steaming, so she suspected Ma had been on the floor for quite a while. 'I think you might have fainted, Ma. You were out cold when I got here.'

At first, she thought her mother was going to deny it. But instead, she opened her mouth to say something, then paused. She took a deep breath, touching the side of her head. Kate could see a lump forming. She must have hit her head when she went down.

'Maybe you're right, love,' she said. 'I... I think I remember feeling a bit dizzy.'

'Oh, Ma. Did you even bother to eat anything today? You've been missing meals, haven't you?' It was clear to Kate she had lost weight.

She shook her head, looking away. 'I've not been hungry,' she said. 'Everything I eat these days seems to disagree with me.'

Before Kate could respond, her father appeared in the doorway. 'What the blazes is going on here?' he demanded as he took in the mess on the floor.

'Ma's poorly, Pa,' said Kate as her mother tried to shush her.

'I... I'm alright,' she argued. 'I'm sorry, Reggie, love. I don't know how I could be so clumsy. Give me ten minutes and I'll get your dinner. Betty Searle gave me a dozen eggs. How about a nice cheese omelette?'

'I'll do it,' Kate began, only to have her father's cursing drown out her words.

'Are you bloody kidding me?' he roared. 'I work my fingers to the bone to put food on this table,' he slammed his fist down on the wooden surface, 'and come home to find good meat all over the floor, you sitting on your arse and offering me a damned omelette!'

Alarmed, Kate stepped in front of her mother, who was crying and cowering in front of her enraged husband. 'Pa, she's ill. She fainted. Look at the lump on her head. We need to take her to the doctor.'

'She's alright,' he sneered. 'Probably fell asleep and fell off her chair, the lazy mare. It's bad enough she's wasted my dinner. I'm not throwing more money away on a doctor. She needs to pull herself together.'

'But—' Kate started to argue, only to be rewarded by a slap. 'Ow! What was that for?'

'Don't you dare question me, girl. You're as bad as your useless mother. Don't neither of you go asking me for any money this week. I'll be needing extra to feed myself tonight, seeing as how she's thrown my dinner all over the damned floor.' He glared at his wife. 'Pathetic.' He shook his head and turned away. 'Clean up this mess. I'm going to the pub.'

The silence after he slammed the front door was finally broken by her mother's soft sobs.

'Oh, Ma, don't cry,' whispered Kate as she wrapped an arm around her mother's thin shoulders. 'It wasn't your fault.'

'Yes, it was,' she wept. 'I didn't have his dinner on the table and he took it out on you.' She stroked a trembling hand down her daughter's cheek. 'I'm sorry you got a wallop because of my clumsiness, my darling girl. You didn't deserve that.'

She certainly didn't deserve it, but Kate wasn't about to agree with her ma and add to her unwarranted feelings of guilt. 'Hush now. Let's get you up to bed. You look exhausted.' She put a finger to her ma's lips when she began to argue. 'I'll clean up this mess and I'll boil a couple of those nice eggs Mrs Searle brought round, eh? We can have a little picnic on your bed.'

After helping her upstairs, Kate was reluctant to leave her ma alone. She was worried about that bump on her head as well as how frail she had seemed as she'd helped her into her nightdress. She silently cursed her pa for being so selfish. He never showed Ma any respect, even though she was the sweetest woman. Instead, he treated her like a doormat and, now it was clear she wasn't well, he'd gone off to the Street Inn and left his wife to suffer alone while he spent money they could have used to get a doctor on more cider.

'Will you be alright for a few minutes while I pop and get Peg?'

'Whatever do you need to bother your sister about at this time of day?' her mother asked.

'She'll want to know you're poorly,' said Kate. 'She can sit and chat with you while I clean up the kitchen.'

Her mother seemed to shrink into the bedcovers. 'Please, Kate. Don't tell Peg or your brothers. I had a funny turn, but I'll be right as rain after a little rest, I'm sure. I don't want you worrying anyone, lass.'

Kate sat on the bed and gently brushed her mother's hair back from her face. '*I'm* worried about you, Ma. I wish you'd let me get Peg.'

She shook her head. 'No, lass. Leave her be. She'll be giving her Will his supper about now. He's her priority now and that's as it should be.'

'And you should be Pa's priority, not his cider cups,' she argued.

Ma sighed. 'It is what it is, Kate. He works hard and deserves the chance to relax after work.'

Kate could barely hold back a snort. She'd never known Pa to do any more than he absolutely had to. He wouldn't even go onto piecework, which would give him the opportunity to earn a lot more money if he only got his finger out and got on with it. Fred said Pa was always finding ways to avoid work, and was often on the sharp end of Mr Clement's tongue when he was caught skiving.

He also took every penny of Kate's wages, doling out a few pennies of pocket money now and again. She didn't even know how much she earned because he collected her pay packets. He'd been doing this since she started work, saying he'd done the same for all her siblings until they got married and left home.

'It's my money,' he'd said. 'I put a roof over your head, food in your belly and clothes on your back. It's about time you paid your way after wasting so much time at school. It never did me any harm, leaving at twelve and earning my crust. Why they let girls stay on until they're four-teen now is beyond me. I told your ma, you don't need no book learning to earn a wage or run a house. But she's soft, that bloody woman, and now you're probably ruined. Mind you don't let on to any lads who come courting that you're too clever for your own good, or we'll never get rid of you.'

No, her pa didn't work hard. He expected everyone else to, though, and more than once when she first started work he'd punished her for wasting thread and having her wages docked. She'd learned fast that keeping her pa happy was just as important as staying in Mr Briars' good books.

When Peg had married, Kate had been brave enough to ask Pa how he would manage when she got wed too. After all, with no other children left at home, the only wage coming in would be his. He'd snarled that he'd send Ma back out to work. 'But don't think you're getting away any time soon, lass. You owe me a few years yet, you ungrateful little madam.'

It was the thought that her ma would be left to the mercy of her selfish bully of a husband without anyone to help her that had made Kate silently promise that she would never marry and abandon Ma. Her friends had been horrified when she'd told them. But Kate had shrugged. 'What's all the fuss about marriage anyway? I'd only be swapping Pa for some other man who'd control my life. Only he'd expect his rights in the marriage bed as well and then keep me tied to the kitchen sink with a load of snivelling kiddies.' She'd shuddered at the thought.

'Promise me, Kate.' Her mother's voice brought her thoughts back to the present. 'I don't want anyone else to know about this. I'm alright. You mustn't go worrying them.'

Kate sighed. 'Alright, Ma. Don't fret. I won't say anything yet. But you must promise me that you'll rest now and if you're not better soon, I'll have to tell them and we'll have to find a way to get you to the doctor. God knows, we can't rely on Pa to look after you.'

That her mother simply nodded and lay back without arguing spoke volumes. By the time Kate had made a boiled egg and brought it upstairs for the patient, she found her mother deeply asleep. She didn't have the heart to wake her.

4

The twins, Peter and John, inhaled their supper as if afraid someone would come and steal it from their plates.

'Slow down, boys,' said their mother with an affectionate smile. 'I spent all afternoon making that pie so I'd appreciate it if you took longer than a few seconds to savour it.'

'It's tasty, Ma,' said Peter.

'Is there any more?' asked John, his mouth still full.

'Manners,' scolded Jeannie. 'No talking with your mouth full.'

'And no seconds,' said Lucas. 'We're not made of money. What's left of this pie will make another meal tomorrow.'

'But I'm still hungry,' complained John.

'Then have a piece of bread,' said Lucas. 'Just stop whining like a girl.'

'A girl wouldn't eat as much as him,' said Peter, grinning.

John grumbled some more as he slathered the piece of bread Ma cut for him with butter and some of the fresh raspberry jam she'd made this week. He fell silent while he ate it, giving them all some peace in which to finish their meals at leisure.

'Hey, Lucas,' said Peter, 'Alfie said his older brother has enlisted.'

Lucas frowned as Jeannie cast an anxious glance at their mother. As she expected, Ma had gone pale. Jeannie wanted to tell Peter to shut up, talking about the war around her. Their mother was prone to terrible anxiety since their pa had been killed in an accident at the factory when the twins were tiny. He'd been helping repair a cargo lift that had jammed. It had fallen on him, crushing and killing him instantly. One day he'd been there, then he'd been gone, and now Ma would often fall into a pit of despair and worry whenever she thought about anything happening to any of her children. The declaration of war had thrown her into a panic and it had taken days to calm her down and assure her that the boys were all too young to fight, and anyway, they were Friends and pacifists. Jeannie just hoped it would all be over soon so that none of the boys were faced with the dilemma of refusing to take up arms.

'More fool him,' said Lucas.

'He said if we all refused to fight, the Kaiser would come for us next and we'll all be killed and anyone left would be slaves to the Germans.'

'Peter,' Jeannie hissed, glaring at him while directing her glance sideways towards their mother. 'Did you pass that arithmetic test you had today?'

Peter's ears went pink and his mouth turned down as he realised Ma was getting upset. 'Er...'

'Of course he did,' said John, looking put out. 'It's not blooming fair. We're identical, aren't we? So how come he can make sense of his numbers and I can't?'

Lucas chuckled. 'You could too if you bothered to pay attention like he does.'

'Promise me, boys,' said Ma, just as Jeannie was beginning to think the change of topic had cleared the air.

'What, Ma?' asked John.

'Promise me you won't fight. None of you. It's wrong and I couldn't bear to lose any of you, or for any other mother to lose their sons at my boys' hands.'

'We might not get any choice, Ma,' said Peter, nearly in tears. 'Alfie says—'

'Just shut up about what Alfie says.' Lucas raised a finger and pointed it at Peter, silencing him. 'He's a kid. What does he know? We have to trust Mr Asquith knows what he's doing and like he says, it will all be over by Christmas.'

'And if it isn't,' said Jeannie, putting a hand on Ma's shoulder, trying to reassure her, 'we will do as every other Friend will do and stick to the Peace Testimony. The Clark family will do the same, I'm sure. So will a lot of people around here.'

John scoffed. 'I'll bet the Clarks won't go to gaol if they won't fight. But who's going to stop us being locked up?'

'Show some respect,' snapped Lucas. 'The Clarks put food on our table and a roof over our heads. They're humble people who will do what is right, and we should follow their lead. If it means going to gaol for our beliefs, then so be it.'

Ma put her hands to her face. 'Please, boys, don't argue over this. I can't bear it.'

Jeannie stood up and began gathering the plates. 'John, go and heat up some water so you can start the washing up. Peter, you can dry up.' She shoved the plates into John's hands. 'Don't argue,' she said when he opened his mouth. She lowered her voice. 'It's your turn. Ma needs a break and we're all sick of hearing you two going on about things we told you not to discuss in this house. So just get on with it.'

She turned to Ma. 'Come on, Ma. Let's sit in the garden for a while. It's still light out and warm enough that we won't need our coats. Are there any gooseberries left on the bushes? Maybe we can do a gooseberry fool for pudding on Sunday. I'll fetch a bowl, shall I?'

An hour later, Ma was calmer and went inside to prepare for bed. The twins had gone down the road to kick a ball around with a friend and would no doubt only come back when it was too dark to see unless Lucas went to look for them. Jeannie remained alone on the wooden bench her father had made, enjoying the cool, late-summer evening.

'You alright, sis?' Lucas came and sat beside her. 'I had words with the twins. They'll not be talking about the war in front of Ma again.'

'Good. The stupid boys should know better. She already suffers with her nerves over the slightest thing.'

'I know. That's why I put them right.'

'Are they expecting you to go and fight?' She hoped not. That would mean they were thinking about going too. Lord knows what it would do to Ma.

He shrugged. 'I've no plans to enlist. I read the Peace Testimony again when we heard the news, and I agree with it, even though I think the Kaiser is wrong and should be stopped. Killing each other isn't going to solve the problem. The government needs to talk to the German government, come to some accord.' He sighed. 'Things are getting tense in the Clicking Room. Half the lads are itching to sign up and rush off to foreign soil, while the rest of us won't go willingly. Some of the old chaps who fought in the Boer War are cautioning against fighting, while others are egging the lads on, telling them it will make men of them.'

'I hate this,' she said. 'Kate says if women could vote, there wouldn't be a war.'

'She's probably right, but I can't see the Suffragettes winning their cause now. All anyone cares about is winning this damned war. Of course, the excuse will be that we men need to protect the womenfolk and giving them a say in affairs of state would weaken our ability to do so.'

She nodded. 'I know. I wonder if German lads are having the same conversations with their sisters?'

He laughed softly. 'Probably. I don't suppose they're much different from us, are they?'

Jeannie shivered as she imagined other brothers and sisters on these shores and in Germany. All frightened – at least, those of them with any sense. None of them wanting this war, yet at the mercy of just a few men who felt it was their right to claim power and decide for everyone else.

'Anyway, let's not fret about it now. There's enough daft boys rushing to prove themselves.'

'Like Alfie's big brother,' she said.

'Mmm. We can't stop them, sis. We can only look within our own consciences and do what we believe is right.'

She nodded, feeling helpless. 'Alright. Let's change the subject. How do you fancy coming up Collard Hill with us on Sunday afternoon?'

'Who's *us*?' he asked, narrowing his eyes.

'Me and Kate are saving Louisa from having to attend the Holy Trinity picnic with Horace from the Counting House. You probably know him; he's your age. Spotty lad, greasy hair, laughs like a donkey?'

He laughed. 'I know him. Why on earth would a lass like Louisa Clements be walking out with him?'

Jeannie knew what he meant. Louisa, with her blue eyes and blonde hair and lovely figure, was one of the prettiest girls in Street. She was far too good for the likes of Horace.

'That's the point,' she said. 'She doesn't want to, but her ma and his have decided they're a good match, so Lou's desperate to escape. Which is why we're going up Collard Hill on Sunday. Say you'll come. If there's a few of us, we can have a good laugh.'

He pulled a face. 'I don't want to hang around with a load of girls.'

She rolled her eyes. 'You wouldn't be the only lad. In fact...' She felt her cheeks getting warm as she formed her next words. 'I was hoping you'd bring Mattie along.' When he frowned, she rushed on. 'And someone else... I don't know, maybe another lad from the Cutting Room, or someone from the Meeting House. Not anyone who goes to Holy Trinity, because Louisa says her ma has already tried to push her towards most of them and not a one has taken her fancy.'

'Why d'you want Mattie to come?' he asked, ignoring everything else she'd said.

She looked down the garden, not wanting him to see how mortified she felt. 'Actually, it was Louisa who asked if he could be invited.'

'Her pa wouldn't approve of Mattie,' he said, still watching her closely. 'He's a Friend, and a bit of a lad, too. You know how he likes to laugh and joke. Mr Clements isn't keen on anyone who isn't serious.'

Jeannie agreed, and hoped with all her heart that this fancy Louisa had for Mattie would die a death soon. But she also had to admit to herself – but never to her brother – that she'd always had a soft spot for Mattie Searle. He was handsome and a charmer. He could always make her smile. She had an awful feeling that Louisa and Mattie would make a perfect couple, and she dreaded the thought of them finally meeting properly, especially if she had to be there to witness it.

'Look,' she said, blowing out an impatient breath. 'I promised to ask, but if you don't want to come, that's fine by me. Us girls can go on our own.' In fact, she'd be relieved. Maybe keeping the two of them apart a little longer would give Louisa the chance to find someone else and leave Mattie to her. After all, Jeannie had far more in common with him than Louisa did and Jeannie had secretly carried a torch for him for a lot longer than her friend had. She stood up. 'I'm going to bed. Can you chase down the twins and get them in? And tell them to do some chores for Ma tomorrow. They seem to think they can lollop in bed or go out with their chums just because it's the school holidays. It's about time they did their bit.'

'Yeah,' said Lucas. 'I'll tell 'em. The garden needs weeding and they can clean the windows.'

'Right. I'll suggest Ma is sure to supervise them or they'll be pulling up her best plants and leaving streaks all over the windows.'

'Like we did, you mean?' He grinned at her and she laughed at the shared memory.

'Exactly! They've got to learn, just like we did.'

She turned and opened the kitchen door.

'Jeannie.' His voice stopped her.

'Mmm?' She looked at him over her shoulder.

'I'll speak to Mattie and maybe Ted Jackson about Collard Hill.'

'Oh! Alright. If you're sure.' Ted was Holy Trinity, but Louisa hadn't mentioned him, and anyway, she was interested in Mattie, so she was sure her friend wouldn't mind.

He shrugged. 'I'll see what they say. Night.'

'Night.'

She climbed the stairs to the room she shared with Ma, feeling both scared and excited at the prospect of an afternoon with Mattie Searle. But she had a horrible feeling that he would never see her as anything more than Lucas's sister.

5

Lucas regretted mentioning the walk to Collard Hill as soon as he saw Mattie's eyes light up.

'So Jeannie's friend Louisa Clements is going to be there?' he asked. 'The blonde one who lives up Somerton Road?'

'And Kate Davis. The brunette one who lives in Silver Road,' he said, keeping his tone bored. 'I said I'd ask, but I don't see the point of wasting an afternoon with some daft lasses.' He knew that most of the lads his age were keen on impressing girls, but he'd never met a girl yet that he thought was anything special. He'd rather spend his free time with his pals. He'd hoped that Mattie would agree with him, but it looked like he wanted to go on this walk.

'I've been trying to drum up the courage to speak to her for ages,' said Mattie. 'This is perfect.'

'You know her pa is my foreman, don't you? And he's Holy Trinity. He'll not want you sniffing around his daughter. He wanted her to go to the church picnic with Horace. That's why her friends have organised this outing.'

Mattie grinned. 'She's too good for that spotty four-eyes. I'm in.'

Lucas suppressed a sigh. 'Really? Wouldn't you rather do something else?'

'When the prettiest girl in the village is begging to be rescued from a fate worse than death with Horace? Not on your nelly, mate. Come on, it'll be a laugh.'

He shrugged. 'My idea of a laugh doesn't include my sister and her giggling friends.'

Mattie shook his head, smirking. 'You know, you're turning into an old man before your time, Lucas, my friend.' He jabbed him on the arm. 'Girls giggle because they like us. You know the easiest way to shut them up is to kiss 'em, don't you?'

Lucas glared at him. 'No one is going to kiss my sister and live to tell the tale.'

Mattie backed up, putting his hands up in surrender. His eyes were wide, although Lucas could see they were still full of humour. 'Woah, hold on there. I wouldn't kiss your Jeannie. I mean, she's a lovely girl, but... well... she's *your sister*. I know better than that.'

'Good.' He felt out of sorts with all this talk of kissing girls.

'But that doesn't mean I wouldn't mind trying to steal a kiss from the lovely Louisa,' Mattie winked. 'I'm more scared of you than I am of old man Clements.'

Lucas groaned. 'No kissing my sister's friends, Mattie. At least, not while I'm there. I'm supposed to be watching out for them, not acting as matchmaker.'

He laughed. 'I'm not planning on wedding her, Lucas. I'm too young to settle down. But don't worry. I doubt she'll let me kiss her until she gets to know me anyway.'

'Huh. If she's got any sense, she'll be even less inclined to let you kiss her once she does get to know you.'

Mattie laughed at Lucas's grumpy tone. 'We'll see. So, who else is going?'

'I thought I'd ask Teddy.'

Mattie looked surprised. 'For your Jeannie? He's Holy Trinity.'

'God, no! I told you. My sister's off limits. This isn't about pairing off with the girls, Mattie. They just asked if we wanted to go on a walk with them. Why would I want Teddy anywhere near Jeannie if I've warned you off her? You're my best friend.'

'I did wonder. So you're not going after Kate Davis then?' He hesitated, frowning. 'Hang on... you're not carrying a torch for Louisa as well, are you?'

Lucas rolled his eyes. 'Of course not!' How could Mattie be so dense? When had he ever shown any inclination to pursue a girl? Fear trickled down his spine as he realised he maybe ought to at least pretend sometimes. He kept waiting for a girl, any girl to spark his interest, but so far... nothing. He'd rather spend time with Mattie and the other lads. It occurred to him that he was more bothered about girls kissing his best friend than he ought to be. 'I just... they're Jeannie's friends. She's my little sister and they're her age. It don't seem right to be looking at them in that way.'

'I can see your point, friend,' Mattie nodded. 'But they're not little girls any more. They're sixteen and a couple of years out of school. But if it bothers you so much, maybe you should look at courting lasses you haven't seen playing hopscotch with your sister, eh?'

'Yeah, maybe,' he agreed. 'Not that I've got any time for courting.' Mattie would understand that. His pa had passed only a year or so ago. With his brother Will married, Mattie had been left to support their mother. His ma had gone back to work in the Trimmings Department at Clarks and they seemed to be getting along alright. Lucas, on the other hand, had to worry about his ma, whose nerves were often too bad for her to be able to work, as well as Jeannie and the twins. Mattie was right. He was becoming an old man before his time.

'But I really fancy my chances with that Louisa,' Mattie went on, oblivious to his friend's burdensome thoughts. 'Did I tell you I see her going to and from work every day? She's been sending me *meaningful glances*, I swear.'

Lucas forced out a laugh. '*Meaningful glances*, eh? Are you sure she's looking at you and not some stray puppy passing by?'

'Oh, she's looking at me, alright.' His grin was smug. 'I'm looking forward to being properly introduced.' He hooked an arm around Lucas's shoulder. 'Let's go and tell Ted the good news. I know he likes brunettes, so it might just be Kate's lucky day.'

6

Jeannie wasn't giggling. It had taken just a moment for her to realise that the attraction Louisa felt for Mattie was mutual. She'd never seen her brother's friend so bashful before. His ears were pink as he smiled at Louisa. His brown eyes were warm as he regarded her. He looked like a man who was totally smitten.

She wanted to cry. For years, she'd been dreaming of Mattie looking at her like that, but he never had. Now he never would. That much was made abundantly clear as he teased her gently (as you would a younger sister) before he began flirting with Louisa as they walked along the lanes towards Collard Hill. It was a three-mile walk to Compton Dundon and the foot of the hill. By the time they'd walked there, spent some time exploring and enjoying the views across the levels, and then walked home, it would be several hours before she could be on her own. Suddenly, the prospect of spending so much time in the presence of her and her brother's best friends no longer appealed. She'd been so looking forward to today, but now, as Mattie and Louisa moved ahead of the rest of them, chatting and laughing with their heads close together, she wished she was anywhere but here.

'You alright, Jeannie?' Kate asked softly.

What could she say? *No, I'm heartbroken?* She smiled, trying to pull herself together. 'I'm fine. Just realising how far Collard Hill is. Maybe we should have chosen somewhere closer. I'm not sure these shoes will survive the trek.'

They both glanced down at her well-worn Clarks ladies' walking shoes. She kept them clean, but nothing could hide the fact that they were old and past their prime. They were her only pair of sturdy footwear. At home, she wore slippers, and she had a pair of rubber boots for rainy weather. She really ought to buy another pair of shoes. But she'd stopped growing now, so her shoes weren't getting too small for her feet. Not like her brothers. The twins were growing like weeds and were always in need of bigger boots. Even Lucas was still growing. At least he could pass his outgrown footwear down to Peter or John, but that still meant they had to buy some more in order to keep all three of them shod. Even buying seconds at a discount, keeping the whole family in decent shoes was costly. So Jeannie and Ma had to make theirs last longer.

Kate linked arms with her. 'Mine are pinching already,' she confessed. 'They've been tight for a while now. But Pa won't give me any money for another pair until these ones fall apart. Maybe today will be my lucky day,' she laughed.

Jeannie felt sorry for her friend. No matter how difficult things were for the Musgrove family since their pa had been killed, at least they pulled together and gave each other the love and support they needed. But poor Kate and her ma were at the mercy of Reggie Davis, who was a drunkard and a bully.

'Is he still not letting you have your wages?'

Kate shook her head. 'Never has and probably never will.' She sighed. 'And to be honest, Jeannie, if he gave me any money now, I'd spend it on getting Ma to a doctor and for any medicine she needs to get better. I can live with a blister or two so long as she's well.'

Jeannie squeezed her arm. 'Is she not any better?'

Kate shook her head, pressing her lips together. 'She's lost more weight than she ought to, and she's always so weak.'

'I'm so sorry. You'll let me know if there's anything me and Ma can do, won't you?'

She nodded but didn't say anything more. Jeannie didn't suppose there was anything to say that would take away Kate's worry.

Ted Jackson appeared at Kate's side, grinning down at her. 'Alright, Kate?'

Jeannie looked over her shoulder to see Lucas glaring at his friend's back.

'Good grief, Teddy Jackson, there's no need to sneak up on a girl like that,' snapped Kate as she let go of Jeannie's arm and clutched at her chest. 'Couldn't you at least cough or something to warn us you're coming?'

'Maybe we should make him wear a bell round his neck,' suggested Lucas. 'Then we'd all know where he is.' His deadpan remark had them all laughing, but to Jeannie, it looked like he meant it. She wondered what had got him in a mood.

'Sorry,' Ted mumbled, looking bashful. 'Mind if I walk with you?'

To Jeannie's surprise, Kate actually blushed. She'd never have believed it if she hadn't witnessed it herself. 'Go ahead,' she said. 'I'll talk to Lucas.' Ignoring the brief flare of panic in Kate's eyes, Jeannie gave her friend a gentle shove to get her walking again and waited for her brother to join her.

'Looks like love's in the air,' she told him softly, wishing with all her heart that someone would look at her the way Mattie looked at Louisa and Ted looked at Kate.

'Bloody hell,' muttered Lucas. 'This was a bad idea.'

She agreed, but if she said so, she was likely to burst into tears and make a fool of herself in front of everyone. Then her friend would pity her, and she couldn't bear that. Instead, she took a deep breath and began walking again, following the two couples while trying to look at anything other than them. Lucas trudged along beside her in silence.

The lanes were bursting with wildflowers and blackberries ripening in the sun. The fields that hadn't already been harvested were full of crops. She could hear the occasional rumble of a steam-powered tractor engine above the steady tromp of their feet on the road. There was a constant hum of insects among the wildflowers and she could see swallows flying high above them. By the time they reached the slopes of

Collard Hill, she was hot but feeling more at peace with the world. The simple act of walking and the conscious effort to focus on her surroundings rather than her companions had quietened her mind. While her heart still hurt, her thoughts were clearer. Mattie wasn't for her. She probably should have known it, but it hadn't stopped her wishing... She had to pull herself together and have faith that God had a plan for her and that one day, she would meet a good man who would look at her the way that Mattie now looked at Louisa. In the meantime, she had a good life with a family who loved her, a good job and the best friends a girl could wish for. Of course, this attraction between them might be nothing more than a flash in the pan, but somehow Jeannie doubted it.

Even though it was painful to see Louisa flirting with Mattie, it was clear to her that she couldn't compete. There was an energy between the two of them that she'd only ever seen between her own parents, who had adored each other.

Another giggle from Louisa and an answering chuckle from Mattie was echoed by Kate and Ted, who were close behind them.

Suddenly, Louisa's father's voice filled the air, telling Mattie to get away from his daughter.

Jeannie startled, spinning round, expecting to see Mr Clements chasing after them. But he was nowhere to be seen. She looked back at her friends, who were howling with laughter.

'It's Ted,' said Lucas. 'He can mimic just about anybody.'

Sure enough, Mr Roger Clark's voice boomed out, causing more hilarity up ahead. Jeannie blew out a relieved breath and began to chuckle.

'I thought we were in trouble there for a moment,' she said. 'He's good.'

He grunted, not impressed. Jeannie realised that she and Lucas had fallen back a way while she'd been searching her heart. It surprised her that her brother hadn't ploughed ahead. He was usually at the front, his long legs eating up the road. She cast a glance at him. He looked thoroughly fed up.

'Lucas,' she began, but he cut her off.

'Enough of this,' he muttered under his breath before he raised his voice and called to his friends. 'When you two have finished acting like girls, I'll see you at the top.' Then he took off, running past them and lightly slapping the lads on the back of their heads as he did so. 'Last one up is a turnip.'

'Hey!' yelled Ted, rubbing where he'd been hit. 'I'll get you for that, Musgrove.'

Lucas laughed as he kept on running. 'Got to catch me first.'

'Come on, Mattie, let's show him!'

'You'll never catch him,' said Jeannie. He already had a head start and he seemed filled with an energy that spurred him up the slope.

'Ha!' said Mattie. 'Watch me.'

And then the race was on. All three lads ran full tilt up the hill, leaving the girls far behind.

'Idiots,' Jeannie muttered as she joined her friends and began walking after the lads.

'They'll be all sweaty, running like that in this heat,' said Kate, wrinkling her nose.

'Isn't Mattie handsome?' Louisa sighed. 'Oh! He's slipped!'

Jeannie rolled her eyes, hiding her concern as Kate burst out laughing when Ted tripped over him and landed in a heap next to Mattie. 'Not so handsome when they're covered in dirt and sweat. Lucas beat them both fair and square.'

Her brother was standing at the top of the hill, his arms raised in triumph. Ted and Mattie wrestled with each other, trying to get up and finish the race. Clearly, neither wanted to be last. Jeannie shook her head as Kate continued to laugh and Louisa rushed forward to make sure Mattie was alright.

'We should've come on our own,' she grumbled. 'I should have known the lads would act like idiots.'

'Ah, come on, Jeannie. At least they're entertaining.'

'Really? You're not stuck with my brother.'

Kate paused and pulled a face. 'Sorry. Were you interested in Ted?'

'No, of course not!' she said. *Mattie. Only Mattie.* But she couldn't say that. She'd never told her friends about her feelings, and now it was too late. She realised that she'd perhaps always suspected that her feelings for him would be unrequited. Telling her friends had seemed wrong. She'd been worried that they'd laugh at her, or worse, pity her. After all, Mattie was such a handsome and popular lad. Why on earth would he be interested in a plain mouse like her? 'You're welcome to him.'

Kate studied her face as they trudged up the hill behind the others. Ted had gained his feet and shot off after Lucas, leaving Mattie to the tender ministrations of Louisa as she fussed over him. Judging by the grin on his face, he was loving every minute of it, the race forgotten. 'Are you sure?'

'Yes, I'm sure,' said Jeannie. 'I... It's just a bit awkward if you two are going to pair off with Mattie and Ted and leave me with my brother. How would you like it if you had to keep company with Fred or George while your friends flirted with other lads?'

Kate linked arms with her and nudged her shoulder with hers. 'I should hate it,' she confirmed. 'I'm sorry, Jeannie. We'll let the lads play the fool and us girls will enjoy ourselves on our own, alright?'

Jeannie sighed. Now she felt petty and mean. 'I don't mean to be a killjoy,' she said. 'If you really want to have fun with Ted, it's fine.'

'It's alright. He's nice enough, but I'm not sure I'm that interested,' she said softly so that none of the others could hear. 'I think I was just flattered he noticed me.'

Jeannie nodded. She understood. She wished that someone would notice her for a change. The thought of her friends having sweethearts filled her with dread. She might be happy for her friends, but it would mean that she'd be left alone and on the shelf. How on earth would she manage to hide her jealousy from them?

7

As autumn approached, work carried on as usual in the Machine Room where Kate, Louisa and Jeannie worked, although the gossip was often about whose sons, brothers and sweethearts were enlisting. There were so many lads rushing to join the fight that Louisa reported her pa was grumbling that the Clicking Room was running short of good workers and he was having to rely on older men and young boys as those of fighting age went off to the recruitment office. It was causing him and the other foremen in the predominantly male departments no end of problems. Only Quaker lads like Lucas and Mattie and married men like Mattie's brother Will and Kate's brother Fred resisted signing up, although a few had left their wives and children to answer the call from king and country. It meant that those that remained had their hours extended in an attempt to keep up with the work. If the Clickers fell behind cutting out the leather for the shoes, or the heel-makers didn't keep up, the whole production process could grind to a halt. Some of the pieceworkers in the Machine Room who sewed the leather uppers were already complaining that they were waiting around for work.

The girls talked about it as they sat outside on the grass during their dinner break.

'They say we're going to have to switch to all wooden heels because the government is requisitioning rubber and leather supplies for army equipment,' said Louisa. 'Mr Roger Clark has been having a devil of a job sourcing sole leather, as well.'

'We'll all be wearing clogs if this carries on,' said Kate.

'Lucas says they're even talking about moving some women into the jobs where they're short of lads,' said Jeannie. 'Has your pa said anything about that, Lou?'

She shook her head. 'He's grumbling, but I haven't heard him mention letting girls work for him.' She smiled. 'But I think Mattie's going to try and get transferred from the stores into the Clicking Room. He thinks he can make a good impression on Pa, so he'll let us start courting.'

Jeannie said nothing as Kate grinned at her. 'I thought you two were already courting,' she teased. 'You mention his name often enough.'

Louisa felt her cheeks go warm. 'Well, I suppose we are,' she confessed. 'But my parents don't know that. It's not like we're going out properly... I mean, we see each other in the mornings on the way to work and he waits for me outside after our shifts and walks me back as far as The Cross. Pa doesn't know because he goes in earlier than us and comes home a bit later. But we aren't walking out at other times.'

'Louisa,' said Jeannie. 'Are you sure it's a good idea? You know your parents don't approve of Friends. Isn't that why they keep trying to pair you off with lads from Holy Trinity?'

'I know,' Louisa groaned. 'I don't know what to do. I really like Mattie. I can't bear the lads they keep pushing me towards.'

'Don't you think you should tell them?'

Louisa knew she was right. But she also knew that once her parents knew about her and Mattie, they'd put a stop to it. 'I know I should. But I'm not ready yet.'

Kate and Jeannie exchanged a glance.

'What?' she asked.

Kate sighed. 'Lou, love. Someone's bound to tell your pa that you and Mattie are walking to work together. You know how fast news travels round here. Wouldn't it be better if you told him before someone else does?'

Louisa's heart sank, even as she raised her chin. It had only been a couple of weeks since she'd been properly introduced to Mattie on the walk to Collard Hill, but they had been the happiest days of her life. He was so handsome and such a sweet lad and she knew she'd never find anyone so perfect for her. They always had so much to talk about and, when his hand sometimes brushed hers as they walked up the High Street to the factory, she felt such a thrill. He didn't hold her hand, of course, and she never took his arm. There were too many people around who'd have something to say about it if he did. Of course, she realised she was playing with fire. It didn't stop her wanting to carry on, though.

'We're not doing anything wrong,' she said. 'We're just friends walking to work together. Pa can't have any objection to that.'

Kate nodded, her expression sympathetic. 'Of course you're not doing anything wrong. You're not that kind of girl. But... well, to be honest, Lou, just one look at you and Mattie together and the whole world knows you're more than friends.'

'She's right,' said Jeannie softly. 'You both glow, like you're lit up from within. It's impossible to miss.'

Louisa felt a mix of elation and panic. He hadn't said anything about his feelings, but she had been sure that Mattie felt this connection between them as strongly as she did. Jeannie's words seemed to confirm that it was a mutual thing, which made her delirious with happiness. She wanted to get up and dance with the joy of it. But then fear overwhelmed her. Kate was right. Someone was bound to mention it her pa, and then he'd forbid her from seeing Mattie and everything would be ruined.

'Not yet. Once I tell them, they'll try and stop us and I'm not ready for it to end.' She paused, silently begging her friends to understand as she felt her tears well. 'I think I love him. What if he's the love of my life and Pa splits us up?'

'Oh, Louisa.' Jeannie's eyes welled too. 'Are you sure?'

She nodded, blinking fast in an effort to stem her tears. It wouldn't do for anyone to see her like this and tell her pa.

'Of course she is,' said Kate, putting her arm around Louisa's shoulders. 'He's a fine lad and he's only got eyes for you. But you have to be careful, Lou. It was hard for Peg when she started courting Will. Ma was alright about it, on account of her friendship with Mrs Searle, but Pa hit the roof. With both of your parents against it, it will be even harder.'

The factory hooter went off and the girls got up. Time to get back to work. They returned to the Machine Room in silence. Louisa was glad of the distraction of work. If the conversation about Mattie had gone on much longer, she was sure she would have burst into tears and made a fool of herself in front of everyone. She just wished she knew what to do. She loved her parents, but if they made her choose between them and Mattie, she wasn't sure if she would be able to bear it.

As Kate left the factory at the end of the day, she heard raised voices. A couple of lads were squaring up to each other outside the gates. One had his fists raised as he yelled at the other chap. There was a small crowd surrounding them. Half seemed to be egging the angry lad on; the others were trying to calm things down. At the edge of the crowd, Ted Jackson watched intently.

'What on earth is going on?' asked Kate as she reached his side.

Her hand on his arm caught his attention. When he saw who it was, he smiled. 'Hello, Kate. How are you?'

She shrugged, her eyes on the lad who was now jeering at his opponent. 'I'm fine. But what's the matter with those two? If any of the directors see them carrying on like this outside the gates, there'll be hell to pay.'

'I know. Idiots.'

The aggressor was in full flow now. 'It's nothing to do with religion,' he shouted. 'It's cowardice, pure and simple. You're hiding behind your ma's skirts and too scared to fight like a man. You want to be talking German when the Kaiser sends his soldiers over here to interfere with our womenfolk? They'll line up all the cowards like you and shoot you. Where will your precious Peace Testimony be then, eh?'

'Oh, no,' Kate muttered. 'Is he really picking a fight over this?'

Ted took her hand and led her away from the crowd. 'Come on, I'll walk you home. No point in hanging around here.'

'But shouldn't someone stop him? You know full well a Friend won't fight back. He could get badly hurt.'

Ted looked over his shoulder. He was quite tall, so could see over most of the crowd. 'They won't listen to us,' he said. 'But it looks like a couple of the foremen have just arrived. They'll break it up. For now.'

They walked away as someone began to berate the man who'd been shouting and the rest of the crowd started to make a sharp exit. No one wanted to be associated with the fracas outside the factory – they all needed their jobs and couldn't afford to be branded as troublemakers. Ted used his height to shield Kate from the people rushing past them and she gave him a grateful smile once the crowd thinned and she could step back a pace.

'Thank you,' she said as they walked side by side along the High Street. 'Whoo, that was... I can't believe people are turning on each other like that.'

Ted shrugged. 'It's been brewing ever since war was declared. Some think it's their duty to fight. Others think it's their duty not to.'

'And which camp are you in?'

He slowed his step and turned towards her. 'My two older brothers have already enlisted. Ma thinks I should too, as soon as I'm nineteen.' The lads enlisting today weren't deployed overseas until they reached that age. 'But Pa fought in the Boer War and he tried to talk my brothers out of going. He couldn't stop them, but says at least one of his sons should stay at home, so here I still am.'

She nodded and they carried on walking. They passed the Crispin Hall, the impressive community hall built by the Clarks. The notice board outside was dominated by a large army recruitment poster. 'How do you feel about that?'

'If I have to go, I will. But I'll wait and see. I've no great desire to fight. There's no orders for any of us to enlist. Not yet, anyways. They're relying on volunteers and say it will all be over by Christmas, anyway. So I don't see the point in rushing off to basic training only to be sent home again in a couple of months' time.' He smiled and held out his arm as they paused to let an elderly man pass on his way out of the tobacconists. 'Of course, if I had nice girl like you on my arm, I might be even less inclined to go off to fight at all.'

Kate blinked in shock. 'What are you saying, Ted Jackson?'

He raised his eyebrows, his arm remained out in invitation and his smile fixed as he stared into her eyes. 'I'm saying I'd really like to walk out with you, Kate Davis. You're the prettiest girl I know and I'd be proud to be your sweetheart. What d'you think?'

'Oh!' She took a deep breath. She'd never been asked out before and she hadn't expected it now. A few lads had flirted with her, but she'd always laughed it off. Yet she did like Ted. He had a sunny disposition and made her laugh. She'd never seen him drinking or getting angry with anyone. He seemed a decent sort.

'I don't know,' she said, hesitating. 'My ma's ill and... well, everyone knows my pa.'

He nodded, some of the hope in his eyes dimming. But he didn't say anything.

'I'm not keen on being told what to do,' she said. 'You'd probably be better off with some other lass.'

He shook his head, keeping his gaze on her. 'I don't want any other lass, Kate. I'm not the sort to tell anyone what to do, so as long as you're not a nag, I think we could get along quite well, don't you?'

'I am not a nag,' she snapped.

His smile, which had been fading, came back even wider. 'Then I think we should give it a try, don't you?'

Kate stared up at him, still unsure. She was tempted. He was fine-looking and seemed kind. She'd found she could laugh with him rather than at him, which was unusual for her. 'I don't know,' she said. 'I haven't really thought about courting. I want to do things with my life. I don't want to spend the rest of my days at the factory but nor am I sure I want to be tied down with a husband and children for a long while yet. I've always said I wouldn't walk out with a lad, because I know he would just take charge and stop me doing what I want to do.'

He sighed. 'Look, Kate. I'm not going to force you if you really don't like me like that. But I'm not your pa and I understand you wanting to be with your ma while she's poorly. I can even respect you wanting to do something more than working in the Machine Room. I'm not keen on being a Clicker all my life either, but then again, I don't know what else I can do.'

'Other than enlist.' She couldn't help but feel respect for the fact that he wanted more out of life than working at the factory. But she wasn't sure she wanted a sweetheart at all, let alone one who rushed off to war. She thought this war was wrong and nothing good could come of it.

'Mmm. Well, I'm not convinced that's the answer either. I'll wait and see. But what I do know is I like you fine, Kate, and I'd like the chance to get to know you better and see if we might just get along. What do you say? We could go to the picture house in Glastonbury and watch a film.'

Kate would love to go to the movies. It was a rare treat. If she went there with Ted, she wouldn't even have to talk to him while the film was showing, would she? It seemed like a good idea.

'Alright, Ted. I'll let you take me out and we'll see how we get along.'

8

'What are you in such a rush for?' asked Mrs Clements when Louisa headed for the door a couple of mornings later. 'They haven't put the girls on longer hours, have they?'

'No, Ma,' she said, reluctant to tell her the real reason she was in a hurry – to spend a little more time with Mattie before work. 'I just thought I'd get on, seeing as how I'm ready. You always said it made a good impression to be early for a shift.'

'Mmm.' Her mother didn't look convinced. Louisa wondered whether she shouldn't have tried to make her hair look quite so pretty this morning. 'Well, you can hang on a few minutes. I want to talk to you.'

'What about?' Louisa tried to remain calm, but she was desperate to get down to The Cross where Mattie would be waiting for her.

'They're looking for young women to be pen pals to some of the lads from Holy Trinity who have enlisted. I think you should do it. They're all decent young men, fighting for king and country. Who knows? You might become fond of one of them and make a match of it after the war.'

Louisa wrinkled her nose. 'I don't mind writing letters,' she said. 'But don't get your hopes up about any matches, Ma. I know all of those lads, and not one of them appeals to me.'

Her ma tutted. 'Don't be so quick to dismiss them. Going to war could be the making of them. They'll come back mature men, not daft lads.'

'If they come back at all,' she muttered under her breath. 'Alright, Ma.' She raised her voice before she could be called out on her attitude. 'Sign me up as a pen pal, but now I've got to get to work.'

She ran down the road, not wanting to miss Mattie, hoping that she wasn't going to arrive at The Cross all sweaty and with her hair all over the place. She slowed a little and sighed with relief when she saw him sitting on the edge of the water trough that surrounded the lamppost in the middle of the junction where the Somerton and Glastonbury roads met the High Street. She walked towards him, running a hand over her hair to smooth it down. Mattie rose and waited for her, his smile warming her cheeks.

'Sorry,' she said. 'Ma wanted to chat.'

'You're worth the wait,' he said as they started walking side by side. 'Everything alright?'

She nodded, wishing she could take his arm like other couples making their way towards the factory. But she daren't. Not yet. 'The church are asking girls to become pen pals for the lads in the army.'

'Why?'

'So they get a bit of cheer from home, I suppose.'

He nodded. 'That makes sense. I'm sure they'll appreciate it. The Friends are already welcoming Belgian refugees. Clarks are giving them jobs and any that can't be placed with families will be housed at The Grange.'

The Grange was a big old house on the edge of the factory. The Clark family had bought it in order to acquire the land on which much of the factory was now built, but none of the family had lived in it. The current building was Georgian, but before that there used to be a priory there centuries ago and rumour had it there was a medieval tunnel leading from it all the way to Glastonbury Abbey. Not that Louisa believed it. How could they dig a tunnel under the River Brue, which flowed between Street and Glastonbury, and manage to get all the way to the Abbey underground? There was definitely a tunnel there – she knew people who'd seen the entrance to it. But apparently no one could follow the tunnel far as part of it had collapsed decades ago, so she didn't suppose anyone would ever find out the truth of it.

'My auntie trained there,' said Mattie. 'She ended up working in service for a rich family in Bristol before she got married.'

'Oh, yes, I'd forgotten they used to have the School of Housewifery there,' she smiled.

'It was that or the factory for local girls in her day. Now there's just the factory for all of us.'

'I suppose so,' she said. 'Although Kate's brother George is working for his father-in-law in his haulage company.'

'Which relies on Clarks for a lot of its business. There's not a business for miles that doesn't rely on Clarks to some extent. Even the local butchers and bakers. All their customers work at the factory. If the factory weren't here, none of us could afford to buy meat or even bread.'

'I know,' she said, glancing around to make sure no one was close enough to hear their conversation. 'I think my pa resents the hold the Clark family have over this village. But I think he's wrong. They're good people and without the factory, where would we be?'

'Dead poor,' he said. 'I suppose he dislikes the fact that they're Friends.' When she didn't answer, he sighed. 'I can't change who I am, Louisa. But I really, really want to be able to court you properly. I want to be able to walk down this road with your arm on mine. I'd love to be able to take you out somewhere nice, just the two of us. Do you think your pa will ever accept it?'

The thrill of happiness that Mattie wanted to be her beau was muted by the realisation that her pa would probably never approve of her walking out with a Friend.

'I don't know,' she said. 'If he only knew you, I'm sure he'd love you. But... he's got this bee in his bonnet about Holy Trinity being the only true church in the village and while he has to show respect for the Friends in public, he's made it quite clear he has no wish to socialise with them.'

'Or see his only daughter with one of us,' he concluded, his expression glum.

Louisa wished she could say something to encourage him, but she had no idea what to say or do. 'To be honest, he doesn't even like me being friends with Jeannie, and she's the sweetest, kindest girl I've ever known.' She felt sick at the thought that he might decide she wasn't worth the trouble and turn his attention to some other lass. 'But, whatever he says, I really would like to be your sweetheart, Mattie. I just don't know what to do.'

Mattie groaned and slowed his steps so that he could turn and look at her. 'What are we going to do? I want to make this work. Unless you think I'm not worth the trouble, that is?'

'Oh, my lord, Mattie, why would I think that? I was just working myself up, wondering whether you'd think the same about me and give me up for someone else!'

He shook his head, a soft smile on his face as he gazed at her. 'I definitely don't want to give you up. No other girl will do. You're the best, Louisa. Just perfect. If I didn't think it would get us into a whole mess of trouble, I'd kiss you right here, right now in the middle of the High Street.'

Louisa gasped at the passion in his voice. They hadn't kissed yet. She wanted to, and now she knew he felt the same, her yearning grew even more. Yet she worried that he'd think her loose if she let him kiss her, and lord only knew what her parents would say if they found out! She was in such a tizzy that she didn't know what to say. Instead, she gave him a small smile and began walking again.

He chuckled and matched his stride to hers. 'Don't worry, I won't do anything that might harm your reputation. I'd never do that to you. But we've got to think of some way to be together soon, or I'll die.'

'I feel the same,' she whispered.

'Good. Then we'll have to find a solution.'

'Even if it means waiting until I'm twenty-one and can make my own decisions?' she asked.

'Even then,' he agreed. 'My ma always says the best things are worth waiting for.'

'She's probably right, but I'm not sure I can wait four whole years to be able to walk out with you, Mattie.' She paused. 'Actually, I've had an idea. Did you know that Ted's taking Kate to the picture house on Saturday?'

'Yeah.'

'What if I tell my parents I'm going with Kate and don't mention anyone else is going to be there?'

He grinned at her. 'You want to sit in a dark picture house with me, Louisa Clements? You know what that will lead to, don't you?'

She giggled. 'I hope so,' she told him as they reached the factory gates.

He winked at her as they parted. 'See you later. I'll talk to Ted. You talk to Kate.'

She nodded, her eyes sparkling, before she turned away and rushed up the stone steps to the Machine Room.

* * *

'So, what do you think?' asked Mattie. He'd tracked Ted down when he delivered supplies from the stores to the Clicking Room. They didn't have much time to talk as Mr Clements would be after them for time-wasting before long.

'A double date?' Ted frowned as he helped Mattie unload the skins and some replacement blade sharpeners from his cart. 'I'm not keen, mate. I was hoping for some time with Kate without her friends around.'

''Course you are,' grinned Mattie. 'And I'll bet Kate's hoping for the same. Every girl's dreaming of some kissing at the movies. I wouldn't want to cramp your style, Teddie boy.'

Ted scowled at him. 'I'm not sure that's what Kate wants.'

'Yes, she does. They all expect it, even when they say they don't. God's honest truth. You can't take a girl out and not kiss her.'

'D'you reckon?' He didn't look so sure.

'Trust me.' Mattie nodded before he glanced around, keenly aware of the danger of getting on Louisa's father's wrong side. 'We won't bother you. I feel the same about wanting some time alone with my girl. Louisa's knocked me for six. I've never felt like this about another girl. She might be the one for me. We'll sit somewhere else. But she has to tell her parents the girls are going together, on their own, or they won't let her go.'

The cart was empty and Louisa's father was making his way through the Clicking Room towards them. Mattie didn't want to hang about. He gave Mr Clements a polite wave and was on his way to the door before Ted responded.

'Alright,' Ted called after him. 'But you owe me.'

Mattie gave him a thumbs up and made his escape. That was one thing on his list of tasks required to win Louisa Clements ticked off. Next, he needed to see what he could do to progress within the factory. If her pa was a foreman, he'd expect any lad who wanted to court her to have some decent prospects. It hadn't bothered Mattie before. He worked to earn a crust and to help support his widowed mother. But meeting Louisa had changed all that. He wanted to be worthy of her. If that meant knuckling down and learning skills that would get him a better job than working in the stores, then that's what he'd do.

He paused on his way back to the stores, wondering what had come over him. All those months he'd been admiring Louisa from afar, he'd never dreamt of anything more than flirting with a pretty girl, maybe stealing a few kisses. He hadn't had any urge to settle down before now, and he would certainly have been put off by her father's disapproval if it had been any other girl.

But, he realised, Louisa was becoming very special to him. She was easy to talk to. She made him feel ten feet tall when she looked at him with those big blue eyes of hers. He wanted to know if her skin felt as soft as it looked. Each day seemed so much better when he saw her. He couldn't stop thinking about her and wanted to spend as much time as he could in her company.

Mattie Searle was in love.

* * *

'Are you sure you don't mind?' Louisa asked Kate.

Kate shrugged. 'Don't make any difference to me,' she said. 'If Ted don't mind, neither do I.'

Louisa squealed. 'Thank you! You have no idea what this means to me.'

Kate laughed and shushed her. 'Just don't go all soppy with him near me.'

She giggled. 'I can't promise that. He makes me feel soppy all the time.'

Kate rolled her eyes. 'I'm not fond of all that lovey-dovey stuff.'

'Then why are you courting Ted?' asked Jeannie. She'd been listening to their conversation, her gaze swinging between the two of them.

Kate shrugged. 'Because I like him well enough. It don't mean I want anything serious for a long while yet, though, and I've told him that.'

'Well, I like Mattie, and I *do* like all that lovey-dovey stuff,' said Louisa. 'So maybe we should sit in different rows? So long as my parents see you and me heading off to the picture house together, they don't have to know we'll be meeting the lads there and going our separate ways inside, do they?'

'Fine by me,' said Kate, turning back to her machine. 'Watch it, Mr B is heading this way.'

The girls put their heads down and focused on their work. Louisa couldn't keep the smile from her face. She wanted to laugh out loud with pure joy. She was sure that, in the dark of the movie theatre, she and Mattie Searle were going to share their first kiss. She couldn't wait.

'Louisa, are you sure you're doing the right thing?' asked Jeannie when Mr Briars' attention was drawn to something down the other end of the Machine Room. 'I mean, what if your parents find out? You still haven't talked to them about Mattie, have you?'

She shook her head. 'I want to,' she confessed. 'But I'm scared, Jeannie. I couldn't bear it if they stopped me seeing him, and I'm sure they will.'

'You know they love you, don't you? They want what's best for you.'

'I know. But Mattie *is* the best for me as far as I'm concerned, and they won't give him the time of day just because he's a Friend. It's not fair.'

Jeannie nodded slowly. 'Well, you must do what you think best. But be careful, won't you? Maybe not telling them will make things worse in the end.'

9

Jeannie was feeling a bit down when she left work on Saturday. It was a half day at the factory, so she and Lucas came home along the High Street towards their cottage in West End via the butcher's, grocer's and green-grocer's, picking up provisions for the family on their way.

'What's up with you?' asked Lucas as they approached home, loaded up with shopping. 'It's the weekend. No work until Monday. Why the long face?'

'Nothing,' she snapped. 'These bags are heavy, and I'm tired, that's all. We should've got the twins to meet us and help carry everything. They've got nothing to do and they'll be eating most of it anyway, the little pigs.'

Lucas laughed. 'You can't be calling them *little* pigs any more, sis. They're taller than you, now. At the rate they're growing, they'll end up taller than me soon.'

'Well then, they're definitely big enough to help carry the shopping home. I'm sick of doing everything and them doing nothing. It's a good thing they'll be working at the factory soon. It's about time they did their bit for the family.'

Lucas regarded her calmly. She immediately felt guilty because he was carrying more than she was, truth be told, and she, Lucas and Ma had all indulged the twins ever since Pa had died when they were so little, so she supposed they only had themselves to blame. But she was out of sorts and in no mood to apologise. She knew the minute they got home, the twins would demand to know what there was to eat before she'd even put the food away. Then she'd have to help Ma cook up the meat into stews and pies for the next few days, and she'd promised Ma to do some clothes mending as Ma's fingers weren't as nimble as they used to be. So much to do. *She* didn't have an outing to the picture house in Glastonbury to look forward to like her friends did.

'I'll talk to them,' said Lucas. 'Is that all that's bothering you?'

She nodded, looking away. She could hardly tell her brother she was suffering from unrequited love for his best friend, who was actively courting her best friend behind her parents' backs, could she? She felt pathetic enough, without being mocked by her brother. She knew full well that any lad would prefer pretty, blonde Louisa to plain, mousy-haired Jeannie.

They entered the cottage in silence. Jeannie let out a sigh of relief when Ma said the twins had gone swimming at Clyse Hole on the River Brue with their pals. All her brothers went there, but Jeannie didn't as the lads would often swim naked and she had no desire to see her brothers or any other lads she knew in their birthday suits. Ma helped her put the food away, planning what to do with the rabbit they'd got from the butchers and tutting over the quality of some of the vegetables.

'We really should grow more of our own,' she said. 'Your pa had green fingers and kept us well provided for, but I've never had the knack. I would like us to try again, though. Maybe you and the boys have inherited his gardening skills. If my joints weren't so stiff, I'd do it myself, but I can't be bending to weed, and the digging is beyond me these days.'

As well as her problems with her nerves since Pa died, Ma had begun to suffer with her joints in recent times – the result of years of working at the factory, trying to keep her family fed after she'd been widowed. Her hands were riddled with arthritis and she had problems with her back from hunching over to work on fiddly shoe trimmings. Jeannie was sure her eyesight was failing as well because she seemed to have lost interest in reading these days, although Ma wouldn't admit it. She was barely in her forties, but she seemed so much older.

'We got the best we could find, Ma,' she said. 'But maybe we *should* grow our own. We could all help. We could ask old Mr Vowles next door for some advice.' Their neighbour kept a fine vegetable garden, although he wasn't keen on sharing his surplus with anyone.

There was a knock at the door as they sat down for a cup of tea. Jeannie jumped up to answer it. Mattie stood on the doorstep.

'Afternoon, Jeannie, is Lucas in?'

Trying to quell her racing heart, she nodded. 'Come in, Mattie. He's in the kitchen. Want a cuppa?'

'Yes, please,' he smiled as he followed her through the parlour to the back of the cottage. He put a hand on her arm before they reached the kitchen, stalling her. She tried not to let him see how his touch affected her, but she knew her cheeks must be going red. 'I wouldn't mind a bit of advice from you, either,' he said quietly.

'Oh? What about?'

'You know I'm meeting Louisa at the picture house later?'

She nodded, looking at the floor so he would think she was listening but wouldn't see the pain in her eyes at the very thought of it.

'Well, I want to take her a little present. You know, a token, to let her know how much I think of her. I thought maybe a little posy of her favourite flowers. What do you think?'

With her heart hurting, she shook her head. She wished they weren't having this conversation, but she was relieved that he'd thought to ask. 'You shouldn't give her flowers. She wouldn't be able to take them home. How would she explain that to her parents? She told you they won't approve on account of you being a Friend, didn't she?'

He blew out a breath and let go of her arm to run a hand down his face. 'Phew, it's lucky I asked you, Jeannie. Thanks. I hadn't thought about that. The last thing I want to do is make trouble for her. You're a good friend.'

She shrugged, still not looking directly at him. 'I don't want to see her get into bother.' Louisa was still one of her best friends and the fact that she'd captured the heart of the lad Jeannie had been swooning over for as long as she could remember wasn't her fault.

'So what can I get her?' he asked. 'I want to make this special for her.'

Jeannie thought for a moment. 'I know that she likes chocolate and her favourite sweets are sherbet lemons.'

He nodded. 'A nice box of chocolates would be a good idea. She could say she treated herself, couldn't she?'

She wrinkled her nose. 'She's not inclined to spend her money like that. Maybe a bag of sweets and a bar of chocolate might be less likely to make her parents suspicious.'

Lucas appeared in the doorway. 'Mattie, I thought I heard your voice. What are you two gossiping about?'

Mattie grinned. 'Your sister's giving me some advice.' He turned to her. 'Thanks, Jeannie. I really appreciate this. Got to keep on the right side of old man Clements until I can win him over, eh?'

Lucas rolled his eyes. 'So you didn't come to see me?'

'Yeah, I did. But you were too idle to open the door when I knocked, so when I saw Jeannie, I thought I'd ask her.'

'About what?' he frowned, his suspicious gaze going between the two of them.

Mattie grinned. 'Getting a nice present for the sweetest girl in the village. I'm taking Louisa out tonight.'

Lucas shook his head, looking disgusted. 'You're daft in the head if you think buying her presents is going to win her pa round. Give it up, man. You're on a hiding to nothing. I'm surprised he agreed to letting her go out with you.'

Mattie looked a bit shifty. 'He didn't. He thinks she's going out with Kate. But she's got a date with Ted and we're going to meet the girls at the picture house.'

'Are you out of your mind?' Lucas exclaimed. 'If he finds out, he'll kill you. You should call it off.'

'Don't fuss, it'll be alright. Anyway, I can't let her down,' he said. 'I think I'm in love. Louisa is the girl for me, I feel it in my bones. I'll talk her pa round, just you watch me. I've already applied to transfer to the Clicking Room. I reckon, if I work hard, I'll impress him. He'll see that I'll be a good provider.'

'You're joking,' said Lucas. He looked really shocked.

'No. I've never been more serious in my life,' Mattie replied, his eyes shining with sincerity.

The grip around her heart tightened at his words. Jeannie didn't know if she could survive this pain. She turned away. 'Mattie wants a cuppa, Lucas,' she said, her voice rasping against the tightness in her throat. 'Now you're here, you can make it. I've got mending to do.' She went into the kitchen ahead of them, scooping up the pile of clothes that needed repairing and the sewing basket. 'I'll take these into the parlour and let you two talk in peace.'

'Don't you think he should call it off, Jeannie?' asked Lucas.

Of course she did. But was she thinking that because she was genuinely concerned that they were going to get into trouble with her friend's parents? Or was she hoping they would split up because she was jealous of Louisa and wanted her own chance with Mattie? She realised it was a little of both and she didn't like herself very much because of it. It wasn't Louisa's fault that Mattie preferred her to Jeannie.

'It's none of my business,' she said, shaking her head. 'But you should be careful, Mattie. Don't hurt Louisa.'

He put a hand over his heart as Lucas scowled. 'I swear, Jeannie, I would never do anything to hurt her.'

'You don't know that, Mattie,' she said, getting angry. 'If her pa can't be persuaded to accept you, you'll break her heart.'

'She's right,' said Lucas, his voice low and grave. 'What's the rush? You're only eighteen.'

'Nineteen soon,' he said. 'Two days before you.' He grinned. It had always been a great joke to him that their birthdays in November were close together but that he was the eldest. He was always teasing Lucas about it, claiming seniority because of those two days.

Lucas shook his head. 'What the heck are you thinking, Mattie? Give it a few years. If she's the one, she'll still be around. You've barely given yourself the chance to get to know her yet. You could change your mind in a month or two.'

Mattie's mouth set into a stubborn line. 'Once you know, you know. Why should we wait? My ma says Pa told her on their first date that he was going to marry her and neither of them ever regretted it for a moment.'

'There's plenty of other couples who rushed into getting wed and lived to regret it,' he replied.

Mattie held up his hands. 'Look, I'm not rushing into marrying her. I just want the chance to walk out with her without having to sneak around in fear of her pa, alright? That'd do me, for now at any rate.'

Jeannie had heard enough. She sidled past them as they continued to argue and shut the door between the kitchen and parlour. She hoped Louisa appreciated the devotion Mattie was showing to her. As she sat down and began to sort the clothes, finding spare buttons to replace ones that were missing and the right colour wool to darn the holes in socks that the twins seemed to destroy with annoying regularity, she tried not to think about Louisa and Mattie at all. But it was hard.

Her ma found her there an hour later.

'My, lass, you've been busy,' she said as she sat in the armchair opposite her and surveyed the neatly sewn buttons, the elbow patch on a shirt that John had torn, and a pile of darned socks.

'Nearly done,' she said, focusing on her needle. 'Then I can help you with supper.'

'No need. There's a stew in the oven.'

'Oh, I didn't realise you were already cooking, Ma.'

'I did pop my head in earlier, but you were in a world of your own, so I left you to it.'

Jeannie was surprised. 'I'm sorry, I didn't even notice.' She tied off the last piece of thread and gave a deep sigh.

'Lucas has gone round to Mattie's for a bit. He said he'll be but an hour or so.'

Louisa nodded and gave another sigh.

Ma sat down in the chair opposite and gave her a gentle look. 'You don't seem happy, lass. What's bothering you?'

At first, she didn't want to say anything. But the love and sympathy in her ma's eyes loosened her tongue. 'Kate and Louisa are going to the picture house tonight with Ted and Mattie.'

'Did you want to go too? I'm sure we can find some money so you can go. I've got a little left from—'

'No,' she said. 'It's not that. I'm not that bothered about seeing a film. It's just... well... my best friends have got chaps asking them out.' She felt her eyes fill with tears as understanding washed over Ma's face. 'No one's ever asked me out, Ma. I feel like I'm going to be left on the shelf.'

'Ah, Jeannie, lass. Your time will come. You're only sixteen. There's no rush.'

'That's what Lucas told Mattie about Louisa.'

Her mother regarded her for a few moments. 'I know you've carried a torch for young Mattie for a while,' she said gently. 'Is that what's really bothering you?'

She was going to deny it, but she couldn't. Instead, she closed her eyes against the tears that fell and nodded. 'He's never looked at me like he does Louisa,' she sobbed. 'I'm just not pretty enough.'

Ma leaned forward and put her hands on Jeannie's shoulders. 'What's this? Not pretty enough? Jeannie, look at me.'

Louisa couldn't deny her mother but she raised her head with reluctance. She didn't want to see pity in Ma's eyes. She didn't expect the fierceness of her expression.

'Now you listen to me, Jeannie Musgrove. Just because a girl's got bright hair, it doesn't mean she's prettier than anyone else. You might not catch a lad's eye straight away like a blonde girl would, but don't you dare put yourself down. Do you know what I see when I look at you?'

Jeannie shook her head, too full of emotion to speak.

'I see a lovely-looking girl with clear skin and warm, hazel eyes and the sweetest smile I've ever witnessed. I see a kind, compassionate, clever young woman who's devoted to her family, and a friend who is loyal and loving.'

She gave her ma one of her sweet smiles, but it was tinged with sadness. 'You're my ma,' she said. 'Of course you'd say that.'

'And it's because I'm your ma that you should listen to me. I'm not giving you a load of flannel, lass. While there are girls out there that turn lads' heads just by walking down the road, none of them have what you have, Jeannie. Your beauty shines through from here,' she touched her daughter's heart, 'any lad worth his salt will see that the moment he starts to talk with you. He'll see your warmth, your sharp mind and your good heart. That's true beauty, which never fades. A pretty hairdo and a bit of make-up will cover a multitude of sins and I'll wager will lead to disappointment in most cases.'

'But Louisa is lovely, inside and out, Ma. I can't compete with her.'

Ma touched her cheek, wiping away her tears. 'You don't need to compete, my love. Mattie's not the one for you, nice lad that he is. No, there's someone else out there for you. You just have to be patient. When you meet the right man, you'll both know it.'

She sniffed. 'In the meantime, I have to watch while my friends start courting and I'm left at home darning the twins' socks.'

The moment she uttered the words and saw the pain they caused her mother, she regretted them. 'I'm sorry, Ma. I didn't mean it like that. I don't mind doing the mending. I know you do what you can for all of us.'

Ma kissed her forehead. 'I know, lass. I'm sorrier than I can say that I put so much on your shoulders. You're the best daughter a mother could ever wish for. I promise, when you meet the right lad, I won't hold you back. I want you to be as happy with your love as I was with your pa. But promise me, Jeannie. Don't you ever go thinking you're not as beautiful or deserving of love as your friends. Trust that God has a plan for you and He will reveal it in his own time.'

'Alright, Ma. I'll try.'

10

'How can you be so calm about this?' asked Louisa. 'I'm shaking with nerves.'

Kate laughed. She'd called for Louisa and now they were walking through Glastonbury towards the picture house, where Ted and Mattie were going to meet them. 'Probably because I'm not so bothered about having a sweetheart as you are,' she said. 'I mean, I like Ted well enough, but I'm still not sure I'm ready to be courting. In fact, I don't know if I'll ever be.'

Louisa frowned. 'Whyever not? I swear I've been dreaming of having a sweetheart for as long as I can remember.'

Kate shrugged. 'I don't see the point, really. Why get all het up about a lad, only to have him turn into your pa the minute he has his ring on your finger?'

'What do you mean?'

'I mean, he'll be expecting you to give up any dreams you have and devote your life to keeping him happy.'

'I don't think Mattie's like that,' she said. 'He's very good to his ma. I'm sure he'd be just as kind to his sweetheart.'

'I hope you're right, Lou. But not every lad is like that. And who's to say he won't change when he's married? Ma says Pa was a real charmer when they were courting. But look at him now, the miserable so-and-so. He's never kind. In fact, he's downright mean. Ma had to sneak me some money for this evening.'

'Won't Ted pay for your ticket?'

'I don't know. Maybe he will. But I couldn't come without enough to pay for my own if he didn't, could I? I've never been out with a lad before, so don't know what to expect.'

'Mattie's already told me he's paying for mine.'

'Good for him. But I haven't got Ted Jackson's measure yet, so I'm not expecting anything.'

'Well, I am,' Louisa giggled. 'I'm expecting Mattie to hold my hand, maybe even give me a bit of a cuddle. And if I don't get my first kiss tonight, I'm going to be sorely disappointed.'

Kate scowled. 'Just be careful. I told Ted I want to take it slow, like. He'd better not be getting all handsy with me tonight. I'm not even sure if I fancy him that way.'

They turned the corner into Magdalene Street and saw the lads waiting outside the Town Hall where the picture house was situated. There was quite a queue lining up to get in.

'I hope no one sees us and tells my pa,' said Louisa, suddenly seeming less excited and more scared as they got closer.

'Don't act like you're doing something you shouldn't,' Kate advised. 'We're here to see the film and just happen to see the lads, who are friends of ours. There's nothing wrong in that.'

'I suppose not.'

'Just make sure he keeps his hands to himself while anyone's looking.'

Louisa nodded. 'Hands to himself. Right.' She paused. 'But we can hold hands in the dark, can't we?'

Kate nodded. 'But no kissing. Someone's bound to see.'

'Mattie says we can sit in the back row, then no one will see.'

She groaned. 'I'm not sitting in the back row. Everyone knows what couples get up to there.'

Louisa didn't comment as they reached the lads. She was suddenly very nervous. Maybe they shouldn't sit in the back row then? But if they didn't, someone was bound to see them kiss.

The look of adoration in Mattie's eyes when he greeted her made her pulse race and pushed all of her doubts from her mind. He was so handsome. She *had* to kiss him tonight. She might never get another chance.

It turned out that Ted and Mattie had already bought tickets for the girls, so they didn't have to queue up. This week's feature included a short Fatty Arbuckle film followed by *Little Lord Fauntleroy*.

'I read the book of *Little Lord Fauntleroy* a few years back,' said Louisa as the credits started for the first feature. 'It's a wonderful story. I can't wait to see the film.'

'I hope you like it,' said Mattie. 'I know I will, because you're here with me.' He took her hand and kissed it.

A thrill rushed through her at the feel of his lips on the back of her hand and she nearly swooned at the romance of the gesture. When he continued to hold her hand as the film began, she gave a happy sigh and sat back. She gave him a sideways glance and saw that he was watching her with a smile on his face.

'Alone at last,' he whispered, making her giggle.

Ted had tried to persuade Kate into the back row near them, but she'd shaken her head and marched down the aisle a few rows. He had followed, his shoulders slumped, making Mattie chuckle.

Louisa leaned closer to him. 'If Ted's hoping for a kiss tonight, he's going to be out of luck,' she whispered.

Mattie inclined his head towards her. 'And am I going to be out of luck, too?' he asked softly, making her shiver as his warm breath caressed her cheek.

She shrugged, feeling shy. She wanted him to kiss her more than she'd wanted anything in her whole life, but she didn't want to say that in case he thought she was going to let him take advantage of her. 'I don't know,' she said. 'I don't want you to think I'm easy, because I'm not.'

'I know you're not. But that doesn't stop me wanting to be lucky tonight, Louisa. It would be a dream come true. I've been wanting to kiss you for months. Every time I see you walking to and from the factory, I want to take you in my arms and kiss you. But if you're not ready, that's alright; I can wait. Because I reckon I'm already the luckiest lad here seeing as how I'm with the prettiest girl in Somerset.'

At his soft words, her doubts and shyness fell away. She touched his cheek and raised her chin, bringing their lips together for their first sweet kiss.

* * *

Kate felt antsy as Ted settled down next to her. She'd been irritated and embarrassed when he'd tried to lead her into the back row. She was ready to give him a good telling off, but his whispered, 'Sorry, Kate,' disarmed her. He looked genuinely contrite.

'There's a better view of the screen from here,' she said by way of her own apology.

As the lights went down, he leaned closer. Kate leaned away, turning to push him away when he put something in her hand.

'What's this?' she asked. It felt like a smallish, flat box.

'Chocolates,' he said. 'It's not much, but I hope you like them.'

The curtains in front of the screen swished open and some of the audience gave a small cheer as the Fatty Arbuckle film began to play. Ted turned towards the screen. In the light reflected from the screen, Kate could see that his ears had gone red. She looked down at the small box in her hands. It was heart-shaped with a picture of flowers on the lid. She'd never been given anything so pretty before and it made her feel awful that she'd been so snappy with him.

'Thank you, Ted. It's very thoughtful of you,' she said, touching his arm. He looked at her and smiled. 'Do you want one?' she asked.

He shook his head. 'I haven't got much of a sweet tooth,' he said. 'They're all for you.'

She opened the lid. There were half a dozen little chocolates, all different. Inside the lid was an illustrated paper listing which sweet was which flavour. She selected a violet crème and popped it in her mouth. 'Oh, my,' she murmured. 'Delicious.'

She put the lid back on the box. She would take her time eating these. In fact, she might save the rest and take them home to share with Ma. A little treat might make her feel a little better. Kate was feeling guilty about leaving Ma alone this evening while Pa went to the Street Inn as usual.

He never bothered to spend any time with his wife – or his daughter, for that matter. Not that Kate was worried about that. She'd long ago realised that her father wasn't a loving man and was best avoided if you didn't want a slap for the slightest reason.

She settled down to watch the film and was soon laughing at the antics. Ted seemed pleased that she found the same things funny and kept smiling at her as they clapped along to the music and cheered with everyone else when the hero prevailed. In the interval, he didn't rush off like some of the lads to chat to their pals, but stayed with Kate, asking after her Ma and telling her about how one of his brothers was already in Flanders and the other had just finished his basic training and would be home for a few days before being shipped overseas.

'I hope they come back soon,' she said. 'My brothers have said they won't go unless they have to.'

'But they're married, aren't they? It makes more sense for the single lads to go first, doesn't it?'

'It doesn't make sense for anyone to go,' she said, feeling frustrated. 'Surely the government could negotiate with the Kaiser instead of rushing into the fight like this.'

Ted sighed. 'You're probably right. But who knows what's been going on behind the scenes? For all we know, they might have been trying to reason with him for months before they declared war.'

Kate blinked in shock. She barely registered the words he said after he told her she was probably right. Not a single man or boy had *ever* said those words to her, even when she'd used the strongest, most logical arguments. They usually told her to shut up because she was a girl and wouldn't understand such things. The fact that he considered what she'd said and actually thought she might be right both shocked and thrilled her.

She looked at him with new eyes. Before, she'd thought he was nice-enough looking and had a fairly pleasant disposition. But now... his brown eyes showed an intelligence she hadn't given him credit for and his actions revealed a kindness and respect for her that she hadn't noticed before.

The lights began to dim, signalling that the main feature was about to start. Ted leaned closer, but not too close.

'Kate, would it be alright if I held your hand?' he asked.

If he'd asked earlier, she'd have said no. But now she felt more comfortable with him. 'Alright,' she said.

He smiled as he took her hand and covered it with both of his. Kate felt something loosen in her gut. This wasn't so bad. His grip was warm and dry and gentle. Not sweaty and too tight like her pa's punishing hands. It was nice. She'd always thought of hand-holding as something someone did to keep you in check, to stop you from running away. But she didn't feel like a prisoner in Ted's hands. She wasn't sure how she felt, but it was quite pleasant. With a sigh, she relaxed and concentrated on the film.

* * *

In the back row, Louisa barely noticed the first film. She was cuddled as close as she could get to Mattie, who was constantly kissing her. He was a good kisser. At least, she thought he was, although she had no previous experience to compare him to. His lips were firm yet gentle, and not too wet – she'd heard girls in the Machine Room complain about sloppy kisses and she hadn't looked forward to receiving one. She'd had to tell him to stop him touching her hair as she didn't want her ma asking how she'd managed to mess up her hairdo. She had a comb in her bag for repairs and could blame so much on the wind, but she didn't want to risk the slightest chance of Ma suspecting that a boy had been running his hands through her hair in the back row of the picture house.

In the interval, she'd rushed off to the toilet before the lights had come up. She'd suggested to Mattie that he didn't wait for her in their seats during the break because they couldn't risk anyone wondering who he was with and seeing them together while the lights were up. They both slipped back into their seats when the lights went down again, Louisa giggling over the subterfuge.

As they settled down again for the main feature, Mattie put his arm around her and held her close, sharing the chocolate and sherbet lemons he'd brought for her. Louisa rested her head on his shoulder and knew she had never felt happier in her whole life.

* * *

About halfway through the film, Kate noticed that Ted was fidgeting.

'What's the matter?' she asked quietly.

'Nothing,' he whispered. 'Just trying to get comfortable.' His legs were so long that his knees touched the back of the seat in front.

'You should have taken an aisle seat,' she told him. 'Then you could've stretched out a bit.'

Someone in the row behind them shushed them. Ted ignored them, leaning towards her ear. Unlike before, she didn't shy away this time. 'If we cuddled up, I could have a bit more room,' he whispered.

She glanced up at his hopeful face with suspicion. 'Just a cuddle,' she whispered.

With a grin, he let go of her hand and put his arm around her, leaning over the armrest to hold her close. He sighed as this gave him the chance to stretch his legs out sideways. 'That's better,' he murmured.

Kate couldn't relax. He was big and it felt hot with his body pressed against hers. But he'd asked politely, and at least he wasn't all squished up against the seat in front now, so he'd stopped fidgeting. She decided she could put up with it and focused back on the film. She couldn't help thinking she'd preferred it when they were just holding hands, though. Being held this close to a male body made her feel vulnerable. The only time Pa got this close to her was to hurt her. It felt as though her body was remembering that and raising her heart rate so that she could flee.

Ted, on the other hand, seemed to be perfectly content. His fingers began gently stroking her neck, just below her ear. She wasn't sure whether he was even aware that he was doing it because when she looked at him, he was watching the film. She shifted her head, trying to dislodge him without being obvious about it. His fingers stopped their movements for a moment, but then they moved to her collar bone and started again... softly... as though she was something delicate to be treated with care. No one but her ma had ever touched her with such gentleness, but she didn't know whether she could trust this. She closed her eyes, willing her heart to slow down, wishing he'd stop while at the same time wishing he wouldn't.

'You're so lovely, Kate.'

His warm breath against her ear as he whispered the words made her start and open her eyes. On the screen, Little Lord Fauntleroy's uncle's widow was scheming to replace the sweet little lord with her own son, who had been born before her bigamous marriage, as the heir to the title. She was lying through her teeth in order to get her own way. As Kate recognised the greed and selfishness in the woman's eyes, Ted's hand slipped lower, touching the top of her breast over her blouse. At the same time, his other hand cupped her cheek and turned her face. He kissed her without so much as a by-your-leave.

Kate gasped, trying to pull away, her skin heating with panic. This wasn't how she wanted her first kiss to be. But Ted was a man on a mission now and he didn't let go. She froze, not knowing what to do.

It was the muttering of the woman sitting behind them that spurred her into action. 'Shameless, young people these days,' she said, flooding Kate with anger.

Her words and disgusted tone that gave her the strength to latch onto his hand at her cheek and wrench it away. At the same time, she arched away from him, breaking contact with his lips.

'Let me go!' she hissed. 'Or so help me, Ted Jackson, I will bite you.'

Still clearly enthralled by the kiss, Ted blinked at her in confusion for a moment before letting her go. Kate immediately stood up, picked up her bag and started down the row away from him. She couldn't stay here another moment. The people in the seats between her and the aisle grumbled as she apologised and stumbled in her rush to get away from him.

'Kate, wait!' he said.

Several people shushed him, others called out for them to sit down. But Kate was desperate to get away. She finally reached the aisle and began to run towards the exit. She didn't stop until she got outside. Only then did she remember that she was supposed to be walking home with

Louisa. She leant against the wall, catching her breath, trying to decide what to do.

Mattie would see Louisa safely home, she was sure. And she would see Louisa in church tomorrow and apologise, but there was no way she could go back into the picture house now, and she wasn't inclined to hang around.

No, she would walk home alone. It was dark, but there was a full moon, so she could see her way well enough.

The door burst open and Ted rushed outside. 'Kate! What's the matter? Are you alright?'

She turned on him, letting her anger overcome her fear. 'No, I'm not alright, Ted Jackson. How dare you?'

He stepped towards her and she took a step back. She was angry, but she wasn't stupid. He wasn't getting close enough to touch her again. When he saw her expression he stopped, raising his hands as though in surrender.

'I don't understand,' he said. 'We were getting on so well.'

'We were, until you started taking liberties,' she snapped. 'I told you, just a cuddle, and truth be told, I wasn't all that comfortable with that. But you agreed, and you seemed trustworthy, so I thought I could rely on you to be decent. Then you had to get all handsy, didn't you? And who gave you permission to touch me like that and kiss me? I certainly didn't. What sort of a girl d'you think I am?'

His shoulders slumped and he lowered his head. 'I'm sorry. I thought you'd like it. A lot of girls pretend they don't want a kiss but they enjoy it when it happens.'

'Who told you that?'

He looked away. 'A friend.'

'Well, he's wrong and I'm not *a lot of girls*, thank you very much.'

He raised his head, his expression earnest as he gazed at her. 'I know you're not, Kate. That's what I like about you.'

'Well, next time you *like* a girl, don't listen to what your pals tell you about what a girl wants and listen to her instead. A cuddle does not mean she wants a... a *mauling*, and it certainly doesn't give you permission to steal a kiss. Half the people in that picture house will know you were taking advantage of me, Ted Jackson. You've probably ruined my reputation now.' She turned away, too angry to cry. 'Now leave me alone. I'm going home.'

He fell into step beside her as she strode quickly down the hill. 'I'm so sorry, Kate. I wasn't thinking straight. Please forgive me.'

'No, go away.'

'At least let me see you home.'

'I'm perfectly capable of making my own way, thank you very much. You've done enough for one evening.'

'I won't touch you, I promise. I was out of order. I know that now.'

'As if I'd let you touch me again,' she scoffed, increasing her pace. 'You were most definitely out of order. I'll never trust you again.'

Even as she said it, she felt an overwhelming sense of sadness. They *had* been getting along until his hands and lips had gotten the better of him, and for a little while she'd been hopeful that... But no. She took a deep breath, aware that his longer legs were easily keeping up with her. She was beginning to get hot and bothered with the rush, whereas he was barely breaking a sweat as he lolloped along beside her – a fact which added to her irritation.

'If that's how you feel, then fair enough,' he said, his expression grim. 'I was a blinking idiot, and I'll always regret it. But it's my own fault, so I'll have to accept your judgement. But I'll not compound my sins by abandoning you to walk home alone in the dark. So you can either stop and we'll wait for Louisa to come out of the picture house so you can walk with her, or you'll have to put up with me until I see you safely to your door.'

Kate was taken aback by his masterful tone. She slowed her steps but was reluctant to stop altogether as she thought about what to do. 'Mattie will see Louisa home,' she said eventually. 'I just hope he's not daft enough to go right to her front door. Her pa will be looking out for her.' But Louisa knew that, so she would make him leave her just out of sight of the house. She and Lou usually parted ways at The Cross, as it wasn't too far up Somerton Road to her house, so Mr Clements would expect to see her coming up the road alone.

'Alright. Then I'll see you home safe.'

She glanced at him sideways. 'So long as you keep your distance.'

'Agreed,' he said, although he didn't sound too happy about it. 'And I hope one day you'll accept my apology and give me another chance.'

She opened her mouth, intending to tell him that hell would freeze over before that happened, but shocked herself by simply saying, 'We'll see.'

The walk from Glastonbury to Street was accomplished in silence. Kate couldn't understand why she'd said that. But Ted seemed content with it and adjusted his long pace to her shorter one as her anger slowly faded and her rush to get away diminished. By the time they reached Silver Road and her parents' cottage, she felt calmer.

She stopped by the front gate, looking up at the building in the moonlight. It was the middle house in a terrace of seven cottages built from the blue lias stone that was quarried locally and used in most of the buildings in the village. The front grass needed cutting. Her brother George was due to come round and see to it soon, but his wife Vi had a baby – little George – so they were a bit busy these days. The paintwork around the door and windows was looking a bit shabby, because Pa refused to spend money on a bit of paint to smarten them up. He said it was the landlord's problem, not his. As the Clarks were his landlords and paid his wages, Kate thought he should show a bit more respect for their property, but she didn't dare say so. She noticed weeds growing in the guttering on the edge of the roof as well.

Ted stood quietly beside her while she contemplated all this. She wondered what he thought of the dilapidated state of the house, made all the more stark by the neatly kept houses and gardens on either side. She knew his ma and pa from church and had been past their cottage a time or two. It always looked immaculate.

'I've been thinking,' he said softly into the silence. 'Will you hear me out?'

She glanced at him. He looked hesitant. 'What are you thinking?' she asked.

'What you said about your reputation. It's bothering me. I don't want anyone to think badly of you because of me acting like an idiot.'

'It's a bit late for that,' she said, crossing her arms over her chest and feeling herself getting cross again. It was bad enough that she was constantly ashamed by her pa's drinking and brash behaviour. The thought that people would think she was a loose woman made her burn with the injustice of it all.

'Maybe not,' he said, his tone thoughtful. 'Not if we were officially courting.' He held up a hand when she opened her mouth to speak. 'I know you don't want kisses. I'm not daft. I've learned that lesson well. But, you know, I like you, Kate, and even if you don't like me in *that* way, I'd still like us to be friends.'

She frowned and tilted her head to the side as she viewed him through narrowed eyes. 'I don't know what you're saying. What d'you mean?'

He ran a hand through his hair, grimacing. 'Sorry, I'm not good at this sort of thing.'

She laughed, a short, sharp, unamused snort. 'You can say that again.'

He nodded, then took a deep breath. 'I just thought that, if we went out – either with other friends or on our own – and people saw us together, they would see we were really courting. Then no one would think you were easy because of that kiss at the picture house. It would save your reputation. What do you think?'

She stared at him, her mind whirling. He was a nice lad, tall and good-looking and he was clean and tidy. He'd brought her chocolates and held her hand and made her feel special. But she'd hated the way he'd got all handsy. Maybe one day she'd want that, but tonight she hadn't been ready, and maybe she wouldn't be ready for a long time.

'No kissing or getting handsy?' she asked.

His face fell for a moment, then he took a breath and looked more determined. 'Not if you don't want it, I swear. Although... people will expect us to hold hands, and maybe share a little peck now and then.'

'Mmm. I'll not have you leaping on me again like you did tonight, Ted Jackson.'

He tried to hide his smile, but couldn't quite manage it. Kate liked that she could read his expressions easily. He knew she was wavering, but he also knew he shouldn't get cocky about it or she'd get mad again.

'I promise you, Kate, I will not kiss you again unless you say I can.'

'And if I only want a peck on the cheek?'

'Then that's what you shall get.'

She sighed. 'Alright. But you step out of line just one more time, then that'll be it. Understood?'

He nodded, no longer trying to hide his smile.

Kate waved goodbye to him as she closed the front door quietly. The light in the parlour was out, but her parents' bedroom light had been on when they'd come up the lane and, as she walked into the cottage, she saw that her father was in the kitchen, sitting at the table with a jug of cider in front of him.

Her heart sank. She'd hoped he'd still be at the Inn, or already in bed in a drunken slumber.

'Where you been, girl?' he demanded when he saw her hesitating in the doorway.

'To the picture house with Louisa.'

He sneered. 'Getting a bit above yourself, gallivanting with the foreman's daughter, ain't you?'

Kate shrugged, not wanting to provoke him. 'She's been my friend since school, Pa.'

He grunted and took another noisy slurp from his tankard. 'Bloody waste, going to that picture house. I suppose she gave you the money for it?' He pointed a grubby hand towards the ceiling.

Kate didn't say anything. It was no good denying it, or arguing with him.

'Well, now you're here, get your arse upstairs and sort her out. Bloody woman's been sick all over my bed. Clean it up and if she does it again, she'll be sleeping in your bed from now on.'

Kate rushed towards the stairs. 'Is she alright?'

"Course she's alright. Probably something she ate. Always looking for attention, that one. Should have made her clean it up herself but the useless mare's just lying there, looking pathetic.'

She was up the stairs before he'd finished, rushing towards her mother's room, terrified of what she might find.

11

On Sunday after church, Louisa knocked on the Davis family's front door. She hoped that Mr Davis was out. He wasn't very nice and he always looked at Louisa with a mix of anger, contempt and lust in his bloodshot eyes, making her feel dirty and uncomfortable. If she wasn't so worried about Kate, she would never come here.

She breathed a sigh of relief when her friend answered the door.

'Louisa,' said Kate. 'What are you doing here?'

'I missed you and your ma at church this morning. I wanted to make sure that everything's alright. I mean, it's not like you and your ma to miss a Sunday, and you must've left the picture house early because we couldn't find you or Ted anywhere. So I just had to come round and check that you weren't ill.'

Kate sighed and shook her head. 'Thank you for thinking of us. It's not me; I'm alright. But Ma's proper poorly,' she said quietly. 'Come in.' She stepped back and opened the door wider so Louisa could pass into the parlour and follow her into the back kitchen, which was filled with steam. 'Pa's out, lord knows where. When I got home last night, he was in his cups as usual. Said Ma had been sick and I had to clean her up, then he went out again. He hasn't been home yet. I've been boiling the water to wash the sheets and her nightdress.' She indicated the piles of linens on the draining board and on the stone floor by the sink. 'I'm on the last one.'

'Is she still being sick?'

'Not at the moment, but I can't get her to eat anything. I'm really worried about her, Lou. Pa won't let me get the doctor, and Ma won't let me tell Peg or my brothers.' Kate scrubbed a hand down her face. 'I've been up with her all night, fretting about her. I don't know what to do for the best.'

'Aw, I'm so sorry, Kate.' Louisa hugged her. 'What can I do to help?'

She rested her tired head on her friend's shoulder for a moment, taking some brief comfort from her embrace. 'Thanks. But there's no need,' she said, stepping back and raising her chin.

'There's every need,' Louisa replied, rolling up her sleeves. 'Let's get these sheets finished, shall we?'

Kate smiled for the first time that day. 'How about you make us a cuppa while I scrub the last sheet? I know how delicate your stomach is. I can't be doing with you emptying your stomach on the kitchen floor after I've just mopped it.'

Louisa pulled a face. 'I can't help it if some things make me heave. But alright, I'll make some tea, and when they're clean, I'll help you put them through the mangle. Will your ma be wanting a cuppa, d'you think?'

Kate shook her head. 'I just checked on her. She's asleep. I'd rather let her rest for now, otherwise she'll be wanting to get up and start fussing about putting a meal on the table for him.' She scowled and lowered her voice. 'I wish he'd fall into a barrel of his precious cider and drown, Lou, I really do.'

Louisa didn't know what to say to that. Her parents were nothing like Kate's. They were strict, but never cruel. She knew they loved her and they certainly didn't hit her like Kate's pa did to her sometimes. Neither of her parents were drinkers either and they cared for each other. She realised how very lucky she was compared to her friend. It made her feel guilty that she was feeling so hard done by lately.

They worked side by side. Kate took a break to drink the tea Louisa made for her and to let the sheet soak in the hot, soapy water so that it would be easier to scrub. She insisted that Louisa sit at the kitchen table while she got on with the job.

'Anyway, I'm sorry I left you in the lurch last night,' she said as she worked. 'I hope Mattie had the decency to see you home.'

Louisa smiled, her face glowing. 'He did, although I made him leave me at The Cross in case Pa was watching, which he was.' She fanned her face. 'Phew! I'm so relieved I thought of it.'

'Just as well you did then,' smiled Kate.

'So, what happened with you and Ted? We couldn't find hide nor hair of either of you when the film finished.'

Kate rolled her eyes as she looked over her shoulder at Louisa. 'You didn't notice all the kerfuffle when I got up in the middle of the main feature and left him sitting there? Or him chasing after me out of the picture house?'

Louisa gaped. She hadn't expected that, and now she felt guilty for being so wrapped up in Mattie that she hadn't noticed. How could she have let her friend down like that? 'Oh, no! Oh, my word, Kate. What did he do? He didn't hurt you, did he?'

Kate turned away, shaking her head. 'If he'd hurt me, I'd have screamed the place down,' she said. 'It's bad enough that Pa's the way he is. If a lad tried to treat me wrong, I wouldn't keep quiet.'

'You're so fierce, Kate,' said Louisa. 'I've always admired that about you. I'm sorry your pa's so awful and I'm relieved Ted didn't hurt you. I didn't think he was the sort, but you never know, do you? So, come on then, tell me, what he did do?'

She paused and looked down at the sheet in the sink and the scrubbing brush in her hand. She began to scrub again before she answered. 'He bought me chocolates in a heart-shaped box,' she said.

Louisa got up and came to stand beside her. She didn't look down at the sink, but searched Kate's face instead. 'That's good, isn't it? I'd say that's very romantic. Mattie got me some sherbet lemons and a bar of chocolate. Ted must be really sweet on you.'

Kate shrugged, not making eye contact as she scrubbed even harder. 'We had a lovely chat in the interval and he held my hand. He seemed like a decent chap.'

Louisa leaned closer. 'So, what happened?'

She sighed and dropped the scrubbing brush in the water. Her hands were red from the heat of the water. They were shaking slightly. She rested them on the edge of the porcelain sink. 'He asked if he could cuddle me and I said yes. It seemed alright at first, although I wasn't that comfortable and was getting a bit warm. But then he started getting handsy and then he kissed me.' Her words came out in a rush as her face flushed as red as her hands. 'It's not how I wanted my first kiss to be.'

Louisa wasn't sure what to say. While all this had been happening, she'd been getting *her* first kiss and she'd loved it. She was upset for her friend that her experience hadn't been as good. She put an arm around Kate's shoulders. 'How did you want it to be?' she asked.

'I don't know,' she sighed. 'I'd have liked a bit of warning for a start, and maybe for him to wait until I was ready. I told him I didn't want any funny stuff, but he just didn't listen.' She looked at Louisa with troubled eyes. 'I like him well enough, but I'm not looking for a sweetheart yet. In fact, I'm not sure I'll ever be. Pa hasn't exactly left me with any faith in the males of the species. Now, it looks like I'm stuck with Ted for the foreseeable future.'

'Whatever do you mean?'

She looked away again and plunged her hands back into the water. She found the brush and began scrubbing again in earnest. 'When he followed me outside, I tore a strip off him. I said he'd ruined my reputation, being all over me like that in the middle of the picture house for everyone to see.'

'I'm sure no one would've noticed in the dark,' said Louisa, trying to reassure her.

'Oh, they did alright. You didn't hear what the woman behind us was saying. I'm surprised it's not all over the village as well as Glastonbury by now.' She took a deep breath and blew it out. 'So Ted reckons we should let everyone see we're a proper courting couple so they don't think so badly of me.'

'You're courting?' Louisa squealed, wanting to jump up and down with excitement while at the same time confused about how unhappy Kate looked about it.

Kate nodded, then shook her head. 'I suppose so. I'm not sure. I don't know if I want to. I mean, I was having a lovely time until he got too close and started getting all handsy and kissy-kissy.' She pulled a face which made Louisa laugh.

'Oh, Kate. Maybe I should get Mattie to talk to him. Ted's obviously not doing it right.'

Kate gave her a sideways glance. 'And Mattie is?'

She beamed at her. 'He's perfect,' she sighed. 'I don't ever want to kiss anyone else for as long as I live.'

Kate groaned. 'God, Lou, be careful. You go swanning around with that smile on your face and your ma and pa will soon know you're walking out with Mattie. You know they'll put a stop to it right away, don't you?'

That wiped the smile from her face. Instead, her brow creased with worry. 'But it's true,' she confessed. 'He's the one for me, Kate. What am I going to do?'

'Just be careful, alright?'

The fear of losing Mattie was stronger than the fear of lying to her parents, so she nodded. 'I will.'

'Good. Maybe we can walk out together and bring some others along? If we're in a crowd, Ted won't be able to get too close to me,' she said with an exaggerated shudder.

* * *

Louisa managed to keep her secret for a couple of weeks. Every day except Sundays, she would 'bump into' Mattie at The Cross on the way to work. They would greet each other politely and then walk together to the factory. With plenty of people around them, they made sure not to touch and rarely even made eye contact – because whenever Louisa caught Mattie's warm, brown gaze, she would melt and blush. But they'd talked, getting to know each other better with each conversation. And with each word, Louisa became more and more convinced that Mattie was the only one for her. She just needed to find a way to show her parents what a good lad he was and how well they were suited. But it wasn't easy, given her pa's prejudice against Friends.

Mattie was doing his bit. He'd applied for and been granted a transfer into the Clicking Room and was now working under Louisa's father. He was working hard, always willing, trying everything he could to impress Mr Clements.

'He's a tough nut to crack, your pa,' he told Louisa on the way into work one morning. 'But he said I was doing a good job yesterday, so I think I'm getting his measure.'

'Don't get complacent, though,' she warned. 'Pa has very high standards.'

'I won't,' he assured her. 'Not when you're the prize.'

She cut a quick glance at him and saw that he was smiling. She loved his smile. Truth be told, she loved everything about him, but she didn't have the nerve to say it before he did. When he saw her looking, he winked. Louisa turned away, trying not to blush.

'I wondered if we could eat our dinners together today,' he said, as cool as a cucumber. 'What d'you think? We could sit somewhere quiet in the canteen. Maybe get some of our pals to make a group of it around us so we don't stand out too much.'

Louisa wanted to say yes straight away, but she hesitated. 'I don't know. Let me talk to Kate and Jeannie.'

'Good idea. I'll be in the canteen at dinner time. I'll get Lucas and Ted along. Everyone knows Kate's walking out with Ted, and her sister's married to my brother. As Jeannie is Lucas's sister, and he's my best mate, no one will bat an eyelid.'

Louisa wasn't so sure, but she was willing to give it a try. 'Alright. See you later.'

They shared an intimate smile, one that said all the things they didn't dare say out loud in public, one that remembered their sweet kisses in the picture house, one that spoke of their hopes for a future together, before Louisa turned towards the stairs leading up to the Machine Room.

That was when she saw her pa and realised he had been standing there, watching them.

Mattie didn't turn up in the canteen at dinner time. Nor was he anywhere to be seen outside the factory at the end of her shift. Instead, Pa found her and told her to get home and tell Ma that his lads were working extra hours because they were behind on their targets and he was staying to make sure they knuckled down and didn't waste company time. She didn't dare ask about Mattie and Pa didn't mention him by name. But she couldn't help worrying that he *would* have something to say as soon as he got home.

She walked along the High Street to The Cross along with the crowds of workers who were heading home. Even surrounded by so many people, she couldn't help but feel lonely without Mattie at her side.

When Pa eventually arrived home, Ma fussed about how long their supper had been kept warm in the oven and how it wasn't right to expect a man to work so hard.

'There's a war on, woman,' he grumbled as he sat at the table. 'We're short-staffed and short-supplied, but we've still got to fulfil our orders. If we lose customers, we'll have a devil of a job getting them back, then we'll start losing jobs at the factory.'

Louisa sat quietly as her mother dished up their meal. She'd insisted that they wait for Pa to get home before they ate. Ma thought it was important for them to eat together as a family every evening and at the weekends. By rights, Louisa should be starving on account of the delay, but since she'd seen Pa watching her and Mattie this morning, she'd been a bundle of nerves and her hunger had fled.

Now, she looked at her plate and wondered how on earth she'd manage to eat it without being sick, she was in that much of a state. Not that Ma had noticed, because she was doing her best to appear as calm as usual. She reasoned that if she acted as though nothing of importance had happened, Pa would forget what he'd seen, or at least decide it wasn't anything he needed to be concerned about.

Pa said grace and began to eat as soon as he said the Amen. Louisa picked up her cutlery and did the same. Ma didn't seem to notice anything out of the ordinary, and chattered on about inconsequential things like the flower rota in the church and how someone's son had tried enlisting but had been rejected on account of his weak chest.

Louisa listened with half an ear, eating slowly and steadily in the hope that her stomach wouldn't revolt. She slowly began to relax and enjoy the meal. She even accepted a small portion of jam roly-poly and custard for pudding.

It wasn't until Pa had finished his meal and had accepted a cup of tea from Ma that he turned to Louisa.

'You seemed mighty friendly with young Matthew Searle this morning, Louisa,' he said.

Ma straightened in her seat and cast a narrow-eyed gaze at her daughter.

Louisa tried not to fidget. She'd almost let down her guard, but thanked her lucky stars she hadn't quite trusted that she'd got away with it. So she smiled and shrugged. 'He's Kate's sister's brother-in-law, and Jeannie's brother's best friend.'

'Yet none of them were talking to him this morning. Only you, lass. You know he's a *Friend*?' He said the word with a slight sneer which made Louisa want to call him on it. But she didn't dare.

'I believe so, Pa,' she said, keeping her voice calm and trying her hardest not to appear too interested. Yet she couldn't help but say, 'I hear he's working for you now. Is he doing well?'

Pa took a sip of his tea before replying. 'He'll do well enough. He's willing to learn and does as he's told.'

She nodded, determined not to reveal the elation she was feeling inside.

'But that doesn't mean I want you getting too friendly with him,' he continued, reducing her hopes to ruins in a moment.

'Goodness, no,' said Ma. 'We'll find you a decent Anglican lad, don't you worry, lass.'

Louisa dropped her spoon into her bowl with a clatter as she felt the blood drain from her face. 'Ma, I've already told you, I'm not interested.'

'Nonsense. Every girl needs to consider her future. And hanging around Quaker lads is not going to do you any good. We need to get you more involved in the church socials now you're older. And I really don't think you should keep on associating with Jeannie Musgrove, Louisa.'

'Whyever not?' she asked, stunned. 'Jeannie's one of the nicest, kindest people I know.'

Pa watched, impassive, as Ma waved a hand in dismissal of Louisa's feelings. 'Oh, she's a nice enough girl, but she's not one of us, is she? I don't mind you working with her, but do you have to spend so much time with her outside of the factory?'

Louisa took a deep breath, trying to calm herself. 'Because she's a Quaker?'

Ma frowned, clearly not liking the fact that Louisa was questioning her. 'Alright, yes, because she's a Quaker. Why, she's got three brothers who will hide behind that Peace Testimony of theirs while good Christian lads are risking their lives for king and country.'

'Her younger brothers are only thirteen and her older brother is the man of the house since their pa died. And anyway, the Clarks will be refusing to fight on account of their beliefs,' she pointed out. 'Would you have me shun them as well?'

'Don't be ridiculous, child.'

'I'm not a child, Ma. How can I be when you're determined to marry me off as soon as you can manage it? As far as Jeannie and her brothers go, I think you're being unfair. The Quakers are as Christian as we are and they're prepared to risk *their* lives to stand up for their beliefs, just as the martyrs in the Bible did. If you can sit back and say nothing while the Clarks stand behind the Peace Testimony, how can you criticise the Musgroves for doing the same thing?'

Pa put up a hand. 'That's enough, Louisa. You will not talk to your mother in such a manner.'

'But—'

Pa brought his hand down on the table, making the plates and cutlery rattle and Louisa and her Ma jump. 'I said enough!'

He waited a few moments before speaking again. 'It is none of our business how the Clarks conduct themselves. They are our employers, not our friends. But it *is* my business who my daughter associates with. Now, while I would prefer you to choose your friends from the young women at Holy Trinity, I do not in all conscience have any great objection to your friendship with Jeannie Musgrove. She's a hard worker, good and conscientious, and her family have lived through difficult times since their father was killed at the factory.'

Louisa relaxed a little. If Pa didn't mind her being friends with Jeannie then Ma couldn't force her to give it up.

'However,' he went on, 'I am very concerned about seeing you being so friendly with young Matthew this morning, and I'll not have it. You must put a stop to that immediately, young lady. He's not one of us and, promising as he seems to be in his work, I'm still not convinced he's a good fit. We shall have to see. In the meantime, I'll not have him associating with my daughter. I don't want to see the two of you together alone again.'

She sat frozen, shattered. She couldn't even argue with him because it would only make things worse. She realised with startling clarity that, in going to work in the Clicking Room, Mattie had made himself incredibly vulnerable. A word from her father could mean he'd lose his job and his whole future. *Pa could ruin him if he wanted to, and it would be my fault. All my fault.*

'Do I make myself clear, Louisa?' he asked.

She looked down at her hands, clasped together in a death grip on her lap. 'Yes, Pa,' she said, her heart breaking.

12

Jeannie and Louisa were sitting in the canteen eating their lunches a few days later when Ted approached them.

'Where's Kate?' he asked.

'She's popped home to check on her ma,' said Jeannie. 'She did ask us to tell you she's sorry. You know she's been poorly?'

He nodded.

'Well, Kate's worried she's not eating properly so she's gone to make sure she has some food.'

Ted frowned. 'Is that right?'

Louisa looked up from where she'd been staring down at her cold meat sandwich. 'What d'you mean?'

He shrugged. 'It's just that I overheard her pa tell her brother there's nothing wrong with the woman. She's just doing it for attention.'

Louisa looked furious, but Jeannie, ever the peacemaker, put a hand on her arm to stop her.

'Ted,' she said. 'You know Reggie Davis, right?'

He nodded.

'So you know he's... well, a bit selfish? Maybe a little too fond of his cider?'

'What are you saying? That he's lying?'

Louisa couldn't remain silent any longer. 'Exactly,' she snapped. 'He's a drunkard and a bully. Not really a man who should have had a wife and family at all. He treats poor Mrs Davis horribly. I've seen for myself how ill she is, and he won't even let them get her to a doctor. Why, if it weren't for Kate, I'm sure the poor woman would have expired from neglect by now.'

'I hate to judge people,' said Jeannie, 'but Louisa's right. Please don't believe anything her pa says, Ted. If Kate thought you did, well, I don't suppose she'd want to associate with you any more.'

'And it would be no more than you deserve,' said Louisa, glaring at him.

Ted sighed. 'Don't get me wrong,' he said. 'I'm no friend of Reggie Davis. But, every time I arrange to see Kate, she's rushing off with an excuse about her ma. She promised to eat her dinner with me today and hasn't even turned up.'

Louisa nodded, her attitude softening a bit. 'Be patient with her, Ted. She's having a rotten time of it.'

He took a deep breath and nodded. 'So long as she's not dumping me,' he said.

'I don't think that's her intention,' said Jeannie. 'But maybe there's something you can... I don't know,' she hesitated.

'What?' he asked.

Jeannie looked at Louisa and wondered whether she should say anything. She was really worried about Mrs Davis, and poor Kate was losing her mind, worrying because she'd had to promise her ma she wouldn't tell the rest of the family how ill she was. She saw Louisa's worry mirrored her own, so she made the decision. She looked up at Ted, who was hovering over them, fretting about Kate.

'Mrs Davis made Kate promise not to tell her brothers and sister that she was poorly because she didn't want them to worry or to get in an argument with their pa. But *we* haven't made that promise.' She glanced at Louisa again, who nodded. 'So, if we tell her sister Peg on our way home tonight, would you mention it to Fred when you see him in the Clicking Room? I hate to think he might believe his pa's nonsense. If they knew, they'd be able to help Kate and... let's face it... if you want to spend time with her, it might help if she wasn't the only one caring for her ma.'

Ted grinned, his whole face lighting up. 'I'll do it,' he said. 'I'll find Fred right now and put him straight. You tell Kate we'll all help her. She shouldn't have to bear all of this on her shoulders.'

'She does it out of love, Ted,' Jeannie pointed out. 'She's a good daughter.'

'That she is,' he agreed. 'She's a good lass.' He turned to leave, then smacked his palm against his forehead and turned back round. 'I nearly forgot.' He reached into his jacket pocket and pulled out a rumpled, folded piece of paper. He offered it to Louisa. 'Someone asked me to give you this.' He winked at her as she took it from him.

Jeannie realised it would be a note from Mattie. Louisa's face lit up. It didn't seem to matter that Mr Clements held the power of Mattie's job in his hands. The pair of them had been passing notes every day for a couple of weeks now. It was going to end in tears, Jeannie just knew it.

Ted strode off and Jeannie focused on the remains of her bread and cheese as Louisa lowered the note under the table and looked around, making sure no one was watching before she opened the paper and read it.

'He says he's going round to your house after work with Lucas,' she whispered. 'He said I should come home with you.'

Jeannie stifled a sigh. She hated all this sneaking about. 'You can if you want, but we said we'll go and see Peg, didn't we? Anyway, are you sure it's a good idea?'

'What do you mean?'

She hesitated. 'It's just... if your pa finds out Lucas is helping Mattie meet with you, he could be in all sorts of trouble. It wouldn't just be Mattie's job on the line, would it?'

Louisa went pale. 'I hate this,' she said. 'I really, really hate it. Why are Ma and Pa being so unreasonable?' She lowered her head, looking at the note again. 'He says he's got an idea about how we can see each other without them knowing. I wonder what he means?'

This time Jeannie did sigh. 'Lucas says he's got a bee in his bonnet about volunteering to help the Operatic Society. They're putting on *HMS*

Pinafore and need lads to make the scenery and lasses to sew the costumes. He wants all of us to go so your pa won't think it's just the two of you.'

It was the last thing Jeannie wanted or needed. Her own ma was doing quite well at the moment, but it was coming up to the anniversary of Pa's fatal accident and she knew that Ma always went downhill around that time. She could slip into a funk for weeks and it would be on Jeannie's shoulders to keep the family going and them fed until she managed to pull herself out of it. Jeannie always hoped that it would get easier for Ma as the years passed, but it never had. She'd loved Pa so much, she simply didn't know how to cope without him, even after all these years. Sometimes, Jeannie envied Ma such a perfect love. Yet, at other times, she cursed it. Surely by now, Ma should be stronger? Why couldn't she be grateful for what she'd had and for her children and pour all her love into life with them instead of giving up the way she did?

She shook her head slightly, trying to banish these thoughts. There wasn't anything she could do about it – lord knew she'd tried.

'Ooh, that's a good idea,' said Louisa, her eyes shining.

Jeannie did sigh then. 'It's not really,' she said. 'It's not like we'll be working alongside the lads – they won't risk getting paint and sawdust all over the costumes, will they? And I'm not sure it's a good idea for me and Lucas to be out in the evenings. It's not like the twins will look after Ma, is it?'

'Oh, please, Jeannie. At least give it a try. You never know, they might surprise you. Anyway, if you and Kate come at first, Ma and Pa aren't to know if you stop going after a couple of weeks, are they?'

'Someone's bound to tell them,' Jeannie pointed out.

'Not necessarily,' she said. 'We'll be careful.'

'I can't see Lucas being keen either,' she said.

'Can you at least talk to him?'

'And Kate won't want to leave her ma alone in the evenings. She's fretting enough about her being on her own while she's at work.'

'That's why we need to talk to Peg, remember?' Louisa put Mattie's note into her pocket and screwed up the brown paper her ma had wrapped her cold meat sandwich in. She stood up. 'Look, if I give you a note for Mattie, I'll go and see Peg on my way home. Maybe she can sit with Mrs Davis a couple of evenings a week.'

* * *

At the Musgrove home that evening, Mattie worked hard to persuade Lucas and Jeannie to join him at the Operatic Society.

'What if they want us to sing?' asked Lucas. 'You know they're always going on about needing more male voices.'

Mattie laughed. 'They can try,' he said. 'But as neither of us can hold a tune in a bucket, they'll soon abandon that idea.'

Jeannie giggled. He wasn't wrong. She supposed it was because they were Friends and didn't spend their Sundays singing hymns. Apart from the odd occasion at school when they'd been expected to sing, none of them had much experience. Jeannie liked to think she could carry a tune, but the lads were tone deaf and sounded terrible.

'I'm not dressing up in those fancy costumes, neither,' grumbled Lucas. 'You won't see me with frills and tights.'

'I'd pay to see that,' said Jeannie, grinning.

Mattie shook his head. 'Not going to happen, my friend. Scenery or nothing. That's all we're offering.'

'You do it,' said Lucas. 'You don't need us.'

'But I do,' he said, leaning forward, his expression almost desperate. 'Lou didn't dare even come here tonight, because her pa wouldn't like it. He knows you and me are pals, so he's suspicious. If we can meet on neutral ground – the Crispin Hall, for example – and with a crowd of people around, then at least I can see Louisa and maybe, just maybe, I can get to walk her home, seeing as we both live in the same direction. You know while we're working longer hours at the moment, I can't even see her going to and fro from the factory.' He ran an agitated hand through his hair. 'Please, Lucas. Be a pal. Help me out on this.'

Lucas glared at him. 'Why? I mean, why go to all this trouble for a lass when it's clear her pa is never going to let you court her? Is it because she's forbidden fruit?'

Jeannie wanted to know as well, but didn't dare ask. She waited, barely breathing, for his answer. She got it before he even opened his mouth. He looked down, his ears went red and he blinked rapidly. When he blew out a breath and looked up, there was no mistaking the passion in his eyes.

'Because Louisa Clements is the love of my life.' He said the words quietly. 'And I'll fight to my last breath to be the best man I can for her.'

Jeannie's last hopes shattered, sending painful shards into her heart. Even Lucas looked shocked.

'How do you know?' he asked.

Mattie shrugged. 'She's all I can think of. When I'm with her, I feel complete. When she's not here, I feel... empty.' He swallowed hard and started to look embarrassed. 'But if you go blabbing this to anyone, I'll deny it and fight you.' He grinned, as though he was joking.

Neither of them laughed. Both Jeannie and Lucas could see that he was sincere. He really did love Louisa.

Jeannie put a hand on his arm. 'I... I think she loves you as well, Mattie. But please be careful. Mr Clements could ruin you. In fact, he could ruin us all for helping you.'

He nodded, giving her a grateful smile. 'I will. I don't want anything to happen to my friends.'

'You're bloody mad,' said Lucas. 'But if you truly mean it, I agree with Jeannie. Watch your back.'

Mattie's smile widened. 'No need,' he said. 'I've got you two for that. So, are we going to help out the Operatic Society?'

Brother and sister looked at each other. Both were unhappy about this, but Jeannie knew they'd both do everything they could to help Mattie and Louisa. She nodded and with a sigh, Lucas did the same, muttering under his breath about blithering idiots.

13

Kate was washing up the last of the pots from supper when her sister Peg arrived.

'What are you doing here?' she asked.

Peg glared at her. 'Am I not welcome in my family home these days?'

'Of course you are. Sorry. I'm just surprised, that's all. Shouldn't you be at home with your husband?'

'We're married, not joined at the hip. I've given him his supper and now he's gone round to see how his ma is, so I thought I'd do the same.' She glanced round. 'Where is she?'

Kate sighed. 'She's in bed.'

Peg nodded. 'How long has she been poorly?'

It occurred to Kate that her sister wasn't surprised. 'A while. She made me promise not to tell you. How did you know?'

'Your friends are worried about you and Ma both. I take it Pa's at the Inn?'

She nodded. 'Where else would he be?' Her tone was bitter but she didn't care. She pulled the plug in the sink and watched the water drain away. She was too tired to move. Peg handed her a cloth to dry her hands.

'Don't be angry with Jeannie and Louisa. They didn't make any promises and we needed to know.'

Kate looked at her, alarmed. 'Have they told Fred and George as well?'

Peg shook her head. 'No. Ted Jackson told Fred and I told Will to pop round to George's on his way home later to tell him. We should all have been told right at the start, Kate. You know that, don't you?'

Her shoulders slumped as she nodded. She dropped her head, not daring to look at her sister. 'I wanted to. I kept asking Ma to let me tell you, but she was adamant. She didn't want you to worry.'

Peg put an arm round her shoulders and led her to one of the chairs by the range and urged her to sit down. 'So that left you with all the worry and responsibility on your shoulders. That's not fair on you, Kate, love. You shouldn't have to take all that on yourself. *He* should be looking after her.'

Kate snorted. 'Don't be daft. When has he ever looked after anyone but himself?' Tears filled her eyes. 'He won't even let me get the doctor.' She scrubbed at her face. 'Oh, Peg, I'm so worried. Ma's so poorly, she barely eats, and all Pa does is shout at her.'

'Best he's out at the Inn then,' said Peg, her teeth gritted. 'Don't you worry. We'll help now. You're not alone, Kate. I promise.' She brushed a stray tear away from her cheek. 'I'm going to make us a cuppa, then I'm going to take one up to Ma so I can see for myself.'

'She'll think I told you and she'll get angry with me.'

'No, she won't. I'll tell her I miss her and came round to see her, which is the truth. I only stayed away because Pa was such an arse about me marrying Will. She doesn't have to know who told me.'

Half an hour later, Peg came downstairs. She'd visited with Ma, taking her a cuppa and some rich fruit cake she'd brought with her. She looked pale when she came into the kitchen.

'She needs the doctor,' she said.

'I know,' said Kate. 'But he won't let me.'

Rage filled her sister's face. 'Damn him! He's killing her!'

'You think I don't know that?' Kate's voice rose as the careful control she'd kept on her emotions all these weeks finally broke and she began to cry. 'I'd take her myself, but he's got my wages and never gives me anything these days. He barely hands over enough to feed us. How am I going to pay for it?'

'Oh, Kate, love, don't cry.' Peg knelt by her chair and hugged her. 'We'll work it out, even if we have to shame him in front of the whole village. We'll get Ma to the doctor, I promise. She'll be right as rain before you know it.'

Kate nodded, but she couldn't stop her tears from falling. She had a horrible feeling that it was too late, and she blamed herself for not defying her father before now to get Ma the help she needed.

By the time Pa rolled in, drunk as usual, from the Street Inn, all the Davis siblings were at the cottage. They stood facing him in the parlour, grim-faced. Kate held Peg's hand, needing to feel her sister's strength as they faced him.

'What are you lot doing here? Bugger off to your own homes,' he grumbled.

'We came to see Ma,' said Fred, the oldest. 'She's proper poorly. We stayed to find out what you're going to do to help her get better.'

Pa sneered. 'There's nothing wrong with her,' he spat. 'She's just a lazy mare. Barely gets her carcass out of bed these days. I have to rely on *her*,' he pointed a grubby finger at Kate, 'to get me supper and clean me clothes, and she's bloody useless n' all.'

'She works all day at the factory, just like you do, Pa,' said Peg.

He glared at her. 'Who asked you? Bugger off back to that lily-livered boy you turned your back on your church and family for.'

George barked out a humourless laugh. 'That's rich, coming from you. When was the last time you set foot in church? And she never turned her back on any of us. It was you who did the turning, Pa.'

'Don't you talk to me like that in my own home. Get out, the lot of you.'

Fred crossed his arms. He was a big man, in his late twenties. He worked in the Clicking Room alongside Pa and Kate had heard he earned heaps more than Pa on piecework because he was a fast and accurate worker. Apart from their hair and eye colour, the two men couldn't have been more different. 'We're not leaving until you agree to get the doctor out for Ma. She's not lazy. She'd never stay in bed like that if she was well.'

'Don't you tell me what to do,' he roared. 'I'm not wasting good money on some quack who'll sell us useless potions and tonics.'

'No,' said George, looking disgusted. 'But you'll waste every penny you have on damned cider.'

'What are you – the Temperance police?' the old man snapped. 'I work hard and I'm entitled to a glass or two in recompense.'

Peg snorted. 'A glass or two? You can barely see straight. More like a gallon or two, while Ma's wasting away to nothing up there.'

'So what?' he spat. 'Your precious ma does bugger all all day. She hasn't *earned* the money to pay for no doctor.'

'No,' said Kate, stepping forward. 'But I have. I want to use my wages to pay for the doctor.'

'Don't you dare talk to me like that! You'll show me some respect in my own house!' Reggie Davis lashed out, a beefy hand catching Kate on the side of her head, knocking her off her feet.

Peg rushed to her side while their brothers restrained their father. Reggie shouted and struggled against their grasp. But his sons were both taller than him now and stronger in their sobriety than he was in his drunkenness. As Peg helped Kate to stand and carefully checked her for injuries, their brothers spoke to Pa in low, angry tones. Kate sank into a chair, despair leaching the strength from her legs.

A noise from the stairs caught everyone's attention and they turned to see Ma there, clinging to the banister. She looked so frail, Kate couldn't understand how she had had the strength to get herself out of bed and halfway down the stairs without them noticing.

'Whatever is going on?' she asked, her voice weak. 'I thought we'd been invaded by ruffians.'

'We was,' said Pa. 'Your bloody spawn have come back to attack me.'

'No one attacked you, old man,' said George. 'You smacked Kate.' He looked up at Ma and smiled gently. 'It's alright, Ma. We're just pointing out that she didn't deserve it and now he needs to show a bit more appreciation for you and our Kate.'

Ma looked troubled. 'Kate?'

She gave Ma a shaky smile, not wanting her to worry. 'I'm alright, Ma.'

Ma studied her with sad eyes before she nodded and turned to Fred and George. 'You shouldn't fight with your father, boys.'

'No fight, Ma,' said Peg. 'Just a discussion. Nothing for you to worry about. We were just talking about getting the doctor round to have a look at you. Why don't we get you back to bed?'

Kate wanted to burst into tears again at the mix of uncertainty, fear and hope in Ma's expression. But Peg's warm hand on her shoulder gave her strength. She took a deep, calming breath and stood up. 'Yes, Ma. Me and Peg will help you while the boys talk to Pa.'

As the sisters approached the stairs, Pa growled, 'She can sleep in Kate's room. I'm sick of hearing her moaning and groaning all night. Then you can all bugger off out of my house.'

Kate didn't want to wait around to hear her brothers' reactions to that. Nor did she want Ma exposed to any more of his abuse. She'd gladly share her room and bed with Ma. At least that way, she could look after her properly. Peg must have felt the same way because she rushed up the stairs with Kate and between the two of them, they practically carried Ma back up the stairs. It wasn't difficult. The poor woman was as light as a feather.

Once in the relative safety of Kate's room with the door firmly shut behind them, Pa's voice and his sons' responses were muted.

Kate spent a sleepless night, watching over her ma, listening to the soft moans of pain that Pa had complained about. It filled her with bitter anger that they were separated by just a thin wall, on the other side of which the drunken beast snored loudly. He hadn't even come in to check on his wife before he'd collapsed into bed.

Her siblings had left not long after that, returning to their own homes, leaving Kate scared and lonely, knowing that Pa was likely to wallop her again when he woke up in punishment for bringing the rest of the family into the drama. He wouldn't believe that she'd had nothing to do with it. Fred and George had told her to tell them if he did hit her, but she knew she wouldn't. What was the point? It would only earn her another punch.

At seven o'clock the next morning, Peg arrived with the doctor. Mrs Searle, Peg's ma-in-law, was hot on their heels. Kate was already up, getting ready for work. Pa was still snoring, comfortable in the marriage bed while his sick wife had been banished to Kate's much smaller bed.

After a quick word with her, Peg took the doctor upstairs. Kate supposed she should have gone too, but she didn't have the heart to be there while Ma was being examined. She was worried sick about how on earth they were going to pay the doctor. She couldn't believe her brothers had persuaded Pa to hand over the money. Maybe they hadn't. She fretted about who was paying for it. But now the doctor was here, she wasn't going to send him away. Ma needed his attention and she'd find a way to pay for it somehow, even if it killed her.

Instead, she made Mrs Searle a cuppa and busied herself around the kitchen, preparing some porridge for Pa's breakfast and wrapping some bread and cheese in paper for her lunch. Pa always took himself off to the canteen and had a hot meal in the dinner break, but never gave Kate the money to do the same. Sometimes she felt more like a slave than a daughter.

'I need to apologise to you, Kate,' said Mrs Searle when she joined her at the kitchen table with her own cuppa.

'What on earth for?' she asked.

'Your ma is a good friend. She helped me no end when my William died. I should have been here for her in her time of suffering. So I'm sorry for that, lass. But rest assured, I'm here now and I'll support you and Peg and your ma as best I can.'

Kate wanted to hug the woman. As a girl, Betty Searle had been at school with Ma and then started at the factory with her at age twelve and they'd worked together in the Trimmings Department until their respective marriages. Mrs Searle had returned to the factory after her husband's death and now worked in Trimmings, often deputising for Miss Florrie Bond, the only female forewoman at Clarks.

Even though Ma was a faithful member of the Holy Trinity congregation and her friend was a Quaker, it made no difference to their friendship. Despite the condemnation of others in the community – including her godless pa – when Peg and Will got married, the two women had been delighted that their children had fallen in love and were making a life together.

'Thank you, Mrs Searle,' she said. 'You're a good friend.' She glanced at the clock on the kitchen wall. 'I'd better wake Pa or he'll be late for work.' She hesitated, not wanting this kind woman to witness her surly father's manners, especially when he found out that the doctor was in the house. 'Please don't feel you need to wait around. I don't want to make you late for work. I know you like to be in early. I can come and find you at dinner time and let you know what the doctor says.'

She had already accepted that she would be late herself. She wasn't leaving this house until she knew what the verdict was. Not that it mattered if she was docked pay for tardiness – the only person who would notice would be Pa when he collected her pay packet. Never once in the two years she'd been working at the factory had she even seen her wages. She had no idea how much she earned – only that if she didn't work hard, Pa punished her for being lazy.

'Don't worry, lass. I'll wait a little while; there's plenty of time to get to work. You go and wake your pa and warn him to mind his manners while the doctor's in the house.'

Kate grimaced. 'I think that's likely to set him off,' she said, heading for the stairs. 'You'd better cover your ears.'

The older woman laughed, but Kate hadn't been joking.

Kate arrived at work twenty minutes late, which meant she'd lose an hour's pay. Not that she cared. Her emotions were in so much turmoil, she barely knew how she got there. Her sister had come with her to the factory, right up to the Machine Room door, even though she didn't work there since she married Will. She kissed her cheek and pushed her towards the bench where Jeannie and Louisa were already busy at work.

'Looks like Mr Briars is in the weekly meeting,' she said softly. 'So at least we don't have to put up with his complaining just yet. Keep your chin up, love. I'll talk to you at dinner time, alright? You get on while I say hello to a few people.'

Kate nodded and approached her machine.

'Kate! Whatever's wrong?' asked Jeannie as soon as she saw her face.

Louisa stopped her machine and stood up. 'Is it your ma?'

Kate burst into tears, uncaring who saw. 'She's dying,' she sobbed. 'The... the doctor says it looks like there's a tumour in her stomach. He says she needs to be in the hospital but Pa won't have it. He said it's point-less if there's nothing they can do.'

Her friends engulfed her in their arms, crying with her as she let out her shock and grief. Then Peg was there too, and before they knew it, half of the Machine Room had fallen silent and women and girls were gath-ering round the sisters to offer comfort.

But nothing could console Kate. She blamed herself for not taking action to get help weeks ago. Now it was too late. Ma was destined to die a painful death. Without Ma, Kate would be alone and at the mercy of her father. She didn't think she could survive it. But maybe that was no more than she deserved.

Mr Briars returned from his meeting, shouting at everyone to get back to work. Peg apologised for the disruption and explained about Ma. Kate didn't take any notice of his reaction. She simply sat at her machine, her misery and grief a heavy cloak around her shoulders, and began to work, losing herself in the repetitive actions, stitching the pieces of the shoe liners together, pair after pair after pair. She took no notice of anything going on around her, even though she was aware of Jeannie and Louisa's concerned glances. She didn't notice when Peg left and didn't want to talk to anyone. She didn't want to say she was alright. She wasn't. She never would be again.

She couldn't help but remember Pa's angry words when he realised the doctor was there, or how rude he'd been to the man and also to Mrs Searle, calling her a busybody. She hadn't even felt the slap Pa had given her when, after he'd declared he couldn't afford medicine for Ma, Kate had pointed out again that he had plenty of money for cider, so why would he not pay for something to ease Ma's pain?

As she worked, she vowed to do everything she could to make Ma's final days as comfortable as possible, to let her know she was loved. She also swore that she would never forgive her father for his neglect of his wife, the mother of his children, who had been a good and faithful companion all these years. No, she would never, ever forgive him.

14

Jeannie was surprised when Lucas insisted on accompanying her to help out at the Operatic Society. She really hadn't wanted to go and was sure her brother felt the same and would come up with an excuse to miss it. But Louisa was desperate and, now that they knew the seriousness of poor Mrs Davis's illness, Jeannie couldn't in all conscience expect Kate to go with Louisa. When she'd mentioned it at home, Lucas had taken her aside and quietly told her he was going too.

'I thought Mattie was joking about it,' he said. 'But he's not, is he?'

'No,' she told him. 'It's not a joke. They're so desperate to see each other without Mr and Mrs Clements finding out what they're up to. You know Kate and Ted went to the picture house with them the other weekend, don't you?'

'I know,' he said, looking grim. 'He's been going on about kissing her there ever since. If I'm not there, he'll be sure to get himself in a whole mess of trouble.'

Jeannie hoped her face didn't give away the pain she felt every time she heard about Mattie kissing Louisa. She really couldn't bear to think about it. While she didn't wish unhappiness upon either of them, she wished they'd get over this... this *infatuation* they had for each other. It hurt too much.

'If Mr Clements gets word of it...' she began.

'He won't,' Lucas assured her. 'Mattie's not daft. He only talks to me about it when there's no one else around to earwig.' He sighed. 'I'm sick of it, to be honest, but he won't shut up about it.'

'Well, I hope they're both careful. I'd hate to see either of them in trouble. That's why I thought it was my duty as her friend to go along with Louisa – to make sure they don't do anything they might regret later.'

Lucas nodded, his expression grim. 'You're right, sis. That's why I'll go too. Keep Mattie in line. He could lose his job over this if he's not careful.'

Neither of them mentioned that their jobs might be on the line as well if Mr Clements had a mind to punish them.

Jeannie was relieved that, as soon as they got to the Crispin Hall for the first meeting, those who weren't already involved in playing parts in the production were separated into groups – the men and boys would be creating the scenery and props, while the women and girls were required to help make costumes. Louisa looked crestfallen when the wardrobe mistress led them to another room.

'I thought we'd be working with the lads,' she whispered to Jeannie.

'It wasn't likely, though, was it?' She sent her a sympathetic look, even though all she could feel about it was an overwhelming relief. The last thing she wanted to do was to witness the two of them gazing into each other's eyes. She'd feel responsible for protecting them, when she really just wished they'd stop it all.

'I don't want to spend my spare time sitting at a sewing machine,' Louisa grumbled. 'It'll be like being at work.'

'Maybe we can ask if we can work on the cutting out or hand-sewing,' Jeannie suggested. 'That will make a nice change, won't it?'

Doing the hand-sewing wouldn't be a novelty for her, Jeannie realised, considering how much mending and darning she did at home since Ma's hands had become so arthritic. But she tried to stay positive. It wouldn't do for Louisa to pout through the whole meeting.

'Why can't we paint the scenery with the lads?' Louisa asked, raising her voice a little. 'I'm very artistic. I could probably do a better job than most of them.'

The wardrobe mistress overheard her comment and gave her a baleful stare over her wire-rimmed glasses. 'There may be an opportunity for girls to undertake some of the finer art work later on,' she said. 'But in the meantime, your assistance is required here. If that does not suit you, Miss Clements, then perhaps volunteering isn't for you.'

Louisa flushed. 'I'm sorry, ma'am. I... I don't mind working on the costumes.'

She subsided in her seat, feeling embarrassed and guilty. The whole point of coming here had been to spend more time with Mattie, and she felt frustrated that their plan had been thwarted. But she couldn't make a fuss, or someone would put two and two together and realise what she was up to. If it got back to her parents that she was keeping company with Mattie, they'd immediately put a stop to it.

She spent the rest of the evening paying attention to what was required of them. Ma would certainly ask how the meeting went and, she realised, being able to tell her about the women and girls there and the tasks they'd been assigned would put her parents off the scent.

She wished that she didn't have to do this – that she could be allowed to walk out with Mattie openly. Some days, she resolved to tell Ma and Pa about Mattie and how much he was coming to mean to her. After all, Ma was so keen on getting her married off, they might be pleased she'd met someone she could love. Mattie was a fine lad – a hard worker and good to his mother. Everybody liked him. But then Pa would make a comment about Quakers and she realised that they would always hold his religion against him and she would fall into despair again.

* * *

In another room, Mattie looked downcast as the lads listened to one of the older men explain the plans for the staging of the production. There would be backdrops to paint, moveable scenery and props to build, and even a replica of the quarterdeck of a sailing ship. He talked about sails and rigging and a ship's wheel while other, more experienced volunteers talked about how these could be fitted and what other props would be needed.

Lucas watched his friend sulk with grim satisfaction. He knew it had been a daft idea, thinking he could come here and sneak off for private time with Louisa. He was relieved to have been proved right, but then worried about what risky scheme his friend could come up with next. He'd never seen Mattie so enamoured of a girl before and it worried him. Mr Clements wasn't an easy man and he was very protective of his only daughter. If Mattie couldn't get over this ridiculous infatuation soon, he'd be for it. The foreman would make his life hell – might even find a way of making sure Mattie lost his job at Clarks, and then where would he be?

He was torn between wanting to protect Mattie and being as jealous as hell of the object of his friend's affections. He didn't want to witness Mattie falling in love with a girl, he didn't want to lose his friend's attention – which he would once he was properly courting, it was clear it was already happening. The two of them had been best pals all their lives. Lucas felt closer to Mattie than anyone, even his own brothers.

The man in charge pinned some drawings to the wall so that everyone could see them, catching Lucas's attention. They were an impression of how the stage would look with the mock-up of the quarter-deck on it. The 'sails' and 'rigging' would be hung from the beams over the stage down to the deck to make it look like an authentic vessel.

'That looks impressive,' he said quietly to Mattie. 'D'you reckon we can build it?'

'I don't see why not,' he said. 'There's enough fellows here to do the job. In fact, it looks like they've got enough people, don't you? Not much point in us coming back, is there?'

Lucas felt a jolt of irritation. 'Well, I think it looks interesting. I'm going to hang around. It'll be good to do something besides work and it'll be a laugh. We don't need girls to have fun.'

'If I can't spend time with Louisa, I don't see the point of being here,' Mattie grumbled.

'Suit yourself,' said Lucas, not even attempting to hide the disgust in his voice. 'I'll come without you.'

* * *

The women and girls had begun to go through the Operatic Society's wardrobe of costumes, pulling out any that might be suitable for the wardrobe mistress to assess. Any that were approved were put in another pile, while discarded costumes were returned to storage.

Jeannie and Louisa were given the job of checking the approved costumes for any problems – buttons missing, loose seams that needed sewing and tears that needed repairing. They were to write down what needed doing to each costume on a piece of paper and attach it to the relevant costume with a safety pin. Others were checking accessories – gloves, scarves, belts and hats, and matching them with costumes.

'We will allocate what costumes we have as appropriate,' the wardrobe mistress explained. 'Some will need alterations to fit the particular *artiste*, while others will have to be made from scratch.'

'*Artiste*?' Louisa grinned at Jeannie, her sulk forgotten now that they were busy. 'Are we going to be in the presence of the stars? I thought it was going to be a few of the office staff and their wives having their day in the limelight.'

Jeannie giggled, earning her a cool stare from the wardrobe mistress, who hadn't heard Louisa's whispered comment. She sent the older woman an apologetic smile and bent to her work again.

'Ooh,' said Louisa, holding up a dress. It was buttercup-yellow silk with a fitted bodice, big, puffed sleeves and a full skirt that fell to the floor. 'Isn't this divine? If I had the nerve to sing in public, I'd try for a part just for the chance to wear this dress.' She held it up against her. 'I could fit into the waist, but I don't think I've got enough bosom to fill the top.'

'Just as well you haven't got the courage to try out for a part then,' laughed Jeannie.

Louisa sighed and laid the dress on the table where she could check it over properly. 'It is. I doubt if I'd be allowed to wear this anyway. Lasses who try out for the first time usually end up in the chorus and this looks like something the heroine would wear.'

They carried on working. Around them were women and girls, some of whom they knew from the Machine Room or around the village. Others they weren't familiar with. The conversations were lively and amusing to listen to. One elderly matron rued the fact that she was too old to try out for the role of Josephine, the young heroine.

'You're more likely to get the role of Buttercup, the Bumboat woman,' one of her friends told her.

Another woman turned to them, outraged. 'I'll thank you not to use that kind of language in here, thank you very much,' she said.

The woman who'd said it laughed. 'Oh, don't get your knickers in a twist, Ethel. It's a perfectly good word that was good enough for Mr Gilbert and Mr Sullivan, so it's good enough for you. A Bumboat woman is one who sells goods to sailors on ships. She travels from ship to ship in the harbour in a little boat.'

'How do you know all this?' she was asked.

'My ma loved singing, particularly Gilbert and Sullivan. She collected the librettos of all their operas. She was always aware of her lack of education, though, so every time she came across a word she didn't understand, she'd find out what it meant.'

'What's a libretto?' Jeannie asked. She immediately went red, feeling foolish, but some of the others nodded, indicating they wanted to know as well.

'It's a book of the words to the opera,' the woman explained. 'Like a script for a play.'

'Ah, I get it. Thank you,' she said. That made sense. She didn't do much singing so she wouldn't have come across such a term. They had no hymns at Meetings for Worship, and she'd never been much for music, preferring silence or the sounds of nature. It explained why the other Friends there didn't know the term either.

Louisa looked impressed. 'What a wonderful way to learn,' she said.

The woman smiled at her, a twinkle in her eye. 'It was. She passed on everything she learned to us children, which is why I know about Buttercup the Bumboat woman in *HMS Pinafore*. 'Tis said she was *the rosiest, roundest, and reddest beauty in all Spithead.*' She nudged the other woman's arm. 'That's why I thought of you, Ethel. We could put a red wig on you and you're the perfect shape for Buttercup.'

Jeannie's eyes widened, expecting Ethel to take offence. But she laughed with the other women, nudging her companion back.

'Go on with you, you're so daft. As if the likes of me could carry a tune!'

The wardrobe mistress had popped out of the room for a moment when Jeannie realised that the conversation on the other side of the room was less light-hearted. A shrill voice cut through the chatter and laughter.

'It's none of your business!'

Everyone stilled and looked in the direction of the voice.

'I was only asking when your lads were going to do their duty for king and country,' said her companion, her voice tight. 'It's not gone unnoticed that they're the only ones in our street – apart from the Quakers, that is – that haven't enlisted. Don't you think it's time you encouraged them to be men and stand up to the Kaiser? Or do you *want* to be speaking German and answering to the evil Hun for the rest of your life?'

'You've still got a lad at home, Hettie Jackson,' said someone else.

Jeannie caught Louisa's eye. 'Is that Ted's ma?' she mouthed.

Louisa nodded, turning back to the drama.

'I've two sons already in the army. My youngest will be going any day now.'

The first woman scoffed. 'I heard that he's more interested in Rosie Davis's lass than fighting.'

Hettie glared at the speaker. 'He'll be off soon enough. He's not serious about that girl. And neither is he a coward. Unlike some mothers' sons around here.'

'You take that back!' The other woman rose and faced Hettie, her hands on her ample hips. 'That's a vile thing to say.' She looked around at the others in the room. 'Did you hear what she said? She's saying if our sons aren't enlisted, then they're cowards.' She rounded on Hettie. 'That's a lie and you know it.'

Hettie wouldn't back down. She ignored everyone else and stood to face her. 'I take nothing back. I'm speaking the truth. If everyone keeps their sons tied to their apron strings, the Hun will be swarming over the English Channel, just like they've charged over France and Belgium, and then where would we be? We need all our lads to go and fight. It's bad enough that the so-called *Friends* won't fight. No doubt they'll be *friends* to the invaders when they get here, licking their boots and making them welcome. But that won't help them when they line us all up and shoot our menfolk and use us women as their slaves.'

Disquiet rippled around the room. Jeannie felt a chill at the picture Mrs Jackson had painted with her words and her sneering tone when she'd said *Friends*. She knew she should stay out of it, but she had the urge to speak, so she stood up.

'We have to have faith in our government to negotiate peace,' she said. 'Fighting isn't the answer.'

Mrs Jackson rounded on her. 'Who are you? One of the *Friends*, no doubt, for I've not seen you in church before.'

'I'm Jeannie Musgrove,' she said, lifting her chin. Just because she was a Quaker and a pacifist, that didn't mean she wouldn't defend herself. 'And yes, I am a Friend.'

'Leave the lass alone, Hettie,' said one of the women.

'No,' said Hettie. 'It's the likes of her and her brother that's trying to persuade my boy not to fight.'

Jeannie swallowed hard. She'd never seen such anger and disdain directed at her before. She shook her head. 'I've not spoken to Ted about this,' she said.

As the older woman opened her mouth to speak, the door opened and the wardrobe mistress walked in. She stilled in the doorway, taking in the tension in the room.

'What's all this? Has everyone finished?' she asked, her voice calm and authoritative. A couple of women shook their heads and most of them turned back to their work. 'I was only gone for five minutes,' she went on. 'I must say, I'm disappointed. If I can't trust any of my band of lady volunteers to work without supervision for such a short space of time, I wonder whether you're suited to this kind of thing.'

Louisa touched Jeannie's arm to get her attention. Jeannie sat down and turned back to her task. She'd been frozen in place by Mrs Jackson's anger. It shocked her that she could be so cruel. She quickly lowered her head and carried on checking the shirts she had on the table in front of her for missing buttons and tears. When Jeannie found a small rip in a seam, her hand shook as she noted it on a piece of paper.

As they worked, the room was silent save for the wardrobe mistress's quiet questions to the other two women who'd been standing, who she'd moved away from the others. Their answers became increasingly loud and shrill as they argued over who was to blame for the disruption that had stopped the volunteers working. Jeannie tried to shut it out, but she was still shaking from Mrs Jackson's attack on her and she couldn't block out their words.

She'd heard about people denouncing the Quaker Peace Testimony as unpatriotic and calling the Friends cowards. It had only been a couple of months since war had been declared and already people who knew nothing about the Quaker faith were attacking it. But here in Street, with the Clark family being both prominent Quakers and the major employers of thousands of locals, it was rare for anyone to be openly hostile to Friends. That it was her brother's friend's ma attacking her directly because of her beliefs was particularly upsetting. Ted was a nice lad; both Lucas and Kate said so. It distressed her that any mother could demand that her son go to war, but when she knew that son personally, it was even more shocking. She closed her eyes, looking within, seeking guidance.

'Are you alright?' Louisa asked her quietly.

Jeannie nodded but didn't look up. 'She's afraid,' she whispered. 'She can't mean it. Can she?'

Lou touched her arm. 'I hope not.'

'I'm not staying here to be insulted by cowards,' shouted Mrs Jackson, making Jeannie jump and open her eyes. 'I'll leave you lot to bury your heads in the sand while the enemy gets closer every day. I'll be devoting my time to doing my patriotic duty, not sewing silly costumes for daft operas.' And with that, she grabbed her handbag and coat and stalked out of the room.

There was utter silence for a moment. Then someone muttered, 'Good riddance.'

'That's enough!' said the wardrobe mistress. 'Ladies, let me make myself clear. I will not tolerate behaviour such as I've witnessed this evening. This is a cultural society, not a debating society. From now on, if you wish to continue volunteering to help with this production, please leave your political beliefs and whatever arguments you may have about the war outside the door. I do not wish to hear them and I will not have my schedule of work disrupted by them. Do you understand?'

The woman who had been arguing with Hettie Jackson nodded. 'Yes, ma'am. I'm very sorry. I'd like to carry on, and now that she's gone, I'm sure the rest of us will get along alright.'

There was a murmur of agreement. Jeannie and Louisa remained silent, watching and listening.

The wardrobe mistress said nothing for a few moments, looking around the room. 'Very well,' she said eventually. 'I'm sorry that I wasn't here to prevent the situation from escalating, but rest assured I shall not make the same mistake again.' She checked her watch. 'I think we've achieved a good deal this evening, all things considered. It is hoped that all the roles will be cast by the time we meet again on Thursday and we shall be in a better position to know which of these costumes can be used and what needs to be created. Thank you for your time, ladies. Please return your completed work to the appropriate baskets and leave any garments that you haven't managed to check yet on the end table.'

Jeannie helped the others clear everything away, relieved that the evening was over. All she wanted to do was go home and crawl into bed.

'What a to-do,' said Louisa as they headed outside. 'I've never heard the likes of it.'

'What to-do?' asked a male voice behind them.

Jeannie jumped, putting a hand to her heart as she turned to see Mattie grinning at them. Lucas stood behind him. He tilted his head to one side when he caught her eye.

'You alright, sis?' he asked.

She should have known she couldn't hide her distress from him. The only thing he never noticed – because she kept up her guard and made sure that he didn't – was how she pined for Mattie.

'We've had a time of it,' said Louisa, moving closer to Mattie, but not so close that people might gossip. 'Ted's ma picked a fight with one of the other women over their lads enlisting, then she started on Jeannie.'

'What?' said Lucas, standing straighter. 'What did she do to you?'

'I'm alright, she didn't touch me,' said Jeannie, taking a step back when he moved towards her. 'She was just cross and took it out on me.

But the wardrobe mistress came in and stopped it. Don't worry. It was nothing. Just a woman frightened we'll be invaded, that's all.'

'Hardly nothing,' said Louisa, looking indignant on her behalf. 'She was vile. She called Friends cowards and she accused you and Jeannie of trying to talk Ted out of enlisting,' she told Lucas.

He frowned. 'I've not. It's not up to me. It has to be his decision. That's all I told him.'

Jeannie nodded. She thought as much. Friends didn't judge or preach. They were required to look within themselves for the light of the spirit and to live according to what that light revealed to them.

'Well, it seems Mrs Jackson is crediting you with more influence than you think over Ted,' she said. She shivered in the cool, autumn air. It had been quite warm when they'd arrived, but now the sun had gone down, she felt a chill. 'I feel sorry for him. From what she was saying in there, I get the impression she's putting a lot of pressure on Ted to enlist.'

'And she was adamant that Ted wasn't serious about Kate,' said Louisa. 'But some other woman said he was probably not going because he was sweet on her.'

'So, what happened after that?' asked Mattie, his usual cheerful manner subdued.

'She left,' said Jeannie. 'Stormed out in a terrible huff.'

'After telling us the Hun were going to invade and the Friends would be traitors and befriend them and all the men would be shot and the women enslaved,' Louisa finished with a dramatic flourish, putting the back of her hand to her forehead and pretending to swoon.

'Blinking hell,' said Mattie. 'Really?' The girls nodded. He laughed. 'Daft old bat.'

'It's not funny,' said Lucas. 'People are getting scared.'

'That's what I said,' said Jeannie. 'She wasn't thinking straight.'

'It's still no excuse to attack you like that,' said Louisa.

Jeannie agreed. But she had a horrible feeling there would be more attacks like this from more people as this awful war progressed. Quakers had been vilified every time there was an armed conflict and refused to take up arms against their fellow men.

The Clark family had struggled with the issue during the Crimean

War, being pressured by the government to supply sheepskin goods for the soldiers. While they didn't want to do anything that might support the war, they realised that the soldiers were dying from the cold during the winter in larger numbers than those dying in combat. In order to save them from such a fate, Clarks finally agreed to take the contract. But every penny of profit they made from it was directed into building the Board School in the High Street and the Clark family were still supporting it today. Jeannie, Kate and Louisa, their parents and all of their friends had been educated there. She wondered what would happen with this war. Clarks had moved from predominantly sheepskin products to boots and shoes these days. As far as she knew, their competitors in Northampton and Leicester had swept up most of the contracts for army boots already.

Jeannie shivered again. 'It is what it is,' she said. 'Let's walk you home.'

Mattie held up a hand. 'No need to go out of your way, Jeannie, love. You and Lucas get on home. I'll escort Louisa home.' He winked. 'At least, as far as I can go without her pa spotting me.'

Jeannie frowned.

'You're playing with fire,' said Lucas. 'Let us walk with you. Then if he sees you, he won't be so suspicious.'

'It's alright,' said Louisa. 'We'll manage. Jeannie's cold. You should get on home.'

Jeannie wanted to deny it, but she shivered again. She had a feeling it was more shock from Mrs Jackson's venom than actual cold, but she didn't want to say that. It would just frustrate Lucas that he hadn't been there to protect her. 'I forgot my jacket,' she said.

Lucas rolled his eyes. 'Well, that was daft, wasn't it?' He turned towards the High Street. 'Come on, then, before you catch a chill.' He looked over his shoulder at the other two. 'Be careful,' he said.

They both nodded, but Lucas had already turned away and Jeannie ran to catch up with him.

15

The chance to walk Louisa home two evenings a week persuaded Mattie to carry on volunteering for the Operatic Society. She was glad of his company as the nights drew in, as there seemed to be a lot of men congregating at the Street Inn these days and, particularly when they were due to leave for basic training, they would get particularly rowdy. She knew that she could go another way – up Leigh Road and down Hindhayes Lane to reach her home in Somerton Road – but it was much darker that way and the lane was a bit rough. She didn't want to fall in the dark. Nor did she agree to let Mattie take her that way when he suggested it as it would mean he'd have to walk past her house to get to his home in The Mead. The risk of Pa seeing him was too great. Instead, he always made sure to see her past the Inn and as close to her house as he dared, keeping her safe.

This worked fine for a few weeks, until just before Guy Fawkes Night. Louisa had been a little late coming out of the Crispin Hall. As they approached The Cross, a group of lads stumbled out of the Inn. One called out to Louisa, offering to buy her a drink in return for a kiss. When they spotted Mattie with her, they started jeering.

'There he is. The biggest chicken in the village. And who's this? Old man Clements's lass, ain't it? What you doing with that fine piece of skirt, eh, Chicken? Hiding beneath her petticoats, I'll wager. She's too good for the likes of you.'

Mattie ignored them, moving so that he was between Louisa and the lads, urging her quietly to carry on walking. She nodded and increased her pace to match his, hating the way they were laughing at Mattie. Didn't they realise that refusing to fight took just as much courage, maybe even more than rushing towards the battle? Louisa had half a mind to stop and give them a good telling off, but knowing they were in their cups, she realised it would do no good, and maybe make matters worse.

One ran after them, standing squarely in front of Mattie to stop him. Before they could go around him, his pals had joined them, surrounding the couple.

'Get out of the way,' said Mattie. He remained calm, looking the ringleader square in the eye.

'Make me,' he said, his face so close to Mattie's that Louisa saw some of his spittle hit Mattie's cheek. 'Oh, wait! You can't, can you? A *Friend* doesn't fight.'

'I won't kill another man,' said Mattie, his voice low and dangerous. 'But I'll protect others and defend myself should the need arise.'

Louisa shifted closer to him, anger and fear making her nervous. 'Leave him alone,' she demanded, trying to make her voice forceful. 'Let us pass.' The final words came out with a squeak, which caused much hilarity amongst their tormentors. She went to push past the nearest lad, but he grabbed her arm. His cider-laden breath made her feel sick as he laughed in her face.

'Don't touch her!' Mattie shouted, lunging for him and catching him by surprise. His grip loosened and Louisa was free of him.

'Run, Louisa!' Mattie shouted.

She hesitated. She couldn't leave him. It was four against one. They'd kill him. Another lad tried to grab her but she swung her handbag at his head. It wasn't until she heard the thud and he fell to the ground, stunned, that she remembered that she had a glass bottle of elderflower cordial in there that Jeannie had given her earlier.

Mattie had bested the first lad and had him pinned to the ground. His pal lay dazed beside him. The others stood by, looking uncertain.

'Get him!' shouted the lad under Mattie.

'Shut up!' said Mattie, cuffing him on the jaw.

The other two moved forward, their violent intent clear.

'Stop it!' Louisa shouted, flinging herself between them and Mattie, waving her bag at them, anger giving her voice more volume than usual. 'I'll tell my father about this, you rotten bunch of louts! He'll have your hides for this!' She pointed at one of the lads. 'I know who you are. You're a Clicker. I'll tell on you, don't think I won't!'

To her surprise and relief, he backed off, as did his friend, the two of them running off down the High Street. Louisa turned, ready to use her handbag as a weapon again if need be, but Mattie had already got to his feet, pulling the ringleader with him, holding him in an armlock that the lad couldn't escape, no matter how hard he tried. Louisa felt a burst of pride at Mattie's strength.

The lad on the ground groaned. Louisa brandished her handbag, ready to hit him again. Somewhere under her anger, she was grateful that she hadn't killed him.

'Now listen here.' Mattie gave the lad he was holding a shake. 'I don't care what you think of me, but if you or your friends ever, *ever* show disrespect to Miss Clements again, I'll make sure her father hears about it. D'you hear me?'

Louisa wanted to melt into a puddle of pride and admiration as Mattie firmly told the lad off. Without his friends to back him up, he was diminished and powerless. If he hadn't been keeping a firm grip on their assailant, Louisa would have rushed over and kissed Mattie.

'What's all this?' said a sharp voice behind them.

Louisa spun round, barely missing her pa with her weighted bag. 'Pa!'

'Louisa, what's going on? I came down to find you when you didn't get home at your usual time.' He looked at the tableau before them – Mattie holding one lad in an armlock, another lying on the ground, groaning. Louisa knew he'd think the worst of Mattie, so she rushed into an explanation.

'I asked Mattie to see me past the Inn because these... these louts were hanging around.' She couldn't keep her disgust out of her voice. 'And it's just as well I did. They started heckling me...' *and Mattie* – but she knew her father wouldn't be interested in that. 'Making lewd comments. And – and him and that one grabbed me.' She pointed at the two louts and shuddered. 'If Mattie hadn't stopped them, I'm sure they would've attacked me. They're that drunk.'

The lad on the ground sat up, groaning and holding his head. 'Bloody hell,' he said, hissing in a breath. 'What the fuck did you hit me with?'

Her father frowned. 'Watch your tongue, boy. You will not use that foul language in the presence of a young lady.'

His head came up at the shock of hearing the foreman's voice, causing him to groan again.

Pa turned to Mattie. 'What *did* you hit him with?' he asked. 'I have to say, I'm surprised at you, Matthew. I've never heard of a Friend using his fists.'

Before Mattie could say anything, Louisa grabbed Pa's sleeve. 'He didn't hit him,' she confessed. 'I did.'

Her father's eyes widened with surprise. 'You did?' She nodded. He shook his head. 'I don't believe it. He's twice your size.'

Louisa hung her head and dug into her bag, pulling out the bottle of elderflower cordial. 'I forgot I had this in here. Mrs Musgrove sent it for Ma. I... he was grabbing at me so I swung my bag at his head.'

The lad groaned again, still holding his head. 'You could've killed me, you stupid bitch!'

'Watch your mouth!' Mr Clements clipped his ear and the lad yelped.

Louisa blinked. Both Pa and Mattie had spoken together, saying the same thing with identical expressions as they glared at him. She bit the inside of her cheek to quell the urge to laugh. It really wasn't funny. Maybe she was hysterical.

The ringleader struggled, trying to get away. He'd kept quiet and tried to keep his face averted ever since Pa had arrived. Now Pa's attention shifted to him and he approached him, grabbing his chin and turning him towards the light streaming out of the Inn's windows.

'I might have known,' said Mr Clements, his anger growing. 'Assault my daughter, would you, Smith? How dare you?'

'I-it weren't m-me, honest,' he stammered. 'I was just talking to 'em. He hit me.' He tipped his head towards Mattie, narrowly missing bashing his forehead into Mattie's nose. 'Unprovoked, Mr Clements, I swear.'

'He did not!' cried Louisa. 'You and your drunken friends blocked our path and you and him,' she pointed at the lad still on the ground, 'tried to manhandle me. He was defending me, you filthy animal!' She took a deep breath, trying to calm down. Shrieking like a fish-wife wouldn't impress Pa. She turned to her father, trying to tone down her hysteria. 'If Mattie hadn't agreed to accompany me, Pa, I dread to think what would've happened. There were four of them. I recognised the others from the factory – they work for you, I'm sure. But thanks to Mattie's bravery, none of them could touch me and the others ran off.'

Pa was silent for a moment, his expression set and angry. 'And what have you got to say for yourself, young Matthew?' he said eventually.

'Nothing to add, sir. Miss Clements has told you the truth. I wouldn't start a fight. I only used force to stop them getting to your daughter. I couldn't stand by and let them manhandle her.'

Pa nodded. Louisa prayed he'd be impressed by Mattie's calm, respectful answer. 'Let him go,' he said.

Mattie obeyed immediately and stepped back. Smith shrugged his shoulders and swivelled his head, as though trying to work out the kinks now that he'd been released from Mattie's strong grip. Freedom gave him a little of his bravado back. He sneered at his captor. 'You was lucky this time, Searle, but you'd better watch your back.'

'That's enough,' Pa said, his tone curt. 'If I hear you're continuing this fight after tonight, lad, I'll be sure to tell the constable about your trouble-making. As it is, if you and your friends want any kind of future in this village, you'll mend your ways, because I'll be watching you close from now on.'

The boy turned an insolent face towards Pa. 'I ain't staying round here like this chicken, anyway. I'm off to basic training next week.'

'Good. Maybe some army discipline will knock some sense into you,' said Pa. 'But if you come back, my lad, you'll find your options at Clarks severely limited. I'll not have troublemakers in the Cutting Room and I'll be sure to let the management know about your behaviour tonight. Now, help your friend up and get out of my sight. I'll be speaking to your fathers tomorrow.'

The lad on the ground whimpered as he was hauled up by his pal. 'Sorry, sir,' he said, almost tugging his forelock at Pa.

'It's my daughter you should be apologising to.'

'But she nearly killed me!'

Pa stared him down. 'Would you rather the constable settled this matter?' he asked.

He took a step back. 'No, sir. Sorry, Miss Clements,' he said, even as he turned and staggered away, Smith dragging him along. 'I didn't mean no harm by it.'

Louisa didn't know whether to laugh or to follow after him and aim a sharp kick to his backside. She'd never seen such a pathetic excuse for a lad, and now she'd seen two – no, four, including the others who'd run away like scared rabbits.

They watched until the lads were swallowed up by the darkness. Then Pa turned to Mattie.

'It seems I'm in your debt, Matthew. Thank you.'

Mattie nodded, keeping his face solemn. 'I'm glad I was here to help, sir. No girl should have to put up with that sort of behaviour.'

Pa nodded. 'My only question is, what were the two of you doing, walking along here together at this time of night?'

Louisa was glad that the only illuminations came from the grubby Inn windows and the lamppost in the middle of The Cross, a few yards away from where they were standing. She was sure she was blushing. Had they been found out?

Mattie's expression remained solemn and open. 'I've been helping build the scenery for the Operatic Society, sir, and, as you know, Louisa and her friend Jeannie have been working on the costumes. When I saw she was walking home on her own this evening, I kept an eye on her. That's how I saw her hesitate when those lads came out of the Inn, so I asked her if she was alright.'

'He did, Pa,' Louisa confirmed. 'And I asked him to escort me past them. It was clear they'd been drinking and I didn't feel safe. Thank the lord Mattie was here.' She shuddered dramatically, hoping she wasn't overdoing it. 'That one I hit got so close, I could smell the cider on his breath. Disgusting.' She shook her head then turned to Mattie. 'Thank you so much, Mattie. You're a real hero.'

Pa frowned. 'Yes, well. I'd better come and get you from now on. I don't want anything like this to happen again. I dread to think what would've happened if you'd been alone.'

'I thought the same, sir. Which is why I'm happy to volunteer to escort Miss Clements home whenever we're at the Crispin Hall. I wouldn't want to see anything happen to her, and it would save you the inconvenience of coming out in the cold.'

Louisa struggled to keep her expression bland. She didn't want Pa refusing. It would be awful if he came and collected her every time. She'd *never* get the chance to spend time with Mattie.

'I'll think about it,' said Pa, giving nothing away.

Mattie nodded. 'Alright, sir. Let me know. In the meantime, I'd better get home and make sure my ma's alright. I don't like leaving her on her own too long. I'll see you tomorrow, sir.' He smiled, bid them goodnight and left.

16

Jeannie joined her ma in the parlour, leaving her brothers to clean the kitchen after their supper. Her friends had been amazed to hear that her brothers had to help with the evening chores, but with Ma so fragile all the time, and Jeannie out at work, Lucas had decided that everyone had to do their bit to help. Jeannie thanked God every day that she had such an insightful brother, otherwise she'd have been left to do everything while the boys loafed about.

Ma had taken up her knitting and was working on some new socks for the twins. 'I swear they grow like weeds, those boys,' she sighed. 'Their toes come right through their socks in no time. I expect they'll be needing new boots again soon as well. Thank goodness Lucas seems to have stopped growing.'

At just turned nineteen, Lucas was certainly more a man than a boy these days. His beard was thick, requiring him to shave daily, and he was filling out in the shoulders. Like the twins, he grew quickly, reaching six foot by the time he was sixteen. Jeannie had a feeling the twins would be even taller than him by the time they stopped growing.

Her progress was slow, on account of her arthritic hands, but Ma swore that knitting was easier and less painful than sewing or darning for her and that she had to have something to do.

'I think I might need a new sole on mine, Ma,' said Jeannie. 'I've a little hole which lets the rain in.' She grimaced. 'I tried putting some cardboard in, but it just got soaked as well.'

Ma nodded. 'We'll take it to the cobblers on Saturday afternoon. With any luck, he can do it straight away.' She sighed again. 'I wish we could get you a new pair, lass, but there's just not enough to go around at the moment.'

'Don't worry, Ma. I'm saving my pennies. If I can get them repaired, I can manage with the pair I've got until I can get some new ones.'

Jeannie gave two-thirds of her wages to Ma, which wasn't much as she was only on eight and six a week at the moment. She bought her own clothes (or rather the material and wool to make them herself) and tried to save a few coppers when she could for necessities like shoes and stockings. Lucas, being older and on male workers' rates, earned a lot more. His pay had risen to nineteen shillings a week on his birthday this month. He'd been the breadwinner of the family since Ma had had to give up work. He handed over most of his earnings to Ma, insisting that he didn't need much. His only expenses were for any clothes and boots he needed, and for his subscription to the Street Shoemakers' Provident Benefit Society. He'd joined the Provident as soon as he could, pointing out that it would provide sick pay if he was too ill to work, and a death levy if he met with an accident like their pa had. 'We never know what's in store for us,' he'd told Jeannie. 'Better to pay it and have peace of mind. I wouldn't want Ma to struggle like that again, being left grieving and with no money coming in.'

Ma nodded and carried on knitting. 'The twins told me Clarks have asked the schools to identify boys coming up to fourteen and ready for work at the factory, on account of the shortage of labour now so many young men have enlisted. Now they're keen to start work as soon as they turn fourteen in January.'

'Shouldn't they at least see the school year out?' asked Jeannie.

'That's what I said,' she replied. 'But you know those two. They've never enjoyed being in the classroom. Maybe they'd be better at work. Lord knows, a few more shillings coming in would come in handy. It would at least cover all the food they eat. And Peter said they'd be offered some schooling a couple of afternoons a week until they were sixteen.' She shook her head. 'Of course, John was cross that he told me that. He's the keenest to leave school. That boy has never taken to his lessons, even though he's as bright as the rest of you.'

'Surely we can manage a little longer before making them go to work? It's not like they'll be earning much at fourteen, anyway,' said Jeannie. It didn't sit right with her. She'd often wished she could have stayed on at school. She'd loved it. But with Ma struggling so with her nerves and the burden of four children, it had been out of the question for her. Both Lucas and Jeannie needed to be at work to support the family. Having the twins leave school before they needed to seemed to her like she and Lucas had failed the family somehow.

'Don't forget, Jeannie, love, boys earn more than the girls. They'll be starting on six shillings a week at fourteen.'

Jeannie scowled. There wasn't much that riled her, but knowing her little brothers would soon earn more than she did, just because they were male and not because they worked any harder or were any cleverer, really annoyed her. It was so unfair. She wanted to contribute as much as they would to the family and worked just as hard as Lucas did. But, just because she was female, she would always earn less than them. But it wasn't Ma's fault, and Jeannie couldn't do anything about it, so she had to stop fretting and complaining about it.

'I know,' she sighed. 'If you think it's alright, Ma, then go ahead and let them. Like you say, a few extra shillings will help feed them. Maybe once they're earning, they'll start to appreciate the value of things.'

Ma nodded. 'I'll talk to Lucas, then I probably will. You two work hard enough as it is. I can't keep on expecting you to bear the burden.'

They sat in silence for a while. They could hear the twins bickering in the kitchen, Lucas's deeper voice giving the occasional order or rebuke above the chink of crockery and the clang of cutlery as they put them away. Jeannie hoped that Lucas was making sure they didn't break anything. In the parlour, Jeannie was lulled by the sound of the clock ticking on the mantle, the crackle of the fire in the grate, and the click-click of Ma's knitting needles.

She was half-asleep when Lucas came in and joined her on the settle.

The twins clattered upstairs to their room, making Jeannie blink and rub her eyes at the noise.

'How are things at the Operatic Society?' Ma asked him.

'Alright,' he said. 'The main parts of the scenery are almost finished, and most of the props are done. The girls say the costumes are nearly ready and ticket sales seem to be going well.'

'Have either of you seen any of the rehearsals?'

Jeannie shook her head. 'We can hear them singing while we're working, but they're in the main hall and we're in different rooms. I don't even see Lucas while I'm there. It sounds lovely, though.'

Lucas snorted. 'Sounds terrible,' he said.

'But you're tone deaf,' she pointed out, giggling at his outraged expression.

Ma smiled. 'And did Mrs Jackson ever come back, Jeannie?'

'No, thank goodness. If she had, I'm not sure half of the women would have stayed.'

'Like you said at the time, lass, the poor woman's scared. She's listening to all that warmongering and propaganda and won't let herself think about how every soldier, no matter what side they are, is a mother's son.'

'It's not just the likes of Mrs Jackson, Ma,' said Lucas. 'Mr Clements made an announcement and said no talking about war or who's enlisting or whatever in the Clicking Room. Said it's interfering with work and he won't have it. If he catches anyone fighting over it, there'll be hell to pay.'

'Goodness me,' said Ma. 'I hope no one is arguing with you, son.'

He smiled and shook his head. 'Don't fret, Ma. I'm bigger than most of the others. They won't be picking on me, or Mattie for that matter, not after his run-in with Timmy Smith.'

'What's this?' She looked worried. 'What run-in?'

'We forgot to tell you, Ma,' said Jeannie, keeping her tone light, narrowing her eyes at her brother. She proceeded to tell the story, making it as funny as they could manage.

'And the word is out that Mattie isn't the pushover some people thought he was, *and* he's in Mr Clements's good books,' said Lucas. 'Now he sees Louisa home to her door from the Crispin, with her father's approval. He's like her official bodyguard and everyone wants to know how he bested Timmy Smith and his gang.'

Jeannie glanced at him. He sounded almost put out by that. But she couldn't tell what was behind his sharp tone. Was he carrying a torch for Louisa as well? Or was he jealous of Mattie's newfound notoriety?

'I thought you said Mr Clements didn't want Louisa spending time with Mattie?' said Ma, looking confused.

'He didn't,' said Jeannie. 'But I think the incident persuaded him that he was decent and trustworthy. He's starting to warm to Mattie. Louisa's hopeful.'

Lucas rolled his eyes. 'I still think he's wasting his time. Old man Clements will never let his precious daughter end up with a Friend.'

Ma looked thoughtful. 'It would certainly be difficult for them. But a love worth having is worth fighting for. If they're meant to be, they'll find a way and, God willing, her parents will come to terms with that.'

Lucas got up, stretching his long body and arms. 'I'm off to my bed.' He kissed Ma on the cheek and flicked Jeannie's ear, jumping out of the way when she would have slapped him, before climbing the stairs to the attic bedroom.

Jeannie sighed and sat back. She supposed she ought to go to bed as well. Her body was tired, but she knew she'd only lie awake while her mind played her pictures of Louisa and Mattie together.

Ma picked up her knitting again, tutting when she realised she'd dropped some stitches. 'Here, Jeannie, lass. Can you pick these up for me?'

She handed the knitting over. Jeannie leaned forward to that she could see by the light of the oil lamp by Ma's chair and deftly put it right.

'There you go, Ma.'

'Thanks, love. You're a good girl.'

Jeannie smiled and sat back, watching Ma working.

'So,' said Ma, not looking up from her needles. 'Louisa and Mattie, eh?'

'Mmm. I'm the only one still single.'

'You're a lovely girl and any lad would be proud to have you on his arm,' she said.

Jeannie shrugged. 'Trouble is, I don't want any lad, Ma. I want someone who's a Friend, so that disqualifies a lot of lads round here. And even among our Meeting, there's not really anyone that has taken my fancy.' *Except Mattie.*

'Except Mattie,' Ma echoed her thoughts, her shrewd gaze searching Jeannie's face.

Jeannie squeezed her eyes shut. 'I'm pathetic.'

'Of course you're not. Don't fret, lass,' she said gently. 'Your time will come.'

When she opened her eyes, she felt her tears well. 'I feel awful, Ma. Louisa's one of my best friends and I want her to be happy. But not with Mattie. Why does it have to be Mattie?'

This time, Ma was careful to push the ball of wool onto the needles to stop the stiches escaping before she put her knitting down. She opened her arms. 'Oh, my darling girl, come here.'

Sniffing, Jeannie got up and knelt by Ma's armchair. Her mother put her arms around her shoulders and kissed her hair.

'I'm so sorry you feel like this, Jeannie, love. I can't imagine how hard it is for you. But I'm proud that you have so much love inside you that you can continue to be a true and loyal friend, even when it's breaking your heart.'

'I don't suppose I'll ever get married now,' she said. 'I'll be an old spinster like Miss Clark or the Misses Impey.'

'There's no shame in that,' said Ma. 'Look at the marvellous works those ladies do.'

Miss Alice Clark was the first ever woman director at Clarks, as well as being a suffragette and a champion of women's rights. At the moment, they said she was in London at a university, writing a book about working women in the seventeenth century. She managed all this, even though her health was poor. Her elderly cousins, the Impey sisters, were stalwarts of the Friends' Meeting House. While one, Ellen, ran the family farm in Street, the other – Catherine – was a pioneer who had created the first journal that spoke against treating people with black or brown skin differently from others. She had travelled across the Atlantic and corresponded with people around the whole world. The sisters had hosted black people from America, who came to England to deliver lecture tours denouncing the lynching of their fellows. The Misses Impey were in their seventies now and still busy and well-respected.

'Or you could be like Florrie Hood,' said Ma.

Jeannie looked up. 'What? Miss Hood in Trimmings?'

Ma nodded. 'She's an example to us all. Never married, but that hasn't stopped her making an impression on everyone who meets her. Clarks have made her the only forewoman. Imagine that! Running her own department, even while she's looking after her elderly mother and sisters. Why, someone at the Meeting House told me that the directors had given her a gift of two pounds to buy a bicycle so that it's easier for her to get home to Glastonbury and back to feed her bedridden ma in the dinner break. They think so highly of her, they want to make her life easier.'

Jeannie wasn't convinced. 'But I'll wager they don't pay her as much as the foremen,' she grumbled.

Ma tutted. 'I wouldn't know about that. It's Florrie's business what she earns. The point is, I'd be happy for you if you meet a good man and fall in love, Jeannie. But I'd be just as proud of you whatever happens. Thanks to Miss Alice and the Impey sisters and Florrie Hood, you're likely to have opportunities here in Street that my generation never dreamt of. Whichever path you take in life, I pray that it will be filled with love.' She kissed her hair again. 'Don't fret, my love. I'm sorry that Mattie wasn't clever enough to see the treasure that was right in front of him, but maybe God has other plans for you. In the meantime, embrace life, seek the light. In these dark days, we all need the light more than ever.'

17

Kate was exhausted. Ma remained in Kate's bed, which she didn't mind because it meant she was on hand if Ma needed her in the night and they could both keep out of Pa's way. But rather than risk hurting Ma if she rolled over in her sleep, Kate now slept on a pallet by the bed. Not that she slept much. She was constantly on guard, listening in the dark for any change in Ma's breathing, terrified that she'd die in the night and Kate wouldn't be awake to be with her in her final moments.

Peg and their sisters-in-law had started coming round during the day so that Ma wasn't on her own while Kate was at work. Pa had refused point blank to let Kate stay home, telling her she needed to earn her keep or she could bugger off and live on the streets. The others had to gang up on Pa at pay day to get him to hand over enough money for food and to pay the rent, otherwise they'd all be out on the street.

She would never leave her ma to his mercies, so she carried on – going to the factory every day, rushing home at dinner time to check everything was alright before running back to work for the afternoon, then running home as soon as her shift was over. Peg stayed until Kate got back, often leaving a hot meal in the oven when there was enough food in the house. Not that Kate was eating much, nor was Ma. Her illness meant that her stomach had become blocked by the cancer, leaving her in terrible pain and unable to keep anything down. She was existing on thin soups and broths, but that wasn't going to be enough to help her survive. But Peg's kindness meant that Kate didn't have to waste precious time she could spend with Ma in cooking a meal for Pa.

Mrs Searle came round most evenings to sit with Ma, as did Kate's brothers when they could manage it. Pa was always absent. He'd come home long enough to eat his supper in sullen silence, then he'd take himself down to the Street Inn, never once bothering to ask after Ma or to go into Kate's room to see his wife. Hours later, he would stagger back, blind drunk, sometimes stinking of perfume. Kate was thankful that Ma's visitors had always left by the time he got home. She was ashamed enough of his behaviour, without having anyone else witnessing it.

At the factory, it was all Kate could do to concentrate on her work without falling asleep. She made a lot of mistakes that had to be corrected. Mr Briars had charged her for spoiled thread two weeks running, until Pa had lost his temper when he'd seen her reduced wages again and slapped her. She hadn't bothered trying to hide the resulting black eye, she was so beaten down. She wondered if that was the reason why Mr Briars hadn't charged her for thread since then, even though she was still making silly mistakes. Whatever the reason, she was grateful and tried her best not to spoil any more work.

Louisa and Jeannie tried to help her. They had taken to bringing her treats – little cakes or biscuits, some apples or plums, and even a jar of Jeannie's ma's blackberry jam, trying to tempt both Kate and her ma to eat. Louisa had given Kate some hair ribbons, saying she had too many and was having a clear out. 'These colours suit your colouring much better than mine,' she'd said as she'd pressed them into her hand. Just thinking about their kindnesses brought tears to her eyes. She was aware that, apart from her selfish monster of a father, she was truly blessed by the people around her.

As she left the factory after her shift this evening, she pulled her coat around her, shivering in the winter chill, and set off for home as fast as she could.

'Kate! Wait a minute!'

She recognised Ted's voice and waved a hand, not slowing down. 'Can't stop,' she said. 'Gotta get home for Ma.'

She felt guilty that she had brushed him off so many times in the past few weeks. But Ma needed her. Ted could wait. If he didn't want to, then so be it. She was too tired and heartsore to care.

Behind her, she heard the clatter of his boots on the road as he ran to catch up with her.

'Can I walk with you?'

'If you like,' she shrugged, still walking. 'I can't hang around, though.'

'How's your ma?'

She took a deep breath, her chest tight. 'Not good.'

'Bugger. Sorry about that. It must be horrible.'

'Yeah.' She carried on, anxious to get home, yet dreading what she might find there; wishing that her pa would drop dead so that she didn't have to live in fear of his fists and his indifference to her ma.

'And how are you, Katie?' he asked. 'I've missed seeing you.'

His soft words shocked her. They'd been getting on well enough after she'd made it clear she didn't want a repeat of the kiss he'd foisted on her at the picture house. He'd been friendly and made her laugh on the few times they'd seen each other since then. But she couldn't in all conscience say she'd missed him. She'd been far too busy, worrying about Ma and making sure Pa had clean clothes and a hot meal at breakfast and supper-time so that he had nothing to complain about and would leave her and Ma alone.

'Sorry,' she said. 'I've been busy.'

'I know,' he said. 'I heard your pa wasn't doing anything, so I was wondering if there's anything I could do to help?'

Kate shook her head. 'It's alright,' she said, touched that he'd even thought to ask. 'Pa would be more of a hindrance anyway. I've got the rest of the family and a few friends helping now.'

He nodded as they strode along. His long legs kept up with Kate's rushed pace easily. While she was getting hot and breathless, he looked like he was out for a stroll, easy as you like. Not for the first time, Kate wished she'd been born a lad, tall and strong like her brothers, instead of being stuck in this feeble girl's body.

'I'm glad you're getting help. You still look exhausted, mind. You're not sickening for something as well, are you?'

She looked up, ready to tear him off a strip for being so personal. But the concern in his regard stopped her. He meant well. She could see that. He wasn't like Pa, who would say such a thing when he was more concerned that she wouldn't be around to fetch and carry for him any more, the selfish old so-and-so. Her heart softened and some of her anxiety faded.

'I'm alright, Ted. Don't worry. I'm just really tired. I watch Ma all night.' She ran a hand down her face, wanting to do nothing more than lie down and sleep, but she knew she wouldn't... couldn't. 'I can't rely on Pa; he's usually too drunk to notice anything,' she confessed, unable to hide her bitterness.

He filled the rest of their journey telling her about the Belgian men that had started working in the factory – all refugees that Clarks had agreed to sponsor and employ. 'They're nice fellows,' he said. 'One of them was a teacher. I'm getting him to teach me a bit of French and Dutch. He says I've got a talent for languages.'

'Why would you need to learn languages?' asked Kate.

He shrugged. 'I don't know. I just like a challenge, you know? And maybe, if I go to Flanders, it will come in handy for me to talk to the locals.'

'If there's any left,' she scoffed. 'It sounds like they're all being forced out of their homes while the fighting goes on around them.'

'I know. Pierre told me they lost everything. The family home has been destroyed, some of his neighbours were killed when they tried to resist the Hun. The school where he worked shut, so he didn't have a job. He barely got out with his life and a few things in a small suitcase. He doesn't know where half his family are, or even if they survived.'

'That poor man. I hope his relatives are alright.'

'Me too,' said Ted. 'Maybe if I go over there, I'll be able to look for them.'

Kate didn't think he'd be allowed to wander around the countryside – he was more likely to be trapped in one of those awful trenches. She hoped he didn't go, but it wasn't her place to say anything.

They reached the Davises' cottage. She was torn between rushing up the path and going inside to see Ma, and lingering at the gate for a few more moments to talk to Ted.

'Will you be at church on Sunday?' he asked.

She shook her head. 'I asked Louisa to deliver a letter to the Reverend, asking him to come and give Ma the sacrament while she's bedridden. She keeps asking when he'll come. She's never missed church before and it's upsetting her that she hasn't taken communion for so long. But I haven't heard back from him.' She sighed. 'I think he's still punishing us for Peg becoming a Friend.'

'That's not your ma's fault,' he frowned. 'You know my pa's on the parochial church council, don't you? How about I have a word with him for you?'

Ted's pa was a foreman in the Mechanics' Department at the factory, and his wife was a stalwart of many a church committee. He'd certainly hold more sway with the vicar than Kate would.

'Would you?' she asked, feeling a splinter of hope enter her weary heart. 'It would mean so much to Ma.'

'I'll talk to him tonight,' he assured her. 'Now, I won't keep you, Katie. But do you think you might be able to come for a little walk with me on Sunday afternoon? Some fresh air might do you good.'

She wanted to say yes, but reluctantly shook her head. 'I'm sorry, Ted. Peg's here Monday to Saturday while I'm at work and my brothers and sisters-in-law are here when they can, but they've got their own families to worry about. I can't ask any of them to come round on Sundays as well. I won't leave Ma on her own because, well... I don't know how long she's got left. I need... no, I *want* to spend all my spare time with her.'

He sighed, but nodded his head. 'I understand. I'd want to do the same. But would you mind if I walked you home from the factory like I did today? It's good to be able to see you and have a little chat. If I can't do anything else, would that be alright?'

She smiled, grateful for his patience and understanding. 'Yes, Ted. That would be lovely.' She put a hand on his shoulder and reached up on tiptoes to place a soft kiss on his cheek. 'Thank you,' she said, blushing now for being so forward. 'Bye.'

'*Au revoir, mademoiselle,*' he said with a grin. 'That's French, that is.'

He watched as she rushed down the path and into the house. As she closed the door, he waved and smiled before marching off down the lane with a spring in his step.

* * *

Louisa rushed round to Kate's house straight after church. Ma and Pa had wanted her to wait until after Sunday luncheon, but she promised it would just be a quick visit and she'd be back in time for the meal. She knew that Kate needed to hear what she had to tell her.

It was Kate's pa who opened the door. Louisa put on a polite smile. He scowled at her.

'Not another bloody do-gooder. What d'you want?'

She kept the smile on her face, despite his rudeness. 'Hello, Mr Davis. Can I have a quick word with Kate, please?'

He tipped his head towards the kitchen. 'She's in there. Don't you go keeping her from making my dinner, lass. She's lazy enough as it is.'

Louisa would have liked nothing more than to point out how hard Kate worked and how ungrateful he was, but she didn't dare. She'd seen the bruises on her friend. Reggie Davis didn't hesitate to hit a defenceless girl. She didn't want to give him an excuse to attack her, or to take it out on Kate after she left.

'I won't keep her, Mr Davis. In fact, I'll help if she needs it.'

'Go on then. Tell her to hurry up. I want some food in my belly before I have to go out. Got people to see.'

Louisa slipped past him, knowing full well he'd be seeing those people through the bottom of his cider glass.

Kate sat at the kitchen table, peeling sprouts. On the range behind her there was a pot of stew and one of potatoes bubbling away. A sweet pie rested on a wooden draining board, fresh out of the oven, if the scent of cooked apples and cloves was anything to go by. The clothes airer hanging from the ceiling was full of newly washed clothes.

'Goodness, you've been busy,' said Louisa.

Kate glanced up. She looked exhausted. 'I've been up since six. Peg offered to do the washing tomorrow, but I thought I might as well get on with it. Keeps me busy. Not much time to think.'

Louisa sat beside her and took the knife from her hand. 'Let me do this. You're dead on your feet, love.'

She didn't argue. She let go of the knife and rested her elbows on the table and her chin in her hands for a moment, watching as Louisa carried on preparing the sprouts. 'Thanks, Lou,' she said. 'Don't think I'm not glad to see you, but what are you doing here? Shouldn't you be at church?'

'I've already been, silly. I came straight from there. I can't stay long, but I wanted to tell you as soon as I could.'

'Tell me what?'

'When we were coming out of church, we were right behind the Jacksons, waiting in line to thank the Reverend for the service, as you do. I don't know why we have to thank him for doing his job, do you? It's not as though his sermons are very interesting, is it? There's always one or two of the older folk nodding off while he drones on.'

Kate chuckled. 'And who can blame them? I've nearly nodded off in church myself before.'

Louisa laughed. 'I think we all have. But that's not why I'm here. I wanted to tell you that Ted's pa spoke to the Reverend about your ma and how she needed him to visit and give her communion.'

'What did he say?'

'Well, at first he acted like he didn't know your ma was ill. So I stepped forward, all innocent like, and said, "Did you not get a chance to read the letter to you from Kate Davis that I dropped off at the Vicarage, Reverend?"'

'Oh, my lord, d'you think he didn't even read it?'

She shrugged. 'Who knows? He wasn't admitting to anything. He blustered a bit, then said he was a bit behind with his correspondence and he'd check his in-tray as soon as he could. Then Mr Jackson said that poor Mrs Davis is suffering greatly and would find great comfort in being given the sacrament if the vicar could find the time to visit her on her sickbed. He pointed out how faithful your ma has been all her life and how the church should offer a good Christian woman God's blessing at her time of need.'

Tears filled Kate's eyes. 'He said that?'

Louisa smiled and wiped a stray tear from Kate's cheek. 'He did, and me and Ted both agreed with him. Even Mrs Jackson and my ma and pa nodded. No one can fault your ma's faith, Kate. Just because the Reverend is in a sulk over Peg leaving the flock, he shouldn't take it out on your ma.'

'I know. But I wasn't hopeful he'd see it like that. Which is daft, seeing as how he never complained when my brother Fred joined the Methodists when he married Vi. Why ignore that, then make such a fuss over Peg becoming a Friend?'

'I think he dislikes the fact that they don't have a minister or services like the other churches do. He thinks it's dangerous for folk to *seek the inner light* rather than suffer through his sermons every Sunday.'

'It's daft and it's cruel. So, is he coming round or not?'

'I think so. Like I say, he blustered a bit, but he had to agree with Mr Jackson and then the vicar's wife said maybe she should go with him to see if there was anything the ladies from the church could do to help. She said she planned to do some pastoral visits on Tuesday. So I think they'll have to come now because she said it in front of mine and Ted's parents and a few other people were within earshot.'

Kate's eyes widened. 'Oh, lord, I hope we're not going to be invaded by ladies doing good deeds. Pa will have a fit. That's if he doesn't throw them all out on their ears.'

'Kate, don't worry.' Louisa put a hand on her shoulder. 'It will be alright, I'm sure. You know the church ladies. Some of them are enough to scare the daylights out of the likes of your pa. He won't dare be rude to them – most of their husbands know him at the factory, some of them foremen like Pa and Mr Jackson, and even he's not stupid enough to upset them.'

Kate took a deep breath, rubbing her eyes with the heels of her palms. 'You're right. And even if he was rude to them, I don't care, so long as the Reverend gives Ma the sacrament so she can rest easy. Thank you, Lou. It means a lot to me.'

Louisa smiled. 'It's Ted you need to thank. He's the one who got his pa to confront the Reverend. He'd never have listened to you or me.'

She nodded. 'Well, I appreciate the part you played. I'll be sure to thank Ted as well, though.' She thought for a moment. 'Are you alright finishing those sprouts for me while I pop and tell Ma? It'll perk her up no end.'

'Go on,' said Louisa, picking up the knife again.

'And I'd better warn Peg about their visit. Maybe George's wife can come round that day for Ma. She's Holy Trinity. I doubt if Peg wants to meet with the Reverend and his wife any more than they want to see her.'

18

Once the costumes were completed for the cast of *HMS Pinafore*, Louisa offered to help at rehearsals so that she still had an excuse to be at the Crispin Hall a couple of nights a week and for Mattie to walk her home. Her parents were still reluctant to give their permission for him to properly court her, so these brief snatches of time alone were all they could hope for at the moment. So Louisa made teas and washed up the cups, kept track of props and generally made herself useful. Eventually, the director asked her to act as prompter when their regular one was indisposed.

'He's asked me to study the libretto and the stage directions so that I can do the job if ever the usual prompter can't come again,' she told Mattie, her blue eyes glowing with excitement. 'I was ever so scared, in case I got it wrong, but he said I did a good job for a beginner and I should sit in on all the rehearsals and practise so I can get better.'

Mattie smiled and looked around to make sure no one was watching before he kissed her cheek. That was all the kissing he could get away with since their visit to the cinema. Louisa had been too scared of her pa finding out and forbidding them from seeing each other again. 'Clever girl,' he said. 'Now you've got a reason to keep coming to the Operatic

Society. I was worried your pa was going to stop you now the costumes are finished.'

'So was I,' she confessed, her cheek warm where he'd kissed her. 'That's why I offered to help when they said the woman was ill.' She pulled a face. 'Is it very wicked of me to hope she doesn't come back too soon?'

'Doesn't matter if she does. The director's asked you to be there to learn from her.'

'He has,' she smiled. 'What a stroke of luck, eh? So how's the scenery coming along?'

'Almost finished. Just some of the backdrops need finishing off. I've volunteered to do a bit of the painting. I used to be quite good at art when I was at school, even won a few prizes for drawing and painting. Seems some people remember it as they were reported in the local paper and some even got put on display. So when I offered, they said I could.'

'Clever boy,' she giggled, looking round before kissing his cheek. 'I loved art at school as well. I still do a bit of drawing. I've even tried to draw you.' She wrinkled her nose. 'I don't think I've got it quite right yet, though. It's hard when you're doing it from memory.'

'Maybe I should sit for you,' he said, striking a pose. 'Clothes on or off?'

That brought colour to her cheeks even as she laughed out loud. 'Matthew Searle, you wicked boy. I'll not be doing any drawings of you without your clothes on.'

'Why not? All true artists paint naked people, don't they? I know I'd like to draw you without your clothes on. You're beautiful, whatever you wear, but I'm betting you're even lovelier in just your birthday suit.'

She put her hands to her cheeks, shocked at the very idea. 'Oh, my word, Mattie, stop it! If my pa heard you saying things like that, we'd never be able to see each other again. He'd probably come after you with a pitchfork.'

Mattie chuckled. 'I know, lass. I'm just jesting.' He paused. 'Or am I?'

'Oh, you!' She slapped his arm and started walking down the High Street. Mattie followed on, still laughing as she huffed at him.

'Sorry, love,' he said softly as they walked side by side, not daring to touch. 'I'm just teasing. I know you're not that kind of girl. I mean, if you were, you'd have let me have another proper kiss by now.'

She took a deep breath, hearing the hurt in his voice. 'You know I want to, Mattie,' she whispered, even though the street was empty and they were cloaked in darkness. 'But if someone sees us...'

'I know,' he said. 'That don't make it any easier, though. You know I love you, don't you?'

She stopped, right in the middle of the street. 'Really?' she asked, not daring to believe him. 'Or are you just jesting again?'

He'd walked on a couple of steps before he realised she wasn't beside him. He halted and turned to face her. 'No jesting. I really do love you, Louisa Clements. You're everything to me.'

Her heart overflowed with happiness. 'I love you too, Mattie.'

He let out a long breath. 'Well, that's a relief,' he smiled. 'Now all we have to do is convince your pa that I'm a good catch and we can get wed.'

Her joy dimmed a little, but she raised her chin. 'It won't be easy,' she said. 'But I don't want anyone but you, Mattie.'

He nodded, his eyes blazing as he clenched his jaw hard and his lips thinned. 'I want nothing more in this world than to take you in my arms and kiss you properly right now. But you're right. We need to win over your pa and being seen canoodling in the High Street won't further our cause any.'

Louisa nodded, averting her gaze from the power of his, full to bursting with love for him. She began to walk again, slanting him a secret smile as she drew level with him. He groaned.

'Lou, darlin', please don't look at me like that. At least not until we can be alone and do something about it.'

They walked on in silence, neither daring to dawdle, knowing that Mr Clements would be standing at the window, looking out for them coming up Somerton Road.

'Mattie,' she said eventually. 'What will we do if Pa never comes round?'

He didn't answer for a moment. She risked a glance at him and saw her own desperation in his grim profile.

'I swear to you, Louisa, I'll do my best to win him over. He's already seen that I'm a hard worker and I'm willing to protect you. I'll keep on trying, I'll be respectful and do his bidding, no matter how long it takes. The only thing I won't do is leave the Friends. It would break Ma's heart, and I'm not comfortable with that.' He shrugged. 'Which makes me see why your church is important to your ma and pa, so I'd never expect you to give up Holy Trinity, either.' He sighed. 'But as far as I'm concerned, God has brought us together and He'll find a way for us to stay together without having to compromise our faith.'

'I understand, and I wouldn't want you to give up your church just because my parents aren't happy about it. If it's good enough for the Clarks, it should be good enough for everyone.'

'I know. But I've seen the problems it's caused for others, including my own brother, so I'm not expecting it to be an easy path for us. But if you love me half as much as I love you, Louisa, we'll find a way, I promise.'

They were within sight of her cottage now. Louisa felt a flash of panic. 'But what if they *won't* come round, Mattie? How will we...?'

He didn't change his pace, kept his eyes on her home – where her pa was clearly visible, standing in the window of the front parlour, watching them, his shoulders hunched with suspicion. Mattie raised a hand and waved, his expression clear and respectful.

'If they won't,' he said quietly, as though if he spoke any louder, Pa would hear him, 'then we'll wait until you're of age and we'll get married anyway. You're seventeen now. Four years seems like a lifetime, but it will pass, love, and then we can be together forever.'

19

It always amused Jeannie that, as soon as the hour of silent worship at the Meeting House ended with an Elder standing and saying, 'Thank you, Friends,' the peace was shattered as the members of the Meeting began to chatter to each other. The level of noise would be low at first as everyone continued to feel the reverence of the silence of the morning's worship. Then voices would raise as neighbours greeted each other and caught up on the latest gossip. It was no different today, the second Sunday of December.

She watched as Ma went to talk to Mrs Searle and some of the other women, nodding a respectful greeting to Mr and Mrs Roger Clark and Miss Alice Clark as she passed them. Jeannie saw that Mrs Esther Clothier – Roger and Alice's sister – was also there with her husband and their little boy, Peter. He was such a poppet. With a nod from his ma, he skipped outside with some of the other children who had been in the upstairs room attending Sunday School while his parents had joined the Meeting.

The twins, who declared they were too old to go upstairs these days, had managed to refrain from fidgeting through the Meeting, but she knew they were unlikely to have been thinking about the Lord or seeking the light within themselves. More likely they were thinking up mischief. As usual, they rushed out as soon as the Meeting ended. They'd been given permission to meet their friends at Victoria Field to play football. The recreation ground had started to look a bit ragged since the groundsman had enlisted, but that didn't stop the lads from having a kickabout there.

Lucas was talking to Mattie, their heads together. They looked serious. Jeannie was tempted to go over and find out what they were gossiping about, but before she made up her mind, they made the decision for her. Lucas looked in her direction and beckoned her over.

It was unlike her brother to want to talk to her here – after all, if he had anything to say, he simply spoke to her at home. Here, he preferred that he be left to the company of his best friend and the other lads. Nor did she feel comfortable around Mattie these days. She was coming to terms with the fact that he loved Louisa, but that didn't stop her feeling a pang in her heart whenever she saw him.

When she didn't move, Lucas said something to Mattie and they came to her.

'Jeannie,' said Mattie by way of greeting. 'We need you to go and see Kate.'

She frowned. Both lads looked serious. 'Kate?' She'd been sure he was going to ask her to pass a message to Louisa – that had happened far too often in recent months and she was getting heartily sick of it. 'Why?'

Lucas leaned in, putting an arm on her shoulder and guiding her out of the Meeting House. 'It's Ted. He's had some news,' he explained quietly as they passed through the door and nodded to the overseer who was there, thanking Friends for joining the Meeting this morning. The three of them shook his hand respectfully and moved away so that they could speak privately.

'What about Ted? Is he ill?'

Mattie shook his head. Lucas looked grim as his friend said, 'No. His brother's been killed. They got the news yesterday. Ma saw the postman. He said he'd delivered an official letter. Mrs Jackson took it, ripped it open, then screamed before she fainted dead away.'

'Oh, my word! The poor woman. Which brother was it?' She knew both of Ted's older brothers were fighting.

'Albert, the oldest. He was at Ypres, we think,' said Mattie.

'Ted said he'd let slip something in one of his letters that hinted that was where he was, but we're not sure,' said Lucas. 'Anyway, it don't matter where he was, does it? But whatever happened, we think you should go and let Kate know. Ted will want her to know.'

She nodded. 'Yeah, 'course I will. Poor Ted. I'll tell Kate.'

'We're going to try and see Ted, but he might still be at church with his ma and pa.'

'Alright. I'll just let Ma know, then I'll go straight round to Kate's. Give Ted and his family our condolences,' she said.

On the walk to Kate's cottage, she thought about Albert Jackson. She didn't know him well, but she knew who he was. Street was a close-knit community where most people worked at Clarks or relied on business from those who did. She thought that Albert had worked in the Big Room, where the different components they made in the various departments of the factory came together and the shoes and boots were finished. He was the first casualty of war that she actually knew. It chilled her to think of how many other young men from around the village had gone off to fight and wouldn't be coming home.

She wondered how Ted was feeling. His parents would be devastated, of course, losing their firstborn and him being so far from home. She thought about Ted's other brother – she thought his name was Stanley, but she couldn't be sure. Did he know that Albert had been killed? How horrible to be stuck there, fighting, when your brother is dead and you're separated from your family by the English Channel.

She pulled her coat tighter, trying to stop the chill that came from her thoughts as much as the December wind.

Kate rushed her through the front parlour to the warm kitchen, not making eye contact with her pa, who sat in an armchair by the window, a jug of cider at his side.

'You'd better not be here to hold up my dinner, Jeannie Musgrove,' he muttered after them. 'A man's entitled to some bloody peace in his own home on a Sunday. Don't need no more bleeding-heart do-gooders round here. You can all bugger off.'

'It's nearly ready, Pa,' his daughter told him, ushering her friend through.

Jeannie didn't say anything, following Kate quickly, praying he would leave them alone. She breathed a sigh of relief when Kate closed the kitchen door behind them.

'I'm so sorry—' They both spoke at once, then laughed a little hysterically when they realised what they'd done.

Kate held up her hand. 'I'm sorry about Pa. He's already in his cups, as you saw. He won't bother to get out of his chair so long as I don't keep him waiting too long for his dinner.'

Jeannie shook her head. 'It's not your fault, Kate. You don't need to apologise. I'm just sorry if me being here causes trouble for you.'

Kate sighed. 'No, it won't. No more than usual, anyway. He's always like that these days. Rude to everyone. I'm just glad Ma doesn't hear half of it. She's ashamed enough as it is.'

'How is she?' Jeannie asked. She almost felt sorry that she had to ask because she knew the news wouldn't be getting any better.

Kate shook her head. 'She's still alive, no thanks to that bugger in the other room,' she said, her voice low and full of bitterness. 'The doctor said she should go to the sanitorium, but Pa won't hear of it, even though he was told Clarks would give a grant towards the cost. They did for Mrs Black, remember, when she had tuberculosis? They paid for a nurse to come for someone round the corner who had typhoid. But Pa told me to shut up and we won't be getting any help for Ma. I don't think he can even be bothered to ask.' She closed her eyes and took a deep breath. 'I know you don't want to hear it because you're a good soul, but I really hate him, Jeannie. I wish it were him suffering instead of Ma.'

Jeannie hugged her friend tight. 'If it were him, your ma would be working herself ragged, looking after him,' she pointed out.

'Yeah, she would. But when she's gone, if he gets ill, I bloody won't look after him. I'll leave him to rot until he goes to hell. I don't care if that makes me as bad as him.' She sniffed and pulled away, turning her back on Jeannie as she checked the pots on the range. 'I'm sorry, Jeannie, you didn't come round here to hear me declare how much I hate my pa.' She glanced at her over her shoulder. 'What did you come for? Aren't you usually still at your Meeting now?'

She felt her throat tighten. 'Lucas and Mattie asked me to come and tell you. They heard that Ted's brother Albert has been killed in France.'

Kate gasped, her hands coming up to cover her mouth as her eyes filled with tears.

'I'm so sorry to bring you more bad news,' Jeannie went on. 'But the lads thought you should know and, well, Ted's not likely to want to be running round telling people.'

Kate shook her head and took a deep, calming breath as she wiped her eyes. 'No, it's alright. I'm glad you did. Poor Ted. I can't imagine how him and his family must be feeling. I wonder if Stanley knows?'

'I wondered that as well. Don't they send brothers to fight together? It would be horrible to see your brother die like that when you're fighting for your own life beside him, wouldn't it?' She shuddered. 'It don't bear thinking about. All those lads... what they must be suffering...' Her eyes welled. 'I can't bear the thought of it.'

Kate sank down into a chair at the kitchen table. Jeannie sat opposite her.

'I don't know what to do, Jeannie,' she said.

Jeannie took her hands in hers, noting that Kate was shaking. It was probably the shock.

'Do you want to go round and see Ted?' she asked. 'Because I can do your pa's dinner and watch your ma if you do.'

Kate thought for a moment, then shook her head. 'He'll be with his ma and pa and maybe people from Holy Trinity. They won't want me there as well.'

'Alright. I can stay for a bit anyway, so if you change your mind, just say so.'

She nodded, looking a bit dazed. 'I heard about all the casualties, but I never thought... I used to see Albert at church with the family. He was a nice lad – a lot like Ted. I can't believe he's gone.' Her tears welled again. 'How many more have got to die before they stop this awful war, Jeannie? They said it would be over by Christmas, but it's nearly that now and they're sending more and more lads out there.'

'I know, love. It's…' Her throat closed up. 'Just terrible,' she whispered.

A shout from the parlour reminded them that Reggie Davis was waiting for his dinner. Kate got up and dished it up for him while Jeannie set the table for one as Kate said she'd eat her meal upstairs with her ma later. Once they were ready, Kate put her pa's meal on the table and he sat down with a grunt, his cider jug beside him. He tucked in: no thanks, no saying grace. The girls went into the parlour and left him to it, closing the door on him.

'I need to write Ted a note,' said Kate. 'Will you take it to him for me? I can't leave Ma while Pa's like this, but I want him to know I'm thinking of him. Ma will want me to send her condolences to the family as well.'

'Of course I will,' said Jeannie.

It took just a few minutes for Kate to write two short notes. When she'd signed them on behalf of herself and her ma, she folded them and handed them to her. Jeannie stood up.

'I'll leave you to it. Go up and rest on the bed with your ma,' she said, stroking her friend's hair. 'Make sure you eat as well. You're worn out. Surely your pa will be off to the Inn once he's eaten, so you can relax for a few hours?'

Kate nodded. Jeannie wasn't sure whether she was agreeing to rest, or simply being polite so that she would leave her alone.

'I'll make sure Ted gets your letters,' she said at the front door.

'Thanks, Jeannie. Tell him I'm sorry. I know I said it in the note, but tell him anyway.'

'I will. They're in for a rotten Christmas, aren't they?'

After delivering Kate's letters, Jeannie walked home in a sombre mood. The drapes had been drawn in the Jackson house and Ted had looked pale and wan, his eyes bloodshot and puffy. She'd heard his ma sobbing and his pa's deep voice trying to comfort his wife. The grief flowing from that cottage chilled her bones and made her heart ache.

20

Kate didn't see Ted until they went back to work in January after the Christmas break. She hadn't expected to, but she missed him and thought about him a lot. She hoped he was alright.

Her own life continued in the same vein as before – lying in the dark, listening to her ma's laboured breathing, then trying to persuade her to at least drink some weak tea or broth when she awoke. She would make Pa's breakfast then rush to work, anxious to get through enough pieces to meet her quotas, rushing home at dinner time to see Ma and Peg – who would force her to eat something – before running back to work before the factory hooter went. The afternoons were the worst. She was exhausted and had trouble concentrating, but she managed to plough through. Mr Briars kept a close eye on her, but, thanks to her friends, she never let him down. Louisa and Jeannie had decided to help her, slipping some of their finished pieces into her basket through the day. When she caught them doing it, she'd protested, but they told her they knew she would do the same for them if they needed it, so she should be quiet and let them get on with it. She'd been too tired and grateful to argue.

As soon as the hooter sounded the end of the shift, she would shed her apron, pull on her coat and run all the way home. Every time she approached the cottage, she was afraid that Ma had died while she was at work. That fear almost crippled her, causing her to sag with relief the moment she saw her Ma's dear face and realised she'd been spared for another day.

Christmas had passed with Kate barely noticing, other than having some days off when the factory closed. Pa was nowhere to be found. Someone said he was spending the holiday with a pal in Glastonbury. No doubt it was someone with a good supply of cider. Kate didn't care. It meant she could devote her time to Ma, storing up precious memories to sustain her when Ma finally lost her fight. It wouldn't be long now. She knew it and denied it at the same time.

It was a Saturday in January when she saw Ted. He was waiting for her at the factory gate. It struck her that his brother's death had changed him. Gone was the easy smile and relaxed stance. In their place was a tense, unhappy young man whose eyes were clouded with grief.

'Ted. How are you?' she asked, wanting to stop and talk to him, to ease his suffering, while every cell in her body urged her to run home to Ma.

He shrugged and turned in the direction of Silver Road, clearly intending to walk Kate home. 'Not good,' he said. 'Ma's taken it badly. Christmas was terrible. I suppose it was for a lot of people. We all thought this damned war would be over, didn't we? But all we're getting are higher casualty rates. Have you walked through the village lately? So many families are mourning. I think this is the bleakest Christmas this place has ever seen. It doesn't help that we haven't heard from Stan.' His long legs set a good pace, which Kate rushed to match, grateful that he didn't want to dawdle, even when he clearly needed a friend to talk to.

Kate touched his arm. 'Surely if anything had happened to Stan, you'd have heard by now, wouldn't you? I'm sure you'll hear from him soon. You know some people are saying that when the fighting is going on, it takes longer to get letters from the front.'

He nodded but didn't say anything for a moment. 'I'm worried about him. They were in the same unit. The letter said only Albert was... you know... but it didn't mention Stan.' He ran a hand through his hair. 'Why didn't they at least say he was alright?'

'Because whoever sent the letter was probably some clerk at the War Office who didn't know your brothers were there together and didn't think to mention Stan. I'm sure he'll be alright, Ted. No news is good news, isn't that what they say? If he's still there fighting, that's all that the government is worried about, not reassuring his family.'

Ted sighed. 'I suppose.' She still had her hand on his arm and he covered it with his other hand. 'Thanks for your letters, Kate. We appreciated them. I know you're busy with your ma. How is she?'

She shook her head, blinking against the tears that were never far from the surface. 'I don't know how much longer she can go on. My brothers clubbed together to pay for some medicine to help with the pain because Pa is being a selfish so-and-so as usual. But they can't keep on doing that. They've got their own families to look after.'

He squeezed her hand. 'If I had any spare money, I'd give it to you, Kate, I swear. But... we don't know if they'll let us have Albert's body back so we can bury him at Holy Trinity. Pa's trying to find out. They say if we do get him, we'll have to pay to bring him home and I don't think we can afford it. There are so many casualties, the only ones coming home for burial are officers from rich families. But Ma's in such a state, we've got to try, even if it takes every penny we have.'

Kate's heart broke for him and his family. 'I understand,' she said. 'I hope you get him home.'

He left her at her gate. She wanted to linger, to comfort him, but her own responsibilities were calling to her. With a sigh, she turned away from the sight of his hunched shoulders and lowered head as he trudged down the lane, and went inside.

'You're such a good girl, Katie,' Ma whispered as Kate gently wiped her face with a warm cloth. 'You and Peg both. Don't know what I'd do without you.' Her voice was frail, her breathing shallow. 'You should be out, courting, living your life, not here.'

Kate put the cloth aside and kissed Ma's forehead. 'I don't want to be anywhere else. I love you, Ma. Being here with you's no hardship.'

Ma rested back on her pillow, worn out by the effort of drinking some broth. She held out her hand and Kate took it, looking down at her from her perch on the side of the mattress.

'Lie with me, love,' said Ma. 'You need to rest.'

Careful not to disturb Ma, Kate lay down beside her, clinging to her hand. She was so frail now, skin and bone, her cheekbones sharp.

'Not long now, love,' she said. When Kate stiffened and would have protested, Ma squeezed her hand. 'No, listen to me, please. Let me speak. I need to tell you... You've been so good to me, I couldn't have wished for a better daughter. But it breaks my heart what this has cost you. Shhh, don't argue with me, Kate. He's made it harder, made more demands than he should.' She sighed. 'He was a good man once, but the cider took its hold. I miss the Reggie I married. That man downstairs is not him.'

'You're too good for him,' said Kate, unable to keep the bitterness from her words.

'No, love. None of us is too good for anyone else. He's lost his way, that's all. I tried to be a good wife, but I think I disappointed him. I was too busy being a mother and he felt neglected.'

'He's the one neglecting you,' said Kate. 'Don't defend him, Ma. He doesn't deserve it. You've always been devoted to him.' She couldn't understand it. He did nothing but belittle his wife and children, demanding they do everything for him, yet giving nothing in return but pain and abuse.

Ma sighed again and closed her eyes. 'I'll at least go to the Lord knowing I did my best. I hope that's enough. I'm so tired. Let's rest now.'

Kate watched as Ma slipped into a doze, her breathing slow and shallow. She wanted nothing more than to close her own eyes and sleep, but she didn't dare. Ma was right, she didn't have long and Kate wasn't about to miss one second of what was left of her beloved mother's time. She lay on her side, holding Ma's hand, keeping vigil.

She must have fallen asleep eventually. In the middle of the night, the slackening of the thin hand in hers brought her awake. She leaned close. 'Ma?' she asked softly, listening for her next breath. But it never came. Her mother was gone.

21

The rest of January and February were a blur of darkness and grief for Kate. Her pa was no good to man nor beast. He stayed so drunk that he missed his shifts at the factory three days running. Mr Clements came round to talk to him. He expressed his condolences to Kate and told her that the management was giving the family a grant towards the funeral expenses, which was a relief. Kate didn't know what he said to her father, but Pa stayed off work until after Ma's funeral. He would have missed that as well if her brothers hadn't forced him into his Sunday suit and marched him between them behind Ma's casket to the church. He sat, stony-faced, through the service and burial, then staggered off to the Street Inn, cursing his ungrateful children and useless, dead wife.

Unlike him, Kate had only missed the one day of work after Ma's passing and also the day of the funeral. Peg had come round in the morning after Ma died to help her lay her out while their sister-in-law had informed the Reverend and arranged the funeral. Neighbours and friends had gathered as soon as they heard the news to pay their respects, bringing food and condolences. Pa had eaten their gifts of food, but thanked no one, ignoring everyone including his own children. Rosie Davis was well mourned by her children and friends. Kate knew no one would be sorry to see the passing of Reggie Davis. In fact, she prayed for it.

She was glad to go to work, to get away from him and be with her friends. With Ma gone, she hated going home. She stayed at the factory at dinner time now that there was no need to rush home. Louisa and Jeannie urged her to eat, sharing their food with her, but she had little appetite.

'You've got to eat something, Kate, love,' said Jeannie when she refused an apple a few days after the funeral. 'You'll make yourself ill. Your ma wouldn't want that, would she?'

Jeannie and Louisa both were worried about Kate. It was as though something died in her when her ma passed. She was like a shadow of the Kate they knew and loved.

Kate shrugged. 'I'm not hungry,' she said. She stood, wobbling a bit for a moment before she took a breath, squared her shoulders and raised her chin. 'I'm going to head back to my machine. I'm behind.'

Jeannie watched her walk away. 'I'm worried about her,' she said.

'Me too,' said Louisa. 'I wish I knew what to do to help her.' She wrapped up her uneaten bread. 'I brought extra, hoping she'd eat it,' she said. 'I don't even know if she's eating at home.'

'Probably not. I've asked Ma if we can invite her for Sunday dinner. Maybe a change will do her good. I hear her pa's barely getting by at work; he's always in his cups. He'll be worse at the weekend and probably won't notice if she isn't there.'

'I don't know,' said Louisa. 'He's quick to demand his hot meals. Lord, I hate that man!' She looked around, making sure no one could overhear them. 'Don't tell anyone, but I know Pa's giving him the benefit of the doubt at the moment on account of him losing his wife. He told Ma that he's had to tell Reggie Davis that if he doesn't sort himself out soon, he'll lose his job. He's already been fined for spoiling work and being late.'

They packed up and left the canteen, both lost in their own thoughts. They didn't notice Ted Jackson until he was standing in front of them.

'Where's Kate?' he asked. 'I haven't seen her for a few days. We're all doing extra hours in Clicking because we're behind on orders. I keep missing her after work.'

Here was another one lost in grief, Jeannie thought. She hadn't seen poor Ted smile since the news about Albert. She gave him a soft smile, trying not to appear too sympathetic. Lucas had said Ted was tired of people feeling sorry for him.

'She went back to the Machine Room early,' she said.

'Is she alright?' he asked.

'We don't know, probably not,' said Louisa. 'She's barely eating and she's so sad.' She shook her head. 'We're worried about her. Do you think you could try and help her?'

He ran a hand through his hair, frowning. 'I'm not sure what I can do,' he said.

'Just talk to her,' said Jeannie. 'And maybe get her out of the house. Her pa's worse than ever.'

'I know,' he said, looking grim. 'Blooming fool's going to get the sack if he's not careful. Mr Clements sent him home this morning. Told him not to come back until he's sober. I wanted to warn Kate.'

'Oh, lord,' groaned Louisa. 'That man.'

'I don't like it,' said Jeannie. 'If he's in trouble at work, he'll be in a temper and he'll take it out on Kate.' She looked at Ted. 'You know he beats her, don't you?'

Ted snarled, 'Lucas said. What kind of monster hits his own daughter? Kate don't deserve that.'

'No, she doesn't,' said Jeannie. 'But we don't know what we can do about it.'

'It would help if you spent some time with her,' said Louisa, giving Ted a sideways glance. 'Maybe give her a break?'

He nodded. 'I'll meet her after work. Can you tell her I was looking for her?'

'Will do.'

He was waiting for Kate when she left the factory. She nodded to acknowledge his presence but couldn't bring herself to say anything. It was too much effort. Everything was. She didn't know if this pain that had wrapped itself round her heart and mind when Ma had passed would ever diminish. Right now, it was all she could do to get through work, keep the cottage tidy and put a meal on the table for her pa when he expected it.

'Mind if I walk you home?' he asked.

She could see her grief mirrored in his eyes. He understood. He wouldn't expect her to pull herself together and smile. Much as she loved her friends, they didn't understand and kept trying to cheer her up. She was hard pressed not to scream at them to leave her alone sometimes. She knew they meant well, but that didn't help. She nodded at Ted. He held out his arm. She took it, grateful to lean on his strength as they made their way, slower than usual, towards Silver Road.

'Did the girls tell you about your pa?'

She frowned. They had tried to talk to her, but she'd kept her head down and concentrated on not wasting thread. 'No. What about him?'

'The foreman sent him home this morning. He was operating a press and damned near caught someone's hand in it. The lad working with him screamed like a girl and old man Clements came running. Your pa stank of cider and was yelling at the lad for making a fuss.'

Kate groaned. 'Did he get the sack?'

'I don't think so,' said Ted. 'Not this time. But I heard Mr Clements tell him if he ever came in drunk again, he would be for it.'

'If he loses his job, we'll lose the house,' she said. She found she didn't care. Now that Ma wasn't there, she'd rather live in a ditch than stay there.

'I think he realised that. He tried apologising, but his words were slur-ring and, well, there was a bit of cursing as well. Clements had a couple of men escort him off the factory premises. Told one of them to make sure he got home and didn't stop off at the Street Inn.'

Kate sighed. 'It won't make much difference. He's always got cider in the house these days.'

'I'm sorry, Kate,' he said. 'You've had a rotten time of it lately and it's about time he acted like a man and started looking after you.'

She laughed without humour. 'He's never looked after any of us. That was Ma's job as far as he was concerned. I don't expect he'll change now. The only person I can rely on is myself.'

'I think your brother Fred is planning on going round to see him tonight.'

Her oldest brother worked in the Clicking Room as well. He'd have seen it all.

'He looked furious,' he went on. 'He spoke to Mr Clements, but I don't know what was said.'

She grimaced. 'I hope they don't get in a fight. Vi will kill Fred if he does. She says Pa's not worth the trouble.'

'No, he's not. But you are. I expect Fred's more worried about you.'

'Nothing he can do.' Nothing any of her siblings could do. 'I can't leave home, even if I wanted. Pa takes my wages, so I've no money.'

'Can't you go and live with one of your brothers or your sister?'

She shook her head. 'They've all got their own families to worry about.' Only Peg and her husband Will were childless, but that would change soon, no doubt. None of them could afford to support Kate. If Pa would give up her wages, she might at least pay her way. But he'd made it clear that he was claiming all her wages until she was at least twenty-one. He'd probably try to keep them after that as well if she was still under his roof. And, of course, while she didn't get her money, she couldn't leave, not unless she got wed to someone who could afford to support her. The thought of being tied to another man who could control her life the way Pa did made her feel sick. So she was stuck between a rock and a hard place. Trapped.

She lifted her chin, not appreciating the pity in his eyes. 'Any news of Stan?'

He looked as though he wanted to talk more about her situation, but she stared him down, not willing to say any more. What was the point? In the end, he nodded and looked away.

'We got a letter. Finally. He's still at the front. Said a sniper got Albert, so it was quick, thank God. He was right next to him. Held him while he took his last breath.'

She halted and put a hand to her mouth. 'Poor Stan. That must have been horrible.'

He looked down at the ground, scuffing his boot. 'Yeah. It was a comfort to us to know he was there for Albert, but I think it upset him something awful. Their unit commander sent Stan to a field hospital behind the lines for a while. He said he was so shocked, a doctor gave him a sedative and he just slept most of the time. Then they sent him back to the trenches. Said he keeps looking, expecting to see Albert there beside him.'

Kate knew how Stan must be feeling. She had become so used to sharing a room with her poorly ma that she could hardly bear to go in there now. Her brothers had swapped out the mattress and she'd laundered all the bedding because she was told she had to. She'd kept Ma's bed jacket unwashed, though, so that she could pull it around her shoulders at night when she was loneliest and be surrounded by her mother's scent. But even that was fading now and soon there would be nothing left of Ma in the house.

They reached the house. Kate took a deep breath, half of her dreading what she'd find behind the front door, the other half beyond caring any more. She turned to Ted.

'Thanks for walking me home.' She offered him a sad smile, averting her gaze when she saw the pity in his eyes again.

He held onto her hand on his arm. 'I think I should come in with you,' he said. 'I don't want you facing him on your own.'

She shook her head. 'I'll be alright. If he's been drinking all day, he'll likely be in a stupor by now. He won't even notice me.'

'Then he won't notice if I come in and have a cuppa with you,' he said, his tone firm. 'I don't want you alone with him. Not today. He was in a right temper this morning.'

Kate rolled her eyes. 'He's always in a temper,' she said. 'Don't you think I've learned how to keep out of his way by now?'

His hand tightened over hers and she looked up at him to see determination in the set of his jaw. 'I've no doubt you have. You're not daft. But I'll stay, nonetheless. At least until Fred gets here.'

She sighed. 'There's really no need. But if you insist, I'll get the kettle on.'

He smiled. '*Dank u wel.*'

'What?'

'It's Dutch for thank you. Remember, I told you I'm learning from that Belgian chap, Pierre?'

'Oh, yes,' she said as she opened the front door. 'I didn't realise you were still doing that.'

She held up a hand to stop him following her immediately and held her breath for a moment as she listened for any signs that Pa was about. The cottage was blissfully silent. With a sigh of relief, she opened the door wider and beckoned him in.

In the kitchen, she filled the kettle and set it on the range, grabbing some coal from the scuttle and banking the fire so that it would boil quicker. She was glad it was still lit – she suspected Peg must have come round earlier to see to it. Pa certainly wouldn't, and then he'd blame her for a cold house and late supper.

'Take a seat,' she said, popping her head into the pantry briefly to find it almost bare. 'I'm sorry I can't offer you anything to eat.' There had been some biscuits in there this morning that someone had given them, but Pa had obviously found them, judging by the crumbs scattered over the kitchen table alongside his empty cider jug. She moved the jug to the sink, rinsed a cloth in water and wiped the table down, embarrassed that Ted saw it like this. 'But Pa only drinks cider these days, so I know we've still got some milk for our tea.' She gave him a bright smile to try and disguise the bitterness she felt.

'I'm alright, Kate,' he said. 'Come and sit down before you fall down.'

She sat opposite him, not sure what to do or say. When he took her hands in his, she didn't fight him. His warm fingers felt nice in her chilled grasp.

'Tell me some more Dutch,' she said, not wanting to talk about her life. What was the point?

He laughed and proceeded to talk what to her sounded like gibberish.

'What are you saying?' she said, laughing. 'Is that even a proper language?'

'It is. I swear. I just told you your pa is an old fool and I really hope your brother can sort him out, because you deserve a better life than you have now.'

'You never did,' she laughed, then immediately sobered. She shouldn't be fooling around like this, not so soon after...

Ted squeezed her hands. 'It's alright to smile, Kate, even to have a laugh. I know it's hard. Every time I find myself jesting about something, I remember that Albert won't ever get the chance to play the fool again and I feel a guilt so terrible, it's like a physical pain. But my uncle came to visit us last week – I'm named for him and he's my godfather – and he took me out for a walk. He told me I can't go on feeling guilty every time I find a little bit of joy in the world. Said Albert wouldn't want me to mope for the rest of my life.'

'He probably wouldn't,' she said softly, remembering the sunny smile of Ted's older brother. 'I think he liked finding joy, didn't he?'

'I know,' he said, sounding choked up. 'So since that chat with Uncle Ted, I've been trying to imagine Albert sitting up there in Heaven, looking down on me and getting cross at me for being such a wet ninny. I try to find a little something every day that makes me feel that life's worth living, even though Albert's not here any more.'

'Like what?' She couldn't imagine anything making her feel that life was worth living without Ma here right now.

He shrugged. 'Nothing important. Just... I don't know... when we were walking, it was a bitter cold day, but there wasn't a cloud in the sky. It was such a nice shade of blue. Uncle took me up the Tor. He always likes to go up there when he comes back to Somerset for a visit. Says it feeds his soul. We stood on the top, our backs to the tower, and looked out over Glastonbury, Street and the levels. It was beautiful. Even in the winter, with no leaves on the trees, it looked so pretty. There was a frost on the ground, 'cause it was still early, and when the sun hit it, it sparkled like thousands of diamonds.'

'That does sound nice,' she said, feeling wistful. 'I haven't been up the Tor in a long time.'

'Then we'll go together,' he said. 'But you don't need to go far to find some joy, Kate. There's snowdrops coming out along the lanes. There's Christmas lambs in the fields.' He paused, cocking his ear. 'Hear that?'

She frowned and listened. 'What?'

'Two things. No, three.' He smiled. 'First – the quiet in here because your pa's gone out. That's got to give you a little joy, eh?'

She huffed out a laugh. 'Idiot. What about the other two?'

'I can hear a child laughing. Is it one of your neighbour's littl'uns?'

She strained to hear, and sure enough, there was a giggle. Her lips twitched. 'Yes, that's Sally from next door. She's a sweet little thing.'

His eyes warmed as he noted her soft smile. 'And third – a definite source of joy for me – is the sound of your kettle boiling,' he said.

Kate gasped and turned to look at the range to see the kettle steaming away on the hob. 'Oh, you.' She pulled her hands away, giving his arm a playful slap. 'I can take a hint. One cuppa coming up.'

'Phew, that's a relief,' he said, wiping his brow and hamming it up. 'A man could die of thirst waiting for a cuppa round here.'

She stood up, giving him a narrow-eyed stare as she went to make the tea. 'Ooh, you do like to live dangerously, don't you, Ted Jackson?' Then she burst out laughing as he grinned and nodded.

'See,' he said. 'Joy. Sights and sounds worth living for.' His grin gentled into a soft smile. 'You bring me joy, Kate Davis.'

She sobered, nodding and turning to busy herself making the tea. Right at this moment, Ted Jackson brought her joy – and even a little hope that things might get better one day. When she'd brought the pot, milk jug, sugar bowl and their cups and saucers to the table, she sat down again and looked at him.

'Thank you, Ted,' she said. 'Before she died, Ma made me promise to try and be happy and I swear I've not had the slightest clue how to do that.'

'It's hard, I know.'

She nodded and served the tea, not looking at him as she blinked back the tears that were always close to the surface. 'But I think your uncle is a wise man, and I'm grateful you shared his wisdom with me.'

'Happy to help,' he said, stirring a spoonful of sugar into his tea. 'Any time. We'll look for joy together in honour of my brother and your ma.'

22

'Hello, Jeannie. How are you?'

Jeannie swung round, searching for the voice behind her. She stopped in the middle of the High Street when she realised it was Douglas Baker, a lad she knew from school. He'd been in the year above her and her friends and although she'd seen him around the factory, she hadn't taken much notice as he didn't seem to even know who she was. Yet here he was, on a Saturday afternoon, calling out and rushing towards her.

By rights, she should be getting the shopping with Lucas, like they always did on a Saturday after work. But the twins had started at the factory now and Lucas had said he'd take them with him to get what the family needed. She'd been glad of the chance to go straight home without having to carry the groceries. So that's why this lad was able to waylay her.

'Douglas?' she said in surprise. 'I... I'm fine, thank you. And you?'

He came to stand in front of her. He'd got taller since school, though he wasn't as tall as Lucas or the twins. But he wasn't as spotty as he used to be and he looked quite well turned out, even in his working clothes.

'I'm well, thank you,' he said. 'You're in the Machine Room, aren't you? I work in the Big Room for the time being, but I'm hoping to transfer to the Mechanics' Workshop soon. Better prospects.' He puffed his chest out as though she should be impressed.

'Oh. Well, good for you. I wish you well with it.' She nodded and turned to carry on walking home. It had been a long week. Despite the hundreds of machines rumbling away all day, it had stayed bitterly cold inside the Machine Room today. Someone said Mr Roger Clark had ordered a man to be at the factory overnight to keep the boiler stoked while the weather was this bitter after too many of the workers complained about how hard it was to work with frozen fingers. She was looking forward to getting home and sitting by the range with a hot drink and letting the warmth seep back into her bones. She pushed her hands deeper into her pockets, blowing out a cloud of breath into the cold air.

'Sorry, I can't stop,' she said. 'If I stand still in this cold, I'll likely freeze to death.'

Douglas fell into step beside her. 'It is cold, isn't it? I'll walk with you, if that's alright?'

She glanced at him, not used to getting any attention. This was odd, but also oddly flattering. She gave him a shy smile and nodded. Together, they trudged along the High Street, their shoulders hunched against the bitter wind, their breath forming little clouds around their faces.

'I... er... heard you helped out at the Operatic Society,' he said. 'My ma and pa were in the chorus.' He gave her a bashful smile. 'They tried to get me to go along. If I'd known you were there, I might have.'

Jeannie felt herself blush and prayed that the fact that her face was already red from the cold would hide the fact. 'I wasn't in the cast,' she said. 'I just helped with the costumes. So you wouldn't have seen me anyway.'

He nodded, walking beside her for a little while. Jeannie felt uncomfortable. She had no idea why Douglas should want to walk with her. She'd known him from a distance for years, yet never shared more than a few words in all that time. She was just about to ask him what this was all about when he put a hand on her arm and halted.

'Would you go to the dance with me at the Crispin Hall next weekend?' he asked. 'My treat.'

Jeannie gasped. 'You're asking me out?'

He looked uncertain for a minute, but then seemed to firm his resolve and nodded. 'I'd really like to get to know you better, Jeannie.'

Part of her was thrilled. No one had ever asked her out before. But then she felt a wave of regret as reality set in. His family attended the Tin Church. She gave him what she hoped was a regretful smile. 'I'm sorry, Douglas. You know I'm a Friend, right? Maybe you should find someone from your church to take with you.'

'Aren't you allowed to dance?' he asked, his tone teasing.

'We can dance,' she said, starting to feel defensive. 'But, well, I don't think there's much point in courting someone if there's no possibility of a future together.'

'I can see how that applies if we were older and thinking of getting wed, Jeannie, but we're both a bit young for that, aren't we? And anyway, how do you know whether you might want me you courting you if you don't go out with me at least once and give us a chance to get to know each other?' he asked. He seemed genuinely interested in her answer.

She shrugged, feeling a bit uncomfortable under his intense gaze. 'What would your parents think about you going out with me?'

He blinked and opened his mouth, then closed it again. That told Jeannie all she needed to know. She shook her head and turned away. 'Thank you for thinking of me, Douglas. But I don't think it's a good idea.'

She walked away, leaving him standing there. She didn't dare look back, but she imagined he would laugh this off and go in search of another girl to take to the dance. She didn't mind, she really didn't. Well, maybe she did, a little.

'Jeannie, wait!'

She halted again, looking at him over her shoulder as he ran after her.

'Look,' he said, a bit breathless. 'Can I be honest with you?'

She nodded, wishing he would, wondering on earth what this was all about.

'I really would like to take you to the dance,' he said. 'I've always thought you were one of the prettiest girls around here.'

She wanted to roll her eyes at him. No one would ever call her pretty, not compared to Louisa and Kate. She was the mouse of the trio. But she couldn't help but be a little thrilled by his words, even if she didn't believe them.

'And... well...' He looked bashful. His ears were pink, but that might have been the cold. 'I'd like to spend some time with you – to get to know you.'

'Really?' He was quite nice looking. Not as striking as Mattie perhaps, although pleasant looking nonetheless. But he wasn't a Friend. 'As a pal, you mean?'

He sighed and glanced around, looking nervous. Jeannie got the strongest impression that he didn't want anyone hearing their conversation, especially when he leaned in a bit closer. 'It's a start,' he said. 'You've got pals who aren't Quakers, haven't you?'

'I have.'

'Well, then. Will you be my pal and go to the dance with me?'

* * *

'What do you mean?' demanded Lucas when he overheard her telling Ma she was going to the dance with Douglas. 'What's he after?'

Jeannie glared at him. 'Is it so unlikely that a lad finds me pretty enough to take dancing?' she asked, her hands on her hips.

'You said you'd only step out with Friends.'

'I'm not planning on marrying him,' she snapped. 'But why shouldn't I enjoy the dance with him? Don't I deserve some fun? Or am I supposed to stay at home and wither away like an old maid because none of the lads at the Meeting House wants to take me out or because you don't approve?'

'Of course you deserve some fun, Jeannie, love,' said Ma. 'Lucas is just being protective of his little sister.'

Ma's soothing tones didn't convince Jeannie as her brother glared back at her.

'He acts like I'm not good enough for any lad to ask out,' she complained.

Lucas put his hands to his head and growled with frustration. 'I didn't say that. I just don't understand how someone like Douglas Baker would suddenly show an interest in you. I mean, have you ever talked to him before?'

She shrugged. 'A few times,' she said, not confessing that those occasions were at school and they were never what she'd describe as friendly. In truth, she was as baffled as Lucas, but also excited that, after thinking no one would want her, a decent lad – albeit not a Friend – wanted to spend time with her. 'The whole point of going to the dance with him is to get to know him.'

Lucas sneered. 'Or it's an excuse for him to get handsy with my sister.'

Jeannie gasped. 'Lucas Musgrove, shut your mouth! No one is getting handsy with me on a first date, I won't allow it. I'm not that sort of a girl. But when *I* decide to let someone get handsy with me, it will be my business and not yours.'

Ma stood up, raising her hands to stop Lucas when he opened his mouth to yell at her. 'That's enough,' she said, her soft voice firm nevertheless.

'But Ma,' Lucas began.

'No, son. Jeannie's right. She's a good girl. She deserves a treat and if this lad wants to take her dancing, it's up to her if she wants to go.' She laid a hand on his shoulder, her expression gentle. 'If you put some effort into finding a nice lass for yourself, you'd have less time to fret over your sister.'

Lucas blushed and looked away. 'I'm too busy to bother with daft lassies,' he grumbled. 'I'm off to Mattie's.'

'I doubt he's got much time for you now he's got Louisa,' Jeannie taunted. She didn't usually act so cruel, but his reaction to Douglas's invitation had hurt and annoyed her. Did her own brother think so little of her that he didn't think anyone would want to spend time with her?

When she saw the hurt in his expression, she nearly apologised. But he didn't give her a chance. With a snarl, he whirled around and left the cottage.

'Oh dear,' sighed Ma, her gaze on the door he'd shut behind him.

'I'm sorry, Ma,' she said. 'He just... Why shouldn't someone ask me out?' she cried. 'He didn't have to be so scathing about it.'

Ma turned and touched her cheek. 'I know, lass. He's been the man of the house for so long, I don't think he knows how to think of you as a grown-up.' She kissed Jeannie's hair. 'But he'll come round. He wants you to be happy.'

'Are you sure?' She wasn't. He'd been even grumpier and snappier lately and she was tired of his bad temper spoiling her happiness.

'I am,' Ma said, nodding. 'You're both growing up and, while most of your friends are in that awkward stage where they're expected to act like grown-ups but they want more time to enjoy life before settling down, you and Lucas have had to take on more responsibility than I'd have liked you to have. Your brother has always taken things far more serious because of it. I'm sorry for that. If my nerves were better, I'd not put so much on both your shoulders.'

'We don't mind, Ma,' Jeannie told her as she hugged her ma. 'We love you.'

'I know you do, and I love you all so much that I thank the light every day for blessing me with such wonderful children.'

'I wouldn't say the twins were wonderful,' Jeannie teased. 'More like lanky monsters, eating us out of house and home.'

Ma chuckled. 'But still wonderful,' she said. 'They'll settle down, I'm sure. Now, if you're off to a dance, we need to get busy. I've got some pretty blue cotton in my sewing box that would make a lovely dress. If we start now, you can have a new dress ready for you by next weekend.'

'Oh! I hadn't thought about what to wear.' Her heart sank. 'Maybe I shouldn't go and you can save the material.'

'Nonsense. I've been hanging onto it for just this sort of occasion.' She put her hands on Jeannie's cheeks. 'I'm so pleased for you, lass. Now, let's look through our patterns and decide what style you want. You're going to be the belle of the ball.'

Jeannie grinned, her excitement returning. 'Hardly, Ma. It's a dance at the Crispin Hall, nothing fancy.'

'Doesn't matter. It's going to be a special time for you and you're going to look beautiful.'

Jeannie hoped so. She'd never felt beautiful. But even if she didn't, seeing Ma so happy and lively for a change made it all worth it. No matter how horrible Lucas was being about it.

23

On Monday evening, Louisa was helping Ma with the washing up after supper while Pa sat by the fire in the parlour with his pipe and newspaper.

'Douglas Baker asked Jeannie to the dance at the Crispin Hall on Saturday,' said Louisa.

'Really?' Her mother frowned. 'He's not a Quaker, is he?'

Louisa turned away to put a clean dry plate on the rack above the new gas stove. She rolled her eyes, trying not to show her irritation. She'd known that would be her first reaction. 'They're not getting married, Ma. He's just taking her to the dance.'

'Yes, well, these things have a tendency to lead to unfortunate situations.'

Louisa burst out laughing. 'Unfortunate situations? It's a dance at the Crispin. They're hardly likely to get up to any mischief surrounded by all those people, are they?'

Her mother sighed and handed her another plate to dry. 'You can mock, Louisa, but you're too young to know about these things.'

'Yet you're constantly sizing up lads as potential husbands for me,' she said, feeling tired and frustrated by the same old arguments.

'I'm looking out for your best interests. You need a good husband to support and protect you.'

'I appreciate that, Ma. But I'm hardly in my dotage and I'd rather make my own decision on what makes a good husband.'

'Huh,' her mother scoffed. 'A handsome face doesn't pay the bills, lass. Don't you forget it.'

'No, but a hardworking lad who has already proved he can protect me ought to be given a chance, shouldn't he?'

Her mother sighed. 'Not again, Louisa. We've already discussed this. Matthew Searle is not our kind of person.'

'It doesn't bother Douglas that Jeannie's a Friend,' she said softly, wishing she could scream it instead but knowing it would do her no good. 'It shouldn't matter what church we worship at. We're all Christians. And anyway, I'm not talking about marrying, I'm talking about going to a dance.'

'I don't know about that.' Another plate was handed off. 'If you want to go to the dance, Horace can take you. I'll speak to his ma.'

Louisa closed her eyes. 'No, thank you.'

'So you don't want to go?'

'Yes. But not with Horace.'

'You'd have a lovely time.'

'No, I wouldn't. I have nothing to say to Horace. Didn't you notice when you invited him to tea? We both sat there like lemons while you and his ma chatted. I've no more desire to spend time with him than he has with me.'

'His mother says he's very fond of you.'

Louisa laughed at that. 'Then she doesn't know her son very well. He thinks I'm stuck up. He told me to my face.'

'He did not! Why would you say such a thing? He'd never be so rude.'

He would. Especially after I told him I wouldn't go out with him if was the last man on Earth.

Louisa shrugged. 'Like I say, maybe his ma doesn't know him as well as she thought, or she's feeding you a pack of lies to land him a decent match.'

Ma huffed and attacked the cutlery with renewed vigour, passing her a handful of spoons to dry. 'Then we'll have to find another suitable lad to take you to the dance.'

'Like who?'

'I don't know. We can't expect Ted Jackson to go; he's still mourning his brother.'

'He's also courting Kate,' she pointed out. 'I'd never do that to her.'

Ma frowned. 'That's not serious, surely? Reggie Davis's girl?'

'Ted's very fond of her and she's one of my best friends,' said Louisa. 'Don't judge her by her father. She's nothing like him.'

Ma handed over the forks to be dried. Louisa caused a clatter as she dropped each one into the cutlery drawer. It was getting on her nerves, this constant runaround with Ma about who she could or should go out with.

'Anyway, Kate's not going either, on account of mourning her ma.'

Ma nodded and sighed. 'Rosie Davis was too good for that man. If her daughter wasn't so like her, we might have put a stop to you being so friendly with her.'

Louisa dumped the knives into the drawer with a crash, making her mother startle and turn to face her.

'Whatever's got into you, Louisa?'

Louisa put a hand to her chest. 'Ma, do you think so little of my judgement that you'd have separated me from my friends?'

'No, of course not.' She looked shocked. 'But it's our duty as good parents to make sure you take the right paths in life. You know what Reggie Davis is like.'

'Of course I do. Everyone does. And you knew Mrs Davis, just as I did.'

'Yes, I did. And that's why this conversation is irrelevant, Louisa. We didn't stop you being friends with Kate, did we? Nor with Jeannie Musgrove. I don't know her mother so well, but your father says her pa was a good man who died in tragic circumstances while working hard to support his family.'

Louisa nodded, praying she could find the right words and not make things worse than they already were. 'Then please, Ma. Trust me over Mattie.'

Her mother was the one to roll her eyes this time. 'Not again, Louisa.'

'Yes!' she hissed, still having enough sense not to shriek like she wanted to. She didn't want to attract Pa's attention. It was a miracle he hadn't come in to see what all the noise was with the cutlery. Better to tackle her parents separately. Together, they presented a united front that was nigh on impenetrable. 'Again, Ma. Because you're not listening to me. You keep pushing me towards these lads who you know I don't like, just because they and their families go to our church. That doesn't make them nice people or right for me. I've tried to be polite about this, Ma, but I will not now or *ever* agree to go out with any of them. I've nothing in common with them and some of them, like Horace, I positively loathe!'

'And you think you have anything in common with Matthew Searle?' Ma all but sneered.

'Yes,' she said, letting her love for Mattie fill her with righteousness. 'We have friends in common; he *listens to me* – we can talk for hours without either of us getting bored; he's kind and respectful, not only to me but to you and Pa and his widowed ma and everyone he meets; *he protected me when lads whose families go to Holy Trinity attacked me!*' She paused, noting her mother's stunned expression. She prayed she was actually getting through to her at last.

Just as she was beginning to hope, Ma shook her head, grabbing a dry cloth and wiping her hands. 'Nonsense. You're too young to understand these things.'

'What?' she asked, stunned. 'What are you saying?'

'Those lads at the Inn weren't our sort of people either. Of course we wouldn't want you associating with them.'

Louisa put her head in her hands. 'Ma, you're missing the point.'

'Am I indeed?' her mother bristled. 'And what exactly is your point, Louisa? For I'm sure I don't know what you're trying to say.'

She did. Louisa was sure of it. But she realised that it wasn't going to do any good. She bent down and picked up the damp tea-towel she'd dropped. She folded it and hung it on the rail of the stove where it would dry. 'My point, Ma,' she said slowly, all hope draining from her, 'is that I have met someone who I'd like to go to the dance with, on whose arm I'd like to walk out on, but you're so set on matching me with someone who will make me miserable that you refuse to entertain the idea.'

'Louisa!' her mother gasped, just as they both became aware that her father was standing in the doorway of the kitchen. Judging by the look on his face, he'd been there a while.

Louisa blew out a breath and let her head fall forward. She wanted to weep, but not even the comfort of tears would come.

'Louisa.' Pa stepped forward. 'Why on earth would you think we want to make you miserable, lass? You're our only daughter and we love you. We want what's best for you.'

'I know you do, Pa. But what you think is best for me is the worst thing you could ever do. I won't be pushed into courting, let alone marrying a lad I don't like or even respect.' She took a deep breath, raising her chin, her determined gaze going from one parent to another. 'I've tried to be patient, knowing you love me. But enough's enough. I need to tell you now – I'm never going to agree to any of these lads because Mattie Searle already has my heart.'

She raised a hand as her mother gasped again and her pa frowned. 'Don't worry. I know I'm still young. Mattie's got responsibilities as well, with his ma. We're not in a rush to get married any time soon. We don't know each other well enough for that anyway yet, and who knows? We might never get to that point. But what we want is to at least be given the chance to see how well we suit each other. If we end up no more than friends, well, that's fine. But don't you see? Pushing us apart like this is making me want him more. Wouldn't it be better to let us walk out together and make our own minds up?'

'Well, I never,' said Ma.

Pa said nothing, watching her.

She closed her eyes for a moment, knowing she'd said all she could. It was up to them now.

'I'm going to bed,' she said. 'I'm sorry I'm not the daughter you want me to be. But please, no more matchmaking, because I won't do it. I'm finished with trying to be polite about it. I'd rather be an old maid than have to put up with the Horaces of this world.'

She left her silent parents in the kitchen and took herself off to her silent bedroom, scared and miserable, praying she hadn't made life totally impossible for her and Mattie.

The next morning, her mother woke her early, telling her only that Pa wanted to speak to her before he left for work so she should hurry and get ready. Louisa washed and dressed with a heavy heart, sure that she was going to be forbidden to see Mattie. She arrived at the breakfast table feeling like her life was about to end.

'Louisa, you gave us a lot to think about last night, lass,' her father said as she sat down in front of the bowl of porridge Ma had made for her. 'I can't say I'm happy about it. Your mother and I have always had high hopes for you.'

She didn't know what to say to that. The weight of their disappointment felt heavy on her shoulders.

'But, above all,' he went on, 'we want you to be happy.'

She nodded, her throat closing as tears threatened. She loved them too, but their idea of happiness was very different from hers.

'I can't say I'm thrilled that you've got this fancy for Matthew Searle,' he sighed. 'Any more than we wanted you come and work in the factory at fourteen instead of staying at school and making the most of the opportunities an education might have offered you.'

She swallowed, trying to find her voice, to apologise, to plead, but she couldn't say anything, so she just nodded. She knew what he meant. Both her parents had said this countless times. But she wasn't clever enough to stay on at school, no matter how much they had wanted her to be. Nothing she said now would make any difference.

Ma sat down, nursing a cup of tea. Louisa could feel the waves of her mother's unhappiness surrounding her, but she couldn't look at her. Instead, she stared at the rapidly cooling porridge, wondering if she could manage to swallow any of it.

'But it was clear last night that you're going to be as stubborn about this lad as you were about leaving school,' Pa continued.

This is where he's going to ruin my life and forbid it, she thought, not looking up.

'So, in the light of your refusal to consider any of the lads from good

families that your ma has been suggesting, we've decided to let you walk
out with Matthew.'

Louisa blinked and her jaw dropped. She looked up at her father.
'Really? Did I hear you right, Pa? Are you letting me go out with Mattie?'

He didn't look happy about it, and her ma sniffed and looked away,
but he nodded. 'I am. But there are conditions.' He pointed a finger at
her. 'I'll be talking to him today to make that clear. There'll be no
sneaking around – we expect to know every time you see him where
you're going, what you're doing and when you'll be home. I do not want
to hear that you've been seen doing anything immodest in public, and
you should make sure there are plenty of other people around you both
at all times. I'll not have my daughter ruining her reputation over a lad,
d'you hear?'

She nodded again, so shocked by Pa's change of mind that she didn't
know what to say. Part of her wanted to leap up and dance and kiss him
and thank him, but the more sensible part of her knew if she did, he
might regret it and change his mind again, then she'd be back to square
one. She didn't even dare smile at him, so precarious was her control and
her so great was her fear that he didn't mean it.

'Thank you, Pa,' she whispered. 'We won't let you down.'

'See you don't, lass. If that boy does anything to harm you, I'll make
his life a living hell. You'll conduct yourself properly and we'll be praying
that this fancy of yours will run its course. In the meantime, your mother
will be talking to you about what we consider acceptable behaviour and
I'll be making sure Matthew knows exactly what he's risking if he tries to
take advantage of my daughter.'

Louisa hoped Pa didn't frighten Mattie away, but she didn't dare say
so. Instead, she nodded again and began to eat her porridge while Pa
finished his tea and stood up. She felt his kiss on her head and looked up
at him with a grateful smile.

'I'm off to the factory,' he said. 'Now listen to your ma and then get
yourself to work. I'll see you tonight.'

She arrived at the factory in time for her shift, her cheeks still burning
from the talking-to her mother had given her.

'You're never going to believe this,' she told the girls as they settled at their machines. 'Ma and Pa said I could walk out with Mattie!' She giggled with pure happiness.

'What?' asked Jeannie. 'But I thought they were set against him on account of him being a Friend.'

'They were – still are, if truth be known. But last night, Ma tried to push me into going to the dance with Horace and I told her straight. I'd rather die an old maid than entertain any of the lads from our church, so if I couldn't go with Mattie, I'd stay home.' She laughed. 'Pa overheard us and I went to bed convinced he was going to forbid me ever seeing Mattie again.'

'But he didn't?' asked Kate, looking confused.

'No,' she grinned. 'I had an awful night of it and then Ma woke me early and said Pa had something to say to me so I went down to breakfast sure it was going to the be worst day of my life. But can you believe it? They'd actually listened to me last night and decided to let me go out with Mattie after all.'

Jeannie frowned. 'I don't understand. Why would they do that when they've been so set against him?'

Louisa turned on her machine, aware that Mr Briars the foreman was doing his usual morning round of the Machine Room. He was at the other end of the vast room right now, but it wouldn't take long for him to notice if they were chatting more than they were working. The others followed suit and they all picked up their first pieces of work and fitted them into the machines, although none of them started stitching as all their focus was on Louisa and her news.

'I told them I wasn't marrying him, just wanted to spend time with him and – this is what did it, I think – I said them trying to stop me seeing him was making me want him more and wouldn't it be better for them to let us go out with their permission, 'cause who's to say we won't grow tired of each other, or find we don't feel as strong as we thought and decide just to be friends in the end?'

'Clever,' said Kate, nodding her approval.

'So you told them you don't you think you'll love him as much as you think you do if you spend more time with him?' asked Jeannie, a strange expression on her face. 'Is that what you really think?'

'Don't be daft,' Louisa giggled. 'I might have told them that, but I truly love him to bits. That's never going to change. But of course, Ma and Pa are hoping that I'll grow tired of him and they think letting us walk out together will make it happen quicker. Hopefully, by the time they realise Mattie's the only man for me, they'll have come to accept it.'

24

By Saturday afternoon, Jeannie's new dress was ready. Ma had helped her cut out the pattern and had found some pretty buttons for it. Jeannie had had to do all the sewing on account of Ma's arthritic hands and at one point, she'd been sure it wouldn't be finished on time. But Kate and Louisa had come round a couple of evenings and helped her and she'd put the last stitch in the hem and the final button on the bodice on Friday night.

Her friends had been so pleased for her and Louisa was excited that they would both be at the dance. Jeannie had smiled and agreed that it would be lovely to be there together, but in truth, she hoped that she wouldn't see much of Mattie and Louisa there. The pair of them had been almost unbearably happy since Mr Clements had given them permission to go to the dance. She'd seen them making eyes at each other over lunch all week and Jeannie had no desire to be a gooseberry on their first official date. She'd rather spend time with Douglas, getting to know him, which was making her nervous enough without having the beautiful Louisa and handsome Mattie around for comparison. She knew she and Douglas could never compete, so why try?

'I wish you were coming with Ted,' she told Kate, who had come round to help her get ready. 'But I know it's too soon for both of you.'

Kate nodded as she gave her a sad smile. 'It is. I really wouldn't feel right, dancing and playing around. Nor would Ted. But I hope you have a lovely time.' She touched Jeannie's new dress, which was hanging on the door of her wardrobe, newly pressed. 'You're going to look so pretty in this.'

Jeannie laughed. 'I don't know about that. I just hope Douglas thinks I've made the effort.'

'He's lucky to have you on his arm,' said Kate.

Jeannie shrugged. 'I'm sure he could've asked loads of prettier girls to go with him. I'm still shocked he asked me.'

Kate put her hands on her hips. 'Don't you dare think like that, Jeannie Musgrove. You're as pretty, if not prettier than any other lass round here.'

Jeannie rolled her eyes. 'I'm mousy and skinny,' she said.

'No one can choose their hair colour, unless you're one of those floozy types who bleach their hair, and who would want to be like that? And yours is light brown, almost gold when the sun touches it, not *mousy*, and there's a lovely natural curl to it. You've got beautiful hazel eyes, and I've always thought you've got the nicest skin – so clear and soft.' She stroked her cheek, making Jeannie smile, even though she couldn't bring herself to believe her friend. 'And you might not have a lot of flesh on your bones, Jeannie, but your bosoms have grown since we left school and your figure looks perfect in that dress. The other lads are going to be dead jealous of Douglas, having you on his arm.'

Jeannie blushed. 'Maybe I should've chosen a different style dress,' she said. 'I don't want to give Douglas the wrong impression.'

Kate burst out laughing. 'Oh, Jeannie, you're so funny. You could wear sackcloth and you'd still look lovely.'

Jeannie blushed, wishing it were true. But she knew otherwise. Kate was only saying these things to make her feel better. Still, it was nice to see her friend smiling and laughing after she'd been so sad for so long.

'What are you going to do this evening?' she asked.

'I'm going round to see Peg and Will,' she said, her smile sad again. 'We've got a lot closer since Ma got ill. Did I tell you Peg's coming back to work in the Machine Room?'

Kate's sister had left the factory when she'd married Will.

'Why?'

'They want to move some women and girls into the jobs they can't fill where lads have gone off to fight, as all the men's departments are falling behind without enough workers. So they put out a call to married women to come back to work. As Peg's not got any littl'uns yet, she's going to. Only she told them she didn't want to work with men, so they're giving her her old job back so they can move someone else over to the other jobs that need filling.'

'It'll be nice to see her at the factory again,' said Jeannie.

'It will.' Kate sighed. 'I think she'd been hoping to have a baby by now. I get the impression her and Will are getting a bit worried it hasn't happened yet. Going back to work will take her mind off it.'

'Aw, poor Peg. Maybe being at work will do the trick. So, you're not seeing Ted tonight, then?'

Kate shook her head. 'His ma's still not good after Albert... She's been clinging onto Ted one minute and telling him he needs to enlist the next. He's been staying home evenings and weekends to help his pa cope with her. His poor pa's at the end of his tether, what with being so busy at work and then Mrs Jackson getting in a state.'

'Poor woman,' said Jeannie, remembering her outburst at the Operatic Society. 'I don't suppose you're seeing much of Ted then?'

Kate shrugged. 'He walks me home from work every day, and I see him at church.' She'd gone back after Ma's funeral. Jeannie thought it was to feel closer to her ma, but they didn't discuss it. 'Although we don't sit together. The Jacksons sit with the other foremen and their families, and I didn't feel right up there, even when Louisa's there.' She grimaced. 'Too many people staring and wondering what Reggie Davis's daughter is doing mixing with her betters.'

'You're Rosie Davis's daughter too,' Jeannie pointed out gently. 'And they all respected her.'

'That's as may be. But she's gone.' Her voice caught on the words. Kate stopped and took a deep breath. 'And Pa's worse than ever, so that's the cross I have to bear now. I'm surprised Ted hasn't been forbidden to see me.'

Jeannie wanted to cry. 'That's not fair.'

'I know. But it is what it is.' She gave Jeannie a hug. 'I appreciate you caring about it. But it's alright. Anyway, I don't have the energy to go to dances and the like, and I don't think he does either. We're good friends. We understand each other. But don't go thinking it's a great love affair like with Lou and Mattie.'

Jeannie sighed. She wasn't looking forward to seeing the couple tonight. But she wasn't going to fret about it. She was more worried about her first date and what on earth she was going to have to say to Douglas Baker.

* * *

Lucas had been waiting by the door when Douglas knocked to collect her. He'd glared at him and told him to keep his hands to himself and get his sister home at a decent hour. Jeannie had never been so embarrassed in her life.

'I'm so sorry about my brother,' she said softly as they walked away from the cottage. She could feel her brother's angry gaze on her back but didn't dare look back or she'd be tempted to turn round and go back and box his ears.

Douglas chuckled. 'Don't worry. It's no more than I'd do if a lad turned up at our door to court my sister.' He held out his arm and she tucked her hand into the crook of it, feeling her cheeks warming again, even in the cool spring air. 'You look lovely, by the way.'

She couldn't help the giggle that escaped her. She felt a bit like Cinderella must have felt after the fairy godmother had done her magic. She wore her new dress, with its fitted bodice, square neckline and softly draping skirt. Louisa had loaned her a pretty coral bead necklace and some shoes, for which she was eternally grateful. She hadn't even thought about what she'd put on her feet until Lou had mentioned it the other night when they were sewing. Louisa had a pair of dancing shoes that matched the blue of her dress perfectly that she offered to loan to Jeannie. Thank goodness they were the same size! Her biggest worry now was making sure she didn't scuff the shoes or lose the necklace.

'Thank you,' she said. 'You look very nice, too.'

He chatted to her as they walked the length of West End and the High Street, past the shops – some festooned with Union Flags to show their support for the war – to get to the Crispin Hall, putting her at ease. By the time they got to the dance, she felt happy and even pretty. When people looked at them as they entered, Jeannie could see they were shocked by her transformation. They were so used to her curly hair being tied into a tight bun or plait instead of falling loose almost to her waist as it was now, save for some tresses from the sides which Kate had caught up with a pretty hair clip (another loan from Louisa) at the back. She also usually wore more muted colours rather than the pretty powder blue of her new dress, and of course, Lou's dancing shoes were far more delicate and stylish than Jeannie's usual ancient, heavy Clark's women's walking shoes. Unlike some of the other girls, she didn't have a lot of cosmetics on her face, although Louisa had given her a pale-pink lipstick that made her feel very glamourous when she'd applied it. It was in the velvet purse that Ma had given her to use, along with a comb and hand-kerchief.

After leaving their coats in the cloakroom, she clung onto Douglas's arm as they entered the main hall. The room was decorated with bunting and looked very cheerful. On the stage, a group with piano, fiddles, drums and double bass were playing as couples and groups filled the space, their excited chatter almost drowning out the band. Cigarette smoke was already forming a layer of smoke above the crowd.

For a moment, Jeannie felt overwhelmed by the noise and heat, but Douglas didn't seem at all bothered about it, leading her over to one of the few tables around the edge of the dance floor that was free. He held out the chair for her to sit down, like a true gentleman. Jeannie offered him a shy smile as she sat. Instead of sitting opposite her, he sat beside her.

'With all this noise, we won't be able to hear each other,' he explained, leaning close and speaking in her ear.

'It is a bit lively, isn't it?' she said. 'Almost as loud as the Machine Room in the middle of a shift.'

He nodded, his warm breath on her neck as he said, 'I know what you mean. There's always a racket going on in the Big Room. Some of the old fellas are stone deaf.'

'Some of the women are too. We all lip read,' she told him. 'Which means we have to be careful as everyone can work out what we're saying.'

He laughed and Jeannie felt a warm glow that she had amused him. A few couples and some small groups of girls were dancing. A few people were clapping along to the music as they watched, while a cluster of lads stood around the edges, glasses of soft drinks in hand – this was a Temperance dance and no liquor was allowed – some with cigarettes between their fingers or lips, no doubt thinking they looked the bee's knees with their slicked-back hair and polished boots. Jeannie noticed some of the girls were eyeing them with coy looks and tempting smiles. It made her glad she was here with Douglas and not part of the flirting. It would have been so humiliating, waiting to see if someone would ask her to dance, expecting to be ignored and left on her own as the other girls were paired off with lads. There were a lot more girls than boys at the dance, on account of so many lads having already enlisted. So she was sure she'd have remained a wallflower if she hadn't come with Douglas.

'Do you smoke?' she asked Douglas.

He shrugged. 'Sometimes,' he said. 'Why, do you?'

She shook her head. 'Oh, no. I don't think I'd like it,' she said. 'Our old neighbour smokes like a chimney and when he's not puffing, he's coughing up his guts. It sounds awful.'

'It's not so bad once you get used to it,' he said.

'I'll take your word for it,' she said, hoping she hadn't annoyed him by criticising something he liked. But he didn't seem put out by it.

'D'you want to dance?' he asked.

Jeannie looked at the crowd on the dance floor. They looked like they were having fun, but she wasn't sure if she could be quite so uninhibited as some of them. The tune playing was a bit fast for her. In her imagination, she'd thought the music would be slower, more romantic and there wouldn't be so many people. If she tried to dance like some of those girls, she'd probably knock into someone and everyone would go down like dominoes.

'Maybe in a minute,' she said. 'It looks a bit busy out there.'

He looked a bit relieved and she wondered whether he had only asked to be polite. She hoped that didn't mean he wouldn't ask her again. They sat in silence for a little while, watching. Jeannie was soon tapping her feet, even though she felt too shy to tell Douglas that she'd like to dance now. Instead, she contented herself with absorbing all the sights and sounds, deciding that her dress was just as nice as everyone else's. She smiled at Douglas as she realised this and felt her cheeks warm at his answering smile. He took that as permission to scoot a bit closer and put his arm around her shoulders. He seemed fascinated by her hair, twirling a curl between his fingers. She relaxed into his embrace, feeling excited and scared at the same time. Did this mean he was going to kiss her tonight? She hoped he didn't do it in front of everyone.

Lads who knew Douglas stopped to say hello, as did lasses who knew Jeannie. Some of them didn't even try to hide their shock that they were there together, which seemed to amuse Douglas, but left Jeannie with mixed feelings. She knew she wasn't a great beauty, but surely she wasn't so awful, was she? Some of the kinder girls complimented her on her outfit and said her hair looked lovely, but others weren't so nice.

'Well, well. Jeannie Musgrove, fancy seeing you here,' said one girl she knew from the Machine Room, standing in front of them with her hands on her hips.

'Hello, Doris,' she said, feeling as though she wanted a hole to open in the floor and swallow her up. She'd never had much to do with her, but she knew that Doris had a reputation for being a bully and delighted in putting other girls down.

Doris turned her attention to Douglas. 'Hello, Dougie. Want to dance?'

He looked confused, so she went on, 'You know Jeannie's a *Friend*, don't you? No drinking, no singing. I doubt she'll even dance with you – far too sinful!' She laughed loudly, as did her pals – two other girls from the Machine Room who had never spoken to Jeannie before.

'I can dance,' said Jeannie, her cheeks warming. 'And sing. I choose not to drink, that's all.'

'Leave her alone, Doris,' said Douglas, sounding bored.

Louisa and Mattie chose that moment to approach. 'Yes, Doris. Find someone your own size to pick on,' said Lou.

It was a deliberate jibe. While both Jeannie and Louisa were slender, Doris was what her ma might call buxom but others might call pudgy. Her ample curves were currently squeezed into a dress so tight that Jeannie couldn't imagine breathing in it, let alone dancing. Now she thought about it, Doris always seemed to be in tight clothes. Maybe that's why she never wanted for male attention, although it seemed that this evening, she was without an escort and holding court with her friends instead.

Doris turned on Louisa, sneering. 'Here's another one, Princess Louisa, slumming it with another Friend.' She pointed at Jeannie and Douglas. 'Maybe you should swap with Jeannie and Dougie here, like with like.'

'No, thank you,' said Louisa, winking at Douglas. 'No offence, Douglas.'

He inclined his head. 'None taken. Why don't you two sit with us? I know you're Jeannie's friend. Not like some people.' He glared at Doris.

'I was just saying hello,' said Doris, looking annoyed.

'Really?' he said. 'I didn't hear that. I just heard you being a witch for no reason.'

Mattie stifled a laugh and Doris's friends giggled, earning them a glare from the girl. 'Give it up, Doris,' he said. 'Go and pick on someone else.'

Much to Jeannie's relief, the girls walked away, Doris in a huff, and Louisa and Mattie sat down.

'Are you alright, Jeannie, love?' asked Louisa.

Douglas squeezed her shoulder. 'Don't pay no mind to the likes of Doris. She asked me to bring her tonight and I turned her down. I'd already asked you.'

'Oh,' she said. 'You could have told me if you wanted to go with her.'

'I didn't. She's got far too high an opinion of herself.'

'But a reputation that says the opposite,' said Mattie. 'Not the sort of girl you'd take home to meet your ma, eh, Doug?'

'Exactly. Forget her, Jeannie. You're the one I asked and the one I want to be here with. She's got her nose out of joint and she's taking it out on you. Sorry about that.'

'Doris is jealous, love,' Louisa told her. 'Especially seeing you in your new dress. Jeannie looks lovely, doesn't she, lads?'

Jeannie flushed scarlet as both Douglas and Mattie agreed, smiling at her. For a fleeting moment, she wondered whether she should have tried harder to look nice for Mattie when she'd had the chance. But seeing him with Louisa, she realised it would have been a waste of time.

'I bet Lucas didn't want to let you out the house,' Mattie grinned.

Douglas laughed. 'He did threaten me,' he said. 'Polite like. But if looks could kill...'

Jeannie covered her face with her hands as they laughed.

'Just make sure you don't try kissing her on their doorstep when you take her home,' said Mattie. 'Trust me. He's my best mate. I know what he intends to do to the first lad he sees kissing his sister. It'll be brutal.'

Louisa poked him in the ribs with her elbow as Jeannie moaned in embarrassment.

Jeannie stood up. 'I need the toilet,' she said.

'I'll come with you,' said Louisa. 'Why don't you lads get us a drink? I'll have an elderflower cordial. Same for you, Jeannie?'

She nodded before turning and rushing through the crowd towards the cloakrooms.

It took Louisa a few minutes to persuade Jeannie to leave the toilet and return to the dance hall.

'Are you sure Lucas didn't tell Mattie to be our chaperone?' she asked. 'Because you can tell him right now, I'll not put up with it. My brother was so rude when Douglas picked me up, I don't think I'll ever forgive him. If he's recruited Mattie—'

'He hasn't, I promise. It was me who wanted to come over. I saw Doris and knew she wasn't there to make polite conversation. I was worried about you.' Louisa paused, her smile growing. 'But it sounded like Douglas was doing a good job of seeing her off.'

Jeannie took a moment to think about it. 'He was quite off-hand with her. And he squeezed my shoulder and smiled at me, made me feel protected.'

'Well, there you are. She's nothing to worry about and he's looking after you. So come on. We've been out here far too long. I want that drink and another dance with my man,' she grinned. 'Oh, Jeannie, I'm so happy. I never thought Pa would let me and Mattie walk out together. I'm so lucky.'

'You are,' she said. 'I'm pleased for you.'

It took her a few moments, as they wove their way back through the crowd, to realise that she actually meant it. She'd always have a soft spot for Mattie, but maybe she was beginning to realise that he wasn't meant for her. But that didn't mean she was destined to be an old maid. Not judging by the warm looks she was getting from Douglas this evening.

'And I'm pleased for you. Douglas is a nice lad.' Louisa linked arms with her as they approached their table. 'Now that's all three of us with sweethearts. Isn't it lovely?'

Jeannie was beaming as she sat down beside Douglas, who grinned back and kissed her cheek. It was just a friendly peck, she knew. But it was a declaration to everyone in the Crispin Hall. Jeannie Musgrove, the plain, frumpy Friend everyone pitied or ignored, was a desirable woman. Maybe the ugly duckling was turning into a swan. Or maybe she wasn't. But tonight, Jeannie felt beautiful and she was happy.

25

'Lucas, friend. Got a minute?'

He turned to face Mattie outside the Friends' Meeting House and nodded. He'd spent the past hour struggling to find his inner light when all he could think about was Mattie and Louisa, and Jeannie going to the dance last night with Douglas Baker. None of it sat well with him, leaving his gut churning and his temper sharp.

He couldn't put his finger on what was bothering him so much. He prayed about it, asking God to guide him, show him the way. He felt so lost lately, and he didn't know what to do or say to his best friend or to his sister.

There were a lot of people around after the meeting, so they wandered across the burial ground and into the orchard beyond it. It was cold but dry and the two of them leaned against the wall separating them from the view of anyone outside the Meeting House.

'What's wrong?' Lucas asked him. He got in first, because the last thing he wanted or needed was for Mattie to ask him the same question. He knew he'd been acting like a miserable beggar lately, but he couldn't tell his best friend why.

Mattie sighed and scrubbed a hand over his face. 'Two things. First, I'm not sure about Douglas courting your Jeannie.'

'Why?' Lucas was immediately alert. 'What did he do?'

Mattie held up his hands. 'Nothing, I swear if he had, I'd have jumped in and protected Jeannie. He was nice to her and she seemed really happy. He even saw off Doris Lambert, and you know what a mare she can be.'

Lucas nodded. Doris was well known as a man-eater and for her nasty tongue when it came to other girls.

'No, it was something I heard one of his pals saying at the bar,' Mattie went on. 'They were talking about how they'd not expect Dougie to walk out with a Friend and especially Jeannie.'

'What's wrong with our Jeannie?' Lucas demanded.

'Nothing. There's nothing wrong with Jeannie, nothing at all, and she looked right pretty last night. But, well, I suppose she's usually more... I don't know... more subdued, most days.'

Lucas frowned. 'What d'you mean?'

Mattie shrugged. 'She usually keeps her hair tied up tight and wears plainer clothes. She's quiet, especially compared to Louisa and Kate, so people tend to overlook her. She don't like to make a fuss.'

Lucas nodded. 'She's humble, like a good Friend should be.'

'That she is. Which is why I think Dougie's pals were surprised he'd asked her to go the dance with him.'

'Alright, I can see that. So, what was the problem?'

Mattie grimaced. 'I'm not sure. It might be nothing. But one of them said Dougie was hedging his bets. That he was thinking that if he was seen to be courting a Quaker lass, he could claim he was becoming a Friend. That way, he could say he was following the Peace Testimony to get out of having to enlist.'

'No one has to enlist,' Lucas pointed out, looking confused.

'Not yet they don't,' Mattie replied, looking sombre. 'But the word is they'll be bringing in conscription one of these days and every man under thirty will be called up. If that happens, Friends would have to request an exemption on the grounds of our Peace Testimony, but who knows whether we'd get it or not?'

'There's been nothing in the papers about conscription. There's always plenty of lads marching off for basic training.'

'I know, and it might not happen. But, let's face it, Lucas, there've been a heck of a lot of casualties at the front. It's not just Albert Jackson who's been killed. Plenty of others from round here have been wounded. A lad from down our road just came home without his arm. I heard about another who lost half of his face. They're keeping him in hospital and talking about him needing a mask to cover what's left of it with. At the rate they're getting through men, the government's bound to need more than are volunteering now. It don't seem like it's going to be over as quick as Mr Asquith says it will. Now, if Douglas is thinking the same thing, he's smart enough and crafty enough that he might well be using Jeannie to get himself recognised as a Friend, or at the very least a pacifist, before they bring in conscription.'

Lucas leaned his head back against the wall and closed his eyes. 'And that's what his pal said?'

'Yeah. He might be wrong, of course. Like I said, Jeannie looked right pretty and he might well have had his eye on her for a while. But I don't know. It just seems odd that he came after her out of the blue like that. It's not like he's been flirting with her as far as we know, has he?'

He shook his head. 'No. I think Jeannie was as shocked as I was when he asked her out.' He remembered how angry and hurt she'd been when he'd been clumsy enough to show his surprise. It didn't mean he thought his sister wasn't a catch for some lad. It was just the unexpectedness of Douglas Baker being the one to pursue her.

'Mmm, that's what I thought.' Mattie paused. 'Look, it might just be his pal trying to sound clever, but keep an eye on it, alright? I don't want to see Jeannie getting hurt.'

Lucas nodded. 'I will. Thanks for telling me. Maybe I should've gone to the dance to keep an eye on them myself.'

Mattie laughed. 'He wouldn't have said anything with you around. I don't think he realised I was there, otherwise he'd have kept his trap shut, I'm sure. And Jeannie would've been livid if you'd turned up to act as chaperone, especially if you was wearing that miserable visage you've been sporting lately. What's up with you? I've never seen you so down. Is it the war? Or are you just worried about your Jeannie?'

Lucas sighed. 'A bit of both, I suppose. I'm sick of the digs from people

who think I should be enlisting. As if killing or maiming another man is
going to make an ounce of difference while our governments are
throwing more cannon fodder at the enemy. And, I don't know, I'm
worried that Jeannie's walking out with Douglas because she's thinking
she'll be left on the shelf if she doesn't find a sweetheart like her friends
have done. But she's barely seventeen. It's not like she's an old maid, is it?'

'She'll be alright, I'm sure.'

'Will she? At the rate lads are enlisting, there won't be many of us left
round here. There's not many our age at the Meeting House, so where's
she going to find someone?'

'The war isn't going to last forever,' said Mattie, his tone hopeful. 'And
anyway, if she's looking for a Friend to settle down with, she can look at
the other Meetings in the area. But, like I say, there's no rush, is there?'

Lucas studied his friend, something occurring to him. 'You know, she
wasn't bothered about finding a sweetheart until you and Louisa got
together. I think she might have had hopes that you might have taken up
with her one of these days.'

Mattie looked startled. 'What? Me and Jeannie? But... she's your sister,
you're my best mate. I couldn't've... you'd have killed me, wouldn't you?'

He nodded. 'I wouldn't have been happy, that's for sure. But at least I
know you and trust you. Not sure I know enough about Dougie Baker,
and I sure as heck don't trust him.' He blew out a breath. 'I'll have to keep
an eye on him. I daren't say anything to Jeannie, or she'll likely run
straight into his arms, just to spite me.'

'I'll watch him too. Maybe me and Louisa can suggest some double
dates so we can both make sure he's not stringing her along.'

'Thanks. It would be good if Jeannie has Louisa there to confide in if need
be.' It also occurred to him that if Mattie wasn't alone with Louisa too much,
he couldn't get himself in any deeper with that relationship. He knew that, up
until now, Louisa Clements had been forbidden fruit. He was hoping that
now they had permission to go out together, Mattie would lose interest in her.

'You said there were two things bothering you,' he said. 'What was the
other one?'

Again, Mattie scrubbed at his face, letting out a tortured groan. 'It's

Lou's pa. I don't know what to do. He's got me stuck between a rock and a hard place.'

'How?'

'You know he had a talk with me. Set conditions?'

'Yeah.'

'Well, most of it was alright – no taking advantage, no sneaking around, make sure we tell him where we're going and I get her home on time.' He grinned. 'I delivered her to his door ten minutes early last night and shook his hand and thanked him for letting me escort his beautiful daughter to the dance. He didn't know I'd got my kisses on the quiet before I took her home.' He sobered slightly. 'It's the other condition that's bothering me.'

'What is it?'

Mattie blew out a long breath. 'He says if I want this to be a long-term relationship, he expects me to be a man and show I can protect his daughter from more than the odd drunk outside the Street Inn.'

'How?'

'By enlisting, of course. The old bugger wants me to go and fight, or he'll withdraw his permission for me to court Louisa after three months and make sure we won't be able to sneak around. I think he's even thinking he can sack me as well.'

'He can't do that. Can he?'

Mattie shrugged, looking fed up. 'I transferred to the Cutting Room to impress him. I might have shot meself in the foot there. Now he controls me. He's already said he's keeping me on day rates for the time being, even though I've proved I'm ready for piece work. He's only got to say the word and he can make me look bad to any other foreman in the factory. I might have to leave Clarks. Then I've even less chance of seeing Louisa.' He shook his head, his shoulders slumping with misery. 'He's made her so happy, letting us go out together, but she has no idea how he's scheming behind her back to make sure we can't stay together, and he says if I tell her, that'll be it.'

'My God, I always thought Mr Clements was a fair man. But that's rotten.'

'I know. He knows I can't go to fight. So he'll do everything to split us up.'

Lucas put a hand on his friend's shoulder. 'I'm sorry, Mattie. But maybe it's for the best.'

Mattie's head came up, his dark eyes blazing. 'Are you kidding me? For the best? Of course it isn't! I love that girl and I want to marry her.'

'Mattie, you're not even twenty. There's plenty of time.'

'Is there?' he asked, beyond reason. 'Do you know what it's like to love someone so much, you can't bear to be away from them? To know that only they can make you feel complete, leaving you empty inside when they're not there?'

He could see from the contempt on Mattie's face that he didn't believe he did. But he was wrong. So wrong. 'Yes, I do,' he said, his voice low and scratchy as his throat tried to close and stop the words escaping. 'I know exactly how that feels.'

Mattie stilled. 'What are you talking about? You've never even been out with a lass.'

Lucas turned away, unable to face him. 'You're right. There's no lass; there never has been,' he said. He looked at Mattie, unable to say anything more, fear keeping him silent. Mattie stared back, a slight frown marring his handsome face. He opened his mouth to say something, then closed it again. He blinked hard and took a step back before turning on his heel and walking away.

'It's you, Mattie. It's always been you,' Lucas whispered towards his friend's back before Mattie disappeared around the corner of the Meeting House, knowing that he could never tell him to his face.

26

The end of the Saturday shift couldn't come around fast enough for Louisa. Once she clocked off at dinner time, they were free until Monday morning, which meant she could finally spend some time with Mattie. She'd asked him to wait for her outside the factory today. It had been four weeks since the dance when they'd had their first official date. She'd expected to have seen a lot more of him than she had, but it was as though everything was conspiring to keep them apart. She was beginning to worry that having her parents' permission to spend time with Mattie made little or no difference to the amount of time they were together.

'What are you two doing this weekend?' asked Jeannie as they finally got the signal to shut down their machines and clean up their work benches so that they would be neat and tidy, ready for work on Monday morning. 'Douglas is taking me to the pictures.'

Louisa shared a smile with Kate over their friend's head as Jeannie blushed lightly.

'Mind you don't end up sitting in the back row,' warned Kate, a teasing light in her eye. 'Louisa did that and didn't see any of the films that night on account of Mattie smooching with her the whole time.'

Louisa giggled. 'She's not wrong. But I don't regret a minute of it. In fact, I might ask Mattie to take me again.'

'Oh, I don't think I want to sit in the back row,' said Jeannie, looking worried. 'I don't want Douglas to think...' Her blush deepened. 'No offence, Louisa. But, even though I like him well enough, I don't really feel like I'm ready for that much kissing.'

'Jeannie Musgrove,' said Kate. 'Are you telling me you've been walking out with him for nearly a month and you've not been kissed?'

Jeannie bristled. 'We've kissed,' she said. 'Just... not much.'

'Why not?' asked Louisa.

She shrugged, looking away. 'I just don't want to give him the wrong idea, that's all. I mean, he's not a Friend, is he?' She looked thoughtful. 'Mind you, he's been asking me a lot of questions about being a Quaker lately.'

'Well, there you are,' said Kate. 'Maybe you'll turn him. Will managed it with our Peg.'

Louisa bit her lip, not sure whether to say anything about Mattie's suspicions of Douglas. If he was wrong, Jeannie could be hurt by the idea that him and Lucas only thought the lad was courting her to get out of fighting when he could well be smitten with her. She'd changed in recent weeks – styling her hair in looser styles and wearing more colours. Nothing brash or brassy, just some pastels that made her skin glow and brought out her natural prettiness. Louisa loved that being courted was giving Jeannie some much-needed confidence.

It was good to see Kate looking a little brighter as well. Not that her life was any better than it was a few weeks ago, but Louisa got the impression that her friend was learning to adapt to her new circum-stances. Her sister had helped her negotiate with their pa about giving her enough money to buy food, pointing out that if Kate couldn't buy the groceries, he would starve. He'd not been generous, but it at least meant Kate could eat as well. That her pa was spending all his spare time in either the Street Inn or one of the taverns in Glastonbury meant she at least had the house to herself most of the time. Her relationship with Ted, someone who understood grief only too well, was helping, she thought. Kate could talk to him about her ma and he could mention his brother without either of them having to put up with pitying looks and useless words, which was all Louisa felt she was capable of giving whenever she thought about what poor Kate and Ted must be going through.

'I don't know about that,' laughed Jeannie. 'It takes more than answering a few questions to make someone into a Quaker. It's not the easiest path, especially while the country's at war. No, I think Douglas is just being polite. I don't think he's all that interested in becoming a Friend.'

'Which means he's more interested in you,' pointed out Kate.

'That doesn't mean I'm sitting in the back row with him tonight,' she said, looking worried. 'D'you think he'll be annoyed?'

''Course not,' said Kate. 'I didn't sit in the back row with Ted, did I? I told him straight. If that was all he wanted, he'd picked the wrong girl. You just be firm with Douglas and don't let him sweet talk you into anything. If he's a good sort, it won't make any difference. If he's stupid enough to get annoyed, then he's not worth having anyway.'

Jeannie nodded, looking more resolute. 'You're right, Kate. I'm not ready for the back row – might never be – and if Douglas doesn't like it, then maybe he's not right for me.'

'Well, I'd love the chance to sit in the back row again,' sighed Louisa. 'Pa's had Mattie doing so much overtime on account of the Clickers being behind on their orders that I've hardly seen him. When I do manage to spend time with him, he's so tired, the poor love. He's trying so hard to make a good impression.' The trouble was, she felt as though it was wearing him down and, judging by Pa's sour disposition, it wasn't doing much good. She was beginning to resent her father for pushing Mattie so much. She knew it was because he had high expectations of any man who might want to marry his daughter, but it was driving a wedge between them because Mattie was so tired and distracted all the time.

'Lucas has been getting extra hours as well,' said Jeannie. 'He's bringing in some welcome extra money, but goodness he's grumpy these days. He's been snapping at us all at home. The twins see him coming and disappear. Even Ma is running out of excuses for him.'

Kate rolled her eyes. 'God save us from miserable men. Pa's been moaning like hell about having to go in early and stay late. You'd think he'd be glad of the money, but no. It's eating into his precious drinking time. At least he's sober at work. I think his last warning finally got through. If Ted weren't so easy-going, I doubt I'd bother courting anyone at all.'

'So, have you and Ted been kissing?' asked Jeannie.

Kate looked a bit uncomfortable. 'A bit. But what with Ma and Albert, neither of us feels like doing much canoodling.'

Louisa put a hand on her shoulder. 'There's no rush. You're both still mourning, love.'

'I know, but... it's just... I like Ted well enough. But I sometimes think I've not got a romantic bone in my body. I see you swooning over Mattie and I just don't understand it. I've never felt like that.'

'Me neither,' said Jeannie, looking sad. 'I'm flattered that Douglas is paying me attention, but... I always thought I was a romantic at heart and I'd go all soft and gooey when I met my sweetheart.' She looked at her friends, studying their faces as though they had all the answers. 'But maybe I'm not. I like holding hands or hanging on his arm. But when he cuddles me or tries to kiss me, I panic.'

'Then he's not the right one for you,' said Louisa, her eyes focused on wiping a smear of oil from her work bench. 'Believe me, when you really love a lad, you can't wait for his kisses and cuddles.' She sighed. 'But even when you get them, things aren't always perfect,' she muttered under her breath.

'What's the matter?' asked Kate.

She looked up to see Kate and Jeannie watching her with concern in their eyes. Louisa should have known her friends would've heard her. She shook her head.

'I shouldn't have said anything. Everything's fine with me and Mattie. It's just... I think Pa's putting so much pressure on him, it's putting him off me,' she confessed in a rush. 'He's been acting strange. Something's bothering him.'

'Have you asked him about it?' said Kate.

'Of course I have. But he says it's nothing, that he loves me and he'll do anything to be with me. Then he starts talking about when we're wed, how happy we're going to be. But it's almost like he's trying to convince himself.'

Jeannie put her hand on Louisa's shoulder. 'Like you just said to Kate, there's no rush. He's probably just tired, that's all. Your pa can be something fierce, so I don't suppose he's easy to work for, especially when Mattie's wanting to marry his daughter.'

Louisa blew out a breath and put away her dusters and straightened her baskets. She leaned in closer to her friends. 'You're right. But it's more than just Mattie that's annoying Pa. Don't say anything to anyone else, but from what I've heard him telling Ma, there's all sorts of ructions going on between the Pattern Room and the Clicking Room. Pa got hauled before the managers about his department being so far in arrears with the work and he had to tell them it wasn't just the shortage of men. The Pattern Room foreman has been holding stuff back until Pa chases it, causing all sorts of rows. Pa was furious 'cause the management blamed both of them for not working together. He says the man is impossible to reason with and nothing but a troublemaker. Anyway, Pa's not used to being told off. As far as he's concerned, he's never wrong, but he can hardly say that to Mr Hugh or Mr Roger, can he?'

The two Clark brothers were directors of the family firm and kept a strict eye on all the operations. The girls didn't have a lot to do with them as Miss Alice Clark was the director in charge of the Machine Room, but she wasn't always around on account of her writing a book at a university in London and all her work with the Executive Committee of the National Union of Women's Suffrage Societies. But when she was, Mr Briars the foreman was even stricter than he usually was.

Jeannie looked upset. 'Everyone's so troubled at the moment. It's as though the poison of the war is spreading, even when we're nowhere near the fighting. Why do people have to take against each other? The Clarks have always been good to their workers, but Lucas said a lot of the men are joining the union, and they're picking on those that don't. It's not fair; not every man with a family to support has money spare for the subscriptions, and some Friends won't join anything where they have to pledge an allegiance that might contradict the Quaker way.'

'I know. Pa's complaining about that as well. Mr Roger got right riled when he heard men were being intimidated, so he proposed setting up a workers' committee to deal with disputes. But the union wouldn't have it as it would mean the men wouldn't need them. They're demanding that their members shouldn't have to work with non-union labour. Can you imagine how angry that made Mr Roger? He said not a single Clarks worker would lose their job should they choose not to join the union. Pa thinks it might end in a strike.'

'Oh, no,' Kate groaned. 'If there's a strike, Pa will be on the cider all day until his money runs out. Then he'll be impossible. He's already pushing for me to go onto piece work so I can earn more. He'll make me work myself to death just to pay for his drink.'

Most of the women had left the Machine Room, so the three friends grabbed their coats and bags and headed down the stone steps. Louisa felt unsettled. It felt like there was conflict everywhere – not just in the trenches. Everyone seemed so angry and taking it out on everyone else. It was like there was something in the air. Even Mattie had snapped at her the last time she'd seen him, although he'd immediately apologised and had been sweetly contrite for the rest of the evening. She just hoped he was in a better mood today.

At the factory gate, Mattie leaned against the wall, his head down, his hands stuffed in his pockets. Lucas was with him, talking earnestly with low, urgent tones, but Mattie wasn't looking at him. Louisa's heart sank.

'See you at church tomorrow, Louisa,' said Kate as she left. 'See you on Monday, Jeannie.'

Both girls nodded and waved, their attention on the lads.

'What on earth's wrong with those two?' asked Jeannie, frowning as her brother put both his hands to his head. 'Have they had a falling out, d'you think?'

'I don't know,' she said. 'Mattie hasn't said anything.' But it certainly looked like it.

As they approached, Lucas took a step towards his friend. 'Mattie, please.'

At that moment, Mattie looked up, his face pale and set. He spotted Louisa and Jeannie coming towards them and pushed himself away from the wall, moving sideways to avoid Lucas and shaking his head. 'Not now, Lucas,' he said and walked towards Louisa. When he reached her, he took her face between his hands and gave her the sweetest kiss she'd ever had.

She forgot that they were in front of the factory and there were hundreds of people around.

It felt like a declaration in front of everyone, but especially Lucas. Mattie poured all of his love into the kiss. It felt like... desperation, thrilling her and frightening her in equal measure.

When he finally let her go, she was in a daze. She looked around, amazed that they hadn't drawn a crowd to watch the spectacle, but most folk were more interested in getting home and enjoying some time off. The world had gone on as normal around them.

Except that Lucas was nowhere to be seen.

27

Mattie looked around, seeming satisfied that his friend had gone.

'What's going on?' asked Louisa. 'Have you and Lucas fallen out?'

He shrugged and took her hand. 'Come on, let's get out of here. I need to talk to you.' He began walking down the High Street towards The Cross, tugging her along with him.

Louisa turned to see Jeannie's frown as she watched them leave. 'See you Monday, Jeannie,' she called out. She tried to give her friend a reassuring smile, but in truth, she was worried. Something was seriously wrong here. As if to confirm her fears, Mattie – her usually gentle and calm Mattie – increased his pace and tightened his grip on her hand. Louisa had to trot to keep up with his long strides.

'Mattie, what's wrong? Where are we going?' She tugged at his hand, trying to get him to slow down, but he didn't stop. 'Mattie!' She raised her voice, trying to dig her heels in. 'For the love of God, stop!'

At last, he noticed her struggles and stopped. He turned to look at her and her heart nearly stopped at the agony in his expression. She stepped closer and put a hand on his heaving chest.

'What is it, love? You're frightening me.'

He closed his eyes for a moment, taking a deep breath and forcing it out again. 'Sorry,' he said, opening them again and catching her gaze with his own. He pulled her into a hug. 'I love you, you know that, don't you?'

'Of course I do. I love you, too, and I hate to see you in a state like this. What's happened, Mattie? Have you and Lucas had a fight? Please tell me.'

He glanced around, as though suddenly aware that they were just yards from The Cross on a busy Saturday. He shook his head. 'Not here. Will you walk up the Tor with me? I promise I'll tell you then.'

It had become a favourite walk of theirs. Long enough to get them away from the village, with an awe-inspiring view at the top. They would sit by the ancient tower – or inside it if the wind was too strong – and talk about their future. They'd talked about where they'd live, how many children they would have, how her parents would come round when they produced beautiful grandchildren for them to love. Louisa smiled at the memories of all those plans they'd made. If Mattie wanted to go up the Tor, then it couldn't be something awful. That was their happy-ever-after place.

'Alright,' she said. 'But can we go a bit slower? I've got a stitch from trying to keep up with you.'

He nodded. 'Sorry, love.'

She tucked her hand in his arm and they set off again at a gentler pace. Neither of them spoke. Occasionally, he stopped to touch her cheek and kiss her. His caress was gentle, but he looked as though he was suffering a terrible torment. Louisa's mind was whirling, trying to work out what had gotten Mattie into such a state today. She wondered whether he was one of those being picked on in the Clicking Room for not joining the union. She hoped not. She also prayed it wasn't anything to do with her pa. She would hate it if he made her sweetheart's life so hard that he decided she wasn't worth the trouble.

The final climb up to the top of the Tor left them both breathless. They moved around the tower to lean against the rough stone walls out of the wind. Even though the April sun was warm after the winter months, there was still a chill in the air. Louisa shivered. Mattie pulled her into his arms, sharing his warmth with her. She smiled and rested her head on his chest.

'Mmm, that's better,' she said. 'I love cuddling up.'

She felt his chest expand under her cheek as he took a deep breath. His heart was racing. She couldn't tell whether it was from the climb or something else. He had been acting so strange all week. One moment loving, the next looking away as though he couldn't bear to look at her. But now that they were here and he'd promised to tell her what was bothering him, she suddenly didn't want to know. She had an awful feeling about it.

He took another deep breath before he spoke. 'You mean the world to me, Lou, you know that, don't you? I thank God every day that He brought us together. It's like you're the other half of me. I'm not whole without you.'

She squeezed his waist. 'I feel the same.'

He kissed the top of her head. 'I'd marry you today if I could.'

'I know. But we'll probably have to wait until I'm twenty-one,' she sighed, closing her eyes and savouring his warmth. 'I just hope you don't grow tired of waiting.'

His arms tightened around her. 'I'll never grow tired of you. I'll wait for you for all eternity if need be. Your pa will have to come round eventually, 'cause I'm not giving up.'

She looked up at him. He was staring out over the levels towards Street. She knew that he could see the factory's red-brick chimney, standing proud above the village, and the blue lias stone buildings – workshops, shops and houses, all built to serve Clarks and its workers. Her heart clenched at the sadness in his eyes.

'Is Pa giving you a hard time?' she asked.

He shrugged. 'You're his only daughter. He's protective of you. I understand that. I expect I'll be just as fierce when it comes to our daughters.' He looked down at her and smiled. 'I hope they take after you. They'll be my little blonde-haired, blue-eyed princesses. But then I'll want to chase off any lad who so much as looks at them. Because they'd be mine – yours – ours.' He buried his face in her hair. 'I swear I will protect you. I'll be worthy of you.'

She put a hand on his cheek, her heart nearly bursting with love for him. 'You are worthy of me, Matthew Searle. You're all I want. I want to be your wife and the mother of your children. I'll give you daughters, but I want at least one son as well – a handsome lad with your brown hair and eyes. A little Mattie who will make us so proud.'

She gave him a soft smile and kissed him when his eyes filled with tears. 'Hush now,' she said. 'It won't be so bad, waiting. Not now we don't have to sneak around. Everyone knows we belong together now.'

He sniffed and blinked away the moisture in his eyes, looking away towards the village again. There were a few other people wandering around the top of the Tor, but they ignored them as they cuddled together against the protective strength of the tower.

After a few minutes, Mattie took another deep breath and squeezed her tight. Louisa felt her heart skip a beat. When she looked up into his beautiful, troubled eyes, her instincts told her that her Pa was likely the least of their problems.

'What is it, love?' she asked. 'Please, tell me what's troubling you. You're worrying me.'

He closed his eyes and rested his forehead against hers. She felt his warm breath on her cheek. 'I'm so sorry, Louisa. I've tried everything. I've prayed and prayed, trying to find a way through this, but I don't have any choice.'

'What about? Mattie, you're not making any sense.'

He opened his eyes and she held her breath. 'I have to show everyone that I'm a man and that I'll protect you. I can't hope to ever prove that if I sit on my hands here, doing nothing.' When she opened her mouth to speak, he put a finger to her lips. 'No. Let me speak. This is so hard, but I've got to tell you, make you understand, before it's too late.'

He took another breath, as though trying to pull the strength to say the words out of the air. 'Don't hate me, alright? But I've thought of nothing else for weeks and last weekend...' He shook his head. 'It doesn't matter about that, but the point is last weekend, I came to a realisation. I'm enlisting, Louisa. I'm going to prove to everyone that I'm a man.'

Louisa felt her knees go weak at the shock of his words. If he hadn't been holding her so tight, she would have fallen. It was the last thing she'd expected him to say. 'No, Mattie, tell me it's not true. What about us?'

'I'm doing it for us, don't you see?'

She shook her head. 'No. You don't need to fight, not for me. I'm yours, no matter what.'

He was silent, his tortured gaze begging her to understand.

'Did my pa put you up to this?' she asked, her anger rising. 'Because I won't have it, d'you hear? I'd rather tell him we're splitting up and go back to sneaking around than let him push you into fighting and risking your life, our future. And what about your Peace Testimony?'

He shook his head. 'Don't blame your pa. It's my decision. I have to follow my own conscience.'

'No, I don't believe it,' she said, her emotions giving her the strength to push him away. He let her go, dropping his hands to his sides, even though his gaze wouldn't release hers. 'You don't have to do this, Mattie. Don't let him do this to us! We'll find a way, no matter what he says.'

He shook his head. She could feel the waves of sadness rolling off him and wrapping its tendrils around her heart, squeezing it until she was sure she would die.

'And what about your ma? What does she say about this?'

He hung his head. 'I haven't told her yet. I wanted to tell you first.'

She closed her eyes against the tears that were beginning to flow. 'You can't leave her. You can't leave me.'

'I have to. Please, Lou darling. I need you to understand.' He put a hand on her shoulder. She wanted to shrug him off, but didn't have the strength. She needed to feel his touch. It was the only thing that made any sense to her right now.

'I can't understand it, Mattie. It's wrong. Going to fight goes against everything you believe in. You'll break your ma's heart, as well as mine.' She grabbed his face in her hands, fear making her tremble and her voice shrill. 'What if you don't come back? How will I go on without you? How will your ma survive?'

He pulled her into his arms. 'I will come back, Louisa. I promise you. I will come back and marry you and spend the rest of my life making you happy.'

'You can't promise me that. Look at what happened to Albert Jackson. Look at the thousands and thousands of casualties listed in the papers week after week. You're not a fighter, Mattie. Please don't go. I can't bear it.'

He held her tight as she sobbed. She felt his own tears dripping onto her hair, but he didn't tell her what she needed to hear. Instead, he whispered promises he couldn't know he could keep, and told her he loved her.

She didn't know how long they stayed like that but eventually she had no tears left. She clung to him, praying that she was dreaming and that she would wake up to find that it wasn't true. That Mattie wasn't going to enlist. But the sun hid behind a cloud, chilling the air, and the wind picked up, swirling around them, bringing her back to reality.

'When do you leave?' she asked, her voice barely above a whisper. Maybe if he didn't hear her, he wouldn't go. But, yet again, her prayers weren't answered.

'Tomorrow,' he said.

She gasped.

'I couldn't tell you before, I didn't want to upset you.'

'You mean you didn't want me to have the chance to talk you out of it.'

'If you like. It's hard enough now. I didn't want my last week with you to be miserable as well.'

She sniffed, realising that there were still more tears waiting to flow. 'I knew something was up. Is that what you and Lucas were arguing about?'

He shook his head, looking away. 'No.'

'He's not going with you, is he?' she asked. 'It would kill Jeannie.' *Just as you going away is making me die inside.*

'He's not going with me. He doesn't know. But he'll understand.'

So he hadn't even told his best friend.

'Will he? Because I don't.' She took a deep breath and stepped away from him again. 'You'd better go and tell your ma. I doubt she'll take the news any easier than I have.'

He scrubbed at his face, wiping away the traces of his own tears, before he looked at her. His eyes were bloodshot and puffy. Then he nodded. 'The last thing I want to do is to hurt either of you,' he said. 'I love you both so much. Please, Louisa, please remember that. But I have to go. It's the only way.'

She shook her head. 'No, it's not, Mattie. There's always another way. You and the Friends taught me that. I don't know why you've decided to do this, and I don't like it, not one bit. You're putting our whole future in jeopardy.' She pinched the top of her nose, trying to stop the throbbing in her head. 'But if you're set to go tomorrow, then you've already signed the papers, haven't you?'

He nodded.

'So now you have to go.'

He nodded again, breaking her heart a little more.

She stood there, the wind whipping around her. She didn't know what to do, what else she could say, to stop this happening. If he'd signed the papers, he was committed to joining the army. If he didn't go now, he'd be arrested and put in jail, or maybe he'd be shot for cowardice. That thought took her breath away. She couldn't bear it. She knew in that moment that she had to let him go because at least then there might be a chance that he'd be able to survive the fighting and come back to her.

This time, it was Louisa who nodded. 'Alright,' she said. She wished she could find the strength to look away. 'You'd better go and tell your ma.' She laughed, the sound harsh and unnatural. 'I'll bet you haven't even started packing, have you? You wouldn't have wanted your ma to realise what you're planning.'

He had the grace to look embarrassed. 'I haven't. You're right. Like I said, I didn't want to spoil this week.'

'Well, it's proper spoilt now,' she said, raising her chin, her tone bitter.

'And I'm more sorry than I can say. But I promise you, it will be alright.'

She shook her head. 'I won't let you make that promise, Mattie. We don't know what will happen. All I ask is that you do your best to stay alive and come back to me.'

'I'll write to you every day.'

She gave him a sad smile. 'You can't promise that, either. Who knows what you'll face there? The Jacksons don't hear from Stan for weeks at a time.'

'I will. I swear. Even if I can't send them, I'll write them and you'll get them in a bundle, even if I have to bring them all home with me.'

She held out her hand, realising that if this was the last chance she had, she wanted to be touching him, feeling his warm skin against hers. 'Come on. I hate it, but you have to get home to tell your ma.'

They walked down the Tor and through Glastonbury holding hands. They didn't speak until they got to the outskirts of Street, close to the end of his road.

'I'll be in basic training for ten weeks,' he said. 'Then I get a few days' leave to come home before we're shipped overseas. So I'll be back in July.'

Hope filled her. 'Maybe it will be over before then. They keep saying we're going to win this. You might not have to go and fight.'

He squeezed her hands. 'Let's hope so, love.'

She stopped him at the end of The Mead. 'You can't see me home,' she said. 'You need to tell your ma. You can't put it off any longer, Mattie. It's not fair on her.'

He sighed and nodded. 'I just wanted to spend as much time as I could with you.'

She leaned into him, letting him hold her for a few moments longer. 'I know. But it's time.'

His lips met hers, and she returned his kiss, pouring all her love into it. Then she stepped back. 'I won't come to the station tomorrow,' she told him. 'I couldn't bear it and anyway, your ma and your brother will need time to say their farewells.' She touched his cheek. 'Keep yourself safe, my love. I really need you to come back to me, Mattie.'

He nodded, covering her hand with his. 'I'll see you in July.'

She smiled, even though her heart was shattered. 'You will.'

'And I will write.'

'I hope so.' She gave him one more kiss, then turned away, hurrying towards home. She didn't look back, knowing that if she did, she would run back to him and beg him not to leave her.

28

After church on Sunday, Kate made her way as usual to Ma's grave. It was still bare earth with a wooden marker cross. They said it was best to let the soil settle before putting in a stone, and that the grass would soon grow over the plot. The Sexton who looked after the graveyard promised to sow some seed as soon as the weather was right.

She was surprised to find Louisa there, waiting for her. She'd seen her in church, but the Clements family sat nearer the front, so she hadn't seen her friend's face. Looking at her now, it was clear that something was wrong. Her eyes were red and puffy and there were dark shadows under them, emphasising how pale she was.

'Louisa, love, whatever's the matter?' she asked as she rushed over to her and hugged her.

Her eyes filled with tears. 'Mattie's gone,' she sobbed.

Kate didn't understand. 'What do you mean, *gone*?' She prayed he wasn't dead. He'd been perfectly fine yesterday. 'Has he had an accident?'

Louisa shook her head, scrubbing at her eyes. 'No. It's not that. He's left, Kate. He's enlisted. He got the train this morning.'

'What?' she gasped. 'I don't believe it. You're kidding me, aren't you? I mean, he's a Friend. He shouldn't go at all, especially not without conscription.'

'I wish I was kidding,' Louisa replied, her voice raspy. 'He didn't tell anyone until yesterday. Now he's gone.'

Kate put a hand to her forehead. 'I don't understand. Why would he do that?'

Louisa took a deep breath and tried to wipe away her tears. 'I think my pa pushed him into it. He denies it, of course, and so did Mattie. But why else would he do something like that? Pa's been giving him a hard time, telling him he needs to prove himself. Pa didn't look surprised when I told him he was leaving today. He says it's because Mattie had to give his notice and he'd asked him not to mention it to me. But I know he must have made him do it.'

'Oh, Louisa, love. I'm so sorry. I would never have expected Mattie to do something like that, no matter how hard your pa pushed him. He must love you such a lot.'

Louisa huffed. 'No! If he really loved me, he'd stay here and stand up to Pa. But instead, he let him bully him into enlisting and God knows when he'll be able to come home or if he'll ever come back. What if he gets killed like Ted's brother, Kate? Or gets wounded? I heard a rumour that the Hun have started using poisonous gas that blinds a man and burns his lungs. Then there's all those stories about men having their arms and legs blown off by artillery fire. Oh, Kate, I can't bear it!'

Kate tightened her arms around her friend, afraid she'd collapse, letting her sob out all her fears and heartbreak. She wished she could find the words to comfort her, but she'd heard all those rumours and stories as well and couldn't deny that Louisa had good reason to fear for Mattie's well-being.

'If anything happens to Mattie, I'll never forgive my pa. I swear, I'll leave home and never speak to him again.' Louisa's voice, shrill and full of pain, filled the air.

A movement across the gravestones caught Kate's eye. She looked up to see Mr Clements watching them. His shoulders slumped as he heard his daughter's words and he hung his head as though in prayer. He stood there for a moment while Louisa cried, unaware that he was witnessing her tears. Kate watched, not sure what to do other than to try and comfort her friend.

After a few minutes, he raised his head and looked up to the heavens, a deep breath filling his lungs before he blew it out again and turned his gaze towards the girls. He slowly approached them, his steps cautious, as though he was walking towards a nervous animal that might bolt at any moment.

'Louisa, love,' he said, his deep voice gentle. 'It's time to go home. Your ma's wanting to get the dinner ready.' He put a hand on his daughter's shoulder. She stiffened and wouldn't look at him. 'Please, love. I swear to you I didn't force him to do anything. He told me he wouldn't, and whether you believe me or not, I truly respected that he was sticking to his principles. I don't know what changed his mind, but I promise you, it wasn't me.'

Much as Kate feared Mr Clements as a man of power – after all, he could sack her own father any time and no one would blame him given Pa's liking for cider and dislike for work – she got the distinct impression that he was telling Louisa the truth. But then again, she couldn't imagine anything or anyone else who might have been able to persuade Mattie to join the army. Like Mr Clements said, Mattie lived by his Quaker principles and everyone expected him to stick to them. Him rushing off to war didn't make an ounce of sense.

She felt the fight drain out of Louisa, as though her tears had washed all the life in her away. Without a word, she let her pa put an arm around her shoulders and lead her out of the churchyard to where her ma was waiting at the gate. People were still loitering along the path, catching up on the gossip. No doubt they would be speculating on what had upset Louisa Clements as her parents led her away.

Kate sighed and turned back to the grave, laying a hand on the marker, missing her ma as always.

'Everything's changing, Ma,' she whispered. 'And not for the better.'

Ted found her there a few minutes later. 'Someone said Louisa was crying,' he said. 'Is she alright?'

Kate shook her head. 'No, Ted, she's not. Did you know that Mattie had enlisted?'

It was clear from the shock on his face that he didn't. His eyes widened and he shook his head. 'You're joking.'

'No, I'm not. He left this morning. Louisa didn't know about it until yesterday afternoon.'

He frowned. 'That's mad. Why would he do that?'

She shrugged. 'No one knows. Lou thought her pa had forced him into it to prove himself. But... I don't know... He swore to her just now that he didn't, and he looked like he meant it. He even said he respected Mattie for sticking to his principles.'

'It makes no sense,' he said. 'I wonder if Lucas knows why he did it?'

'He might.' But she wasn't so sure. 'We saw them arguing outside the factory yesterday. It looked like they'd had a falling out.'

Ted thought about it for a bit. 'Mmm. Come to think on it, I don't think they've been talking to each other much all week.'

Kate sighed, giving her ma's grave marker a final loving stroke before she turned away. 'I've got to get Pa's dinner on the table, then I'll go round to the Musgroves and see if they know anything about it.'

'Want me to come with you? Ma and Pa expect me to be home for dinner, but I could come over as soon as I've eaten.'

Kate smiled. Ted didn't realise how easy his life was in that respect. He wouldn't be expected to cook or even help clear up after the meal – his ma ruled the house and did everything for her family. No son of hers was going to do what she regarded as women's work. Kate, on the other hand, had every intention, if she ever married – which she doubted – to ensure that any husband and sons of hers would know how to help in the house. She'd spent all yesterday afternoon and a couple of hours before church cleaning the house and doing laundry as well as getting the food ready for Sunday dinner. She wasn't inclined to be another man's slave in this lifetime. It was bad enough that she had no choice while living with her pa.

One day, I'll escape from there and I'll be free, she told herself. *I'll answer to no man, unless he proves himself to be a decent, fair and true partner in my life.*

'Alright, I'll wait for you. Don't leave it too late, mind.' She was hoping she might get a few hours to relax with a good book later today.

He grinned. 'I'll be as quick as I can,' he promised as he kissed her cheek and set off.

* * *

Jeannie sighed with relief when she opened the door to find Kate and Ted on the step.

'Have you heard about Mattie?' Kate asked as soon as she greeted them and let them in.

She nodded, hoping she wasn't going to cry again. 'His family weren't at the meeting this morning. Ma had a sewing pattern she'd promised Mrs Searle, so she asked Lucas to take it round and to make sure everything was alright. He found Mattie's ma in tears and his brother told him Mattie's already gone.'

'Did Lucas know about it?' asked Ted. ''Cause Saturday, when we clocked off, I told Mattie I'd see him on Monday and he never said a word.'

Jeannie led them into the kitchen. Ma's nerves had got the better of her and she had taken to her bed, and the twins were playing football with their pals as usual. Lucas had gone out, she didn't know where.

'Lucas didn't have a clue. He's really upset.'

'None of us can believe it,' said Kate. 'Louisa's in bits. He only told her yesterday afternoon. It was a terrible shock for her, the poor love. She's blaming her pa, although he's denying it. But if it wasn't him, what on earth would persuade Mattie to go and fight?'

Jeannie felt a wave of sympathy for Louisa. She was finding it hard enough, having admired Mattie from afar for as long as she could remember. But it must be so much harder for his sweetheart. She turned away and began making a pot of tea. It was good to be busy.

'I don't know. Neither does Lucas. I had to do most of the Sunday dinner,' she told them. 'As soon as he came home with the news, Ma started fretting that Lucas was going to enlist as well and got into a terrible state. He was hard pressed to convince her he wouldn't, but she made him swear it. He said if he'd known what Mattie was planning, he'd have stopped him.'

Ted nodded. 'We all would've. Maybe that's why he kept it secret until the last minute.'

'Stupid fool,' Kate muttered.

Jeannie brought the pot to the table and poured their drinks. 'I hope he's alright. I can't imagine what he was thinking. It's not like Mattie at all.'

'Louisa's convinced her pa was behind it, despite what he says,' said Kate. 'But... I don't know. I think he was as surprised as we were.'

'It's Mrs Searle I feel sorry for,' sighed Jeannie. 'It would break my heart if a son of mine went to fight.'

'Was our Peg round there?' asked Kate.

Jeannie nodded. 'I think so. Lucas said Will was there, and none of them were at the Meeting House this morning, so I expect she was.'

'I'll pop in on my way home to see how they are,' she said.

Of course, Kate was related to the Searles by virtue of Peg's marriage to Will. Jeannie felt a pang of jealousy that she didn't have that excuse to go to Mattie's house. She supposed she could have gone round as a Friend, but with the boys all disappearing, she had to stay at home in case Ma needed her and someone had to clean up after their meal. Not that Ma, Lucas or Jeannie had eaten much. Only the twins seemed unmoved by Mattie's departure.

'I expect word has spread by now,' said Ted. 'There'll be a crowd round there, offering sympathy and collecting gossip.' He winked at them to let them know he was teasing. 'At least this has distracted my ma for a bit, although it might set her off again, what with Mattie being a Friend.'

'What d'you mean?' she asked.

He took a sip of his tea before replying. 'She's fretting that I *haven't* enlisted while she feels it's a lad's duty to go and fight. She wants me to go out there straight away to make sure our Stan's alright. Been on at me day and night over the past few weeks on account of his letters being a bit odd.'

'Odd in what way?' asked Kate, looking confused.

Ted took another sip, as though he needed time to get his thoughts in order. 'We don't hear from him often. But when we do, he sounds... troubled. Not himself.' He pressed his lips together. 'Look, I shouldn't be saying this, so don't go telling anyone else, alright?'

Both girls nodded.

'Sometimes the letters are short and sharp. *I'm still here. Wish this damned war was over.* Things like that. Then there are others that are long and rambling and don't make a lot of sense. Sometimes he talks as though Albert's still alive – says he saw him or heard him laughing with his comrades. Then we got one where he says the Hun have taken Albert prisoner but we're not to worry because he's making plans to creep into the enemy trenches one night to bring him back.' He put his elbows on the table and his chin in his hands. 'I don't know what to make of it. I mean, he was next to Albert when he was shot. He held him as he died.' He rubbed at his eyes. 'Pa thinks he might be having some sort of nervous breakdown and should be pulled back from the front. He's tried writing to someone at the regiment, but all they say is that he's fit for duty and must carry on.'

'Poor Stan,' said Jeannie. 'You must all be worrying about him something awful.'

Ted nodded, lowering his gaze to where he was using a finger to trace the grain of the wooden kitchen table, all trace of humour gone. 'We are,' he sighed. 'And I'm stuck in the middle between Ma and Pa. She wants me to enlist in his company and go and be with him and she's fretting that I'm taking too long about it. She's convinced he'll be alright once I'm there to keep an eye on him.' Ted didn't look convinced. 'Then there's Pa, insisting he's not willing to sacrifice another son if he doesn't have to and I should wait and see if they're going to bring in conscription like some folk are saying they will. To be honest, I don't know what to do. I mean, if Stan couldn't save Albert, how can I save Stan? I can't stop a bullet or a shell.'

'Not unless you stand between them and your brother,' said Kate. 'Which you shouldn't be expected to do. Your pa's right. You shouldn't go.'

He reached out and took her hand across the table. Jeannie's heart swelled at the understanding that flowed between the two of them. Kate had been through so much; it was good to see her with Ted. And he needed someone on his side at the moment. They were good for each other.

'I know,' he said. 'But it's not easy when they're arguing over it. Ma's not been right since we lost Albert. She's convinced God won't be so cruel as to take another son and that I need to be there to help Stan through this.'

'It's not God that's cruel,' said Jeannie softly. 'It's the war that's pitching man against man. That's the real cruelty.'

He nodded his agreement.

'But what about you?' demanded Kate. 'Who's going to help you through it? They say it's hell on earth over there. It don't sound like Stan's up to taking care of himself, let alone you as well.'

Jeannie could understand her friend's indignation. Nothing to do with this war made any sense. A wave of despair flowed through her as she thought about Mattie, gone to fight a war he didn't want or agree with. She wished she could understand what had made him do it.

Ted shrugged. 'If I'd known Mattie was going, I'd have asked him to look out for Stan. If any of you hear from him, let me know and I'll write to him. It might calm Ma down a bit if I do that.'

The girls agreed. 'I expect Louisa will hear first,' said Jeannie.

Kate frowned. 'He won't be sent straight to the front anyway, will he? How long is the training? Ten weeks?'

Ted nodded.

'And don't they get some leave to come home for a few days after their basic training?'

'That's right,' said Ted. 'So he'll be back sometime in early July for a bit. Maybe I can talk to him then.'

They all finished drinking their teas, none of them inclined to chat. Jeannie couldn't stop thinking about Mattie.

'Do you think he's joined an Ambulance Unit?' she asked. 'Only I heard Mr Hugh Clark has gone to France this week to serve with one. I didn't think any of the Clarks would fight, so I suppose he thought this was a better option.'

Ted shook his head. 'Those units are mainly volunteers who're paying their own way. Mr Hugh has had his own car converted into an ambulance. Mattie couldn't afford to do that, could he? No, if he got the train this morning, he'll be joining one of the Somerset infantry battalions.'

'Cannon fodder,' muttered Kate. 'The fool.'

'Who knows?' Ted shrugged. 'No one knows what he's been thinking, do they? But Mattie's not daft; he must have had his reasons. Maybe he'll tell us in July.'

They hadn't noticed the back door open, but a movement caught Jeannie's eye and she turned to see Lucas standing there. He looked terrible.

'Lucas,' she said. She wanted to ask him where he'd been, but didn't want to have this conversation in front of anyone else. 'Want a cuppa? There's some still in the pot. It might be a bit stewed, but—'

'No. I don't want anything,' he said, sinking into a chair next to her.

'Alright, fella?' asked Ted. 'This is a turn up, ain't it? Never expected that of Mattie.'

'No one did,' he said, not looking at any of them. 'Where's Ma, Jeannie?'

'Taken to her bed,' she said. 'Maybe I should make a fresh pot and take her a drink?'

He stood up. 'I'll do it.' He checked the kettle on the range and, satisfied there was enough water in it, picked up the pot and emptied it. His movements were slow, as though he was in pain, as he spooned tea leaves into the pot and poured on the water. Once he'd put the lid and cosy back on, he leaned against the sink, staring out the window, his back to them.

'Lucas,' Jeannie said softly. 'You're not thinking about going after him, are you?'

'No. What would be the point?'

'None,' said Kate firmly, startling Jeannie, whose attention had been so focused on her brother that she'd forgotten about their visitors. 'Now he's in basic training, there's no going back for him.'

'Not unless they reckon he's unfit for fighting,' said Ted. 'Which is unlikely. He'll have already had his medical and from what I hear, they'll take anyone these days, just to get more boots on the ground.'

Lucas got a cup and saucer out of the cupboard and poured the tea, not saying anything. Jeannie got up and brought the milk jug to him from the table. He took it with a murmur of thanks, then handed it back to her, all without looking at her.

'I'll take this up to Ma,' he said.

'Are you coming back down?' she asked him softly.

'I dunno. Probably not.'

'But—'

'Just drop it, sis,' he said, raising his voice. 'I don't want to talk about it, alright? He's gone. Didn't even have the courtesy to tell his friends. That's the end of it. If the damned fool wants to get himself killed, that's his business, but I'm not going to spend the rest of this bloody war yakking on about it.'

He walked out of the room with the cuppa for Ma, leaving Jeannie stunned.

'Well, that's told us,' said Ted.

'You alright, Jeannie?' asked Kate.

She blinked and realised she'd been staring at the door Lucas had closed behind him. Taking a calming breath, she turned back to her friends and sat down again, trying to smile. 'Sorry about that. He's not normally so snappy.'

Ted shrugged. 'It's understandable. I was put out that Mattie kept quiet, and I'm only a pal. Lucas is his best friend. No wonder he's so angry about it.'

The three of them chatted on for a few minutes, but Lucas's outburst seemed to have drained the air out of the room, leaving them all struggling to act normal. In the end, Kate stood up and Ted followed suit.

'We'll leave you to it. Hope your ma feels better soon.'

Jeannie nodded. She wasn't so sure Ma would bounce back quickly. The fear that Lucas – who always followed Mattie's lead – might do something daft lingered in the house. Jeannie could feel it and was struggling to deal with it. Ma was so prone to her nerves that it might take weeks to convince her she had nothing to worry about.

* * *

Ted walked Kate home. When she tried to talk to him, he merely grunted, obviously deep in his own thoughts. When they reached the cottage in Silver Road, he waited at the door as usual, while Kate checked whether Pa was home or not. She was relieved to find the house empty.

'Want to come in for a bit?' she asked.

He hesitated for a moment, then nodded. 'Alright. Another ten minutes won't make any difference.'

They sat in the parlour. Ted still seemed preoccupied. Kate reached over and took his hand.

'I'm sorry things are difficult at home,' she said.

He shrugged, squeezing her hand. 'It is what it is. I thought it couldn't get much worse after we lost Albert, but this business with Stan...' He shook his head. 'Ma thinks I don't care, but I do. It's just... what if I get there and he gets killed anyway? She'd never forgive me.'

'It's not just Stan who could get killed, Ted. Please don't go.'

He sighed and pulled her closer, putting his arm around her and resting his chin on the top of her head. She snuggled in, enjoying the cuddle. It was strange how she'd come to enjoy Ted's embraces after her horror of being held by him on their first date. She supposed it was because she knew him better now and knew he'd never hurt her.

'I don't want to, Katie girl, I really don't. But I might have to. I'm not sure how much longer I can put up with Ma's constant demands.'

'Won't she listen to your pa?'

'No. He's tried. You wouldn't believe the shouting matches they've had. Pa's finding excuses for being out the house – he spends most of his time at his allotment, even when it's too cold or wet to dig. I reckon he's hiding out in his shed there, just to avoid another row with Ma. In the meantime, she's helping organise fundraisers at the church for the troops and knitting socks and baking fruit cakes to send out to them. If she could, she'd be out and about, recruiting lads off the streets to take the colours. Did I tell you she's joined the White Feather Movement?'

'No.' Kate's heart sank. 'It must be so hard for you, being in the middle of all that.'

She felt him nodding, his chin still resting on her head.

'It is. And I just know she'll use the news about Mattie to have another go at me about it.' He sighed. 'I don't know what to do, Katie. I know I might have to go and fight one day, and I'll do my duty. But while Ma's intent of me going to save Stan, I feel like I'm damned if I do and damned if I don't. What if I get there and he dies anyway? I don't think I could bear to see him fall, like he did with Albert. So I've been putting it off. Maybe that makes me a coward. I don't know. I'm not afraid of fighting, just letting my family down. I even thought about asking you to marry me. They're encouraging the bachelors to go first. If we were wed, it might give Ma something else to think about. She might be more interested in us giving her grandchildren.'

Kate had gone still at the mentioned of getting married. The idea both tempted and scared her. The idea of being able to escape her father's house appealed. But then they'd have to live with Ted's parents and she could well be swapping one cage for another. Mrs Jackson was a fierce woman and from what Ted told her, she wouldn't be easy to live with.

Ted chuckled, kissing her hair. 'Breathe, Kate. It was only an idea. I know that's the last thing you want.'

She hadn't realised she'd stopped breathing until he said that. She blew out a breath and put a hand to her racing heart. 'Phew! Don't frighten me like that, Ted Jackson.'

He laughed outright at that. 'I knew I could get a rise out of you.' He lifted her hand from her chest and kissed her knuckles. 'Thanks, love. I needed a laugh.'

She laughed too and shook her head. 'Would have served you right if I'd taken you seriously, you daft beggar.'

'Maybe one day, you will.'

'Don't hold your breath,' she muttered.

'What, like you did?' he teased.

They were both laughing when Pa stumbled through the door. Kate's heart sank as he took in the two of them sitting cuddled together on the settle.

'What's he doing here?' he demanded, rounding on Ted. 'You better not be taking advantage of my daughter, you little sod. Get your hands off her.'

Ted raised his hands, his expression calm and respectful as he got to his feet. 'No, sir, I'd never take advantage of Kate.'

She scrambled up and stood next to him. 'Leave him alone, Pa. He's not doing anything he shouldn't. He's a decent lad.'

Reggie Davis sneered. 'No, he ain't. He's sniffing round you like a fucking dog after a bitch.'

'Pa!' Kate was used to his filthy language, but she was ashamed that Ted had to hear it.

'Shut up, you. Get your arse in that kitchen and get my supper. And you,' he pointed a grubby, shaking finger at Ted and scowled, 'get out of my house. I've had enough of the bloody Jackson family. D'you know, your damned ma is standing outside the Inn, handing out white feathers? Stupid cow.'

Kate grabbed Ted's arm when he stiffened and went to step towards Pa. 'Leave it,' she whispered, hoping he remembered what she'd told him about how there was no reasoning with Pa when he was in his cups.

Ted glanced at her. She tried to keep her expression blank so he wouldn't know how worried she was.

'Just go,' she said quietly. 'Please.'

He hesitated for a moment while she silently willed him to leave without making a fuss. She squeezed his arm. 'I'll be alright.'

He didn't look convinced, but he respected her wishes. He turned to Pa. 'I'm sorry about that, Mr Davis,' he said. 'Ma's been a bit keen on sending us all to war since our Albert got killed.'

Kate breathed a quiet sigh of relief when Pa nodded.

'I heard,' Pa grumbled. 'But it don't mean the woman should interrupt a man's drinking time. You tell her from me she needs to stay at home and mind her own business.'

'I'll try, sir,' said Ted as he took his leave. 'See you at the factory tomorrow. Bye.'

He was looking at Pa, but Kate knew he was talking to her. She smiled at him and nodded.

The moment the door closed behind him, she rushed into the kitchen. 'Supper won't be long, Pa,' she called over her shoulder.

'See that it ain't,' he growled, sinking into his armchair. 'And bring me a cuppa while I'm waiting. Some bugger's drunk all me cider. Better not have been that Jackson lad, or I'll knock his block off.'

Kate rolled her eyes. No one but him drank in this house. But trying to convince him of that was a pointless exercise. She only hoped he'd drunk enough wherever he'd been all afternoon that he'd fall asleep as soon as he'd eaten his supper. Then she might finally get a bit of time to herself.

This business with Mattie was worrying her. She couldn't help but feel sorry for everyone who was upset by Mattie's sudden departure. So many people were affected by it. How could he do that to all the people who loved him? She also had a lot of sympathy for Ted's ma, even though she didn't agree with her about sending her youngest son after his older brother in the trenches. But she supposed grief affected people in different ways.

She hoped both Mattie and Stan and all the other lads they knew who'd enlisted would stay safe and that this horrible war would come to an end soon. God only knew how many prayers were being offered up, begging for that very thing. She just hoped He bothered to listen.

29

Jeannie didn't think her brothers could be more exasperating, but the following weeks proved otherwise. While Ma had been nervous and edgy in the days after Mattie's departure, she was slowly rallying and spending less time in her bed. That made things easier for Jeannie, not having to run up and down, trying to get her to eat while trying to keep the twins in line at the same time. At least now everyone sat down for meals together again.

Not that mealtimes were easy. With Ma being incapable of doing anything when her nerves overtook her, the burden of getting food on the table fell solely on Jeannie. The twins were worse than useless when it came to helping around the house and Lucas had become surly and uncooperative, not even bothering to do his share, much less making sure the twins did their bit. At first, she had made allowances for him, knowing how much he'd been hurt when Mattie had gone away. But now she was beginning to resent the fact that they were all expected to tiptoe around him. He wasn't the only one upset by Mattie leaving.

'You lads will have to do the washing up tonight,' she announced as they ate supper. 'I'm going out.'

'That's nice for you, love,' said Ma. 'Are you seeing your friends, or that lad? What's his name?'

'Douglas, Ma. Yes, I'm seeing him. He asked me to bring round some books and pamphlets about the Friends. He's really interested to know more about our faith.'

'Oh, my. That is good news,' Ma smiled.

Lucas scowled and muttered under his breath. She couldn't catch what he said, but his tone was obvious. Something inside Jeannie snapped and she turned on him.

'What?' she demanded. 'If you've got something to say, Lucas Musgrove, just spit it out. I'm sick and tired of you moping and complaining all the time.'

'Jeannie, love.' Ma held out a hand. 'Please don't.'

Jeannie took a shaky breath. She was trembling, so angry and frustrated, she wanted to scream. 'I'm sorry, Ma. But Lucas has been so wrapped up in his misery since Mattie left that he's forgotten to be civil to those of us who are still here. It's not our fault he's gone, but he's taking it out on all of us. It's about time he pulled himself together and remembered he's got responsibilities here.'

'I haven't forgotten,' he snapped, not even bothering to look at her. 'Any more than you've remembered who's the man of this house.'

She laughed at that. 'What?' She shook her head. 'I haven't forgotten, Lucas. But you have. You've not lifted a finger for weeks. It's like your body's here, but your heart and mind have taken off for foreign parts.'

One of the twins giggled and Ma shushed him. Jeannie would have preferred to have this conversation with Lucas without an audience, but now she thought on it, she might as well get it off her chest now.

'I do my bit,' he replied through clenched teeth. 'I got the shopping on my own on Saturday afternoon, while you were off playing happy families with *Douglas*.' He said his name with a sneer.

Jeannie stood up, hands on hips. 'Once. Once in how many years? I was invited to tea by Douglas's ma and you begrudge me even a couple of hours? I've been doing the shopping on *my* own for the past month because every chance you get, you take yourself off to God knows where so you can sulk in peace.'

'She did ask you if you minded, love,' said Ma. 'Please don't fight over this.'

'I'm not sulking,' he insisted, ignoring Ma's pleading. 'I just need time to myself to think.' He glared at the twins, who were sniggering at all the drama.

'You are sulking,' said John. 'Just 'cause Mattie ran off to play with guns.'

Ma groaned and buried her face in her hands. Jeannie, at the end of her tether, reached over and clipped John's ear.

'Ow! What was that for? You said he was sulking first.'

'You're not helping. Make yourself useful.' She picked up her plate and Ma's and shoved them into his hands. 'Both of you can wash up and put away. And keep your childish opinions to yourselves.'

Peter got up silently and collected the other plates, nudging John to move over to the sink and get on with their chore. When his twin would have argued, he hissed at him to shut up. Jeannie wasn't sure whether it was her wrath or the black look that Lucas directed at John that persuaded him to do as he was told for a change, but whatever it was, he glared back at them before following Peter.

With the twins' backs to the rest of them, Jeannie turned her attention back to her brother. The sharp words on her tongue dissolved as she saw the pain in her brother's eyes. With a sigh, she sat down again.

'Look, I know it's difficult, Lucas. We all miss him. But even Louisa is pulling herself together.' *Not very well*, she thought. *But at least she's trying.* 'And she's certainly not snapping and snarling at everyone.' His hands were clenched together on the table in front of him. She reached over and covered them with her own. 'We don't deserve the way you've been carrying on, Lucas. It's not fair.'

He looked up, first at Jeannie and then at Ma. 'I've been an idiot, haven't I?' he sighed.

At the sink, John's snigger was cut short by an *oooff* as Peter jabbed an elbow into his twin's ribs.

'Yes, you have,' said Jeannie. 'And it's upsetting everyone, including Ma.'

'Oh,' said Ma. 'I don't blame you, son. It's just... I hate to see you like this.' Her eyes filled with tears, as they often did when she was in the grip of her nerves.

Lucas ran a hand through his hair as he let out a long sigh. 'I'm sorry. I'll sort myself out, I promise.'

'See you do,' said Jeannie, keeping her voice firm even as she wanted to cry with relief. 'Now, can I leave you to manage them,' she nodded towards the twins, 'while I go out?'

He nodded, but when she went to stand up, he touched her arm, halting her. 'Are you sure you can trust Douglas?' he asked.

'Of course. Why wouldn't I?'

He hesitated. 'I'm not sure. I worry he's taking advantage of your good nature.'

She laughed. 'As if I'd let any lad take advantage of me. I wouldn't.'

He shook his head. 'Not like that. He knows better than to try anything with you – I've already had that conversation with him.'

'You what?' she shrieked.

'Calm down. You're my little sister. Without Pa, it's up to me to make sure no lad shames you. Ask anyone with sisters. We know what lads are like, so we make sure they know not to mess with you.'

Jeannie shook her head, her emotions all over the place. She was relieved that Lucas was actually talking to them at long last; she was mortified that he'd *had that conversation* with Douglas, yet she also felt grateful that her brother cared enough about her to want to protect her, even though she didn't welcome his interference. It had been hard enough to find a sweetheart, without Lucas chasing him off before she had a chance to enjoy a little romance.

'Well, next time,' she said, 'credit me with enough sense to say no, alright?'

He shrugged. 'I know you have, sis. But, like I said, I know what lads think about. You wouldn't believe what some of them say about lasses. Half of it's lies, I'm sure, but it can ruin a girl's reputation. So any of us with any decency have to let them know our sisters are off limits.'

'Don't be angry with him,' said Ma. 'He loves you.'

Another grunt came from John. Jeannie looked over to see Peter hissing in his ear. He'd obviously stopped him from commenting on the conversation. She hid a smile, not wanting to encourage John by laughing.

'I know he does, Ma,' she said. 'But I can take care of myself. Douglas is a decent lad. He hasn't tried anything he shouldn't.'

On the walk to Douglas's cottage, she thought about that. He hadn't done much of anything at all. Douglas was friendly and polite. He let her hold his arm or he held her hand. They'd danced a couple of times at the Crispin Hall, and he'd kissed her a few times. But he'd always been a perfect gentleman, apart from one time when he'd tried to touch her and she'd made it clear she wasn't that kind of girl. He'd apologised right away and hadn't tried it again.

Lucas made it sound like lads were beasts who could barely contain their passions, but she'd never seen any evidence of it when she was with Douglas. Not like she'd seen when Mattie and Louisa were together – they practically vibrated with the need to touch each other. Sometimes their powerful feelings had been embarrassing to be around.

That thought brought her up sharp for two reasons that occurred to her at the same time. First, she realised that seeing Mattie with Louisa had made her uncomfortable, not because she was jealous and wanted him to be like that with her instead of her friend – but, in fact, it was because she'd been quite relieved that Mattie hadn't directed so much passion towards her, even though she'd been convinced she loved him.

The second thing to occur to her was that she really didn't mind that Douglas hadn't tried to act like that towards her again either. She didn't mind his rare kisses, but she had no desire to have him as desperate for her as Mattie was around Louisa.

Her steps slowed as she turned into Wilfred Road where Douglas lived. Those two revelations forced her to look into her heart. Was she walking out with Douglas because she saw him as a potential husband one day? As soon as she asked herself the question, she knew that she didn't. He was nice enough and she'd enjoyed spending time with him. But, if she were honest with herself, she might have to admit that going out with Douglas had been far more attractive to her because her friends had sweethearts and she'd been scared that she was going to be left on the shelf. It wasn't because he lit up her heart like Mattie did for Louisa. The thought of him touching her *like that* filled her with horror.

The bag she carried suddenly felt heavier. In it were the books and pamphlets Douglas had asked her to bring him. They'd had conversations about the Friends and their way of life and he'd been genuinely interested. He'd even hinted that he would like to come to the Meeting House one Sunday. 'I'd love to see what it's like,' he'd said. 'Maybe it's the way for me.'

She thought back to when he'd first asked her out, when she'd tried to refuse on account of him not being a Friend. Over the weeks they'd been seeing each other, she'd made it clear to him that she would always be a Friend and that she would only marry a Friend.

And now he's wanting to read books and come to Meetings and talking about turning his back on his own church. He's even taken me home for tea to meet his ma and pa.

She stood at the gate to his family's cottage, her heart sinking. If Douglas was seriously thinking about following Jeannie's faith, did that mean he loved her and wanted to marry her? The thought filled her with dismay.

The front door opened and he stood there. 'Jeannie, love. Don't stand out there, come on in.' He smiled and held the door wide.

With a nervous smile, she opened the gate and walked down the path, following him into the house.

'I'm so glad you're here,' he said, cupping her cheeks and kissing her.

Jeannie closed her eyes, all her attention on his lips on hers. She waited for some spark, some *joy* to fill her heart. If Douglas loved her, then her prayers for a good man to spend her life with had been answered.

But there was no spark. No joy. His lips were warm and dry and gentle, but they did nothing to heat her blood.

She opened her eyes and stepped away from his embrace. 'I brought you the books,' she said, digging into the bag and pulling them out. 'But if you're really serious about finding out about becoming a Friend, you should speak to one of the Elders or Overseers at the Meeting House. They'd be happy to guide you.'

'I am and I will,' he said. 'But I'd rather find out more from you first. After all, you're the girl who inspired me.' He smiled. 'You know I love you, don't you?'

She swallowed hard against the tightening in her throat and ignored his declaration. 'I wouldn't dream of suggesting anyone change their faith,' she said. 'It wouldn't be right. What would your parents say if they knew?'

He laughed and put an arm around her shoulders. She thought he was laughing with her, but deep down, she got the feeling that he was laughing at her, so she couldn't bring herself to join in. She looked up into his eyes, not even sure what she was looking for. He glanced down at her, but she couldn't read his expression. It was as though he was wearing a mask. Not like Mattie, who wore his heart on his sleeve for everyone to see.

'I've told Ma and Pa what I feel and they understand,' he said. He spoke softly, his tone warm and encouraging, as though he were explaining something to a child. 'They want me to be happy.'

She noticed the silence in the rest of the house. 'Where are they?' she asked.

'Gone to see my grandma in Walton. So we can enjoy some time together, just the two of us.'

As he kissed her again in his parents' front parlour, Jeannie knew with a clarity that could only come from the inner light that she didn't love Douglas and, though she liked him, she didn't want to marry him. But she also realised that Douglas's feelings for her were far stronger – so strong in fact that he was prepared to walk away from his church for her. He'd even got his parents' blessing, for goodness' sake! If she broke up with him now, he'd be devastated. She felt guilty, just thinking about it. She couldn't let him go now, could she?

Jeannie's soft heart broke as she realised that her selfish desire to have a sweetheart and be like her friends had brought her to this point. And now she had to live with the consequences.

30

'Who's that talking to Ted?' asked Louisa.

Kate looked in the direction her friend was pointing and frowned. Just outside the factory gates, Ted stood with a young man and an older gentleman. She knew he was a gentleman because he was wearing a very smart suit and wore a hat. He was leaning on a silver-topped walking stick.

'The young chap is Pierre, one of the Belgian refugees,' she said. 'Him and Ted are good pals. He's been teaching Ted French and Dutch. Not sure who the older one is. His friend's pa, maybe?'

'French *and* Dutch?' said Jeannie. 'Whatever for?'

Kate shrugged, still watching the trio. The older man was speaking to Ted while Pierre looked on. Ted was listening and nodding earnestly, focusing on what was being said, his expression serious. 'He likes it,' she said with a shrug. 'Says it's a challenge that he enjoys.'

'I'll bet he's good at languages,' said Louisa. 'He's a good mimic, isn't he? He fooled me again the other day – I thought it was my pa coming up behind me and calling out, but it was only Ted. I smacked his arm for that one.'

The factory hooter sounded, signalling the end of the dinner break, and those who were lingering outside started to move inside. Kate saw Ted shake the man's hand before the gentleman walked away up the High Street.

'Come on, Kate, or we'll be late,' called Louisa.

Kate turned towards her, expecting Jeannie to be rushing for the staircase to the Machine Room after Louisa, but Jeannie had stopped and was staring at something. As she drew level with her, Kate looked in the same direction and saw Douglas standing very close to Doris Lambert. They were laughing about something and he was bending towards her, his hand on her waist, whispering something in her ear. They looked far too cosy for Kate's liking. She glanced at Jeannie, who looked confused.

'Come on,' she said, grabbing her arm and pulling her inside. 'Or we'll be running up to the third floor instead of walking, just so Mr Briars don't dock our wages. I don't fancy spending the afternoon all sweaty, thank you very much.'

Jeannie followed her, saying nothing.

'You alright, Jeannie?' Kate asked as they reached the top and clocked back in.

Jeannie nodded, looking thoughtful. 'He doesn't laugh like that with me,' she said.

'I'm surprised he seems so friendly with Doris. I mean, she's a flirt, no doubt about it. But she's not the sort of girl a decent lad would want to take home to meet his ma, is she?'

They reached their machines. Louisa was already working, not even looking up. That was all she seemed to do these days – work, eat, sleep. Not that she seemed to be eating much. She'd been pale and wan since Mattie left, only brightening up when she read a letter from him. Like he'd promised, he wrote every day. Kate was sure it was the only thing keeping Louisa going.

Jeannie sighed as she switched on her machine and picked up the next set of linings to stitch. 'Maybe not. But they seemed to be enjoying themselves. He's always so serious with me, like it wouldn't be right to have some fun.'

Kate leaned around Louisa to study her expression. 'If you're not happy with him, you should break it off, Jeannie. There's no point walking out with a misery guts, especially if he's getting his entertainment from the likes of Doris.'

Louisa, catching her last word, looked from one to the other. 'What about Doris?' she asked. 'Has she been picking on you again?'

Jeannie shook her head. 'No, I haven't spoken to her. But she was outside, laughing and whispering with Douglas. He had his hand on her waist.'

'What?' Louisa looked outraged. 'And what does he have to say for himself?'

'Nothing yet,' said Kate. 'She didn't have time to talk to him. But I'm sure Jeannie will ask him, won't you, love?'

Jeannie rolled her eyes. 'Probably.'

They settled down to work. As from this month, all three of them were on piece work, so they knew they needed to keep up their numbers, or it would reflect in their wages. Kate's pa had been rubbing his hands together at the thought of a rise in her pay, telling her she'd better not slack off or she'd feel the back of his hand. Not wanting yet another beating, Kate knew she needed to knuckle down. It burned her guts like acid to know that every penny she earned would go into Pa's pockets. He threw a few shillings at her to buy their food, then ate most of that as well. She'd had a piece of stale bread for her dinner, while Pa went into the canteen and bought himself a hot meal. She felt a wash of shame again, remembering the pity in her friends' faces when they'd seen what she had, both of them immediately offering her some of their food. She'd felt so sick with humiliation that she'd just smiled and refused, saying truthfully, she wasn't hungry anyway.

She hoped Jeannie was as calm as she seemed to be about seeing Douglas and Doris getting so chummy. That girl wasn't popular as she regularly flirted with lads, not caring whether they had a sweetheart or – so she'd heard – even a wife. She knew that Doris's brother Sid worked with Ted and Lucas in the Cutting Room and both lads had warned Kate and her friends to give him a wide berth. Knowing how nasty Doris could be if she got you in her sights, they'd all been happy to avoid her brother.

It worried her that Douglas was in Doris's sights. If she hadn't seen it with her own eyes, she'd have been hard pressed to believe he could ever bother with a girl like her when he had a lovely girl like Jeannie on his arm. But she *had* seen it, and it gave her an uncomfortable feeling about his trustworthiness. She didn't want him to break Jeannie's heart. If he did that, he'd have Kate to answer to. She'd tell him exactly what she thought of him and she wouldn't care who heard her.

She sighed as she finished another lining, took it off the machine and put it in her basket before collecting the next set of pieces. She didn't need to think much about what she was doing as she worked because she'd done the same thing, day in, day out, surrounded by the noise of three hundred machines and the smell of oil and leather and waxed thread. As a result, her mind wandered as her fingers worked.

As she worked, she remembered the gentleman that Ted had been speaking to and wondered who he might be and what business he had with Ted. It had seemed like a serious conversation, rather than an exchange of pleasantries. Ted certainly hadn't been acting like his usual charming self. He'd been sombre and thoughtful. She hoped the man hadn't been bringing bad news.

There was a crowd of men outside the gate when the girls left at the end of their shift. They looked angry and some were shouting.

'They're from the Big Room,' said Kate, recognising a few of them. 'I heard there was trouble in there.'

'They're on strike,' said one of the women nearby. 'Won't work with non-union men.'

'That's not fair,' said Jeannie. 'Not every man can afford union subscriptions. And a lot of Friends don't believe they should join anything that requires them to follow rules that might contradict their faith.'

'So we're all expected to just do what the Clarks say and not stand up for our rights like every other worker around the country?' someone demanded. 'We're on lower wages than a lot of places.'

'And higher than a lot of others,' Louisa pointed out with the authority that came from having a father who was a foreman. 'And Clarks provide a lot more benefits than most firms. We wouldn't have the

Crispin Hall, the new electric street lights, or even the Board School if it wasn't for them. And who built most of the houses in the village? I think we should be counting our blessings.'

'Huh, what would you know, young miss, apart from what you've heard your pa say?'

Louisa blushed. 'I'm a worker here too. I can think for myself, thank you very much, and I've got no complaints.'

Kate nudged her with her shoulder. 'Come on. No point in getting in an argument.'

With Jeannie standing on the other side of Louisa, the three of them walked away, skirting around the mob outside. Kate searched the crowd for anyone from the Cutting Room, but didn't see anyone she knew.

'I hope it doesn't spread to the Clickers,' she said.

'Me too. Lucas hasn't joined the union. He said there's no rush for lads to join; it's the men who are being pressured into it.'

Louisa nodded. 'There's only a handful of them in the Big Room who haven't.'

There were nearly five hundred men and boys working in the Big Room. If they all downed tools for more than a few hours, it would have an effect on every other department at the factory. Kate worried that it would affect their wages now they were on piecework. Maybe they'd have been better off sticking to day rates.

'Pa said the managers are annoyed because they wanted to set up a workers' committee so that they could deal with any disputes through that, but the union refused,' said Louisa.

'Why?' asked Jeannie. 'I thought the whole point of the union was to let the workers have their say.'

'It is, but it seems like they only want it to go through the union's appointed representatives. If Clarks talk to a committee instead and decide things with them, the union has no power, does it?'

'Are the non-union men in the Cutting Room being picked on to join the union as well?' asked Kate.

'I'm not sure,' sighed Jeannie. 'Lucas hasn't said. But he's quieter than usual. I thought he was just missing Mattie, but maybe...?'

'Ted hasn't said anything,' said Kate. 'But then again, he doesn't usually talk about work. He said it's a job, not something he wants to do for the rest of his life, so when he finishes his shift, he likes to walk away and forget it until the next shift. I've no idea whether he's joined the union or not.'

Louisa moved a bit closer to them and lowered her voice. 'I think they are picking on the men who won't sign up, from what Pa tells Ma at home. He's getting really annoyed about it, and so is Roger Clark. He was the one who offered to set up the committee. Said it was far more democratic than expecting men to kow-tow to a union.'

Kate spotted her brother Fred walking around the mob with her brother-in-law Will. 'I'm going to see what they say,' she said, nodding in their direction.

'I need to get home,' said Louisa. 'I should have another letter waiting for me.'

'And I promised Ma I'd set her hair for her,' said Jeannie. 'But let us know what they say, alright?'

'Will do. See you tomorrow.'

She ran over and joined them. 'Are you on strike?' she asked.

Fred shook his head. 'Not us. Just the Big Room are. I just hope it don't spread round the factory. If they cause too much trouble, it could cost some people their jobs. Then the only choice we'll have is to enlist if we want to feed our families. Bloody fools. I wish I'd never joined the union now.'

Kate felt a chill run down her spine. She didn't want her brothers going to war. But the news wasn't good lately. The Hun had sunk a ship called the *Lusitania*, with the loss of over a thousand lives – women and children mostly, seeking a new life in America. Then there'd been those Zeppelin airships over London. They were reporting that seven people had been killed and now everyone in the city was living in fear of more attacks. If the Allies couldn't win the war on the Continent, the Hun would be landing on English shores next. It made this dispute seem even more pointless.

The crowd roared at something the union man was saying. The three of them all glanced over, spotting Reggie Davis standing in the middle of the mob, cheering.

Kate groaned. 'Oh, no! I hope Pa don't vote to strike. If he's not working, he's not earning. I doubt he'll even give me any housekeeping money.'

'I'd say come round to ours for your meals,' said Fred, 'but I'll be in the same boat. I just hope the damned union can support us all if they want this strike so bad. From what I've heard, the management have said they'll not give in on this, so it could go on for a long time.'

Will looked grim. 'I've not joined the union and I'm already getting snide remarks. I just don't see how a union run from another part of the country can do any better negotiating with Clarks than a workers' committee.'

Fred shrugged. 'What persuaded me was the fact that the union knows what's happening in every other boot and shoe factory in the country, so they can make sure everyone gets the same rate of pay for the same job. I thought it would improve our pay and conditions.'

'I still don't see the point. There've been enough men moving to Street to work at Clarks, even if it meant taking a pay cut because they know Clarks look after their workers better than most,' Will pointed out. He nodded his head to the crowd behind them, still making their presence felt. 'That union could ruin everything with their rabble-rousing. We're under enough pressure as it is with so many lads running off to fight. We haven't got time to down tools every time the union man tells us to. At this rate, the Clark family could throw in the towel and shut the factory. Then where would we all be?'

A shiver of dread ran down Kate's spine. All of her family depended on Clarks for their livelihood. Even her brother George would be affected as his father-in-law's haulage company did a lot of work for Clarks. Without the factory, they'd all have to leave Street to find work where they could or they'd starve.

'Out on the streets, that's where. This place would become a ghost town. Surely the Clarks won't give it up?' she said, wanting some reassurance.

'Of course they won't,' said Fred. 'Although they might well suffer stiff losses between the war and the union. It could still mean some jobs being lost. But Clarks'll live on, mark my words. They've been through tough times before and survived.'

Will sighed and ran a hand down his face. 'Yeah, you're probably right,' he told Fred before turning to her. 'Sorry to have scared you, Kate, love.'

'It's alright. It's good to know what's going on.' She blew out a breath. 'I just want Pa to keep his job so I know where he is from eight 'til six and that he can't be drinking.'

They laughed at that before saying their goodbyes and heading off to their respective homes.

Someone must have persuaded Pa to go straight to the Street Inn after the meeting outside the factory, because he didn't come home for his supper. She put a plate over his sausage and mash. She could heat it up if he wanted it when he finally arrived. If not, she'd wrap up those sausages and take them to work for her dinner tomorrow. With any luck, he'd come home so drunk, he wouldn't notice.

It was still light outside when she'd finished eating and tidying up, so she decided to go for a walk. She'd not seen Ted after work, which was unusual, and she was dying to know who that stranger he'd been talking to was. She thought she might wander over to his house, see if he was around.

But when she got there, there was a motor car outside the house. It looked like an army vehicle, a fact that was confirmed when she spotted the soldier sitting in the driver's seat. A few neighbours were hanging around by their gates, chatting, their eyes trained on the Jacksons' cottage.

'What's going on?' she asked one of them.

'Don't know, lass. We think something's happened to Stan. An officer went inside to talk to 'em.'

'Oh, no!' she gasped. She wanted to run up to the front door and knock to see if Ted was alright. He must be feeling awful right now. She hoped and prayed his Ma wasn't blaming Ted for not enlisting. That would be so unfair. Ted loved his brothers, but he shouldn't be held responsible for keeping one of them alive.

She felt terrible for Mr and Mrs Jackson, too. To lose one son was bad enough, but to then lose another... it didn't bear thinking about. She wondered how many other families were suffering similar losses because of this horrible war and her heart wept for them.

'I don't think he's dead,' said one woman, staring at the house. 'They haven't drawn their curtains like you do when there's a death in the family.'

She was right. Maybe he was just injured. That would be terrible too, but not as bad as dying. That was so final. At least if he were alive, he had a chance of being healed. It might actually be a blessing in disguise, bringing him home where he'd be safe and taking the pressure off Ted to enlist.

'How long have they been here?' Kate asked, nodding towards the motorcar.

'About half an hour. I heard the motor and glanced out. It's not like we get a lot of cars round here, is it?'

That was a long time to deliver bad news. From what Kate had heard, the Ministry of War usually just sent a letter. That's what they'd done when Albert had died. So why would they send someone in person this time, when casualties in the trenches were higher than ever? They surely couldn't do that for every soldier, could they?

Kate was getting more and more confused. She knew she shouldn't hang around. Much as she wanted to, she couldn't go and knock on the door, not now. She felt bad, waiting around and listening to gossip. But she was worried about Ted. What should she do? Would knocking on the door be wrong? She was his girlfriend, after all. A couple of the neighbours who'd seen her with Ted encouraged her, no doubt hoping she'd come out and tell them everything. *Well, that's not happening*, she thought. *It's none of their business. If the Jacksons want people to know, they'll tell them themselves. But I do want to make sure Ted's alright.*

She approached the gate and hesitated, still unsure. But before she could move, the front door opened. Ted was showing out a man in uniform, his father standing behind him. The officer saluted them before turning and heading for his car. Kate moved away from the gate to get out

of his way. The driver got out and ran round the car to open the door
for him.

'Kate.' Ted spotted her and beckoned her in. 'What are you doing
here?' he asked as he guided her into the house and closed the door
behind them.

'I... Pa wasn't home and I fancied a walk. I saw the car and the neighbours thought... Is everything alright?'

'We've been better, lass,' said Ted's father. 'But it could be a damned
sight worse.'

Kate startled. She'd forgotten he was there. 'Mr Jackson, sorry, I didn't
mean to intrude.'

He shook his head, looking weary. 'Don't fret, lass. I know them busy-
bodies out there are no doubt conjuring up all sorts of stories about why
a car pulled up outside our house, but they can carry on guessing as far
as I'm concerned. But I expect Ted will want to explain what he can to
you.' Father and son shared a look for a moment. Kate had no idea what
was going on, but as serious as they looked, she was relieved that neither
of them seemed in the throes of grief, and she couldn't hear anything
from Mrs Jackson beyond the sound of her washing up some crockery in
the kitchen, so it couldn't have been the worst news. 'I'll be in the kitchen
with your ma. You and Kate can have the parlour.'

'Thanks, Pa.'

Ted led her to the settee and sat next to her. It was a nice room, with
crisp white antimacassars on the chair backs and doilies under the orna-
ments on the sideboard. It smelled of beeswax and the fresh flowers on
the mantlepiece. The Davis house had been as nice as this when Ma had
been well. Kate tried her best, but with no money, no energy and nothing
but hindrance from Pa, it was an impossible task.

'D'you want a cuppa?' he asked.

She shook her head. 'What's happened, Ted?'

He sat back. Kate was perched on the edge of her seat, nervous about
what he was going to say. He held out his arm and gave her a serious look.
'Can we cuddle while I tell you? I need you to keep my head straight.'

'Oh, you daft ha'p'orth,' she said, but she moved closer and snuggled
into his embrace. 'Now spit it out.'

He took a deep breath and blew it out. 'It's been a day of it, I can tell you. Did you hear about the strike?'

'Yes, but I'm not interested in that. What was that officer doing here? Is Stan alright?'

Another sigh. 'Not really. But he's alive, which is what's important right now.'

'Is he hurt?'

He nodded, pulling her closer and resting his chin on her hair as he liked to do. 'Yeah, he's hurt. He's broken, Kate. He finally snapped. His company had been under bombardment for days and they all had the jitters, but Stan was the worst. He climbed out over the top while he should've been on guard duty and tried to get through the barbed wire between our trenches and the Huns. He was convinced he could hear Albert calling out to him to come and get him. But he couldn't get through and someone saw him and dragged him back. He was so upset they wouldn't let him go to save his brother, he tried to fight them. He lost his rag when they told him Albert was dead and he'd been imagining things.'

'The poor man.'

'It gets worse,' he said. 'Apparently, he ran off – went behind the lines this time, thank God, into some woods. An officer sent a couple of men after him to bring him back. They caught up with him just as he was about to hang himself from a tree with his belt.'

'Oh, no!' Kate cried. 'Please tell me they stopped him.'

He nodded again. When he spoke again, his voice was thick with emotion. 'They were his pals, comrades in arms. There was no way they were going to let him do that to himself. They saved him and had to tie him up to stop him running again. Got him to a hospital unit. The nurses patched him up – he was scratched and bloody from the barbed wire, and the doctor sedated him. He's diagnosed psy...' He frowned. 'Yeah, *psychosis*, that's the word, brought on by something they're calling "shell-shock".'

'I've never heard of that,' she said. 'But it sounds serious.'

'It is. The Major explained it's a new term the medical people have just started using. Men suffering from it end up in an asylum.'

She held onto him, not knowing what to say for a bit. She'd never been to an asylum, but she'd heard they were frightening places. He clung to her, not speaking either. She couldn't imagine how dreadful it was for Ted and his parents right now. And for poor Stan, of course.

'Will he get better?' she asked eventually.

He shrugged. 'They don't know. To be honest, I don't know whether his comrades did him a favour saving him. The army are talking about putting him on trial for desertion and cowardice. If they did, he could face a firing squad.'

She pulled away from him in order to see his face. 'Tell me you're joking. They can't do that! Hasn't he suffered enough?'

His face was deadly serious. 'He has. But the top brass can't afford to let men think they can desert without consequences, no matter how badly they're suffering. That's what the Major just told us. But don't worry. They won't be using my brother as an example.' His expression had hardened as he said the words.

'Are you sure? I mean, they sent an officer here. They didn't even do that when Albert...'

'And they wouldn't have done that this time, if it weren't for Pierre's uncle.'

Kate frowned. 'Pierre, your Belgian friend? I saw you with him at dinner time, talking to a man in a suit.'

He nodded. 'His uncle. Turns out he's an important man. Works with the British Government on behalf of the Belgian Government in exile. Pierre told him he was teaching me the languages and that I was doing a good job of 'em. He came to visit Pierre and to test my skills. Spoke to me in Dutch and French the whole time. I didn't think he could speak English until he switched to our language to tell me I was a very clever young man with a great gift for communicating.' He gave her a half-smile. 'Me, a daft Clicker who left school at fourteen.'

'You are clever,' she said, touching his chest. 'You've got an ear for voices.'

He scratched his cheek. 'Yeah, well. Turns out Pierre's uncle went straight off to find a telephone and made some phone calls. That Major was here as much to see me as to talk about Stan. But I can't tell you about that.'

'Why not? I don't understand.'

He pulled her against his chest, cuddling her close. 'I know you don't. I don't know if I do yet. But the truth of it is, I can't tell you anything else, so please don't ask.'

'Why not?' she repeated.

'I mean it, Kate. The Major said it all has to be kept hush-hush as lives are at stake, the most important to me being my brother's. They've given me a way to make sure he'll be safe in a hospital and won't face trial.'

The dread she'd felt when he was telling her about what had happened to poor Stan came back ten-fold. 'Tell me. I won't tell a soul, I swear, but I have to know, Ted.'

He look down and studied her face. 'I'm sorry, Kate. But I can't tell you the ins and outs of it. I had to sign a paper. All I can tell you is I'm enlisting. The Major promised me that if I do this, they'll go easy on Stan. Move him home where he can get help. Otherwise, he'd be sure to face a firing squad.'

'That's blackmail, pure and simple. They can't do that!'

He shrugged. 'They can. They already did. I signed the papers tonight and I'm to report for duty in three days' time.'

'No! You can't enlist,' she said. 'What about your ma and pa? You're their only son left intact! You can't leave now.'

He stroked her cheek, still holding her tight. 'They know I have to go.'

She began to tremble. 'No, Ted. How could they be so cruel?' She wasn't sure whether she was talking about the army or his parents.

He kissed her forehead. 'War is cruel, darling. But I have to go. If it's the only way to bring Stan home, then I have to do it.'

'But it's so dangerous.'

He rested his forehead on hers. 'I know. But if what I do can help shorten this damned war, then isn't that a good thing? It might save more lads from ending up like Albert or Stan.'

She began to cry, knowing that his mind was made up. 'Three days?' she asked.

'Three days,' he nodded, looking grim.

She clung to him, not wanting to let him go. 'You'll be in basic training first, won't you? That's ten weeks, like Mattie's doing. You'll overlap with him. D'you think you'll see him at the camp?'

He hesitated. 'I dunno. I don't know where they'll be sending me. There's lots of camps training soldiers right now.'

'They said this damned war would be over by Christmas, and now it's nearly summer again and they're still fighting.'

Ted sighed. 'I don't think it's going to end any time soon. Not unless we can find better ways to defeat the Hun. They're using nasty tricks these days.'

'Like poison gas. What if you're gassed?' She felt sick at the very thought. 'Oh, God, Ted. I wish you didn't have to go.'

He sighed. 'It is what it is, Kate. No point trying to fight it. I've got to go and that's that. I'll have to deal with whatever happens when it happens. If I go out there fretting about all the things that might occur, I'll be joining Stan in the asylum before long.'

Kate couldn't look at him. Her mind was a whirl of thoughts – most of them fearful. *What if he's killed like his brother? What if he goes mad like the other one? How will I cope without him being around to cheer me up when Pa upsets me again?* She didn't dare say any of it. She buried her face in his chest, breathing in the now familiar scent of him.

'Will you write to me?' she asked. 'So I know you're alright? I'll write to you every day, I promise.'

She sensed a change in him. As though he'd made a decision – another decision, for he'd made the biggest decision of all tonight to risk his life to save his brother's. She felt his hands move to her shoulders and force her back, so that they weren't touching. She sat back, confused.

'Ted?' she asked.

He stood up and took a couple of steps away towards the hearth, then he turned and looked in her direction. 'I don't think that's a good idea, Kate,' he said.

She realised he wasn't looking at her, but rather at a spot on the wall behind her. His jaw was set and he looked tense. 'It doesn't have to be every day,' she said, assuming he was worried about committing to regular correspondence. 'I mean, I can do that. But I know you'll be busy. So, maybe you could drop me a line every week or so?'

He closed his eyes and shook his head. 'That's not what I meant,' he said, dragging a hand down his face. 'Look, Kate. You're a lovely lass and we've had some good times together. But I have no idea how long I'm going to be away. I think we should call it a day now. Then you can find another lad and I won't have to worry about upsetting you because I haven't written to you.'

She wasn't sure she had heard him right. 'Don't you want any letters?'

He squeezed his eyes shut, as though he was in pain. Then he opened them again and looked straight at her. 'There's no point,' he said. 'Even if I survive the war, I'm not sure I want to come back to Street. Haven't I always said I don't see myself working at Clarks all my life? Well, I think maybe now is the time to draw a line and leave Street behind.'

She felt as though a rock had landed in her stomach. 'Ted, are you breaking up with me?'

For a moment, she thought he was going to deny it. She hoped he'd laugh and tell her not to be so daft. She knew she wasn't the prettiest or the sweetest lass. But her and Ted understood each other – at least, she'd thought they did. Maybe she didn't know him at all.

When he didn't say anything, she stood up and faced him. 'What have I done?'

'Nothing,' he sighed. 'I just don't want to be tethered to this place. I want to see the world, make something of myself. This is my chance.'

'And you think I'd hold you back by writing a few lines with news of home?'

He shrugged. 'I don't want you waiting around, expecting me to come back.'

She blew out a breath, wishing the weight in her stomach would go away. 'Has it ever occurred to you that I might want to get out of here as well? I mean, what have I got to keep me here apart from a drunken brute of a father?'

He frowned. 'You've got your brothers and sister and friends.'

'Who all have their own lives and families,' she pointed out, her anger rising, burning away the hurt. 'I thought we were...' She shook her head and turned away. 'I thought you understood, Ted. But you don't, do you? You're running away as fast as my brothers and sister did.'

Out of the corner of her eye, she saw him raise a hand towards her, but then he dropped it again. She waited, wanting him to say something, anything, that told her he cared.

'I'm sorry, Kate,' he said eventually. 'I didn't mean to hurt you. But I won't make promises I'm not sure I can keep. You need to get on with your life.'

He sounded really sad, but that was no consolation. In fact, Kate didn't think he was sorry at all. He'd probably been trying to think of a way to break up with her for weeks and this was the perfect excuse.

'I thought we were friends,' she said. 'But now I'm thinking maybe I should be apologising to you. You didn't have to hang around me out of pity, you know. I'm not so pathetic I can't look after myself. I thought we were helping each other with our grief. I didn't realise you couldn't wait to get away from me. You only had to say.' She huffed out a bitter laugh, holding up her hand when he went to speak. 'No, let me say this. I should've realised, shouldn't I? A bright lad like you with lots of dreams wasn't ever going to be satisfied with Reggie Davis's lass, were you?'

He hung his head and shook it. 'Kate. It's not...' He rubbed at his eyes. 'I can't... Look, I'm sorrier than I can say. I wish it could be different, but—'

'But nothing, Ted Jackson. That's what we've got. Nothing. All these months, you've just been marking time, haven't you? Waiting to get away from here, from me.' She moved towards the front door. 'Well, more fool you. If you'd just said, been honest, I'd not have bothered you.' She put her hand on the doorknob and took a deep breath. She turned and looked at him, pride keeping her hurt and despair hidden. 'You do what you have to do, Ted. I hope Stan gets better and it was all worth it.' She paused, wanting to cry, to beg him not to go, not to leave her – not like this. But she couldn't. Her pride was all she had left. Instead, she took a deep breath and opened the door. 'Stay safe,' she whispered as she slipped out and closed it behind her.

She didn't even notice whether any of the neighbours were still hanging around outside. She didn't cry, not even when Pa got home later that evening in a foul mood and hit her just because he could.

The realisation that everyone she loved always left her hardened her heart. She'd thought Ted was different. But he wasn't.

I'll never rely on anyone else ever again, she decided. *The only person I can rely on is myself. Love is a fool's game. I'll never trust another man as long as I live.*

31

June was hot and dry, but Jeannie's usually sunny friends were both different girls at the moment, brought low by worry and hurt. Kate's Ted had gone off in early May and no one had heard a word from him. His mother continued to hand out white feathers, although in the village, Ted's departure was hardly noticed what with all the fuss there had been around the Big Room strike at the same time. The unions had underestimated Clarks, resulting in a very public exchange of stern letters in the *Central Somerset Gazette* between Messrs Page and Lavers, the union men, and Mr Roger Clark under the heading that said:

Street Factory Strike Fiasco

The men had gone back to work after a week when Page and Lavers and the dozen other union officials at the factory were forced to sign a non-molestation agreement that Clarks had insisted upon to protect the non-union men. They also had to agree not to strike without proper negotiation and at least seven days' notice of action. Strikers didn't go unpunished, either. They lost three weeks' worth of allowances Clarks had been paying them voluntarily under the war bonus provisions, which didn't help the union's cause.

Kate had been disinclined to talk about Ted, saying only that they'd decided not to bother waiting for each other and no, she wasn't going to be writing to him. She seemed angry, but wouldn't discuss it. Instead, she followed Louisa's lead and focused on her work, increasing her numbers, much to the approval of Mr Briars, the foreman.

Louisa was counting the days until Mattie came home on leave, while fretting that, once those few days were over, he would be sent off to the trenches. Stories of poisonous gas attacks, relentless bombardments and horrific conditions were floating around, contradicting the positive tone of the government communiques reported in the newspapers. Jeannie didn't know what to believe. All she did know was that war was cruel and wrong and solved nothing.

With both of her friends being without their sweethearts, Jeannie was inclined to spend more time with them, like in the days before Mattie and Ted had come into their lives. Douglas didn't seem to mind; in fact, he seemed to encourage it.

'It must be hard for them,' he'd said. 'I can't understand why the lads have gone off like that, especially Mattie Searle. You know, the more I study the Quaker way – and especially the Peace Testimony – the less I want to have to do with this war.' He'd smiled at her fondly. 'I'm so glad I've got you to guide me, Jeannie. You're changing my life. I love you so much.'

She'd smiled, unable to return the sentiment in all honesty, even though he'd sworn that she'd been completely wrong about what she'd seen when she'd asked him about Doris. He insisted he was holding Doris away from him, not caressing her, and he'd been especially attentive to Jeannie ever since. When he'd talked about her changing his life, she'd been dismayed and a little embarrassed that he was giving her so much credit. All she'd done was lend him some literature and then introduced him to one of the Overseers at the Meeting House. Douglas had begun to attend Meetings, beaming at her across the room as he sat down to begin the silent worship.

She'd noticed, though, that he would soon grow bored as everyone bowed their heads and looked within themselves, seeking the inner light. She didn't like to be unkind towards anyone, but she couldn't help telling her friends about how she was sure Douglas had dozed off at last Sunday's Meeting when the three girls gathered one evening in the late sun by the River Brue.

'I swear, his head was starting that funny bobbing motion you see when some folks can't stay awake in the silence.' She demonstrated, slowly dropping her head forward until it reached a certain point, then pulling up sharply with a startled look on her face. Kate and Louisa giggled. 'Then one of the Friends near him stood up and called out, "Friends, the spirit compels me to share my thoughts with you!" Well, I'm not joking, poor Douglas nearly fell off the bench,' she laughed. 'The look on his face was priceless. Maybe I should've warned him that happens sometimes.' She covered her mouth with her hand. 'Am I being cruel?' she asked. 'I know that worshipping with Friends is harder to get used to for people who aren't born to it. But it was hard not to laugh at the time.'

'I never thought Douglas Baker would end up joining the Friends,' said Kate, looking thoughtful. 'From what I hear, he was never what you'd call enthusiastic about church.'

'Well, he hasn't joined us yet. He's what we call an Attender. To join the Quakers, he needs to get the approval of the Elders.'

'Do you think they will give it?'

She shrugged, combing her fingers through the grass around her. 'He seems to be trying hard to impress them. But you never know with the Elders. They'll be watching him, looking for signs that he's sincere in his desire to become a Friend.'

'Are *you* sure he's sincere?' asked Kate. She was lounging on her side, propped up on her elbow. She'd picked some buttercups and had fashioned them into a garland which now rested on her head.

'I wondered that as well,' said Louisa as she lay on her tummy, resting her head on her hands. 'I didn't want to say anything because you seemed to be getting on so well. But, well, I know Mattie was suspicious of him.'

'So was Ted,' said Kate.

Jeannie frowned. Lucas was as well, but she put that down to him being her big brother and not trusting any lad who came near his sister. 'Why?' she asked. 'Has Lucas been turning them against him?'

Louisa looked at Kate, who grimaced. 'No. Although we know Lucas is worried. It's just they thought it was odd that he'd never talked to you before and was suddenly keen to court you. Someone suggested he was hedging his bets in case they brought in conscription.'

Jeannie groaned. 'Does Lucas think that as well?'

They nodded.

'Yet not one of you thought to talk to me about it until now.' She sat up straighter, put her hands on her hips and glared at them. *And none of you can believe a nice-looking lad might actually find me attractive enough to want to pursue me.*

The girls squirmed as though reading her thoughts. 'Sorry, love,' said Kate. 'We knew you liked him and we might have been wrong. We didn't want to upset you. But, to be honest, since we saw him talking to Doris, I've had serious doubts about that lad. I know he explained himself to you, but anyone who's chummy with that trollop isn't likely to be having decent thoughts, now, is he?'

'Has he tried anything with you?' asked Louisa. 'You know, touching and stuff?'

Jeannie blushed. 'Only once. He tried to feel my bosoms, but I slapped him away.'

'Dirty beggar,' muttered Kate. 'What happened?'

She shrugged, not really wanting to talk about it. 'I just told him I wasn't that sort of girl and if that's what he was after, he should find someone else.'

'Did he get annoyed?' asked Louisa.

She shook her head. 'Not really.' Now she thought about it, he seemed a bit fed up for a brief moment. Then he seemed to pull himself together and apologised. She looked at her friends. 'He hasn't tried anything since. In fact, we don't even kiss much. I thought it was because he respected me, but...' The memory of his encounter with Doris at the factory seemed to rise up between the three friends.

'But maybe he's getting his fun from the likes of Doris instead,' said Kate, looking disgusted.

Jeannie was beginning to wonder about that. 'I don't think he is. I mean, it doesn't make sense,' she said, frowning. 'If he's gallivanting with

Doris, why bother courting me? It's not like I'm going to act like her, even if we were married. I mean' – her blush deepened – 'I know he'll expect certain things in the privacy of our marriage bed, but I'm not going to turn into a flirt and be all over him in public, even if that's what he wants.'

'He doesn't deserve you, Jeannie,' said Kate.

Louisa sat up on her knees and put her hand on her shoulder. 'Jeannie, love, if you were really keen on him, you'd be more inclined to want to flirt and mess around with him, so maybe you're not as fond of him as you thought. I know Mattie thinks he might be using you to get approval from the Elders. Maybe he thinks if he's courting a Quaker, the Elders would be more likely to accept his sudden interest in becoming a Friend? If the government brings in conscription like everyone says they will, and he can claim to be a Friend, he might manage to get out of fighting.'

'But that's daft!' she said. 'It might never happen. He's been courting me for months. How do we know he's not genuine in his belief in the Peace Testimony?'

'We don't know,' said Kate. 'But he's not daft. He's seen dozens of lads from round here going off to fight, and some of them have come back wounded and others will never return. Mrs Jackson and the others in the White Feather Movement are seeking out lads like Douglas and putting pressure on them to enlist. Right now, there's nothing they can do to force him, but I'm betting he's hedging his bets and trying to make it look like he's sincere about being a Friend and a pacifist so he doesn't end up in trouble when conscription comes in. And let's face it, everywhere you look now there's recruitment posters and recruiters are turning up at dances and theatres, urging lads to enlist. With all the casualties, the army's desperate to keep up the supply of soldiers to fill the trenches. Douglas strikes me as the sort who would take it all in, realise what's to come and make a plan to keep himself out of it.'

Jeannie sighed, putting her head in her hands.

'But you never know, we might be wrong,' said Louisa, patting her shoulder and trying to look cheerful. Jeannie wasn't fooled, though. 'We might all have misunderstood what was going on with Doris,' she went on. 'He might be so in love with you he's prepared to change faith and wait for marriage before he...'

'Has his wicked way with her?' Kate smirked. 'That might be the case. But somehow, I doubt it. You can't trust any lad these days.'

Jeannie looked up to see that Kate was scowling as she said that.

'Kate, I've got to ask. What did Ted do? You've been dead set against men since he went away. What happened?'

Her scowl deepened. 'He did nothing like that. He just wasn't honest with me, that's all. I felt like a fool when I realised. He hung around me out of pity. I won't be taken for a ride like that again, I can tell you.'

'I'm so sorry,' said Jeannie. She was surprised by that. Ted had always seemed like a decent sort.

'Anyway, forget about him. He made his choice. He's gone and that's that. It's you and Douglas we need to be worrying about. If he's taking you for a ride, Jeannie, I'll have words with that lad, that's for sure.'

Jeannie lay back on the grass and looked up at the sky. It was still warm even as the sun was slowly beginning to go down. There wasn't a cloud to be seen. The air was filled with the sound of the swallows rushing through the warm air above them to feed on the insects over the fields before the light failed. It was nearly midsummer, so it would stay light for another hour or so, but she was tired and thought she ought to get up and go home before then.

She sighed. The things her friends were saying were no more than she was already beginning to suspect. She just didn't know what to do about it. If they were wrong and she confronted Douglas, she could hurt him a lot and that was the last thing she wanted. But if they were right, she really didn't want to have anything to do with someone who could be so dishonest as to take advantage of her good nature to finagle his way into the Friends in order to avoid being called up. It occurred to her that, if Douglas and lots of other lads did that, it would soon become evident and the government might renege on their agreement that genuine Friends and pacifists could expect to have their beliefs taken into account and they would not be forced to fight.

'He says he loves me,' she said. 'What if he really does? Surely he wouldn't lie about something like that, would he? And if he thought I didn't trust him, he might get really upset. How can I know for sure whether he's truly in love with me or just using me?'

Kate scoffed. 'Love is as love does,' she said. 'If he truly loved you, he wouldn't be sniffing round the likes of Doris, would he? He'd want to spend all his spare time with you.'

'It was only that one time,' said Jeannie, still trying to think the best of him.

Kate scoffed. 'That we know of. If he was getting chummy with her in front of everyone at the factory, what's he getting up to in private? He could be with her right now and you wouldn't know it.'

Louisa glared at Kate before turning to Jeannie. 'The question you should be asking yourself is, how do you feel about Douglas? Do you love him?'

She hesitated, remembering how she'd felt when he'd said he loved her. That seemed answer enough for her friends.

'So why are you staying with him?' demanded Kate.

Jeannie sighed and shook her head. 'I don't know. He's kind to me, makes me feel pretty. No one's ever paid that much attention to me before.'

'But he doesn't make you tingle, does he?' said Louisa, no doubt thinking of Mattie. 'You don't feel like you want to be with him all the time.'

Jeannie observed her friend's dreamy expression and felt a wave of envy that she quickly suppressed. Even though she'd admired Mattie for years, she'd never felt that *tingle* that had Louisa in its thrall, and she certainly didn't feel it with Douglas. 'No,' she admitted.

'Oh, Jeannie, love. No lad's worth hanging around with if he doesn't make you feel like that.'

Jeannie closed her eyes and covered them with her arm, blaming the low sun in her face for the tears that threatened. 'What else was I supposed to do when you two were courting and I was left with no one?'

'And look how much good that's done us,' said Kate. 'Both been deserted by our lads.'

'Mattie will be back soon,' said Louisa.

'Well, Ted won't.'

'Don't say that, Kate,' said Jeannie, sitting up to look at her friend.

'Please. We're all praying for his safety. I'm sure he'll be back when he can.'

Kate shook her head. 'No, he won't. He told me. He said he wanted more out of life than to be stuck in Street. He's not intending to come back here again, no matter what.'

'Surely he'll come back to visit his ma and pa?' said Jeannie.

'Maybe,' she shrugged. 'But he won't be staying and he won't be coming to see me.'

'Is that why you're so angry?' asked Louisa.

She shrugged, not looking at either of them. 'That, and Pa. I'm sick of being at his beck and call and getting nothing but abuse for my trouble.'

Jeannie wanted to comfort her friend, to offer her a solution. But she had no idea how Kate would ever get out from under her pa's influence. He was a bully and a thoroughly unpleasant and violent man, but until Kate was twenty-one, he had absolute power over her. It worried her sometimes that she might not survive that long. They were seventeen now, so she had nearly four years before she could claim her independence.

'I'm sorry, Kate,' she said, not knowing what else to say. 'Is there anything we can do?'

Kate shook her head. 'Don't worry about me. It's you we need to sort out. If you don't love Douglas, why are you staying with him? Especially now the two of us are on our own.' She pointed between herself and Louisa. 'We don't need a lad sniffing around any of us if it's not going anywhere, do we?'

'Speak for yourself,' said Louisa, looking annoyed. 'Mattie might not be here right now, but he's still my sweetheart and we'll be together forever when this damned war is over.'

Kate rolled her eyes. 'Good for you. But that don't mean me and Jeannie have to put up with any old dog who just wants to use us, does it?'

'I suppose not,' Louisa conceded. She looked thoughtful as she studied Jeannie's face. 'Please be careful with Douglas, Jeannie. Like Kate says, love is as love does.'

'I know,' she sighed. 'I'll think on it. When I'm away from him, I can see that what we have isn't what I want and isn't likely to go anywhere and I'm determined to end it. But when I'm with him, he's so sweet and kind that I can't bring myself to say anything because I'm sure it would really hurt him.'

'Which is exactly what he wants,' said Kate. 'He's making sure he keeps you sweet. Don't trust him, Jeannie.'

'Like I said, I'll think on it. We're supposed to be going to the next dance at the Crispin Hall on Saturday. Maybe I'll be able to decide by then.'

'I think we should go as well,' said Louisa. 'Then we can keep an eye on you.'

'I can't,' said Kate, scowling. 'I've no money and nothing to wear.'

Louisa nudged her with her shoulder. 'You can borrow something of mine and I'll treat you. It's nearly your birthday, isn't it?'

'Oh, do come, Kate,' said Jeannie before she could protest. 'Knowing the two of you are there will give me some courage if Doris starts in on me again.'

That seemed to decide it. Kate nodded and the three friends made plans to go to the dance.

* * *

Louisa rushed into the Machine Room the next day as the others were switching on their machines.

'You'll never guess!' she told them, joy radiating from her. 'Mattie says he's written to Pa, asking if we can get married when he's home on leave! He said he can't wait any longer.' She did a little dance around their bench. 'I'm so excited!'

'Time to work, Miss Clements,' Mr Briars' voice boomed across the benches.

Louisa giggled. 'Sorry, sir,' she called back, sitting down and switching on her machine.

'Congratulations,' said Jeannie. She was relieved to realise she meant it sincerely. 'I'm so happy for you, Lou.'

'You've not got a lot of time to plan a wedding,' said Kate.

Louisa waved a hand as though batting away her remark. 'We'll manage. Me and Ma will get our heads together when I get home tonight.'

'So your ma and pa have agreed?'

Louisa shrugged as she picked up her work and fed it into the machine. 'I don't know if Pa's even seen the post yet. He'd left for work before me. I read my letter on the way here. I had to stop in the middle of the street and read it again. I couldn't believe it. I'm so happy.'

Kate glanced over at Jeannie, who realised she was probably thinking the same thing that she was.

'Lou, love. Are you sure your pa's going to agree to this? I mean, you're not even eighteen yet, and who knows how long Mattie's going to be away?'

'Of course he'll agree. He told me he respected Mattie, didn't he? It's obvious how much we love each other. What's the point of waiting?'

Jeannie wasn't so sure. Given Mr Clements's objections to Mattie being a Friend, she had a horrible feeling he wouldn't be quite so happy as Louisa was about this plan. But maybe she was wrong.

'Will you get married at Holy Trinity?' she asked.

Louisa frowned. 'I expect so. I hope that's alright with Mattie's family. We'll have to see the vicar tonight and arrange to have the Banns read. He'll be home at the beginning of July, so there's no time to lose.'

Kate grimaced. 'Lou, don't get your hopes up, love. The vicar wouldn't agree to our Peg marrying Will unless he agreed to take a course of instruction and got confirmed. That's why they got wed at the Meeting House.'

'Then we'll do the same,' said Louisa. 'Me and Ma can go and see Mrs Searle and work out what we need to do.'

They worked steadily through the day, Louisa bubbling over with excitement and plans. She thought she'd probably stay at her parents' house until Mattie came home for good, then they'd live with Mattie's ma. She'd carry on working until he got home – 'There's no point in being a housewife if my husband isn't home every night.' She was so sure that it would all work out that neither Jeannie nor Kate had the heart to question it.

* * *

Louisa's dreams all came crashing down around her that evening when her parents refused point blank to agree to Mattie's proposal.

'No daughter of mine is going to have a rushed wedding,' said Ma. 'What will people think? You'll wait until the war's over and have a proper do, and that's the end of it.'

When she protested that she didn't want a fancy wedding, Pa said she was too young to know what she wanted. They argued back and forth for what seemed like hours, but her parents wouldn't be moved.

'I'll speak to Mrs Searle tomorrow,' said Pa. 'She'll agree with us. You're both too young and it would be foolish to rush into this. No, Louisa, if you still want to marry this lad after the war, we'll discuss it again. But the matter is closed now. You can see Matthew when he comes home on leave, but there'll be no wedding.'

32

'You need cheering up,' said Kate. 'And, lord knows, so do I.'

After learning that they wouldn't be allowed to get married when Mattie came home on leave, Louisa had been downhearted and hadn't wanted to go to the dance after all. But Kate wasn't having any of it.

'We can't let Jeannie down,' she pointed out. 'Now we've planted the seeds of doubt, we can't just leave her to work it out for herself, can we? You know how soft she is. If Douglas starts acting all heartbroken, she might well end up agreeing to marry him, just to make him feel better.'

Louisa rolled her eyes. 'Alright. But I'm not dancing with any lads.'

'Me neither. We can dance together if we want to. There's never enough lads to go round these days, anyway. I'm more bothered about making sure Jeannie's alright.'

Louisa nodded. 'D'you think we should talk to Lucas?'

Kate shook her head. 'No. If he comes along, he'll just sit there glowering at Douglas and Jeannie will get upset with him. Then there's no telling what will happen. She might feel like she's got to defend him against her brother. We don't want that, do we?'

Louisa frowned. 'But what if he really does love Jeannie? I'd feel awful if we're telling her she should break up with him if he has real feelings for her.'

This time it was Kate who rolled her eyes. 'It don't really matter what he feels about her, does it? Jeannie doesn't love him but she's too kind to break it off. It's our duty as her friends to help her find the strength, or she'll end up trapped in a relationship she never wanted in the first place.' She sighed. 'I reckon that's what happened to Ma. She always said Pa was a real charmer when they first met. Maybe by the time he showed his true colours, they were already married and it was too late for her to get away. I don't want that for Jeannie.'

'No, neither do I,' Louisa agreed. 'Alright, we'll go to the dance and see what happens.'

* * *

It was interesting to Jeannie that, as more and more bad news came back from the front line, the mood at the Crispin dances got livelier. It was as though folks were throwing themselves into the spirit of the dance in order to forget the reality of the war. The band tonight were playing some of the Ragtime tunes that came from America and the dancers were doing all sorts of crazy steps – waving their arms around and wiggling their bottoms – and laughing like loons. She found it all so strange and a little bit intimidating.

Thankfully, Douglas wasn't a great dancer, so he was happy to sit out most of the wilder dances. Instead, they sat side by side and watched. They didn't say much as the level of noise was such that it was difficult to hold a conversation without shouting. Douglas held her hand. She wished he wouldn't because his palm was quite sweaty, but she didn't know how to pull her hand away without being rude.

Louisa and Kate were doing the Turkey Trot, throwing themselves into the dance and having a rare old time. It made Jeannie smile to see them both enjoying themselves. They'd both had such a rotten time of it lately. They saw her watching and beckoned her over, but she shook her head, not wanting to embarrass herself. While she was alright doing the basic dances like the waltz and the two-step, she didn't have the confidence to try what the girls were doing. She was sure she'd fall flat on her face and never live it down.

To her relief, Douglas let go of her hand. He leaned close so she could hear him when he said, 'I'm going to have a quick chat with my pals. D'you want another drink? Dandelion and burdock, right?' he asked.

She nodded and watched him head out to the bar where only soft drinks were served. She knew that some of the lads and lasses brought their own beer or cider to the dances, although they kept them hidden so they wouldn't be told to leave. It was always clear who was drinking what they shouldn't, though, and Jeannie made sure to give them a wide berth.

Around the hall were couples like her and Douglas. Some were dancing and having a fine time. Others were sitting at tables, gazing lovingly into each other's eyes. Some were kissing, which had shocked Jeannie at first. She had nothing against it, but she had no desire to do it in public where everyone could see. That's how girls got a bad name. It only took someone to start talking about them and word spread like wild-fire. Jeannie wasn't one to gossip, and she tried not to judge. But she also had a fear of someone talking about her, so she never let Douglas kiss her in public.

Another tune began. Douglas was taking his time bringing their drinks, but she wasn't surprised as it was busy tonight. She expected he'd be chatting for a bit, then there'd be a queue at the bar – the dancers were working up a thirst, that was for sure. She decided to visit the toilet while she waited for him. She'd probably be back before he was.

She skirted around the crowd on the dance floor, heading for the door.

'Jeannie!' called Louisa. 'Come and dance!'

She shook her head and smiled, pointing in the direction of the toilets, leaving her friends to throw themselves into the steps of the next dance. She envied them their high spirits, although she suspected both of them were putting on a good show even though life was difficult for them at the moment. She wished she could be like that, but she'd always been shy and took things seriously. Since she'd talked to them about the situation with Douglas, she'd been feeling anxious and unsure.

She reached the toilet and had to wait in line for longer than she expected. A few of the girls said hello to her and she responded in kind, but she didn't know them well enough to indulge in conversation.

Around her, they were gossiping about the couples who were canoodling in the dance hall, as she suspected they would.

Jeannie was thankful when one of the cubicles became vacant and she locked herself inside.

She could hear the girls in the queue whispering and giggling, although she couldn't make out what they were saying. She prayed they weren't talking about her, but a cold feeling of dread in her stomach told her they might be.

She had finished her business and knew she couldn't stay there much longer given the size of the queue for the facilities when she heard Kate's voice outside. With a sigh of relief, she pulled the chain, checked that she hadn't got the back of her skirt caught in her knickers, and unlocked the cubicle door.

'There you are,' said Kate, pushing her way around the little clique of gossipers to reach her side. 'Lou's gone to get some drinks. Come on.'

As she turned the corner behind Kate, her friend stopped dead. Jeannie bumped into the back of her and knew immediately why she'd halted in her tracks.

In a quiet corner, Doris Lambert was leaning against the wall, clinging to Douglas while he kissed her. Jeannie stood there, looking over Kate's shoulder as his hands wandered from Doris's waist to her bottom, pulling her closer to his body as his tongue delved into her red-painted mouth. If she'd been shocked by the couples kissing in the dance hall, that was nothing to the revulsion she felt as these two groaned and writhed against each other. They were so involved in each other that they were oblivious to anything else.

Kate glanced over her shoulder at Jeannie. 'You alright?' she asked softly.

Am I? She wasn't sure. She couldn't take her eyes off the couple, nausea rising within her.

'Breathe,' Kate whispered.

Jeannie took a shaky breath, surprised that she'd actually stopped for a moment. As she blew it out and took another one, her mind cleared. The first thing she felt was relief. The second thing was anger. She went to turn away, but as she did she noticed a tray on the window-ledge next to the couple. She realised that it held the drinks Douglas had promised to bring to their table after he'd had a *quick chat with his pals*.

Douglas groaned, one hand creeping up and squeezing Doris's ample bosom. That was all the incentive Jeannie needed to move. She stepped around Kate towards the tray, picked up the two drinks and threw them over the couple.

Doris shrieked as the cold liquid hit her. Douglas let go of her and spun around.

'Jeannie! It's not what you think!' he gasped, trying to wipe away the dandelion and burdock dripping down his hair and onto his shirt.

'So you didn't have your hands all over her and your tongue down her throat?' she responded, too angry to care that Doris's shriek had attracted an audience, including some of the girls who had been in the ladies.

'You mad bitch!' screamed Doris. 'What did you do that for?'

Kate laughed. Hearing her friend's guffaw made Jeannie giggle.

'You looked like you needed to cool down,' she said, quite proud that her voice sounded strong.

'Jeannie.' Douglas reached out a damp hand towards her but she backed away, holding her hands up.

'Don't you touch me, Douglas Baker!' she shouted, too disgusted with him to lower her voice. 'Not after you've had your filthy paws all over her.'

'But—'

'But nothing. You're a liar and a cheat and I want nothing to do with you.'

Doris touched his arm. 'You don't need her, darling. You said she was frigid anyway. You only pretended to court her so you could—'

'Shut up!' he snapped, shrugging her off, his eyes not leaving Jeannie's.

'Jeannie,' he tried again. 'I swear—'

'Don't you tell me to shut up.' Doris grabbed his arm this time, dragging him round to face her. 'You've been leading me a right dance, letting her think you liked her just so you could claim to be a Friend to get out of fighting, making me sneak around so the stupid bitch didn't catch on. And what do I get for my trouble? She tips her bloody drink over me.'

She pulled her top away from her chest. 'This is my best blouse and it's ruined!'

Behind Jeannie and Kate, the growing crowd were starting to snigger and cat-call. Douglas looked up, the realisation that his ruse had been exposed for the whole world to see clearly hitting him at that moment. Jeannie felt a moment of satisfaction as she saw his expression change.

'Just shut up, will you?' Douglas shouted, glaring at Doris. 'You stupid cow! Look what you've done now.' He turned away from everyone, his shoulders slumped.

Jeannie was glad that she finally knew the truth. She could walk away from him now with a clear conscience. He hadn't denied it and was clearly guilty. She might feel humiliated tomorrow that so many people had witnessed his betrayal when she'd had the chance to let it sink in, but right now, she felt nothing but relief.

Doris, however, clearly felt otherwise. With a snarl, she grabbed his hair and twisted, causing him to yelp as she pulled until she could see his face.

'Don't you blame me, you bloody sod! It's your fault for being such a coward. If you'd been a real man, you wouldn't have bothered with that silly mare in the first place, you'd have enlisted like anyone else.'

He tried to loosen her hands but she continued to pull at his hair, much to the amusement of the crowd as he struggled against her. 'What are you talking about? Even your brother won't enlist. Let me go, you daft mare, or so help me, I'll—'

'You'll what?' she shouted. 'Do this?' The crowd gasped as she let go of him and swung at his face. There was a horrible crunch as her fist connected with his nose and Douglas screamed.

* * *

'I can't believe I missed it,' said Louisa as the three girls stood outside the Crispin Hall. 'I was in the queue for a lemonade for so long, I had no idea what was going on until I heard Douglas scream. Did she really break his nose?'

'Yes,' said Kate. 'And he deserved it. Fancy carrying on like that while he was supposed to be there with Jeannie!'

Louisa turned to her. 'Are you alright, love?' she asked. 'It must have been a terrible shock.'

Jeannie looked into her friend's concerned face and smiled. 'I'm fine,' she assured her. 'In fact, it's a relief. I was such an idiot to have believed he really loved me. It's not as though we had anything in common, is it?'

'Not if he fancies carrying on with the likes of Doris Lambert,' said Kate. She giggled. 'Their faces when you chucked them drinks over them, that was priceless!'

Louisa looked between the two of them. 'Is that why they were wet?' she asked, sending her friends into peals of laughter as Jeannie nodded.

'I thought they needed cooling down,' she gasped through her giggles.

'Doris was not amused,' laughed Kate. 'Jeannie ruined her best blouse.' She flung an arm around Jeannie's shoulders. 'I'm so proud of you, Jeannie. You told him good and proper. Put him right in his place.'

Jeannie grinned, not in the least sorry. 'So did Doris,' she said. 'I wonder if his broken nose will spoil his good looks?'

'He'll have black eyes and bruises for sure,' grinned Kate.

Louisa shook her head, smiling at their mirth. 'Handsome is as handsome does,' she said. 'Even after his bruises fade, I've a feeling that Douglas isn't going to be quite so attractive to the girls round here from now on. Not now everyone knows what a sneaky beggar he is.'

'Come on,' said Jeannie, suddenly feeling exhausted after the high emotion of the past half hour. 'Let's get away from here before everyone else comes out. I'd better let Ma and the boys know what's happened before they hear from anyone else. No doubt the story will get exaggerated in the telling. I expect by Monday, the whole village will know about it.' She frowned. 'I hope people don't think badly of me.'

Louisa put her arm round her other shoulder so that all three friends stood together. 'Are you joking? Didn't you hear what they were saying? You're a heroine, Jeannie. No one likes a cheater. Every girl in that place thought you were right to call them two out and they're delighted Douglas got his nose broke.'

Kate nodded. 'Yeah. And between you and Doris – not that I want to give her credit for anything, but let's face it – the pair of you sorted him out good and proper and sent a message to every lad there tonight that it's not alright to mess around and lie and cheat. While none of them would have been surprised that Doris made a scene, no one expected quiet, sweet little Jeannie Musgrove to turn into an avenging angel. It'll make them think twice about how they behave with their girls from now on, you mark my words.'

Jeannie wasn't so sure until a group of girls walked past them and called out.

'Well done, Jeannie,' said one of them. She was one of the girls who'd been in the toilets. 'You can do much better than him.'

'She certainly can,' said Kate. 'So can we all, eh, girls?'

They agreed and took their leave, laughing and chatting about what a good night it had been.

'See?' said Louisa. 'You're a heroine.'

'I'm not really,' she said. 'But I can't pretend I feel bad about it. I was just so angry. If I hadn't thrown the drinks, I might have bashed him over the head with the tray.' She covered her face with her hands. 'I wanted to. I never thought I could be so violent.'

'But you didn't,' Louisa pointed out. 'Though they deserved it. So don't you go feeling guilty, Jeannie. It's them who were in the wrong.'

'I know,' she sighed, suddenly feeling deflated. 'Well, that's that. I'm single again. I don't suppose I'll ever get married now. There's not a lad for miles around who won't hear about what I did. They'll steer clear of me, that's for sure.'

Kate chuckled. 'If you standing up for yourself worries them that much, then they're not worth bothering with,' she said. 'Don't you fret, Jeannie. We don't need a lad on our arm if they're that soft.'

The friends said goodnight and headed off in different directions. Jeannie walked quickly, not wanting to be stopped by anyone. She was usually overlooked by people but she'd realised quickly that the incident tonight had thrust her into the spotlight and she was going to get a lot more attention until someone else did something daft and caught every-one's interest.

As she approached her house, she saw that the light was still on in the parlour, which meant either Lucas or Ma were waiting up for her. She sighed, knowing she had to tell them what had happened. She only hoped Lucas didn't get mad and start a fight with Douglas when he saw him.

She needn't have worried. Once Lucas had finished laughing at her deliberately comic recalling of the incident, he asked her if she was upset.

'Not at all,' she said. 'In fact, I'm relieved. I was trying to find a kind way to break up with him, but he saved me the trouble.'

'Good for you, sis,' he said. 'You deserve better than him. But if he'd broken your heart, I would've kicked his backside.'

'No need,' she giggled. 'Doris sorted him out, good and proper. He won't be fooling any other girls round here, that's for sure.'

If Doris wasn't such a nasty girl, Jeannie might have sought her out and thanked her. But, she decided, it was probably better if she left her well alone.

33

The days until Mattie got home on leave after his basic training dragged for Louisa. She couldn't sleep or eat and she could barely bring herself to be civil to her parents. It was too late now to arrange a wedding because the Banns would have to be read out in church for three weeks before the ceremony could take place. Louisa blamed her Ma for that. She didn't care that Louisa was more interested in being Mattie's wife than having some fancy wedding that would impress the neighbours.

'I'll not have my daughter getting wed in some hole-in-the-wall ceremony. I don't care if there is a war on. You know what they say: *marry in haste, repent at leisure.*'

Pa had agreed.

'I'll not be repenting,' Louisa had said. 'And I don't want a fuss.'

It wasn't strictly true. She'd dreamt of her wedding since she was a little girl. She had wanted to marry in early May so that she could have a garland of apple blossom in her hair. But now, it didn't matter. Only Mattie mattered. She missed him so much.

At last, the day arrived. Mrs Searle had been kind enough to invite Louisa to join her, Will and Peg as they walked to the railway station at Glastonbury to meet Mattie's train. Louisa had had to force herself to walk at a gentle pace so as not to rush Mattie's ma, when all she wanted to do was run as fast as she could.

Despite going at what seemed like a snail's pace, they arrived on the platform with five minutes to spare. Louisa was such a bundle of nerves, she was shaking.

'It's so good of you to let me come with you today, Mrs Searle,' she said, trying not to stare down the line to spot the tell-tale plume of steam that would signal that the train was drawing close.

'Ah, bless you, lass.' Mrs Searle patted her cheek. 'I know how much you think of my Mattie and how fond he is of you. He'll be wanting to see you the first chance there is.'

Her eyes filled with tears. 'I've missed him so much,' she said. 'I wish he was coming back for good.'

Mrs Searle nodded, her smile sad. 'You and me both, lass. You'll come back to the cottage with us? Me and Peg have put on a fine spread to welcome him back.'

'If that's alright?'

'Of course it is,' said Peg in the same no-nonsense tone that Kate often used. 'You're practically family.'

A shrill whistle sounded and Louisa thought she would faint. Her heart was pounding as the train pulled into the station. Almost before it had come to a halt, the doors were opening and a flood of lads in khaki flowed out onto the platform.

She didn't see him at first, there were so many people. For a moment, she panicked, afraid he hadn't come. But then he was there in front of her, dropping his duffle bag at his side as he opened his arms to her.

'Oh, Mattie! My Mattie!' She rushed into his arms, completely forgetting she had been determined to hold back while his family greeted him first. Then his arms closed round her and he was swinging her off her feet.

She laughed and cried as she clung to him and people thronged around them, breathing in the scent of him, her soul coming alive again at the feel of his body against hers. He set her back on her feet and buried his face in her neck.

'Oh, God, I've missed you,' he sighed, kissing the skin below her ear and making her tingle. Then, without letting her go, he raised his head. 'Good to see you, Ma.'

Mrs Searle rested a hand on Louisa's back as she leaned in to kiss her son over her shoulder. 'Welcome home, son.'

'Sorry, Mrs Searle,' said Louisa, feeling embarrassed. 'I'll get out of your way.' She went to move out of Mattie's arms, but he didn't let her go far. He held her tight against one side while hugging his ma with his free arm.

'My two favourite girls,' he said, his voice warm with satisfaction as he kissed his ma then turned back and kissed Louisa, holding tight to the pair of them.

'Make that three favourite girls,' said Peg, grinning at him as she leaned in between them to kiss Mattie's cheek. 'And I might let you eat the special fruit cake I made.'

Mattie's eyes lit up. 'You made me a cake?'

'She did,' said Will, who had retrieved Mattie's bag and slung it over his shoulder. 'Welcome home, little brother.' He ruffled his hair with his fist in that daft way that brothers did. 'Had to cut your mop, I see.'

Louisa had barely registered Mattie's much shorter haircut. She looked at it now and briefly mourned the loss of his lovely thick hair, but she supposed it would grow back soon enough. As he responded to his brother and answered his mother's questions about what he'd been eating, she studied him, noting the subtle differences between the boy who'd left for basic training and the soldier who had returned. He stood more upright, his jawline was sharper and – impossible as it might seem after only ten weeks – his shoulders seemed broader. As she wrapped her arms around his waist, she noticed that his body seemed harder than before. When he turned his gaze to her, his smile was the same, but... his eyes... She couldn't put a finger on it, but it seemed that while the love was still there, Mattie's boyish innocence was gone.

'Alright, love?' he asked as they began the walk back to Street. His ma was holding onto one of his arms, while he kept the other firmly wrapped around Louisa's shoulders, keeping her close. Will and Peg walked in front of them, his brother carrying Mattie's duffle.

She nodded. 'I'm so glad you're here.' She leaned her head onto his shoulder briefly. 'I'm sorry we couldn't organise a wedding in time.'

He shrugged. 'It's a shame,' he agreed. 'But no matter. I've stated my intentions now. We'll get there in the end.'

Even his voice seemed different – deeper, the words more clipped. She didn't mind. He sounded more manly and mature, more sure of himself. If her pa bothered to talk to Mattie while he was home, he'd be impressed, she was sure. She snuggled into his side, grateful he was checking his pace in consideration of his ma, who smiled at the two of them fondly as they walked along.

Other families were on the road, welcoming their sons and brothers and sweethearts home. Louisa recognised some of them and was glad to see them. But she couldn't help the dread that filled her heart as she wondered what Mattie and all these other lads would face in the coming weeks.

I mustn't think on it now, she told herself silently. *I must make the best of the time we have.*

They had a joyful time of it at the Searles' cottage and the old, teasing Mattie came to the fore as he joked with his brother and told them stories about daft things that had happened during basic training. No one talked about what came next, or asked how long he would be away for after this week. It was as though, if they didn't discuss it, time would stand still and Mattie would stay home forever.

Louisa had been in the kitchen helping Peg make some more tea when she walked into the parlour to find that Mattie had pulled his shirt off and was standing there in his vest, flexing his muscles. Mrs Searle was laughing and shaking her head as Will did the same and started posing.

'What on earth's going on?' asked Peg, trying to look stern. 'Put that away, Will Searle. You too, Mattie.'

Mattie and Will turned to them with identical grins and poses.

'Look, Peg, love,' said Will. 'Ten weeks he's been working on them muscles, but he's not a patch on me, is he?'

'I don't know about that.' Peg rolled her eyes, putting the tea tray down on the sideboard, winking at Louisa when they couldn't see her face. 'But I do know you're both as daft as each other. Now put your shirts on and sit down before the neighbours see.'

Louisa giggled, thinking to herself that Mattie definitely looked more muscly than his brother. She couldn't wait to get him alone so that she could run her hands over his wide chest and shoulders and flat stomach. Her cheeks glowed red as she helped Peg give out the cups of tea and pieces of the promised fruit cake. They'd had quite a feast for their dinner and she wasn't sure if she had any room left for cake just a couple of hours later, but she didn't want to be rude, so she accepted a small piece. She could always slip some of hers to Mattie – he was always hungry.

The afternoon was the happiest time Louisa could remember in a long time. She felt welcome in the midst of this family. It still made her heart ache that she and Mattie weren't getting married this week, but she was determined to make the most of it regardless.

Mattie was at her gate the next morning to walk her to work. It was reassuring to see him in his normal clothes instead of that awful khaki.

'Just like old times, eh, sweetheart?' he smiled.

'Not quite,' she said. 'Before, we had to sneak around to avoid my pa and didn't even dare hold hands. Now, I can hold your arm and be proud that everyone can see I'm yours.'

'Even better, then.'

'Definitely,' she beamed at him. Her smile slipped a little. 'I wish I didn't have to work this week.'

'Me too. But it can't be helped. I hear it's busy at the factory, with too few men and shortages of leather.' He sounded almost wistful.

She nodded. 'And the union causing trouble. But I don't care about any of that; I just want to keep walking with you all day and forget everything else. If I wasn't trying to earn as much as I can for my bottom drawer, I'd say to hell with it and skip off work.'

He chuckled. 'Started to fill your bottom drawer, have you? What's in it so far?'

She blushed. 'Well, you did say you'd made your intentions clear. I'm earning a bit more on piecework and Ma said she didn't want any extra for my keep, so I've been getting some little bits. Just the essentials, you know? I've got a nice tea set, some pillowcases and a tin-opener so far.'

Mattie burst out laughing.

'What's so funny?' she demanded.

He shook his head, still chuckling. 'Nothing at all, love. I'm just thinking that at least we can have a cuppa, open a tin of sardines and then have somewhere to rest our heads. I can't wait to use them.'

'Oh, you,' she giggled, poking him in the ribs. 'My ma always said you need to be able to feed and water your man, then he'll need his rest.'

'Sensible woman, your ma.'

Louisa scowled. 'Too sensible. If she wasn't, we'd be getting wed right now. I'm so cross about that I could spit.'

'Aw, come here.' He wrapped his arm around her shoulders and pulled her close, kissing her temple. He took no notice of the people around them as they passed The Cross, all walking in the direction of the factory. 'I'm disappointed about that as well. I want nothing more than to make you my wife. But I reckoned this might happen. I mean, your pa's hardly overjoyed about the prospect of me as his son-in-law, is he? I just thought it was worth a try. Sorry, love. I didn't mean to get your hopes up.'

'It's not your fault,' she said, still feeling resentful. 'It's theirs. Ma's determined I should have a big wedding at Holy Trinity. But honestly, I don't want a fuss. I just want to be Mrs Matthew Searle.'

He kissed her cheek. 'You will be. As soon as I get back. I promise.'

They reached the factory gates. Louisa was reluctant to go in. She didn't want to let him out of her sight.

'What are you going to do with yourself today?' she asked.

He shrugged. 'Thought I'd just walk. Revisit the village, maybe climb up the Tor.' They both flinched slightly at the memory of their last trek up there. 'Anyway, I can be back here at dinner time if you like? I could bring a couple of meat pies and some cakes for us to eat.'

'That would be lovely,' she smiled. She had some bread and cheese and an apple in her bag, but she could give those to Kate.

The hooter went and the crowds filing into the factory thinned as everyone disappeared into their departments. Mattie kissed her on the lips this time before letting her go.

'Go on,' he said. 'Don't be late. There's still plenty of room in that bottom drawer to fill. I'll see you in a few hours.'

That first morning set the pattern for the following days. Mattie walked her to work, brought dinner to share with her, then would be outside the factory when she finished her shift.

Much to her parents' annoyance, she had supper and spent her evenings at his ma's cottage in The Mead. Louisa didn't care what they thought. It wasn't as though they bothered to invite him to their house and anyway, she couldn't expect to take him away from his ma in the evenings. It was the only time Mrs Searle got to spend with her precious son. Louisa was only grateful the woman was happy for her to be there to share her time with Mattie.

It surprised Louisa that Lucas hadn't been round as soon as Mattie got home. But when she asked Mattie about it, he just shrugged. 'I expect he's busy. The Clickers are all doing overtime to keep up, aren't they? And didn't Jeannie say their ma's nerves were bad lately?'

She finally saw Lucas on Wednesday at dinner time. He was talking to Mattie when Louisa came out of the factory. She hung back, letting them chat, content to be able to see the friends together again. She knew they'd parted on bad terms before Mattie had gone away and she wanted to give them a chance to put things right between them. After a few minutes, Lucas put out his hand. Mattie shook it, then pulled his friend in for a hug, patting him on the back. Louisa breathed a sigh of relief and approached them with a smile on her face. Mattie's face lit up at the sight of her. Lucas turned and nodded before he took his leave of them. For the first time since Mattie had gone away, she thought his friend looked less troubled.

'Alright?' she asked Mattie as he watched Lucas walk away.

'Yeah. All good,' he said.

By Thursday, Louisa could feel the tension building. Mattie was expected to return to base early the next day, ready to be shipped overseas. They were both quiet on the walk to the factory that morning. It wasn't that she'd run out of things to say, but that she had so much she wanted to tell him, but didn't know where to start.

She worked like a woman possessed that morning, her mind a whirl.

'Slow down, Lou,' said Kate. 'You're putting us all to shame.'

It took her a moment to register what her friend had said. She paused before picking up her next piece. 'It's our last day,' she said. 'I've got to do something.'

Kate frowned. 'What?' she asked.

She sat up straight, surveying the pile of finished linings in her basket. 'Mattie's leaving at dawn tomorrow. I'm going to tell Mr Briars I'm feeling poorly and need this afternoon off.'

Jeannie was immediately sympathetic. 'Are you alright?'

She shrugged. 'Not really.' She felt feverish and anxious.

'But you're really not sick, are you?' said Kate. 'You just want to spend some time with Mattie?'

She nodded. 'It's the last chance we've got for God knows how long. I can't just sit here. I want to be with him.'

'But you'll lose money,' Jeannie pointed out, looking worried.

Louisa didn't care about that. The only thing that mattered was spending some precious time with her love.

'Not really,' said Kate. 'Look at how much she's done this morning.' She grinned as she pointed at Lou's overflowing basket. 'Now I understand why you've been working like a Whirling Dervish.'

She nodded. 'Even if I haven't done a full day's quota, I don't care. I'm taking the afternoon off.'

'You could get into trouble,' said Jeannie. 'What if you lose your job?'

Kate scoffed. 'She won't.' She turned to Louisa. 'Don't bother telling Mr Briars. Just go at dinner time. I'll tell him you took poorly and had to go home when we clock back on.'

'Thanks.' Louisa gave her grateful smile.

The moment the dinner hooter went, she flew down the stairs to find her love. He was waiting for her in his usual spot, leaning against the wall just to the left of the factory gates. She walked into his arms, slipping her hands around his waist and resting her cheek on his chest. She breathed in his scent and felt herself relax for a moment.

'I've got the afternoon off,' she said as he kissed her hair.

He lifted her chin so he could see her face. 'How did you manage that?' he frowned.

'I worked like the devil this morning to finish my quota. Now Kate's going to tell Mr Briars that I've taken sick and had to go home.'

He laughed and shook his head, but she could see he was pleased. 'Miss Clements, you are a very naughty girl.'

She giggled. 'Not really, just desperate.'

He hugged her close. 'So, am I supposed to take you home to your ma?'

'Not likely,' she scoffed. 'You'd better take me to your place before anyone notices. I'm not wasting these few hours before your ma finishes work.' She stepped back, grabbed his hand and tugged him in the direction of The Mead. 'Come on.'

He laughed and matched her urgent pace. 'I love you, Louisa Clements.'

'Good,' she said. "Cause I'm relying on you to prove it to me this afternoon.'

34

It was Louisa's birthday on the first Saturday in September and Jeannie and Kate were determined to make it a happy occasion for their friend. They made her cards, put together a pretty bouquet of flowers for her from their gardens, and planned a picnic for the three of them by the River Brue on the Saturday afternoon.

'This is so kind of you,' she said when they arrived at her house an hour after she'd arrived home from work with their gifts and a picnic basket. 'It'll be good to get out.' She leaned closer, looking over her shoulder to make sure neither of her parents were listening. 'They're driving me mad,' she whispered. 'Can you believe they wanted me to go to the dance tonight with Horace's cousin? As if I'd be any more interested in him than I was in Horace. I've told them time and time again I'm with Mattie now, but they still go on about me finding a sweetheart at church.' She rolled her eyes. 'Ma thinks I'll forget about him now he's away, but I won't.'

It was seven weeks now since he'd left for the front. When she thought back to that last afternoon, it was with a mixture of agony and ecstasy. They had savoured every moment together and the memory of that day sustained her in her darkest moments. When he'd finally walked her home, he'd stopped just out of sight of her parents' cottage and they'd poured all their love into their farewell kisses. Since she'd left his arms, Louisa had felt cold, bereft. She had cried for days. Her parents' insistence on acting as though Mattie no longer mattered hurt a lot. But, with each letter that arrived, her love for him grew. And in each letter, he repeated his promise that, when he came home, they would be together forever, no matter what.

After Mattie's departure for the front, Louisa had devoted herself to working hard and putting by the extra money she earned to pay for essentials to give their marriage a good start. She ignored all of her parents' efforts to encourage her to socialise with the remaining lads at Holy Trinity, politely but firmly refusing any invitations, although judging by what she was saying now, she was fast losing patience.

'I can't believe they're still thinking that way,' said Kate. 'It must be horrible.'

'It is,' she agreed. 'I wish I was twenty-one this birthday, then I could get on and make my own arrangements for my wedding without needing Pa's consent.' She huffed out a breath. 'But no matter. They won't change my mind, so I just have to be patient.'

'Let's not fret about that now,' said Jeannie. 'It's your birthday, we've got a lovely picnic and the sun's shining. Let's make the most of it.'

They left Louisa's cottage and headed towards their favourite picnic spot. They were soon sitting by the riverbank on a blanket that Jeannie had brought along.

'It's been so long since we've done this,' said Kate as she hugged her knees. 'We've all been so busy this past year, haven't we? I can't believe all the changes that have happened. We've been at war for over a year now. They said it would be over by Christmas in 1914, but it doesn't seem like it's going to end any time soon, does it?'

'No,' said Louisa. 'Mattie can't say much about it in his letters, but he says it's truly terrible over there. And the less he says, the more I worry.'

Jeannie dug into the picnic basket and brought out three bottles of cordial. 'Come on now. It's your birthday. We have to talk about happy things.'

Louisa took her bottle and opened it, taking a sip of the sweet and tart liquid. Jeannie knew it must be hard for her when every waking moment, she was worrying about Mattie and wishing he was home safe.

'It's hard, though,' Kate echoed her thoughts. She was staring out over the fields back towards the village. 'We've all been through so much, haven't we? I never imagined this time last year that we'd lose Ma so quick.'

Jeannie reached across and squeezed her shoulder. 'I'm sorry, Kate. I know how hard it's been for you. I was glad that Ted was there for you then. I was too young to really remember much about when my pa died. I felt like at least Ted's grief for his brother was fresh, so he'd understand what you were going through.' Lord knew, Kate's pa was no help. If anything, he made his daughter's suffering worse.

'Yes, that's what I thought, too,' said Louisa. 'I wanted to help you, but I've never lost anyone I'm close to, so I had no idea what it feels like or what to say to you. I know you hate pity, so I was afraid of getting it wrong and upsetting you.'

Kate turned to them, a sad smile on her face. 'You have helped. You've both been good friends to me ever since we sat together in school. You helped me by just being by my side in the days when Ma was ill and then when she passed.' She sighed and looked away again. 'Ted helped too. But then the daft bugger decided to enlist and he left me as well.'

Jeannie shared a glance with Louisa before asking, 'Have you not heard from him at all?'

She shook her head. 'No. He said he wouldn't write.'

'But why not? It doesn't make any sense. You and him were getting along well, weren't you? Why just cut you off like that?'

Kate frowned, reaching out and smoothing a wrinkle in the blanket. 'I don't know. Like you said, we were getting along fine. I've been trying to figure it out, but I just don't understand. That last day, it was like he was holding something back. Something he wouldn't share with me.'

Louisa nodded. 'It seems strange that Mattie didn't even know Ted had signed up. All the lads from round here are usually sent to the same camp for basic training, but Mattie says he didn't see Ted there, even though he mentioned meeting up with a few other lads who'd enlisted at the same time as Ted, and no one said anything about him. It's like he's disappeared off the face of the earth.'

'Surely his ma and pa must have heard from him?' asked Jeannie. 'Have you asked them?'

Kate shrugged. 'I tried when I saw them at church a few weeks ago, but they just said he's doing his duty for king and country and they're proud of him. I don't think they have heard from him, though, because Peg said she was chatting with the postman and he mentioned the Jacksons don't get any letters from either of their sons. He said he'd noticed it because he's so busy delivering letters to most families with lads who're away. I can understand that Stan might not be able to – from what Ted told me, the poor lad's gone completely doolally, so I doubt he's capable of writing to anyone. But what's going on with Ted? Where is he?' She growled. 'I swore I'd stop thinking about him after the way he broke up with me, but none of it makes any sense and it's driving me bonkers. I wish he'd just been honest with me, that's all.'

'I heard that Pierre – you know, that Belgian refugee who was teaching Ted his languages? – well, he's gone, too,' said Louisa. 'Just up and left. They say he's gone to join a resistance group in his country. But I can't see it myself. I mean, he's just a teacher, isn't he? What would he know about leading rebels?'

Kate frowned. 'I hadn't heard that, though now I think on it, I haven't seen him for a while. Seems a bit daft to go back when he managed to escape in the first place. Another idiot.'

'It must have been hard for him, knowing some of his family are still there. Maybe he's gone to try and find them? Anyway, I hope him and Ted are alright,' said Jeannie. 'Maybe you'll hear from him soon. I can't believe he'd just cut you out of his life like that.'

'Maybe Ted didn't want you to have to worry about him,' said Louisa.

'Huh! Maybe, maybe. It's more likely he was lying all along and didn't want to carry on walking out with me anyway. Well, I've learned my lesson. I've had enough of men using me. I'll steer clear of them all from now on.'

Jeannie frowned, suddenly worried she'd misunderstood Ted's regard for her friend. 'Kate, he didn't... you know... take advantage, did he?'

'Take advantage?' Kate laughed. 'Oh, Jeannie, whatever do you mean?'

She felt her cheeks grow warm at her amusement. 'You know what I mean. You just implied he was using you. I know you were kissing, but did he do more than that? I wouldn't have thought he was like that, he seemed decent enough, but maybe he wasn't the lad we all thought he was.'

Kate's expression softened as she observed Jeannie's embarrassment and concern. She shook her head. 'No, don't fret, love. It was nothing like that,' she said. 'I made it clear on our first date that I wasn't going to stand for any nonsense, believe me, and he accepted it.' She paused and sighed. 'That's why the way he treated me at the end don't make any sense. If that was what he was after, why carry on going out with me at all?' She scowled. 'It better not have been out of pity.'

'I don't suppose you'll ever know unless he comes back one day and explains himself,' said Louisa.

Kate snorted. 'I'll not hold my breath waiting for that,' she said. 'He said he's not planning on coming back, whatever happens. No doubt, if he survives the war, he'll head for Bristol, or maybe even London, intent on making his fortune. Him and hundreds of others, no doubt. The idiot. Well, he can get on with it. I'm not pining for him and I'll make my own way, thank you very much. I'm taking inspiration from the women round here who are leading good lives without the need for a man. Florrie Bond is a forewoman in Trimmings now, and Mrs Searle's doing alright for herself as her deputy, isn't she? I don't need to stay chained to my machine for the rest of my life. I might even become a suffragette like Miss Alice Clark. It's about time women had the vote. We can't do any worse than the men, can we?' She nodded to herself, clearly satisfied with her thoughts. 'I have to put up with Pa until I'm twenty-one, but the minute I can claim my own wages, I'll be off and standing on my own two feet. I'll live on my earnings and never depend on a man for anything.'

Jeannie sighed. 'I doubt if I'll find a man now. Not after all that business with Douglas.'

'Don't let the likes of him put you off finding a sweetheart, Jeannie,' said Louisa.

'Oh, I haven't been put off,' she said. 'I still dream of getting married and having a family of my own. But I doubt any local lads will want to have anything to do with me now. They tend not to want a lass who acts like a shrew.'

'You were provoked,' said Kate. 'Most lasses would have done the same in the circumstances. A lot would've done worse.' She sniggered. 'I know I would've.'

'Definitely,' agreed Louisa.

Jeannie shrugged. 'I know you and lots of girls have been on my side. But I've noticed lads either laugh when they see me, or they scuttle out of my way. Even my brothers have been teasing me about it.'

'Tell 'em all to bugger off,' said Kate. 'If a lad doesn't know how to handle a strong lass, why would any of us want to be seen on their arms? And as for your brothers, they should be proud of you.'

'Mattie says he wished he'd seen it,' said Louisa. 'He said he'd have cheered for you.'

Jeannie groaned and hid her face in her hands. 'He'll have told all the lads he knows in the trenches by now, won't he?'

'Probably,' Louisa grinned.

'Which means none of them will want anything to do with me when they get back,' she sighed.

Kate and Louisa laughed, not understanding her concerns.

'Like Kate says, if they're like that, they're not worth having. Don't worry, Jeannie. You'll find a decent man to love you. You're a good catch.'

She wasn't so sure. She'd already made the decision not to go out with anyone who wasn't a Quaker. At least a Friend would understand and share her values. She wasn't keen on the idea of a drinker either. Mr Davis had put her off anyone who frequented the Street Inn.

'Maybe,' she said, knowing that she wouldn't be able to persuade them otherwise, although it was a bit rich of Kate to swear off men and then insist she'd find someone who was worth hanging onto. 'Anyway, I thought we were going to talk about happy things. Did you get any nice presents, Lou?'

Louisa reached into her bag and brought out a lovely leather-bound notebook. 'Mattie sent me this. Said he managed to buy it from an art shop in Salisbury before they shipped out.' She opened it to reveal pristine white pages of good-quality art paper. 'He knows how much I love drawing and painting, so it came with a nice set of pencils and a box of watercolours. Look, I've already started my first drawing.' She turned to the first page. 'It's not finished. I was just working on it when you arrived.'

The girls leaned closer. Even though there were only a few lines on the page, they both recognised the face.

'Mattie!' said Jeannie.

'I'd recognise that grin anywhere,' said Kate. 'You're really good, Lou. You always were the best at art at school.'

'Thanks.' Her cheeks glowed with pleasure. 'I wanted to make a good likeness as I don't have a picture of him.' Her glow dimmed a little as she looked at the picture. 'I miss him so much. I feel so alone without him.' She was silent for a moment. Neither Jeannie nor Kate said anything. What could they say?

Louisa took a deep breath and squared her shoulders. 'But it's no use complaining about it. It is what it is. He'll be back one day and we'll get married and be together forever.' She smiled. 'I plan on filling this notebook with drawings to show him when he comes home, and in the meantime, I'm going to do some little paintings on card – local views that he'll recognise. I'll send them to him to remind him that he needs to keep safe so he can come back and see those places for himself.'

'That's a lovely idea,' said Jeannie. 'He'll love that.'

'You should draw us now,' said Kate. 'So you remember this birthday picnic and our afternoon by the river.'

'Ooh, good idea,' said Louisa, digging into her bag for her pencils. 'Get comfy, girls, and don't move until I tell you that you can.' She opened a fresh page and began to draw.

Jeannie sat up straighter. Kate poked her in the ribs.

'She said get comfy,' she said. 'You're looking like someone's shoved a broomstick up your bottom.'

Louisa giggled. 'She's right, Jeannie. You don't need to pose all stiff and formal like you do for a photograph. Just relax. You can lie back on the blanket if you like. It'll make the composition more interesting.'

Jeannie laughed, a little embarrassed. 'I've never even had my photograph taken, let alone had someone draw me.' She lay back, but that didn't feel right, so she rolled onto her side and propped her head on her hand. That felt a bit more comfy.

'Me neither,' said Kate. 'Maybe one day we can all go to a photographic studio and have our pictures taken. Wouldn't that be grand?'

Louisa nodded, her eyes darting between her friends and the page as she made pencil marks. 'I wish I'd thought to do that with Mattie before he went away. That's why I'm trying to draw his likeness. I'm scared he'll be away so long, I'll forget what he looks like.'

'I pray for him every night,' said Jeannie softly. 'For Mattie and Ted and everyone fighting this horrible war. I don't know what God's plan is, but I hope he'll shine his light on the men in charge soon and guide them towards peace.'

Louisa's eyes filled with tears. 'Thanks, Jeannie. I appreciate it, and so will Mattie.'

'We all want peace,' said Kate. 'It makes no sense, all this fighting. It's not getting us anywhere.' She sighed. 'Mind you, have you heard Mrs Jackson spouting off to anyone who'll listen? According to her, we're fighting the war to stop the Kaiser taking over the world and murdering us all in our beds – after his soldiers have had their wicked ways with us.'

Jeannie closed her eyes tight, not wanting to cry in front of the others. 'I thought we were going to think about nice things,' she said. 'We can't tell what's going to happen, so we need to focus on what's good in our lives.' She rolled onto her back, forgetting she was supposed to be posing. When she remembered, she opened her eyes and looked over at Louisa sitting cross-legged with her notebook on her lap as she sketched. She held up her hand and nodded that it was okay for Jeannie to stay where she was, so she relaxed and closed her eyes again.

'I'm happy that the sun is shining on our afternoon off,' she said. 'And that I'm here with the best friends a girl could ever have. I'm grateful for my ma's love, for my brothers – even though they drive me potty sometimes – and for my job. I might not be very ambitious, but it wouldn't be much fun if everyone was, would it? No, I'm happy to carry on working in the Machine Room until I meet a nice man.' *If he ever arrives*, she thought. 'Then I'll be content to be a wife and mother and watch my family grow.'

'Aw, that's nice,' said Kate. 'You'll be a really good ma. You're always so kind and patient with everyone.'

'Except Douglas and Doris,' sniggered Louisa, making them all laugh.

'Well,' said Kate. 'I'm not sure I've much to be grateful for at the moment. But I'm grateful for my ma, even though I'm angry at God for taking her too soon. I'm grateful for my sister and brothers, although I wish I saw more of them. And I'm grateful for you two, my friends forever. They say what doesn't kill you makes you stronger, so maybe I should be grateful for what I've been through.' She frowned, tilting her head to one side as she thought about that. 'Mmm. Not sure I *can* be grateful about that. We'll have to see.'

They relaxed in the sun as Louisa continued to sketch. The only sounds apart from the soft scratch of her pencil on the paper were the occasional pop of a trout surfacing in the river and the swallows above them, swooping to catch as many insects on the wing as they could before their epic journey south began at the end of the summer.

'You didn't tell us what you're grateful for, Louisa,' said Kate eventually, startling Jeannie out of the doze that had begun to overtake her.

'That's right,' she said. 'Come on, Lou. It's your turn.'

Louisa paused and stared out across the fields towards Street. 'I'm grateful that I found my true love,' she said, a soft smile on her pretty face. 'I'm grateful that you're both here with me today so that I don't die of loneliness while he's away.' She sighed. 'Sorry, that sounded selfish and miserable. I mean, I can hardly talk to Ma and Pa these days, so I'm grateful that I have the two of you to share my thoughts with. I know you will listen and not judge me or try to make me change my mind.' She put down her pencil and leaned back on her hands, raising her face to the sun. 'I'm grateful I have a summer birthday so we can enjoy picnics like this.' She sat up straight again and looked at the notebook on her lap. 'And I'm grateful that I've discovered my love of drawing again so that I can capture moments like this and remember them forever.'

'Have you finished it?' asked Kate. 'Are you going to let us see?'

Louisa nodded and handed over the book. Jeannie moved closer to Kate to have a look. With just a few strokes of her pencil, Louisa had drawn the two of them lounging on the picnic blanket, the remains of their meal around them. In the background, she had drawn in the river on one side of them and in the other direction, they could see the chimney from the Clarks Shoe Factory and the building where they worked in the Machine Room standing proud above the cluster of other buildings that made up the village of Street.

'That's beautiful, Lou,' said Jeannie. 'I'm grateful you made me look so pretty.'

'Oh, you,' Louisa laughed. 'I've only drawn what I can see.'

'It's lovely,' said Kate, handing it back to her. The church bell at Holy Trinity tolled five o'clock and she sighed and stood up. 'I need to get home and get Pa's supper on the table.'

The friends gathered their things and began to walk back towards the village.

'I'm sorry to cut the afternoon short,' she said as they reached The Cross. 'But you know what he's like. If there isn't something on the table when he gets there, I'll be for it.'

'We know, love,' said Jeannie.

'Don't worry about it,' said Louisa. 'I've had a lovely birthday, and I wouldn't want you to get into any trouble on my account.'

Kate nodded, hugging both her friends before they went their separate ways home. 'I wouldn't mind so much, but some Saturdays, he hasn't even bothered coming home and the food gets wasted. But the one day I didn't bother because I thought he wouldn't be there, he blinking went and turned up. I got a wallop for being lazy and making him wait.'

'He's a monster!' Louisa exclaimed.

'He's so cruel,' agreed Jeannie. 'I wish you could get away from him.'

'You and me both, love,' said Kate. 'And I will. One day. In the meantime, I'm going to wrap the memory of this afternoon around me like a comforting shawl. I'll remember what we're all grateful for and try not to think about putting rat poison in Pa's supper.'

The friends laughed. Jeannie knew Kate wouldn't do such a thing, but even if she did, she doubted anyone would blame her. Louisa took her leave of them and walked up Somerton Road. Kate and Jeannie carried on up the High Street until they got to the corner of Goswell Road, where Kate had to turn off to get to her home in Silver Road.

Jeannie hugged her. 'It was a good idea, the picnic, wasn't it?' she said. 'I think Louisa liked it.'

'She did,' Kate agreed. 'So did I. We should do it more often.'

They said their goodbyes and Jeannie carried the picnic basket and blanket towards the Musgroves' cottage in West End. It had indeed been a strange year. The war had made life difficult for the whole of Europe, even though some had welcomed it as a chance to do something different with their lives, like Ted.

Kate was still grieving for her ma while her pa continued to make her life hell, while Jeannie had come to terms with the fact that Mattie Searle wasn't the man for her and learned to be happy for him and Louisa. She'd gained some confidence, only to lose it again when she discovered the truth about Douglas.

All three of the girls had found sweethearts only to lose them again. At least, God willing, Louisa would get Mattie back once this rotten war was over. And maybe Ted would come home too eventually. But in the meantime, the friends were all single again.

Jeannie prayed every night and at every Meeting for the safe keeping of the lads overseas and her friends and family at home. But she also prayed that one day soon, she'd find a love like that which Louisa and Mattie shared. She knew that Kate had gone off the idea for herself, but Jeannie prayed for her to find love as well. Lord knows, she deserved it after the year she'd been through.

As she walked into the cottage, Ma was singing. It was one of her good days. Jeannie smiled, truly grateful for the blessings in her life.

ACKNOWLEDGEMENTS

When I moved to Somerset in 2018, to a house built on land previously owned by C & J Clark and the site of one of their many shoe factory buildings, I had no idea that I would be writing this story. I would like to thank my friend and fellow Boldwood author, Lizzie Lane for inspiring me to do so. As a result, I have learned so much about Street and the incredible influence that the Clark family has had, and continues to have, on this community, and I decided I wanted to show this through the eyes of the workers at the factory in the early twentieth century.

Along the way, I have met many residents of Street, the home of C & J Clark, who shared their stories with me. They told me about the history of this wonderful community. Through my research at The Alfred Gillett Trust, which holds a treasure trove of archives from C & J Clark and numerous local organisations, I built a picture of life in the shoe factory during the war. The dedicated volunteers and Friends of Street Library, the ladies at Walton Women's Institute, the retired workers at the Clarks Social Club, and the members of the Street Quaker Meeting House have also been incredibly kind and generous in helping me to build up a picture of life in Street. I am grateful to everyone who has helped me. Any mistakes in this book are my own, for which I hope I will be forgiven.

Most of the characters are fictitious, but I have included some real people in the story – Mr Roger Clark and his sister Miss Alice Clark, who were both directors of the company at the time when this story is set, are both featured, as is their sister Mrs Esther Clothier. I also mention Miss Florrie Bond, one of very few women to reach the level of foreman in the early twentieth century and the only one during the First World War, and the Miss Catherine Impey, a cousin of the Clarks, whose influence on the world was astonishing and criminally under-reported.

I would like to thank my wonderful editor at Boldwood Books, Rachel Faulkner-Willcocks for helping me to make this book the best it can be; the super marketing team led by Claire Fenby for spreading the word about it, and the family of Boldwood authors who have welcomed me with open arms and cheered me along. I'm delighted to be part of the Boldwood family and look forward to a long and fruitful relationship with you all.

Finally, thank you to you for reading The Clarks Factory Girls at War. I hope that you enjoyed it. Look out for the next book in the series, with more of Jeannie, Kate and Louisa's story to come.

ABOUT THE AUTHOR

May Ellis is the author of more than five contemporary romance and YA fiction novels. She lives in Somerset, within sight of Glastonbury Tor. Inspired by her move to the area and her love of social history, she is now writing saga fiction – based on the real-life stories of the Clark's factory girls.

Sign up to May Ellis' mailing list for news, competitions and updates on future books.

Visit May's website: www.alisonroseknight.com

Follow May on social media here:

- facebook.com/alison.knight.942
- instagram.com/alisonroseknight
- x.com/Alison_Knight59
- bookbub.com/authors/alison-knight

Sixpence Stories

Introducing Sixpence Stories!

Discover page-turning historical novels from your favourite authors, meet new friends and be transported back in time.

Join our book club
Facebook group

https://bit.ly/SixpenceGroup

Sign up to our
newsletter

https://bit.ly/SixpenceNews

Boldwood

Boldwood Books is an award-winning fiction publishing company seeking out the best stories from around the world.

Find out more at www.boldwoodbooks.com

Join our reader community for brilliant books, competitions and offers!

Follow us
@BoldwoodBooks
@TheBoldBookClub

Sign up to our weekly deals newsletter

https://bit.ly/BoldwoodBNewsletter

9 781835 330180